THE HAPPINESS RECIPE

Stella Newman is the author of *Pear Shaped*. She lives in London and is a freelance copywriter and keen amateur cook. She blogs about restaurants, food and writing at www.stellanewmansblog.blogspot.com.

By the same author:

Pear Shaped

STELLA NEWMAN

THE
HAPPINESS
RECIPE

avon.

Published by AVON
A Division of HarperCollins*Publishers* Ltd
1 London Bridge Street
London SE1 9GF

www.harpercollins.co.uk

This paperback edition 2018

First published as 'Leftovers' in Great Britain in by HarperCollins*Publishers* 2013

A catalogue record for this book
is available from the British Library

ISBN: 978-0-00-831785-0

This novel is entirely a work of fiction.
The names, characters and incidents portrayed in it are
the work of the author's imagination. Any resemblance to
actual persons, living or dead, events or localities is
entirely coincidental.

Set in Bembo MT Pro by Palimpsest Book Production Ltd, Falkirk, Stirlingshire

Printed and bound by CPI Group (UK) Ltd, Croydon, CR0 4YY

MIX
Paper from
responsible sources
FSC™
www.fsc.org   FSC° C007454

To George Hanna, with thanks

'We've arrived at the top of the staircase, finally ready to start our lives, only to discover a cavernous room at the tail end of a party, most of the men gone already, some having never shown up – and those who remain are leering by the cheese table, or are, you know, the ones you don't want to go out with.'

Kate Bolick, 'All The Single Ladies',
The Atlantic magazine

I am a Leftover.

Well, according to this ridiculous quiz in *Style and Food Magazine* I'm a Leftover:

Bridget Jones is so mid-90s! Today's 30-somethings manage hedge funds, plan mini-music festivals and bake macrobiotic Red Velvet cupcakes, all without breaking a sweat! Answer these four questions to discover which tribe you belong to:

1) Work – Do you:
   a) Run your own multi-million pound start-up, mentor young entrepreneurs in your lunch break and still find time for power pilates and a blow-dry before end of play.

b) Have a trust fund – you don't need more cash; even so, you'll be launching your first shoe collection in Harvey Nicks this spring.

c) Plod along on a treadmill non-career doing long hours for average pay while younger, more thrusting colleagues are promoted all around you.

2) Love and Sex – Are you:

a) Blissfully married to a man you still find ferociously attractive (the sex just gets better every year!) and tiger-mothering four kids under 10 who perform Mozart quartets together.

b) Heavily loved-up with your DJ boyfriend, and having loads of rampant, gymnastic sex, sometimes in public but mostly in Mr & Mrs Smith hotels.

c) Still recovering from your last failed relationship, living a non-voluntary celibate existence because your sad, jaded aura can be spotted from space.

3) Your weekends are spent:

a) Flicking through the FT's 'How to Spend It' with one hand, buying Lanvin on Net-A-Porter with the other, only pausing to bake gluten-free alfalfa flatbreads.

b) Glamping, and on mini-breaks in Copenhagen/ Babington House, religiously avoiding wheat and dairy.

c) Planning what you're going to do if you ever stop feeling so goddamn lonely, while eating and drinking too much of everything.

4) Your role models are:
   a) Nicola Horlick, Karren Brady.
   b) Kate Moss, Florence from Florence + the Machine.
   c) You have no role models. You have given up all hope. All that's left is anger.

Mostly As – You're an Alpha Alfalfa!
Mostly Bs – You're a Gluten-free Glamorista!
Mostly Cs – You're a Leftover!

Quiz by Khloe B

Well, Khloe, I have four things to say to you:

1) I am due to be promoted this Christmas, which is now only 307 days away. (It's a week after Valentine's, and we've just brainstormed our XtraSpecial Xmas poster concepts: Turkey Cran-Apple-Stuffing Ball Pizza anyone?)

2) *Everyone* has failed relationships. Perhaps not quite as fail-y as mine; still, your mistakes, your failures – they make you who you are, don't you know?

3) Eating alfalfa is about as much fun as eating a handful of baby's hair. And gluten-free? I happen to

3

be a *huge* fan of gluten: bread, cakes, pasta. Some of my best friends are pasta. So no, Khloe, there will be no gluten-free alfalfa flatbreads.

4) Who actually spells Khloe with a K? Someone who doesn't know how to spell Khloe, that's who. Is *your* role model a Kardashian?

And another thing, Khloe: anger has nothing to do with anything. You shouldn't try to pigeonhole people, that's all. It's stupid. Really stupid. In fact I'll tell you something else that's stupid: quizzes like this. Stupid quizzes in crappy magazines. Sorry, make that stupid kuizzes in krappy magazines.

I am not a bloody Leftover.

w/c 5 March

Monday

Show me someone in London who loves a Monday morning and I'll show you someone who doesn't take public transport, doesn't work at NMN Advertising, and doesn't make ads for Fletchers pizzas; pizzas that you wouldn't feed to a dog. Not unless you'd been having an ongoing Mafia feud with that dog and his entire family for several generations. Even then you'd probably only feed that dog a single mouthful of pizza before taking pity on him and reaching for the Pedigree Chum.

This morning the tube was delayed, so I was delayed, and by the time I reach the glass revolving doors of NMN, just off Charlotte Street, it's already 7.34 a.m. Free breakfast, courtesy of NMN, runs strictly from 6.30 a.m. to 7.30 a.m. Free breakfast is one of the few perks still left in this office. Obviously there's no such thing as a free breakfast and these breakfasts are a trap, designed to lure you in to work prematurely. However (and it is an important however): Sam, Head of The Post Room, has proved beyond doubt that the egg and bacon croissants NMN use as bait *are* worth coming in early for.

For a bloke who's spent ten years dossing around in a mail room, Sam's remarkably good with computers. Last summer he was so bored, he created an interactive 3D model on his Mac. He programmed in all the variables:

- Croissant Induced Happiness versus Joys of a Longer Lie-in
- Relative Density of Commuters on the Northern Line 06:00 to 08:00
- Financial and Emotional Costs of an Inferior Breakfast from Somewhere Else

Then he did some sums and an A3 colour printout: the croissants won. I had never even considered putting egg mayo and bacon into a croissant. Fried egg and bacon between two slices of a fresh white sandwich loaf? Sure, that's a classic. But egg and bacon crammed into a seductively flaky French buttery croissant with melted cheese on top? If I were Robbie Doggett, NMN's Head of Creative Thinking (and King of Trying to Be Down With the Kids even though he's forty-nine), I'd say *OMG*, or *hashtag ooh la la brekkie*.

I don't say either. I'm thirty-six, I don't txtspk out loud, I don't wear £200 customised Nikes and I don't spend all day Tweeting shite. I would simply say 'great croissants';

but I can't, because it's four minutes past the freebie and they've been removed. Instead I head for the mail room.

Sam's sitting in his swivel chair wearing his favourite Bowie t-shirt and distressed jeans. ('Distressed', due to the fact that he's worn them constantly since 1993; unlike Robbie Doggett's jeans, which are made to look distressed by a team of under-age Cambodian fabric workers who are, I suspect, genuinely distressed.)

'Seven letters, spice from crocus . . .' Sam says, looking up from the crossword and giving me a brief once over. Sam is annoyingly cute: green eyes, light brown wavy hair, and a permanently amused smile that's the result of him being privy to every last thing that goes on in this agency. It's a good job he's lazy, rude and smokes all day, which work against his natural attractions and mean I don't have to fancy him. Much.

'Hold on, I know it, Sam, I do . . . nutmeg?'

'One letter short.' He shakes his head in mock disapproval. 'And there's me thinking you might be hungry . . .' He points his finger at a stash of goodies hiding under a paper napkin on his desk.

'You saved one for me! You can be such a charmer . . .'

'I didn't save one for you, I saved one for whoever solves eight across,' he says. 'Come on, Suze, sixth letter's an O, you're always good on the food questions . . .'

'O . . . o . . . Saffron. It's saffron.'

He nods, then slides his chair over to the pile of goodies

and whips the napkin away like a toreador. Not only has he saved me a croissant, he's also snaffled a chocolate muffin. Best of all, he's ordered in some of those nice Muji fibre-tip pens that are strictly contraband in our new cost-cutting regime, and a brand new pack of turquoise Post-it notes!

This is what my life has come to: elation over a pack of stolen Post-it notes. (It's been a bad couple of years.) I could almost hug him, but Sam doesn't do touching at all – unlike every other man in this building who does far too much touching.

'Thanks Sam, I owe you.'

'Yeah, yeah . . . just bring me in some of that chocolate pudding next time you make it.'

'Which one? The roulade?'

'Which one's that?' he says.

'Round, in slices, had raspberries in it last time.'

'Oh no, not interested in fruit. The one with the brownie bits on top.'

'Ultimate death-by-brownie cheesecake bake?'

'Yep.'

'You didn't think it was too sweet?'

'No, it was good. Death by brownie. Good way to die. Better than car crash or drowning.'

'Happy Monday to you too.'

*

Monday morning means updating The Status Report:

w/c 5th March
- 'Project F' – client briefing – venue TBC
- Brief creative team

I live my life in w/cs. Week commencings.

For example, I know that w/c 23rd April we will be shooting our new TV ad for 'Project F' whether I like it or not. And I do not.

Devron from Fletchers is briefing me tomorrow. We haven't even started the project yet, but according to the timing plan we're already two months late. Devron keeps changing his mind about the brief. It's probably going to end in disaster, but hey – *'Tight deadlines are what keep this business fun!'* That's according to my boss, Berenice: a woman whose idea of fun is Excel. Excel the spreadsheet, not ExCel the conference centre, though she is a woman who loves an industry conference. Networking is one of her middle names: Berenice Robot-Psychopath Networking Davis.

Which reminds me, w/c 4 June I'm being roped in to The Tasty Snacking Show, again. Last year Fletchers forced me into fancy dress to publicise their new 'Pizza Spagnola!' range. Words can't describe the humiliation of getting stuck in the ticket barrier at Earl's Court tube dressed as a Spanish sausage. Take my word for it, there's no obvious place to stick an Oyster card when you're a chorizo.

W/c 16 July – a week in Centre Parcs Cumbria to brainstorm Christmas 2015.

W/c 3 September, birthday week – I shall be on holiday, somewhere hot, preferably with a man but more than likely with Dalia. (That's if I can persuade her to be parted from her on-off-off boyfriend for long enough to board a plane.)

W/c 17 December – get my bonus, pay off my debts and finally get promoted to the board, thus proving to my parents that I am not a failure and I am not a quitter. Then quit. Work out my three-month notice period in a state of sheer unadulterated bliss, every day a rainbow. Release myself into the free world just in time for spring and start doing what I was put on this earth to do. (I'll have worked out what that is by then. Definitely.)

My whole life spent, living in the future.

The one good thing about Mondays? They go fast.

The hours are eaten up by a sequence of pointless, infuriating, navel-gazing meetings:

Team Meeting, Floor Meeting, Department Meeting, Production Meeting and finally Meeting-Planning Meeting. Yes. Just when you think it's safe to go back to your desk at 6.30 p.m., the account directors have a meeting just to talk about the rest of the week's meetings. Still, tonight we're finished by 7 p.m., and I race out of the door before Berenice can make her usual *hi-larious* joke – 'half day, Susannah?'

With any luck Upstairs Caspar will be out for the night.

10

If it wasn't for Caspar my home would be perfect. I live in a cosy one-bed flat on the fifth floor of Peartree Court, a six-storey U-shaped block with a little square of garden in the middle, with, yes, a tree, with pears on. It's in Swiss Cottage, a pleasant area of North London that is not remotely Swiss, nor full of cottages. The flat belonged to my granny, who left it to me and my brother when she died seven years ago. My brother now lives in a big house in Chester where his wife is from. I give him half the mortgage equivalent every month and I get to live here.

Peartree Court is looked after by Terry the Caretaker. If he wasn't in his sixties and missing two important front teeth we'd be in business. He's a total sweetheart – he's even given me a secret key to the roof terrace. It has amazing views of the whole of London. Residents aren't supposed to go up there – health and safety. But as long as I'm discreet and don't let myself get spotted by the busybody Langdons on the third floor then Terry's fine. (The Langdons actually complain every autumn when the pears start to fall from the tree. They don't like the mess of everyday life. Then again, who does?)

Terry's kind to all the old people in the block and tolerant of all the 4x4 driving yuppies who move in every time one of the oldies kicks the bucket. Yuppies like Caspar. Love thy neighbour's not working out too well for us. Caspar moved in just over a year ago. He is an actuary. I don't actuary know what this means, other than that at thirty-one

11

he can afford two cars (Porsche, Range Rover) and has enough free time to play a lot of tennis. I frequently bump into him in the lift in mini-shorts, thinking he's Nadal. Except unlike Nadal, Caspar is pasty, blond and snotty. Grand-slam snotty.

I know this because two weeks after my ex, Jake, ripped out my heart, Caspar ripped up his carpets, installing tropical hardwood flooring instead. Due to the acoustics of this flooring I hear Caspar flob up whatever's in his throat every single morning at dawn, like vulgar birdsong. Caspar spent four years in Hong Kong and he informs me that in Chinese culture it is a *good* thing to loudly hack up one's phlegm. Good for him; not so much for me.

Along with the coughing there's the shagging – his, not mine, obviously. Never optimum to hear your neighbours getting it on. But Caspar's sex life . . . it's so terribly audible. And it's always the same routine: Michael Bublé goes on the Bang & Olufsen. Then I hear Caspar bang and olufsen. I've repeatedly asked him to at least put some rugs down, but he tells me that my ears are too sensitive. So now I've resorted to whacking up the volume on my Adele CD – it's that or else I hear everything.

The only part of his routine that ever changes is the girl. He has a taste for drippy blondes, and because he's a rich, cocky little bugger he seems to have no trouble pulling. Sometimes I see him strut to his Porsche, an interchangeable girl scurrying a few metres behind him like an obedient little mouse. I never ever want to go out with a man who marches ahead of me down the street.

Tonight I'm in luck: Caspar's out, which means some peace. I head straight for the kitchen: the only thing that can undo the damage to my soul that a Monday at work has done is a good dinner. The cupboards in here are a bit of a mess – I'm rubbish at throwing things away – but behind the Hobnob tubes and huddles of geriatric spices I find exactly what I'm looking for.

My grandma always told me that a bowl of pasta is the answer to most of life's problems. She was Italian. Statements like that always sound a little more profound in a foreign language: *Un piatto di pasta e' la risposta a quasi tutti i problemi della vita.* All you have to do is pick the right pasta for your circumstances. For example, tonight I'm tired and feeling lazy. So nothing too complicated: a tomato-based sauce, thirty minutes' cooking time, max. However today, being Monday, was dull, so I'm craving a little lift. The solution? A bit of chilli in the sauce, and a pasta shape that conjures up excitement: fusilli. Lovely and twirly, like a kids' fairground ride.

I check in the fridge and find a pack of bacon that's a week past its use by date. My mum brought me up to believe that a use by date is arbitrary – a random sequence of numbers and letters, designed to trick you into throwing good food away before its time. It might as well be in Cyrillic. If it looks fine and it smells fine then it is fine.

I fry a red onion in butter and olive oil till it's soft and starting to turn golden, then add the bacon and a pinch of red chilli flakes and stand over the saucepan inhaling like a teenage glue-sniffer. After five minutes I pour in a tin of tomatoes, a pinch of salt and sugar, reduce the heat to a low simmer and head to my bathroom.

Make-up comes off, I have a bath and I even manage to apply a Liz Earle nourishing face mask, which promises to brighten my tired, dull complexion. If only Liz could make a potion to brighten the other parts of my tired, dull existence . . .

OK. Pyjamas: on. Baggy, slightly moth-bitten cashmere sweater: on. Horrendous yet cosy Ninja Turtle slippers, a gift from my brother in 1987: on (I'm serious – I never throw *anything* away). Pan of salted water for the pasta: on.

Eleven minutes later – absolute happiness. Twirly pasta with a spicy tomato and bacon sauce with loads of melted cheese on top. Eaten on the sofa in front of an episode of *30 Rock*. Just me, Tina Fey and Alec Baldwin.

My grandma was right about the pasta. My mother was right about those use by dates. And all is right in my world.

Tuesday

All is about to be a little less right.

When I reach my desk the light on my phone is already flashing. It's 7.42 a.m., which can only mean one person: Berenice. I have been summoned. Always ominous with Berenice; she has a way of making you feel like a mass-murderer just by saying your name on an answering machine. I suspect one day I'll break down in her office and admit to kidnapping Shergar, shooting JFK and hiding Lord Lucan under my bed.

I rush to the ladies' to check in the mirror. Could be worse: Tuesday morning bed hair gets pulled back into a bun. Make-up is fine; the early days of the week always see fresh mascara. Catch me on a Friday though and chances are it's Thursday night's face. I'm wearing a respectable M&S knee-length burgundy dress that could pass for Jaeger, in the dark. No cleavage or knees on show – extremely important, in light of Berenice's latest paranoid fixation . . . Jolly good – I look like a tired, non-sexual, overworked thirty-six-year-old woman who is not having much fun. A carbon copy of Berenice, only five years younger.

I take the lift up to the fifth floor. Her PA must be at Early-Bird Zumba so I hover awkwardly outside Berenice's office, waiting for her to notice me through the glass wall. Maybe Sam's right, I think, as I look at the crown of Berenice's head. Last week Sam informed me that Berenice has her colour done every nine days at that place off Sloane Square where Cate Blanchett goes to when she's in town. I have never seen a trace of a dark root in Berenice's hair. It is always perfect: placid, unthreatening, shoulder-length blonde. Not sexy blonde. But grown-up, good taste, all-my-glassware-comes-from-Conran, ash blonde. Personally I favour brown. Slightly unruly, all-my-glasswear-comes-from-Ikea-or-was-borrowed-from-my-local-pub, mousy brown.

Sam also told me that Martin Meddlar, our CEO, gets his hair bouffed at Nicky Clarke once a week and puts it down as a work expense. When I asked Sam how he came by this business-critical information he merely raised an eyebrow and said 'Exactly!' (Either he's hacking into Finance's expenses file, or he's hacking into London's chichiest hairdressers' Hotmail accounts. He's capable of both.)

I glance over to see if Martin and his bouff are in their vast corner office, but no, the plush leather chair is empty.

16

Generally Martin comes in at 11 a.m., lunches from 12 p.m. with a senior client, then returns slightly drunk at 3.50 p.m. just in time for his driver to take him home at 4.00 p.m. on the dot. ('The A40 gets totally gridlocked after 4.30 p.m.')

Berenice must sense movement, as she finally looks up and beckons me in. She's been the head of my department for six years and yet I still feel slightly sick with fear every time I have a meeting with her. 'Susannah, take a seat,' she says.

My name is Susie. I know it's the same name. I know it's not a big a deal. But the only other person who calls me Susannah is my mother when I've done something earth-shatteringly wrong (borrowed her car and forgotten to reset the rear-view mirror; failed to be a successful and married dentist like my brother).

'Fletchers OK?' says Berenice, staring down at her notepad.

Good morning, Susie. Are you well? You look a little tired. I know that we work you terribly hard, but we do so appreciate your labour on behalf of our bottom line. Would you like a cup of tea? A posh biscuit? Maybe even some eye contact? To be honest, I'm happier without the eye contact. There is something hostile in Berenice's grey eyes that I can only assume is the by-product of her being bullied by Martin Meddlar. That's just a rumour – he's only ever been nice to me. Too nice, in Berenice's opinion – hence my dowdy dress. Anyway, allegedly he bullies her, and she bullies me:

a pretty little daisy chain of bullying that entwines the three of us.

'Fletchers is great,' I say. 'Spanish pizza sales are up twenty-three per cent, and the digital campaign's tracking well.'

She nods. 'How's Jonty getting on?'

Aaah, Jonty. The I-d-iot she's allocated to help me out with print ads. The lazy, cocky red-jeaned idiot who is Berenice's best friend's godson and therefore couldn't possibly be an idiot.

'Yup. I think Jonty's enjoying himself.'

'Glad he's helping you out. Now. I know you're looking to progress by year end.'

'Yes, absolutely,' I nod. 'I've been an account director for six years now, so I'm definitely ready . . .' And have been for the last two years since I first asked you for a promotion and you first waved a little carrot near me, before smashing me with a stick of Fletchers pizza.

'And I believe Devron at Fletchers has mentioned Project F to you already.'

'Briefing's tomorrow. What's it all about?'

She flinches. 'I can't share that information, I've signed a non-disclosure agreement.' I bet if I asked her where her PA keeps the Earl Grey teabags she'd say she's signed an NDA on that too.

'Berenice, can I just check, it is still a pizza brief, isn't it?' It had better be. Pizzas are bad enough. (I've also done time on Jumbo Pasties and Asian Cuisine, which for some reason included Polish dumplings.) Just please, please, please don't put me on Dog and Bog. The worst possible fate for anyone here is to be moved to Dog and Bog. (Household department: pet food and loo roll.)

She sighs. 'Basically it's their *biggest* launch of the financial year. Super-high-profile, game-changing, mega-strategic. Lots of . . . fun.' She says the word 'fun' like other people say the word 'herpes'. She squints at something on her notepad. It's the only thing on her desk other than a white porcelain vase with a narrow neck that is currently strangling a single pink orchid. My desk looks like a crime scene. Berenice associates messiness with stupidity, which might explain why she always talks to me like I'm nine years old.

'Susannah. This is your opportunity to prove yourself. It's time to put clear blue water between you and your peers. That's if you want to notch it up to the next level. You've got people like Jonty at your heels, champing at the bit for projects like this.'

My peers? Jonty thinks spaghetti grows on trees. He actually does.

'This project will define you,' she says. 'If you get this right . . .' She looks at me with almost a smile. Of course she will not say 'If you get this right *I will promote you*' for that would amount to a sentence (in mid-air, if nowhere else) for me to clutch onto in my darkest hours. Two years ago Berenice said 'If you prove yourself on pizzas . . .' She never finished that sentence and I never pinned her down; cowardice stopped me. Well, cowardice has not served me well – it's time for a change of tack.

'Are you saying that if I get this right then at Christmas you'll promote me?' I say, as softly and gently as a human voice can deliver a sentence.

Her almost-smile disappears instantly. 'Let's not get ahead of ourselves.'

'I don't mean to push you, but I'm just trying to be clear what I need to do to . . .' What was her awful buzz-word? Mirror her awful buzz-word, speak Berenice back to her. 'What I need to do to *notch* it . . . *to the next level* . . .'

She stares at me as if she's trying to decide between two identical shades of white paint, neither of which are satisfactory. 'I need you to exceed my expectations. I need to see a step-change in your performance. I need to be convinced you're ready for this. You are ready for this, aren't you, Susannah? I need to see that you're hungry. Are you hungry?'

'Oh I'm hungry, Berenice. I'm hungry.'

I'm always hungry.

I'm the hungriest.

'Can we go and eat?' I say to Rebecca as I hover over her desk at the end of the day. Rebecca and Sam are the only two reasons I've stayed borderline sane at NMN and arguably that border has been crossed a few times of late.

'Not bothered about food but I could murder a drink,' she says, pointing to a presentation on her screen titled 'Shlitzy Alcopops – Nurturing The Brand Soul'.

'How can you always drink on an empty stomach?' I say.

'I'm a professional,' she says, shutting down her computer and grabbing her coat. 'Where's good on a miserable rainy Tuesday?'

'Hawksmoor? Killer cocktails and their burgers are meant to be amazing.'

'First round's on me,' she says. 'Let's make it a double.'

Is Rebecca a Leftover then? She's thirty-three, single, does a bullshit job, drinks a little too much. She happens to be gorgeous: she has huge brown eyes with naturally long, thick curly lashes. She never needs to wear mascara, but when she does, people just stare at her as if her eyes can't be real. Plus she's curvy, and leggy! Honestly, if I didn't know her I'd hate her. But I do know her. So I know that along with being naturally beautiful, she's also funny, kind and loyal.

What I don't know is why she's single. Other than that she's playing a numbers game and hasn't found that mythical 'one' yet. And with Rebecca it definitely isn't for lack of trying. Well, who knows what's around the corner?

★

'Best Piña Coladas in London, hands down,' I say, fishing a yellow cocktail umbrella from my glass and sticking it behind my right ear. Perfect! A little friend for the pink one behind my left.

'Try this,' she says, holding out her Martini glass. 'It says on the menu that it's *an anti-fogmatic*, and that in the 1820s, doctors recommended it be drunk before eleven in the morning.'

'And you'd be drunk before eleven in the morning, Berenice would love that . . . Did the barman say he uses coconut sorbet in this?'

'I wasn't listening to him, I was just looking at him.' She grins. 'Did you see his body?'

'Becka, he's like twenty-two years old.'

She shrugs. Rebecca has no qualms about letching over younger men. I don't do it for fear of looking like a cougar, but Rebecca's not yet old enough to be branded a cougar. Besides, the barman couldn't keep his eyes off her either.

'Let's do Piña Coladas every Tuesday,' I say, taking another swig of my drink. 'This is almost like being on holiday!'

'This place is great,' she says, taking in the dark wood panelled walls and old-fashioned table lamps.

'Isn't it? We're two minutes from all that tourist crap in Covent Garden but we could be in a New York speakeasy. Where's my burger, how long since I ordered?'

'Never mind the burger, I think we've got company,' she

says, smiling her perfect Juicy Tubed smile at someone behind me.

Bingo. It never takes more than a couple of drinks in any social setting before Rebecca has attracted male attention. She's the perfect wing-man. (Wing-woman sounds weird, like a low-budget super hero; Wing-Woman! She has wings and she's learning to fly!) 'Pulling partner' isn't right either technically, as Rebecca invariably pulls and I don't. But that's because she always gets the hot guy and leaves me with the sidekick. Fair enough, I guess I'm the sidekick too. Still, even the leftovers don't want other leftovers.

And here we go again.

'Can we buy you beautiful ladies a drink?' says the better-looking one to Rebecca.

'Have a seat,' she says. 'I'll have a glass of champagne, my friend Ella Umbrella over there will have another Piña Colada.'

'No, I'm fine, thanks,' I say. I'm tipsy already – two strong cocktails on an empty stomach have done me in.

'And a couple of Jäger Bombs too,' says Rebecca, giving me the look. The look that says 'Don't complain your life is boring if you refuse to join me in Living It Up and Getting Pissed On A School Night. Booze! Boys! What more could you want?'

'Rebecca! You know they don't agree with me . . .'

Sixty minutes, two Jäger Bombs and another Piña Colada

later, I'm trying to work out where to stick my new green umbrella.

In Danny, the handsome guy, for *droning on* about the transfer window?

In Rebecca, for faking interest so brilliantly, thus leaving me stuck with The Douche Bag?

Or straight into The Douche Bag? I mean, come *on*: we both know the deal. We're meant to politely chat and let the other two get on with flirting. But no.

I now know Jason is forty, a Virgo, but on the cusp and actually *way* more Libran.

He works in equities at a small Swiss firm near London Wall. He's not being arrogant or anything but he's bloody good at his job – it's just a fact.

He lives in Putney, drives a BM, doesn't much like films or books unless they're about real life crime.

He listens to XFM, thinks Katy Perry's got nice tits but Adele should lay off the doughnuts.

He goes down the gym – David Lloyd, Fulham – three to four times a week and does forty minutes on the tread-mill at fourteen kilometres an hour 'cos he likes to look good. It's where he met his last girlfriend, Megan, twenty-five, who was super hot, beautiful blow job lips, ri-di-culous body (the *greatest* arse in London), but after two years she was pressuring him to commit and he just wasn't sure she was enough for him and he doesn't miss her 'cos London's full of fit birds. Mind you, you don't want to be dating a woman who's over thirty. There's a reason why they're single.

I am yet to find Jason's redeeming features.

He thinks my name is Ella, and I haven't bothered to correct him. Partly because he's done nothing other than talk about himself for an hour. And partly because I'm now severely drunk. My burger hasn't turned up and all I can think about is how hungover my Wednesday morning is going to be. I'm a little dizzy and I really should have a glass of water but Jason is now desperately chatting up the tattooed, red-lipsticked waitress and I don't want to interrupt. She's humouring him, playing along, because the cocktails here aren't cheap, and if Jason orders a few more then her tip might reach double digits.

'Oy, Danny,' he says, pulling at his friend's sleeve as the waitress heads back to the bar. 'Did you clock that waitress's mouth?'

'Saw her tramp stamp,' says Danny. 'You dirty dog, Jase.'

'I think she's up for it,' says Jason.

'I think she's a good waitress,' I say, thinking that *I* couldn't flirt with this tosser just for the sake of a bigger tip.

'Those bright red lips! I bet she's filthy . . .' he says, nudging Danny.

'For God's sake, just because a woman wears red lipstick doesn't mean she's filthy,' I say. 'Where's my burger?'

Jason takes a swig of his drink. 'Yeah well in my experience red lipstick's a good indication that a girl knows what she's doing down there.' He grins. 'The more lipstick, the dirtier!' He winks at Rebecca.

Good grief. 'Sorry,' I say. 'Are you actually suggesting that red lipstick indicates a girl is good in bed?' Rebecca gives me a warning look: you're drunk.

He shrugs and looks at his mate with a raised eyebrow, as if he's said the most intelligent thing short of $E = mc^2$.

'Because, Ja-son, if that's true, then why don't you run off and join the circus?'

'What?'

'Go join the circus, Jason. Date a clown. They wear loads of red lipstick – it's all over their face. By your logic that makes them at least twice as filthy as that poor waitress. Yeah, Jase, go and date a nice dirty clown with a squeezy plastic flower and those funny stripy trousers.'

There is an embarrassed silence, filled eventually by Rebecca. 'Sorry guys, maybe those Jäger Bombs weren't such a good idea . . .' she says. Jason is staring at me like I've said something . . . I don't know, what *is* that word now . . . weird?

'You know what, Jase?' I say. 'Maybe you don't have to wait until the circus comes to town. You might get lucky. Maybe there are some clowns hanging out down the David Lloyd, running on the treadmill with their long slutty clown shoes.'

I see Rebecca shaking her head more violently in my direction.

26

'Gosh, clown shoes must make running a *real* challenge. Bet they can't do "fourteen kilometres an hour" like you can . . . Oh! And step class must be a nightmare! So embarrassing, always tripping over their own feet. Poor, sexy, slightly scary clut-slowns.'

'Clut-slowns?' he says.

'Clut-slowns. Clut-slowns, slut-clowns, you know what I mean!'

'Are you a lezza or what?' he says.

'What?!' I haven't been accused of being a lesbian since I refused to snog Elliot Johnson at the school Christmas disco when I was fourteen. 'Jason . . . You know Maggie?'

'Maggie who?'

'*Hello?* Your ex-girlfriend Maggie? Wow, fickle! Two years together and you can't even remember her name!'

'That's because her name's Megan.'

'Oh. Was it? I thought you said Maggie? No?'

He shakes his head.

'Are you sure?'

'Pretty sure . . .'

'Anyway, "the *greatest* arse in London" – *that* one – well, Jason, I've got news for you, my friend: *you* are the greatest arse in London!'

'Suze . . .' says Rebecca, putting her hand on my arm. 'Let's get you some food . . .'

'I think you should take your mental rug-munching

27

friend home – get her back on her meds,' says Jason, heading to the bar in pursuit of the waitress.

'Yeah, send my love to . . .' I rack my brain for the name of a famous clown . . . er . . . how come I don't know *any* famous clown names? Now *that* really is embarrassing. 'Send my love to . . . to Coco!' I shout after him. Yeah. Coco. That'll do. He was a boy clown. I think.

Danny whispers something to Rebecca and follows his mate to the bar. Rebecca just stares at me.

'What?' I say, twiddling my umbrella and checking whether the up-down mechanism on it works. Cool, it does! I love the fact that these umbrellas could actually function as mini parasols, for ladybirds or something . . .

'Bloody hell, Suze,' she says. 'You need to stop doing that.'

'Doing what?'

'Being insane and aggressive when hot men are chatting us up.'

'He wasn't that hot. Anyway you fancy the barman more than you fancied him.'

'Not the point.'

'Come off it, he was booooring. And his nob-head friend was rude about Adele. I'm standing up for womankind. And he made that moronic comment about lipstick and I was merely trying to explain to him that . . . you know . . . you shouldn't objectify women, and lipstick doesn't make a girl sexy . . .'

'Shall I tell you what else doesn't make a girl sexy, Suze?'

'What?'

'Verbally attacking random men.'

'Random dipshits more like . . .'

'Whatever. Either way, you come across as angry.'

'Becka, I'm only angry when I'm provoked.'

'Look, I know you've had a drink . . .'

'That's your fault! You're a bad friend! You made me have *five* drinks on a Tuesday night and you know I don't get along with Jägermeister at the best of times, hideous Alpine medicine . . .'

'Hang on a minute . . .' she says.

'What?'

'The lipstick thing . . .'

'No, it's not what you're thinking!' I hold up my hand to stop what she's about to say.

'Isn't Jake's girlfriend a . . .'

'Rebecca, it has nothing whatsoever to do with that.'

'You're not *still* looking at her stupid blog, are you?'

'No.'

She looks at me.

'Not really,' I say.

'You are. Oh Suze, why are you doing this to yourself?'

'I'm not. There was some stupid piece in *ES Magazine* last week about Spring's New Make-Up Looks. I saw her name, and then there was a little photo of her with her bloody Birkin bag like some wannabe Victoria Beckham,

29

doing some model's lip gloss at a show . . . I wasn't Googling her, I really wasn't.'

'Oh Suze, she is so irrelevant.'

'They're still together, Rebecca. She's posted some new pics on Facebook. God, I need some carbohydrate, I feel dreadful.'

She shakes her head and puts her arm round me. 'Come on, you drunken, crazy fool. Let's get you home for your meds.'

'Only if by meds you mean two McDonald's cheese-burgers for the road? Please, can we?'

She nods, resignedly.

She's a very good friend.

Wednesday

I will never, ever let Rebecca order me a Jäger Bomb, ever again.

I wake up in my clothes with half a pink umbrella in my hair, a splitting headache in my left eye and the taste of McDonald's dill pickle in my mouth. It's fine. I'm not late for work or anything. But as I lie here in bed, talking myself out of chucking a sickie, I can't help but think 'Why, oh why am I still working at NMN?'

I've been there for six years. I moved there from BVD, an even crappier agency, where I worked on a yellow fats account. (Yellow fats = butter, anything that behaves like butter, or that you'd say was butter-y-ish if you had no taste buds/someone put a gun in your mouth. In fact a gun in your mouth would taste more like butter.) I moved agencies because I thought the problem was BVD and yellow fats. But I've come to realise that the problem wasn't my old agency. It wasn't the spreadable butter-replacement solutions. It's this business full stop.

Oh I know what you're thinking: daft cow, of course advertising is full of tossers! Since the 1980s, ad 'folk' have been second only to estate agents as figures of hate. But in recent years two things changed all that. First, bankers and politicians (never high on your Christmas card list), made a running sprint, like at the end of the Grand National, for Public Enemy spots number one and two. The guys from Foxtons slipped down to third place, and ad folk – well, we fell off the podium.

And second: *Mad Men* came on TV. The men were chauvinists but sexy chauvinists. The women looked like actual women. Everyone smoked and drank and had sex with everyone else in the office. The industry suddenly looked glamorous and grown up and intellectually stimulating. And suddenly people seemed to forget that *Mad Men* is a made-up TV show rather than a documentary, and started thinking maybe advertising wasn't so bad after all.

Friends began asking if it was anything like *Mad Men* at NMN. To which the answer is surprisingly twofold: *a bit*, and *not at all*. *A bit*: the men are still chauvinists. Everyone drinks. Some still smoke. Everyone still has sex with everyone else in the office (apart from Sam and me). But glamorous? Grown up? Intellectually stimulating? See '*not at all*' for details. And as for women who look like actual women? I'm one of only four females in the building who's bigger than a size eight, and two of the others are pregnant.

Anyway – I think, as I force myself to crawl out of bed – it's all going to be fine because I have THE plan: execute this new brief perfectly, stay out of trouble with Berenice, get my bonus and promotion at Christmas, then go and find something fun and fulfilling to do in the world of food instead. And no, I will not be serving fries with that.

It could be a lot worse, I figure as I head to the tube. At least I don't work *at* Fletchers.

Fletchers is a rubbish supermarket. They're the seventh biggest in the UK. They used to be fourth, but they've steadily cut the quality of their food and staff. If you go into a Fletchers after 2 p.m. on a weekday, chances are they'll have run out of milk and bread and you'll be lucky to find a chicken in sell by date. They're plagued by bad PR stories: the guy on the meat counter filmed by an undercover *Sun* reporter picking his nose and then touching the pork belly; donkey meat in the burgers; the relabelling of mutton as lamb; the job-lot of tomatoes from China that were genetically modified in an old nuclear plant.

They're still pretty popular with shoppers though. Why? Here's why: firstly, you can feed a family of four for two pounds at Fletchers. Secondly, a large proportion of the British public *love* the Fletchers 'brand'. Devron, Fletchers' Head of Foods and Marketing, is on record as saying 'If you crossed James Corden with a can of Tango and a Geordie hen night, that's what our brand stands for: down-to-earth, honest, cheeky fun.' And all that cheeky fun is down to the advertising we've done for them over the last six years. Advertising that I have, in some small way, been involved in. Good job I don't believe in re-incarnation or I'd be coming back in the next life as a vajazzle.

Fletchers hired NMN as their agency because we are the diametric opposite of Fletchers. We look classy (from the outside at least). We are big. Shiny. Expensive. We do ads for famous beers and jeans; for deodorant that is in every bathroom cabinet in the nation.

Our offices are plush and tasteful. They reek of sobriety. *We're not wacky*, soothe the white walls in reception.

We are solid, reassure the marble tiles in the first-floor client loos. *We won't take your overpriced t-shirt brand and 'sex it up' so that next year the only people wearing it will be gypsies on a reality TV show. Gosh no – not our style at all.*

Take a closer look, whisper the spot-free windows in the second-floor boardroom. *Here, borrow this ruler so you can measure how thick the chocolate on our client biscuits is. See? Isn't that wonderful? Everything's going to be just fine.*

(It's a good job clients never take the lift above the second floor. Up on fourth, the creatives inhabit their own little Sodom. Management up on fifth is Gomorrah. The smell of fire and brimstone is masked by copious amounts of Jo Malone Red Roses air freshener but that doesn't fool me.)

And then we come to my desk, here on the third floor – home of the account directors. It's a metaphorical floor plan. Below us are the clients, when they come in for a meeting. Above us, the creatives. We are stuck in the middle of two warring factions, the filling in a sandwich that you would be well advised not to eat.

I dump my bag on my chair and take a deep breath. Right: I've made a decision. Today is going to be a good day. Yes, I'm hungover, which isn't ideal. But I have a large white coffee in one hand, and a brown paper bag with buttered white toast and Marmite in the other. Caffeine. Salt. Fat. Carb. Chair. Those five nouns: what more could a girl ask for?

Even better! Jonty's not here. He's off on a course all week learning how to manage his workload. Bless, I don't think he needs any help on *that* front, he's given it all to me.

And in other good news Rebecca is out too, on a shoot, so she won't be able to nab me over lunch break and try to make me talk about last night. Rebecca is one of those friends who thinks it's important always to *confront the truth*. Doesn't she realise no one ever thanks you for telling them the truth? Denial is a healthy psychological state, designed to protect us from ourselves, and should be respected accordingly.

So no lunchtime shaming. In fact, today's lunch is going to be the start of the rest of my life: Devron's finally briefing me on Project F and I'll be on the road to promotion. He'll phone me in a bit to tell me where he wants to be wined and dined. My mother is always telling me how lucky I am that I get to go to the occasional posh restaurant and not have to pay. Maybe it does sound glamorous. Except it's not like going somewhere fab with your friends. No. It is going somewhere fab with a compulsive freeloading rude buffoon who is a stranger to the concept of shame.

Sure enough, my phone rings at 10.57.

'S-R,' he says. Berenice calls me Susannah. Devron calls me by my initials, S-R. He doesn't think women other than secretaries should be allowed in the workplace and I figure it's his subconscious mind trying to pretend I'm not a girl.

'So Devron, where do you fancy today?'

'Hawksmoor,' he says, 'in Covent Garden. Hello? Are you still there, S-R?'

'Uh-huh . . .' I say, trying to replay exactly what interaction I had with the bar staff last night . . . Did that waitress overhear any of the clown stuff?

'I want steak,' says Devron. 'Hawksmoor. It's a beef place.'

More than familiar with it thanks, Devron – familiar with the barman, the waitress, the cocktail menu, the cocktail menu . . . Actually, playing it all back in my head, I don't remember embarrassing myself in front of the staff . . . However, I also don't remember whether I took a cab or the tube home last night . . . Not worth the risk. 'We can't go to Hawksmoor,' I say, a little too forcefully.

'What do you mean, *can't*?' says Devron, a hint of irritation creeping into his voice. Damn. There goes the golden rule of my job. Never *ever* use the c-word in front of a client.

'It's just . . . we might have trouble getting a table at such short notice . . . it's very popular.'

'Janelle's on the other line getting us one now,' he says.

Quick . . . think. 'Tell her not the Covent Garden one! There's a new one! In Air Street! It's meant to be . . . much . . . airier?'

'What're you on about? The one in Covent Garden's ten minutes away.'

'If you fancy beef let's go to Gaucho's. They do that lovely Argentinian rib-eye . . .'

'Nah, been there loads. Plus, they're Argies. Hold on . . . one o'clock? Yeah, Janelle's got us in at one, in the bar area. See you there.'

I hang up and have a terrible, paranoid, hungover thought. I check my wallet. Nope. No receipt. I start texting Rebecca to ask if she paid for our drinks last night because I definitely didn't. That's all I need: turn up and find myself on a Wanted poster. Rebecca's on a shoot though so she'll have her phone off till lunch.

No choice: I'm going to have to adopt a disguise, fake

moustache not an option. Off to the loo. Right, let's see what we've got to work with today . . .

Well, one *good* thing about having mousy hair and bluey-grey eyes is that you don't leave a striking physical impression at the scene of a crime. I have the sort of neutral features that you'd describe as nondescript if you were being bitchy; or chameleon-like, if you were Jake, trying to be poetic on our third date. Nothing is too big or small but nothing is special either. If I apply make-up really well I can scrub up to a 7 out of 10. If I'm tired or have no blusher on, these days I can sink to a 3.

I'll have to rely on subtle styling. OK, hair was down, or was it up last night? It smells of smoke. Rebecca must have been smoking, so my hair was probably down, which is why it smells of Marlboro Lights. Fine: I'll stick it up in a bun.

Yesterday I was in my burgundy dress and heels; today a navy jacket, cream t-shirt and trousers. That's good, less showy. And I'm in flats so a totally different height, five foot six now, and yesterday I was at least five foot eight.

Face. OK, not much we can do about this. Yesterday's eye make-up is still on, but a bit smudged under the eyes, not too bad. I could pop to Boots and buy some red lipstick – oh, the irony . . . Pass myself off as French . . . Mind you, red lipstick will only draw attention, and I always feel ridiculous wearing it, like a little girl pretending to be her mother.

girlfriend. Berenice doesn't mind – she'll sign off any client-related expenses without a quibble, even lapdances at Stringfellows when the luxury car team take their client out on a mega jolly. But try to expense a taxi home at 11 p.m. on a rainy winter's night and she'll send round an all-staff email, titled 'KEEP CALM AND CATCH THE TUBE! – AUSTERITY TIMES!' naming and shaming you.

'What are we having?' says Devron, handing me a menu. He does mean *we*, not *you*. Devron is one of life's sharers. Well, a one-way sharer. I too am a sharer. I want other people to try the food I love. I put things on their plates; I eat from theirs. In fact I have no problem eating from a stranger's plate. Jake and I once had a massive row because he thought I was flirting with a man on the table next to us, when all I really wanted was a taste of his cherry pie.

However, I cannot share with Devron. When I first started on Fletchers we went to The Ivy. I was so excited, I'd never been. The waiter had barely laid down my pudding when Devron licked the entire back of his spoon like an eight-year-old boy trying to out-gross his sister. Then, as if in slow motion, he plunged it into my untouched choc-olate fondant. Since then I've developed an over-sensitivity to him touching my food. And he always does touch it. It's just a question of when. In the past I've tried different strategies to avoid him ruining our meals together. Tried pulling the plate away. Tried saying I'm developing a cold sore. Tried licking my own spoon copiously. To no avail.

'Get the burger,' says Devron.

'Don't fancy it,' I say, looking down the menu for the least Devron-friendly dish. 'You get the burger.'

'I want steak. Get the burger.'

'I had a burger last night, I'll have grilled fish.'

'You can't order fish in a steak restaurant. Come on, S-R, look at how good that looks!' he says, pointing to the table to my left.

Devron is right though. The burger looks terrific. And I am badly in need of something more substantial than a sliver of white fish. Plus, a MacDonald's cheeseburger – perfect for a drunken snack – is as much about the excitement of unwrapping that greaseproof paper as anything. This Hawksmoor burger is in a different league: a thick, char-grilled patty of Longhorn beef on a brioche bun, all the trimmings. And it was supposed to be mine last night. Brainwave! If I keep a tight grip on it Devron won't be able to nick any!

Devron beckons the waiter over. 'We'll start with lobster, then I'll get the Chateaubriand, triple cooked chips, beef dripping chips and she'll have a burger.'

'Any sides?' says the waiter.

'Macaroni cheese,' says Devron.

'Good choice,' says the waiter, sticking his pencil back behind his ear when he should be reaching for his sharpener.

'Then bone marrow . . . creamed spinach . . . and talk me through the ribs,' says Devron.

41

'Tamworth belly ribs, sir? Tender pork, marinaded in maple syrup, chipotle and spices.'

'Yeah, one of those with the lobster. And we'll do puddings now – I'll have the peanut butter shortbread, she'll have . . .'

'I haven't even looked yet . . .' I say.

'Sticky toffee ice cream sundae,' says Devron.

Gross. Don't get me wrong. I'm greedy. I love food. I like to try a bit of everything. I just can't stand waste. Maybe that's why I never throw anything away. It's obviously not like I was a war baby, but fundamentally it offends me to see good food go in the bin. I think it's because I come from feeders. In my mother's kitchen food equals love: why would you throw that away, even if it is slightly on the turn?

'So! Big brief!' says Devron, pulling his chair closer to the table. 'Super-high-profile, game-changing – mega-strategic!' I wonder if he stole this phrase from Berenice, or she stole it from him? I wonder how long I can avoid having to use it myself . . .

'We're developing a range that's going to do-mi-nate the pizza market!' he says. (The last 'market-dominating' idea Fletchers came up with was savoury chewing gum.) 'We want TV ads, Twitter, the works. Budget's mega – four million quid. This time next year we'll have wiped the floor with every other retailer. Asda? As-don't, more like. Dominos? Domi-no-nos!'

'Good one, Devron.' (I know. It's bad. But if Berenice were here she'd have fake-laughed for a full minute.)

'Our research guys report massive growth in low-cal treats, women worrying about cellulite but still wanting to nosh on comfort food.' He gives me a knowing look as the waiter approaches with our starters. 'Huge gap in the market and we're going to fill it with a range of *half-calorie pizzas*! It'll be bigger than Fearne Cotton's arse.'

Does he mean Fearne Cotton or Fern Britton? Fearne Cotton doesn't even have an arse, as far as I'm aware. (Devron left his wife and kids for Mandy, a girl he met on a boys' night out at Tiger Tiger. By all accounts Mandy is an avid follower of celebrity culture. In an attempt to look 'with-it' Devron often references celebrities, but he some-times gets a little confused.)

'Let's get Fearne Cotton for the campaign,' he says. 'Have you got her agent's number?'

'Devron, I think if you mean Fern Britton she actually did Ryvita already . . .'

He pauses, a chunk of lobster flesh half way to his mouth. 'Oh. Well you guys can fine-tune the celeb, it was just a thought.' He reaches for the plate of belly ribs and grabs one in his fist. 'Well? What do you think?'

I think if you're going to have a pizza, have a pizza. Do things properly or don't bother.

'How do they cut the calories so significantly?' I say.

'Sell punters half a pizza, ha ha ha!' says Devron.

'Seriously, how?'

'Something to do with fat sprays, flavour substitutes . . . ask Jeff the recipe guy.'

'What's the name of the range?'

'Legal are checking trademarks, I'll confirm end of next week, but it's a goody,' he says, waggling a rib in the air like it's a sixth finger, Anne Boleyn but with pork.

'Have you researched it?' I say.

'No need, I feel it in my gut. Head, heart, guts.' This is one of Devron's favourite phrases. It's the title of some management book he's obsessed with and every time he wants to justify anything moronic he reels it out. His other favourite phrase is *JFDI*. Which is like the Nike slogan, *Just Do It*, but with added swearing.

I smile weakly as the waiter clears our plates.

'Can I see the wine list?' Devron says to the waiter, though there's practically a full bottle on the table.

'Don't you like the Bordeaux?' I say.

'I just want to look at the list. Do me a favour? Go call Tom, fix up a meeting for Friday with him and Jeff to talk you through the range.'

'Shall I do it after lunch? Our main courses will be here any minute.'

'JFDI.'

There's no reception down here so I pop upstairs and out onto the street. Opposite the restaurant is a dance studio and I pause to watch a class of ballerinas stand at the barre

44

warming up. Beautiful. Their bodies are not like normal people's bodies. They move so fluidly, it's impossible to imagine them doing anything other than dancing. I wish I had an innate talent, other than the ability to eat a little bit too much.

I take my phone out to call Tom, Devron's underling, and find a text from Rebecca: 'I think the guys paid last night?' Great. That's exactly what *won't* have happened. I've got away with it now, but still . . . I phone Tom and leave a message, then go back to join Devron and discover the real reason he sent me upstairs. There is now a second bottle of the same Bordeaux open on the table next to the first which is barely touched. I am witnessing a master at work. I'd forgotten that I have to watch Devron like a paranoid hawk at all times. Yet this is a new low – an act of such shameless greed that I almost have to take my hat off to him. Except he'd probably nick my hat and sell it on eBay while I was blinking.

'Ah look, the mains,' he says, nodding at two waiters en route with large trays.

The waiter puts my burger down in front of me. I immediately put my master plan into action: grab the burger and hold on for dear life. If Devron wants any he'll have to fight me for it. For once he is not going to ruin my lunch. Devron looks at the burger. He looks at me. His brain goes into overdrive. Even though it's dark in here, I swear I can see his pupils dilate. Hell, I can actually see the cogs inside his brain start to rotate. My grip on the burger tightens.

In my years at NMN I've learnt a smidgen about Greek mythology; board members often quote the Greeks as a way of making themselves look like intellectuals rather than men who spend all day fantasising about shagging the grads. One thing that comes to me, as my fingers sink into the bun and I struggle to contain the meat, lettuce and tomato inside, is the concept of the Pyrrhic victory. Named after a king who won a battle but lost a war, it loosely equates to a tiny gain offset by a gigantic loss. For, after two delicious bites, my over-tight grip causes the beef to slide from my bun, and Devron, quicker than a Venus flytrap, reaches out, stabs the beef and drags it across the table to his own plate. Game over, and he didn't even blink.

'So, Devron . . .' I say, wondering how it's possible that I'll be paying two hundred pounds for this meal and I'll still need to pop to M&S for a sandwich on my way back to the office, 'this brief. Is the airtime still planned for the start of May?' He nods.

'OK: I'll brief a creative team next week,' I say. 'That'll mean shooting the ad after Easter and, and . . . and . . .'

'And what?'

And the barman from last night's just walked in.

'And . . . yes . . .' There he is, talking to my waiter, and now he's turning and shit, yes, he's looking this way. 'And . . . yes . . . good, yes, Easter.' Shit. 'Easter.'

'Yeah, shoot after Easter,' says Devron. 'Blah . . . blah . . . blah . . . timing plan,' he carries on.

Oh God. The barman is totally staring at me, and now smiling. No, that's not a smile, that's a grin! He is *grinning* in a way that does not bode well.

'Blah . . . blah . . . blue sky thinking . . . blah . . . blah . . . Nike ad . . .' says Devron.

'Absolutely, Devron,' I say, nodding. Oh no! Now the barman's scribbling something down . . . the bill!

'Blah . . . blah . . . super-tight deadlines . . . share the process early . . .'

'Yes, of course . . .' I nod. Oh good grief no! He's coming over. Get back behind the bar, this is not on!

He's half way across the floor heading towards us. I've got to move. Right now.

'Blah . . . blah . . . three weeks on Friday, yes?' says Devron.

'Sure, yes, whatever you want, back in a sec,' I say, darting out from behind the table and heading speedily towards the toilets, head down.

Christ. Lucky escape. How long can I hide in here for? Too little time and the barman will still be lurking. Two and a half minutes? La-di-dah . . . Quick make-up check . . . Oooh, nice wall tiles in here, didn't notice those last night. White rectangular subway tiles, very classic . . . Right, I think that's about time.

I pull the bathroom door open to find the barman

47

standing waiting for me, arms folded. He really is embarrassingly good looking: thick black hair and green eyes, with thick lashes. And that body! His black t-shirt stops at the perfect mid point of his arm, showing off perfect, not too large, but very defined, tanned biceps.

'You again! I couldn't believe it when I saw you in here!' he says. Ditto.

'Well . . . Sorry,' I say, 'but I have to get back to my table . . .'

'Hang on a minute,' he says. 'I'm glad you're here, there's something I didn't manage to give you guys last night, you ran out before I could get over to you!'

Hurry up and get this over with then.

'Yep, sorry about that . . . just give it to me, I'll sort it,' I say, holding out my palm and turning slightly away so that Devron can't see what's going on.

'Cool! I didn't want to hand it over at the table, I thought it might not be appropriate,' he says, handing me a little green paper umbrella. Ah, nice touch. Giving me the bill inside the umbrella, that's a classy move. I look over to see if Devron's watching but he's otherwise occupied, knuckle-deep in my sundae.

'Aren't you going to open it?' he says.

'Bad luck opening an umbrella indoors,' I say.

He smiles. 'Go on, before you go back.'

I quickly open the little parasol, and sure enough, there's a figure written down inside. Except there's no pound sign.

And no decimal point. And while the drinks here are expensive, they're not *that* expensive. This number's eleven digits long.

His phone number. Oh my goodness. This super-hot young barman is giving me his phone number. The game is not over yet! – I have *still* got it going on! I must stop being so hard on myself. Evidently I don't look bedraggled at all. I look good. Better than good: Very Good. Sexxy. Hot enough to attract this chisel-jawed guy who looks quite like David Gandy. I don't think anyone this handsome has chatted me up for years. Maybe I'm entering a pre-Mrs-Robinson stage of allure? A little firework of delight goes off inside me. I try not to show a reaction but I'm already grinning like an imbecile.

'What's her name?' he says.

'Susie,' I say. 'It's Susie.' Hang on. *Her* name? What? Whose name? *Oh no.*

'Susie.' He says it like a handshake. 'Sorry if I was staring at you girls last night, I just think your mate's properly beautiful. If it isn't too cheesy, would you ask her to call me?'

I nod silently, trying to keep my smile up.

'I'm Luke by the way. What's your name?'

I feel a substantial part of my self curl up into a ball and start to howl, though I stay standing, one arm resting on the door frame, pretending not to be acutely embarrassed.

'I'm also Susie actually.' I say, realising that I'm about to

49

pay the bill with my credit card, which clearly says Susie Rosen on it. 'We're both Susies.'

'That's funny,' he says.

'Isn't it just,' I say. 'Ha! We're like the Two Ronnies . . . you know, well actually she's more a Sue-becka. Some people even call her . . . Becka . . . Subecka . . . her middle name's Becka, that's why . . . just to tell us apart . . .'

'Subecka! Sounds Japanese! Well anyway, say hi from me.'

'Will do, got to go!' I say, heading back to Devron, who is arranging with the waiter for his two bottles of wine to be re-corked and put in a bag for him.

'Bit young for you, wasn't he?' says Devron, as I sit back down. 'It's good ice cream, have some,' he says, poking his spoon at my sundae glass.

'I'm stuffed,' I say.

'Right: see Tom and Jeff end of the week and get scripts to me three weeks on Friday.'

'That soon, Devron?'

I'm pretty sure the Amish can erect a wooden house in twenty-four hours. Apparently God created the Universe in seven days. But it takes our creative teams one month to write a few piddly scripts.

'That timing's too tight, Devron.'

'You said it was OK a minute ago!'

I have zero recollection of agreeing to anything of the sort. And if I did it was only because I wasn't listening to a word he was saying . . . OK, let me think: if I brief a team early next week I might manage it, if Robbie gives me one of the more amenable, mature creative teams. Maybe lovely old Andy Ashford.

'Theoretically it's possible . . .' I say.

'We're good, right?' he nods.

'It does depend on the team's availability and workload, I'll do everything I can . . .'

'You're late on this project already.'

'To be fair we haven't had your brief yet. And we haven't got a name for the range. And we haven't seen the products either.' So technically, Devron, I should be the one sitting across the table giving you a menacing look, not the other way round . . .

'So that's a yes then,' he says nodding again. (Last year Devron spent a week on a 'How to Influence People' course. He spent five days glued to YouTube videos of Tony Blair and Obama. Now whenever he wants something unreasonable he nods like a plastic dog in a car. Horrifically, this technique seems to work.)

I nod back at him. 'Yes, Devron,' I say, 'yes, that's totally fine.'

I have a nasty feeling in my head, heart and guts, that I shouldn't have just said that.

The first thing I do when I'm back at my desk is fill out my expenses – two hundred and forty quid with that second bottle of wine! Just once before I quit I'd like to do what

51

Steve Pearson, Board Director on pessaries, does regularly: take the person I'm having an affair with out for lunch and bill it as a client lunch. (Sam – premier source of intel, as per usual.) I'd never actually fake my expenses; more to the point, there's no one here I'd have an affair with. What am I even talking about? I would never have an affair *full stop*. Why can't anybody ever leave anybody without another body to go to?

I wander down to the mail room to see if Sam's around. I fancy a coffee and a gossip but he's nowhere to be found. He's probably in the pub with Jinesh from IT, swotting up on some dodgy new computer software that can read your emails from outer space.

Finally (and this should have been first, but I've put it off because it's the least fun) I take the lift up to the creative floor to visit Robbie Doggett's secretary, Alexis. It's impossible for me not to associate anyone called Alexis with Alexis Colby Carrington from *Dynasty*. So even if this Alexis wasn't already a cold, manipulative bitch, I'd probably project that onto her anyway. She's lying on the leather sofa outside Robbie's office, wearing sequinned hot pants and her favourite Patti Smith t-shirt. Sam's the only man in the building who doesn't think she's the most beautiful woman in W1. As a consequence she hates him. She hates him even more since last year's Christmas party when he asked her – in front of her new pop star boyfriend – to name a single Patti Smith song.

She's deep in concentration, studying *Grazia*.

'Alexis. Have you got a sec?'

She puts her magazine down on the floor and checks out my outfit. Her gaze lingers briefly on my belt, then moves swiftly back to the mag. 'Hi babe,' she says wearily.

'Can you please ask Robbie to allocate me a team for the Fletchers brief asap?'

'Babe, he's shooting in New York, not back for a week.'

'Yes. I know.' And as far as I'm aware they do have telephones and the internet in America. It might just be a rumour but I'm pretty sure it's true. 'He knows the brief's urgent.'

'He didn't mention it to me,' she says, flicking over the page. She pulls her head back as if she's seen a burns victim. 'Look at this cellulite!' she says, her fingers tracing the thighs of some poor A-lister as if the paper were her own skin.

'And tell him Devron wants scripts three weeks on Friday.'

'You'll *never* get that,' she says.

'I'll call him myself and explain?'

'Babe, you know that I'm The Gatekeeper. Leave it with me.' End of conversation.

It's pitch black outside by the time I finish, and a particularly cold March evening with no sign of spring in sight. All I want to do is head home and have a large glass of wine and a curry, but I'm trying not to drink every night.

Plus I can't justify splashing out on a mid-week take-away when I'm meant to be saving for my eventual escape.

Theoretically I should go home via Sainsbury's. Try to be good, buy something healthy and full of beta-carotenes and Omega 3s. Is it Omega 3s or Omega 6s? Can't I just eat double the 3s? A piece of salmon, some leafy green veg. I could make some form of cleansing broth. If I slipped in some udon noodles, it'd be almost like pasta . . . I should also pop in to see my neighbour, Grumpy Marjorie. I try to see her once a month and I haven't been round for a while. The guilt is building up.

Then again, *The Apprentice* is on tonight. If I go straight home I could be in bed with Sir Alan on iPlayer by 9pm. Not in bed with Sir Alan, that wouldn't work at all.

Decision made, I walk quickly to the tube station. I promise myself I'll go round to Marjorie's this weekend. Or maybe next weekend. And I'll eat green leafy veg another day.

Right. Let's start over. Stressful day, happy pasta shape needed. Farfalle! Butterflies are happy! And there's the other half of that pack of bacon from Monday. I was planning a vegetarian dinner after watching Devron demolish a piece of bone marrow with his fingers earlier. Still bacon's not really meat-meat. Pigs are more like chickens than cows, when you think about it.

And I'll chuck in some frozen peas, they're definitely vegetables . . . and there's that carbonara recipe that doesn't need cream – just one egg and an extra yolk – but it still tastes mega creamy: easy, peasy carbonara! Perfect. Crispy bits of bacon, little bursts of fresh, sweet peas, topped with lovely salty parmesan.

My stomach is rumbling on the tube and the minute I walk through my door I start the pasta and pour myself a little glass of wine. It's just one glass. An hour later I'm in bed and I'm content. This is the best way that this day could end. I have three things that I really wanted. Good food. Good wine. Good TV.

I am thankful for these nights, when I am so exhausted, I can almost forget that I've ever been in love. I can almost forget the whole concept of having another person to share my life with. The good stuff, the bad stuff, a photo of ballerinas, the story of Devron and his wine. I've almost forgotten what it feels like to fall asleep next to someone and wake up the next morning feeling happy and calm. I've almost forgotten all of these things. Except in these moments in the dark before sleep comes. And who ever really does forget, really?

Jake, my ex, used to have this thing about foreign catchphrases and quirks in other languages. For example, he thought it was hilarious that the English call condoms 'French letters', but the French call them English hats, '*capotes Anglaises*'. He'd often try to amuse my male friends with this fact, to the point where I'd have to leave the room from sheer repetition.

Another phrase he loved was '*Metro, boulot, dodo*'. *Metro* = subway. *Boulot* = French slang for 'the grind', i.e. the day job. And *dodo* = sweet slang for '*dormir*' = to sleep; like you'd use to a child, i.e. sleepy time. The line is taken from a poem by a French writer, Pierre Béarn, about the tedium of monotonous work: tube, the grind, sleep. Welcome to my world.

Some mornings when I'd be struggling out of bed at 5.30 a.m. for a pre-meeting with Berenice where my sole purpose was to lay pencils for her in Boardroom Two at perfect right angles to the pads, Jake would grab my hand and try to pull me back into the warmth.

'Why do you do that bullshit job? It's Metro Bullshit Dodo, Susie, I don't get it.'

'I'm thirty-three, it's the only job I've ever done. I'm not qualified for anything else.'

'Your skills are totally adaptable, there's loads of other jobs you could do.'

And then a year later, 'Jake: I am thirty-four. That's too old to change careers. I couldn't afford to go back to college now, even if I wanted to.'

'Stop being so negative. People older than you re-train to be doctors or even architects.'

'I can't stand the sight of blood, and I'm not smart enough to be a doctor or an architect.'

'I didn't literally mean those two jobs. I meant you could do anything – even if it takes a few years to get there.'

And then last year, 'It's easy for you, Jake! You're naturally talented, you love your job and you're paid loads to do it. I am average at everything. I have no hidden talents. What am I good at?'

'Food. You just need to figure out a way to make it into a career.'

'Yeah right, chip shop assistant number three, minimum wage and the boss gets to grope me behind the deep fat fryer . . .'

'I don't know. You could run your own café, do a mix of English and Italian classics, just simple, beautiful stuff. You're such a good cook, and you love all that.'

'Do you know how expensive it is to set something like that up? And do you know how many catering businesses fail in their first year? And if you think I'm busy and do horrendous hours now, what do you think that would be like?'

'You could write a cookbook! Or do a recipe blog, or a blog all about pasta! That girl at work I was telling you about, she's started doing a blog about make-up . . .'

'Which girl?'

'You know . . . my friend who does make-up.'

'Who? Leyla Dempsey?'

'Uh-huh.'

'The one whose dad bought her a flat in Notting Hill and a Birkin bag, and pays all her bills for her, but you say she's not at all spoiled and she's really down to earth? That one?'

'Oh Susie, stop it.'

'Stop what? No, it's fine. I'm glad she can afford to spend her days writing about eye shadow, I'm sure it's deeply enthralling, but you know, my dad didn't buy me a flat and he doesn't pay my bills and buy me handbags that cost a year's salary in the chip shop.'

'Well actually you do live in a flat that your grandma gave you.'

'No, I don't! She did not *give* it to me, that's ridiculous. I pay seven hundred and fifty pounds a month to my brother, I have never asked my parents for money since I was twenty-one and I never would. Not least because my parents would tell me to get stuffed, and be a grown up.'

'Well, why don't you?'

'Why don't I what? Ask them for money?'

'No. Why don't you be a grown up?'

'What are you talking about?'

'Man up. Grow some balls. Stop wasting your time in a job you don't even like. You've got no respect for most of the people you work with.'

'That's because they're all letches or bullies. Anyway I do like Rebecca. And Sam . . .'

'You'd still be mates with them if you leave. They might leave before you. Have you ever thought about that?'

'Sam's never going anywhere.'

'Sam's a loser, but he's not the point.'

'Don't call Sam a loser,' I say. 'So your *friend's* blog, presumably she doesn't make any money out of it, it's just some little vanity project? Oh, that'd be a great name for a beauty blog, The Vanity Project . . .'

'Stop having a go at some girl you've never even met just because she's got off her arse and is doing what you want to do.'

'Are you saying I'm jealous of some twenty-three-year-old who writes about bloody lip balm?'

'I'd say you're clearly jealous, yes. And a bit vicious as well.'

'I think it's a really good idea if I go to work now.'

'Yeah, I think that's a really good idea.'

'Am I seeing you later?'

'Not sure . . .'

'Why not?'

'There's a work-drinks thing in Soho . . .'

'Oh . . . the whole company?'

'A few of us, yeah.'

'Oh. Well let me know if you pick up any brilliant tips on how to apply mascara. Am I supposed to look up or down? Gosh, it's all so terribly confusing . . .'

'Go to work.'

Sometimes I have an overwhelming urge to call him, to tell him that I'm finally going to hand in my notice, as soon as they promote me. I want him to know that at long last I'm about to be brave, jump off this treadmill, very soon. I am. But then he'll ask me when, and what I'm going to do instead, and I don't know yet, so I can't, and I'll look foolish.

And also if I call him, he'll think I want him back. Which truly I don't. After what happened? I couldn't forgive him. And also she might answer. And that's one voice I don't ever need to hear again.

are 'Stretchy Friends'. Guys on tills are 'Customer's Best Friends'. And the truck drivers are 'Friends On Wheels'.

The worst thing about this? NMN came up with all of it over the course of a six-month consultation process, called, oh irony, 'Cut The Crap'. Cut The Crap involved a lot of digital mood boards and much talk of empowerment. Fletchers paid us a £130k fee. Devron wrote the cheque in the same week Fletchers announced they'd no longer pay their work experience teens a minimum wage for shelf stacking, sorry, make that 'Stretchy Friending'.

I tell reception I'm here to see Tom, get my security pass, then sit down and prepare for the wait. Regardless of who I'm meeting at Fletchers they will always make me wait twenty-three minutes in reception. I can set my watch by it. It's a basic power play. I am an agency serf: they are the Client Masters. Therefore they will make me sit there while they're sitting at their desks on Facebook or laughing about last night's *Made in Chelsea*. And when their little egg-timer goes off at twenty-three past Meeting Time, they'll saunter down, pick me up and never once acknowledge this whole charade. I once made the mistake of asking Berenice why we couldn't just turn up twenty-three minutes late and I could see her right eyebrow twitching with fury as she struggled to restrain herself from slapping me.

The thing is, I don't mind waiting. It's a rare chance to have twenty-three precious minutes to myself. If Berenice were sitting beside me now she'd be on her iPhone, frantically mailing the office about Five Year Plans for World Domination. Thankfully she's not, so I can relax. I consider trying to source a glass of water. Except that's an impossible dream because I haven't got two pound coins on me. Yes, that's right. If you want a glass of water while you're waiting in reception, you have to insert two pound coins into a vending machine, which then spits out a small bottle of branded tap water. The trout on the front desk will not give you tap water even if you've just run the marathon for Children in Need dressed as Barney the Dinosaur.

No water. So instead I sit and wait. There's a copy of the *Times* on the table and I flick briefly to the food pages. In the 'My Favourite Meal' column, there's a recipe from Celina Summer, some pop star's wife who's just launched herself as the next celebrity chef. She's done a recipe for a chicken sandwich: chicken, lettuce, bread – no butter, not even low-fat mayo. Inspiring stuff, thanks, Celina. Oh great, and your new book, *Eat Music, Dance To Food* has gone straight into the charts. Still, you do look terrific in a bikini, which is ultimately the thing that matters most in a chef.

You know what? It's all very well Jake telling me to write a recipe book, but unless you're skinny and beautiful you're not going to be able to compete with these food celebs. Maybe I should flirt more with Devron, persuade him to put me in the next TV ad. No - I'd definitely rather work in the chip shop than flirt with Devron. Or Tom for that matter. Grim, it'd be like flirting with a teenage boy.

'Jeff. Jeff the chef?' I say, holding out my hand and stifling a giggle.

'You think that's funny?' he says, shaking my hand firmly. 'The cleaner on the fifth floor's called Katrina.'

'Really?'

He nods. 'And when I lived in New York I had a doorman called Norman.'

'You're making that up,' I say.

'True fact,' he says, grinning. I sneak a glance at his wedding finger. Yay! No ring.

'We used to have a gardener called Norman!' says Tom. 'That was in the old house. When we moved to Oxshott my mother had to let him go.'

Jeff raises an eyebrow at me. 'Shall we head to the kitchens then? I'm sure you can't wait to see the product,' he says, with a trace of sarcasm.

'Oh no!' says Tom. 'I really wanted to show Susie my slides that set up our brand rationale positioning.'

'Uh-oh, Thomas. Is this another one of your Death by PowerPoints?' says Jeff. His tone is light, but Tom bristles nonetheless.

'This is a mega-strategic, super-high-profile, game-changing project. A lot of rigour's gone into the thinking.'

'Mega-strategic *and* game-changing? That sounds very important indeed,' says Jeff. 'I thought we were just trying to flog some pizzas?'

'You don't have to see the presentation, Jeff. I can take

her through the slides and we'll meet you in the kitchen after?' says Tom.

Jeff looks me straight in the eye. It is a look filled with conspiratorial naughtiness. *You and I are the same. We are not like Tom. Let's have some fun.*

'I'll come with you,' says Jeff. 'I might learn how to be mega-strategic and game-changing. But will it be quick? I've got another meeting at 10 a.m.'

'That'll be fine,' says Tom.

'Can you do me one favour though, Tom?' says Jeff.

'What do you want?' says Tom warily.

'Can we do your presentation over coffee in the canteen? The fluorescent lighting in those meeting rooms makes me lose the will to live.'

Tom weighs this up as if it's a trap. He takes a breath, then nods. 'OK. I'll go and fetch my laptop and meet you guys up there. Grab me a soy chai, would you Jeff?'

'Will do,' says Jeff. 'Take your time.'

We walk through the building to the central lifts. Somehow it feels like we could be on a date, walking in the park rather than in a concrete office block with giant photos of grey, veiny prawns bearing down on us. There's a crackle of something between us that feels almost visible. I know it's ridiculous, we only met a few minutes ago, but he is most definitely flirting with me. And not just normal flirting. Mega-strategic, game-changing flirting. Flirting in a way that is totally caveman and presumptive: I, Man, flirt with you. I fancy you. You, Woman, flirt back. You fancy me. Let's go to the toilets, take our security passes off, and take it from there.

Of course this is probably all in my mind and yet . . .

'I like your earrings,' he says. My hand immediately moves to my ear, and I find myself twirling with my hair.

'I've forgotten which ones I put on,' I say. 'Are they the amber ones?'

'They're a sort of moonstone,' he says. 'They make your eyes look more blue than grey. You've got those sort of eyes that change depending on what you're wearing, don't you?'

I am definitely not imagining this.

'So is it Susie with an *ie* or with a *zy*?' he says, as we get in the lift.

Lift, for once, could you please get stuck, please? I've been trapped in these buggers at least once a year for six years, and never, ever with anyone remotely attractive.

'Susie with an *ie*,' I say.

'I once went out with a Suziii who spelt her name with three Is. She used to put little flowers instead of dots on them. It was never going to work out,' he says.

Aha! Proof that he's straight too. Excellent. 'So is it Jeff with a J or a G?' I say.

'J, like Jeff Bridges, though obviously he's got a bit more hair than me. Have you seen *The Big Lebowski*?'

67

'Like ten times,' I say. 'I think The Dude is based on this guy Sam who I work with . . .'

Jeff laughs a low, deep chuckle. 'And there's me thinking The Dude was based on me.' he says. 'Did you see that film the Coen brothers did a few years back, the Western?'

'*No Country For Old Men*?' I actually thought it was a touch over-rated but it looks like Jeff loves it, so I don't want to say I didn't like it . . .

'No,' he says. 'I thought it was over-rated. I meant *True Grit*, also with Jeff Bridges.'

'Oh I loved *True Grit*, with the young girl with the plaits. So great!'

OK, enough of this time-wasting. I need to find out if he has a girlfriend. We're now entering the canteen. Tom'll be at his desk already, I haven't got much time. I'd better ask some smart, open questions.

'Do you go to the cinema much?' I say. See if he replies with a 'we' . . .

'Not as much as I'd like,' he says. 'You?'

'Same. I don't seem to have much time, you know, day job, and then I'm quite busy. With *my friends* . . .'

'Yeah, I know what you mean. Work seems to take up far more energy than it used to when I was in service.'

'The army?' I say, looking at his chest. He's so broad-shouldered, I could totally see him running through a muddy field in camouflage, carrying an injured colleague on his back to the medi-tent . . .

'The army? God no. Why would you think I was a soldier?'

Because I'm totally carried away in some insane fantasy based on your fit body?

'Me?' he says. 'I'm a total wimp. No, I meant service, as in restaurants. I used to run my own pub up in Suffolk. Local, seasonal food, nothing fancy. So, what coffee would you like, young lady? You're not into this soy chai malarkey too, are you?'

'Black coffee, thanks.'

'Good, a proper drink. And any cake or a flapjack?' he says, eyeing up the selection of goodies on the counter.

In all the years I've worked on Fletchers, neither Devron nor Tom has once offered me a piece of cake. I think I love Jeff. Or maybe I just don't love Devron and Tom. Or maybe I just love cake.

'That chocolate sponge looks delicious,' I say. 'But I can't be eating cake for breakfast, it sets a bad precedent, don't you think?'

'Nonsense. A girl like you should totally have cake for breakfast! Besides, it looks like a giant Suzy Q.'

'A what?'

'A Suzy Q! Your name's Susie and you've never heard of a Suzy Q?' I shake my head. 'Little American cakes, cream in the middle? Mos Def name-checks them? Go on, get the Suzy Q. You have to, it's practically named after you. It's your namesake. Your namecake.'

I let out a pathetically girly little giggle.

'Go on, it'd be rude not to,' he says.

'Really?'

'Tell you what, if I share it with you does that make you feel any less naughty?'

DO YOU HAVE A GIRLFRIEND? I sincerely hope not, because this conversation amounts to more foreplay than I've had in a year.

'Deal,' I say, grinning, and then rapidly not grinning as I see Tom waving to us from across the canteen. 'Tom's just walked in.' I feel like we've been caught mid-snog.

'He's here already?' he says. 'Oh. Right, well I guess we'd better get back to work . . .'

The man behind the counter comes over to us and gives Jeff a broad smile and a high five. '*Hey amigo, qué pasa? What can I get you guys to drink?*'

'Hey Miguel, how's it going? *Me pones dos cafes solos y un "soy chai" por favor?*' he says, rolling his eyes as the man laughs. 'Miguel's teaching me Spanish, and I'm teaching him knife skills. That's a good deal, isn't it?' he says to me.

'Knife skills! Did you learn those in combat too?' I say.

'Those training kitchens at the Little Chef can be deadly!' he says.

'I'm terrible at chopping,' I say. 'Whenever you see chefs on the telly and they're looking at someone else while they're chopping an onion at a hundred miles an hour – it makes me break into a sweat. I'd have my arm off if I did that.'

'Nonsense, it's dead easy. You just need to practise. It's all about confidence. I could teach you some basic skills, it'd take me half an hour?'

'When?' I say, too quickly.

'Anytime. You'll have to give me your number,' he says, grinning.

Tom is hovering a few metres away from us, glued to his BlackBerry. Nodding mostly, but also saying, 'Sure sure, Devron. Fully strategic' a lot.

'So tell me – what do you do at the agency then?' Jeff says. 'Do you come up with the ideas for the ads?'

'No,' I say. 'A creative team does that.'

'That's a relief!' he says. 'So you weren't responsible for that terrible Perfect Bottom pizza campaign? Find your perfect bottom, we'll give you the right stuffing . . .'

'Actually I did work on that,' I say, blushing. 'But I didn't come up with the idea.'

'Oh,' he says, 'sorry. But they were so cheesy.'

I agree. 'Sold a lot of pizzas though,' I say, shrugging my shoulders in despair. 'Double-digit growth, your boss was very happy with those ads.'

'So what do you do exactly?' he says, gesturing to Tom to get off the phone, and pointing at his watch. It's 9.45 a.m. and I'm sure Jeff had to be somewhere at 10 a.m. . . . .

I reach into my wallet and hand him my business card. That way he has my number and my email too. On the front of the card is a black shiny NMN logo, the legs of the three letters melded together so that the whole thing resembles one big, scary, slightly embossed praying mantis.

On the other side it says:

Susie Rosen
Account Director

That should actually say:

Susie Rosen
Person with the greatest responsibility in the western world (yes, Obama, that is me, not you). The quest for world peace is one thing. But do you have any idea how challenging it is to ensure that there's always a brand new bottle of Heinz ketchup on hand for Devron's bacon sandwich when he comes in for a breakfast meeting?

On the flip side it should have a little note from my mum:

Really, Susannah
You should have gone to dental school like your clever brother. I don't care that teeth freak you out. And now you're wasting your life away at that agency while Marian Bentley's daughter's just been awarded an OBE for her charity work. And did I tell you Sylvia's daughter now heads up the cancer ward at UCH? And she's three months younger than you!

I'd need an A4 business card.

Jeff stares at my job title. 'Account Director,' he says. 'Like accounts as in finance?'

'No, accounts as in Fletchers is the account, I look after it. Basically I try to make sure a client's happy with an idea; if there are any changes I then need to make sure the creatives are happy. Once that's all happened I try to get the ad made, on time and in budget.'

'Sounds reasonably straightforward,' he says.

'If only,' I say. 'The problem is that usually clients and creatives have opposing opinions, so it can feel a little bit like piggy in the middle.'

'Piggy in the middle; I used to hate that game,' he says, smiling warmly.

'Me too.' I smile back.

His face crinkles for a minute. 'Actually do you mean piggy in the middle? Aren't the two sides both on the same side in that game?'

I think about it. I've been trotting out this analogy for years but of course he's right.

'I am an idiot!' I say. 'I'm going to have to think of a different game where two sides attack one person . . . How about dodgeball, where you're just getting hit all the time?'

'Nah, in dodgeball there's no one's in the middle. I think you mean you're a whipping boy. Or a whipping girl!' he says, with a mischievous look.

73

'That sounds a bit *Fifty Shades*!' I say. 'Oh look, Tom's done, I think . . .'

Tom comes over looking mildly flustered.

'So shall we go through these slides then, Tom?' I say.

'You know what?' says Jeff. 'I've got a better idea. We're not going to get through these slides in eight minutes and still have time to talk through product. I'm doing some work on cheese next week, but let's meet up the week after to go through the pizzas. You and me. The product should have moved on by then anyway.'

'Good idea,' says Tom. 'I'll set up a time.'

'No, that's OK, I'll do it with Susie directly,' says Jeff, smiling at me. 'We can do it together. Just the two of us. If that's OK with you, Susie?'

'Yes!' I say. 'If that's what you want. That would be more . . . efficient. And you're so busy, aren't you, Tom? That's a great idea, Jeff,' I say, meeting his look with a smile.

'I think I should be there,' says Tom. 'To answer any questions.'

'No!' I say. 'I mean, of course you're welcome to come but I can email you afterwards if Jeff can't answer something . . . if that's OK with you, Tom?'

'S'pose so . . .' says Tom.

'Listen,' says Jeff, touching my arm lightly. 'I've got to run. Great to meet you, Suzy Q. Good luck with the whips and I'll see you in a couple of weeks.' He looks again at my business card, smiles, then tucks it into his trouser pocket.

'I'm sorry about that,' says Tom, after he's gone. 'Jeff's quite outspoken, he's a bit of a maverick.'

'Don't be silly, that's fine,' I say. I like mavericks, especially hot ones. 'Do you know Jeff well then?' I say.

'What do you mean?'

Do you know if Jeff has a girlfriend?

'I mean do you work closely with him?' I say.

'Not really. He's only been here about six months. Right, can I show you these charts?'

If you must. And for the entire hour that Tom's taking me through the forty-eight slides he's prepared, the only thing I can think about is the way Jeff touched my arm. And that sly smile on his face when he put my card in his pocket. And the way he looked at me; really looked at me.

It's been a long time since someone's looked at me that way.

Saturday

Some Saturdays I wake up, and before I've even managed to get out of bed a little grey cloud comes to join me under the duvet. The weekend should be the highlight of your week, should it not? Should. Now there's a word.

When Jake and I split up, my best friend Polly told me something her therapist had said after Polly's first husband, Spencer, walked out on her when she was seven months pregnant:

'"Should" is the worst word in the English language.'

Funny, because I always thought the worst word was 'jism'.

But no: 'should' should be eradicated from the dictionary. (Although you see what just happened there?) 'Should' means you want people or situations to be a certain way. But they're not that way at all. 'He shouldn't have abandoned his pregnant wife.' But he did. 'I shouldn't still miss my ex.' But I do. Weekends 'should' be the highlight of the week.

Yet some Saturdays when I wake up, all I can see before me is a vast stretch of time that I'm supposed to fill up with 'stuff'. And 'good' stuff. Fun, meaningful, stimulating stuff. Not just lying in bed, watching DVDs, eating ice cream stuff, because that would make me a loser.

As much as I hate my day job, at least there's always stuff to do. Stuff I'm paid to do. Pointless stuff. Soul-destroying stuff. But at least it's stuff that I have to do *or else* there'll be a repercussion involving immediate pain. If I stay in bed all weekend watching Ryan Gosling movies there's no pain. In fact there's the opposite of pain. But where will it ever get me?

I'm lucky though. I have good friends. Friends from school, from uni, from all over. Yet when I stand back and look at how our lives have turned out, it seems that I'm the only one still hanging out here on the ledge of single-ness. Everyone else has been busy, busy, busy. They've been having babies and twins and sometimes up to three babies, though not all at once. They've been moving to bigger houses, moving to the country. Buying Farrow & Ball paints, building glass extensions, razing, gutting and expanding into loft space. The only thing gutted in my flat is me.

Of course they haven't all had a smooth ride. Take Polly, who's coming round for dinner later with our friend from school, Dalia. After Polly's first husband walked out she spent two years bringing up her little girl Maisie on her own. But Polly would never think of herself as a leftover; she got on with life without a fuss. Maybe when you have a kid whom you have to put first then it's easy, though it didn't look easy.

And then she met Dave, and Dave is amazing and it didn't bother him in the slightest that Polly wasn't young and perfect and baggage-free. He proposed after three months, down on one knee, singing Sinatra's 'All of Me', in their local curry house. The wedding's in six weeks' time and I cannot wait to dance away the ghost of Spencer and celebrate Polly and Dave's union. If anyone deserves all the happiness it's Polly. And men like Dave restore your faith in the universe. Shame there's only one of him in the universe.

And then of course there's Dalia: successful and gorgeous and thick as four short planks where men are concerned. *'Better to have loved and lost . . .'* That is so entirely not true when it comes to Dalia and Mark. Honestly I think Tennyson would have developed writer's block when faced with making sense of the on/off relationship between Dalia and that douche 'property-developer' (i.e. trumped-up estate agent) Mark Dawson.

Perhaps, after considerable pondering, with quill in mouth, Tennyson might have come up with the following:

'Better to have never loved. In fact better to have stayed home watching *TOWIE* repeats than to have wasted so much time at the beck and call of an odious man-boy who tells you, through word and deed, that you're not quite good enough for him. Where is thy self-respect, girl? The man is clearly a cock-head.'

But I don't suppose Tennyson would have used a word like cock-head.

So yes, there are worse things than being single. And there are worse things than being alone.

The girls are coming round at 7 p.m., and even though Polly's meant to be on a pre-wedding diet, she's asked me to make spag bol – her favourite. Dalia is off the carbs, since Mark poked her in the thigh a few weeks ago and just shook his head. But it pains me that a paunch-laden forty-four-year-old man dares criticise my friend's weight. She's been shrinking ever since she met him.

So I'll make the spag bol. And if Dalia wants to eat the bolognese sauce on broccoli instead of spaghetti, that's up to her. But after a glass of wine she'll probably be herself again, at least for a while. And I'll make the brownie pudding. Then I can take some in for Sam on Monday morning.

First things first though, chores: put the laundry on, tidy the flat, do the recycling. I head to the recycling bins round the corner armed with my cardboard wine delivery box, filled with bottles. Thank goodness no one I work with lives in my area and has ever witnessed me at these bins on a Saturday morning. Every time I stand here I curse myself for not having removed the thick tape from these boxes back in my flat, and yet I never do. Because now, not only do I look like an alcoholic (six glass bottles smashing the message home) I also look like I'm drunk. I mean, like I *am currently drunk at 9 a.m.*, not just I *am a drunk*. I try to tear the tape but it won't come off so I try to pull the box apart but it's tougher to rip than the Yellow Pages. I stand wrestling with it like an old souse in a pub brawl. I grunt a bit, pull and shake it, then try to bash it through the slot, even though I've tried this twice already and I know it doesn't quite fit. Then I jump on it, kick it, manage to tear a tiny corner off it and end up grunting again, before throwing it in despair onto the pile to the right of the bins where all the less civic-minded people simply dump their cardboard in the first place.

I'm exhausted. That's more than enough interface with the real world for one day. I return home, put Prefab Sprout loudly on the stereo in a pre-emptive move against Caspar and head to the kitchen to start making dinner. It's barely breakfast time, I know, but the key to making a bolognese this delicious is to start as early as possible on the day you're going to eat it. (In an ideal world, you'd make it the day before, so that the flavours can develop overnight, but work tends to get in the way.) For best results, the sauce needs to cook for at least six hours, preferably more. If you can leave it to its own devices in the oven on a very low heat for twelve hours, you'll have the best bolognese you've ever eaten in your life, and I can guarantee that or your money back.

Everyone has a recipe for bolognese that they love. And in Italy, every region has a slightly different recipe. In some areas they sweat the vegetables in butter and olive oil – they insist it makes it sweeter than olive oil alone. Some people don't even use celery, just carrot and onion as the base. Then there's the dairy brigade who insist on cooking out the meat in milk, to help cut through the acidity of the tomatoes. Others swear that white wine, not red, is the key to perfection. And don't even start on the subject of tomatoes. Fresh or chopped or passata or puree? All of the above, or no tomatoes at all?

Every Italian swears that theirs is the best recipe. What's more, if you don't make your bolognese in the same way they do, that means your father must have been dropped on his head when he was a baby and your grandmother was probably the town slut. Naturally I use my Italian grandmother's recipe, and I know for a fact that she wasn't the town slut. I know this because shortly after she gave birth to my mother, my grandfather ran off with the *actual* town slut, a woman by the name of Lucia Mollica, which means 'crumb' in Italian. Which seems fitting, as my grandmother took all of his money, along with my infant mother, and left him with just a loaf of bread in the kitchen and a note saying 'Don't eat it all at once'. She boarded a train, then a boat, and ended up in Glasgow, where her uncle ran a successful ice cream parlour, in which one Saturday, a year later, she met my 'real' grandfather. Until the day she died, whenever she saw or heard the name Lucia, Nonna would curse both her first husband and his mistress in the most lurid phrases you've ever heard come out of the mouth of a pensioner. (My grandfather had taught her to swear like a Glaswegian navvy, so she was pretty professional.)

Nonna's recipe isn't difficult but it does require two ingredients you can't buy off the shelf: love and patience. First you have to chop your vegetables into very fine dice. And of course you can't use a food processor, because the ghost of Nonna is watching, and she wouldn't like it. Cook the veg in olive oil for at least half an hour, on a heat so low you have to keep checking that the gas is actually on. Then add garlic, and sweat some more. In a separate pan, dry-fry some pancetta – salty pig meat being the base for so much that is good in this world. Then in the same pan, brown some beef mince, then half the amount of pork mince again. Add it to your *soffrito* along with a bottle of passata, fresh rosemary, salt and pepper. And then the secret ingredient that truly makes this dish: an entire bottle of red wine. Pour that in, put a lid on the casserole dish and put it in the oven for the whole day, stirring every couple of hours.

This is the perfect dish for a day like today. The weather's miserable, I've got nothing better to do, and I can justify not setting foot outside again with the excuse that I have to babysit the dinner. At around 4pm I rouse myself from a mid-afternoon doze and head for my A4 files of recipes. They're the one organised thing in my flat. I'm always fiddling with recipes, and the only way that I remember these tweaks is if I've scrawled them on a piece of paper. Aah, here we go: chocolate brownie cheesecake bake. It's one of the more obscene puddings in this file, but I've never met anyone who didn't go back for seconds. First you make the brownies, and Lord knows there are as many brownie recipes as there are Hindu deities. Normally I'd go straight to my friend Claire's recipe, which produces the ultimate squidgy yet chunky brownie. But the brownies in this pudding need to stay in neat squares so I use a Nigel Slater recipe that is foolproof and produces a more cake-like brownie, better fit for purpose.

While the brownies are in the oven I make the cheesecake base – full-fat Philadelphia, mascarpone and vanilla, whipped together and poured onto a base of crushed dark chocolate digestives mixed with melted better. That's my favourite part of the whole process – spreading the biscuit base out into the tray with a spatula, like it's wet sand. The brownies come out of the top oven and in goes the cheesecake for forty minutes, then the heat goes off and the cheesecake stays in the oven to cool and set. I give the bolognese a quick stir, then head back to the sofa for another little lie-down. I can't wait to be an old lady when all this mid-afternoon snoozing will be deemed socially acceptable.

The girls are due at 7 p.m. so at 6.30 p.m. I open a bottle of wine and start drinking – I might as well air the wine before they get here.

Polly's the first to arrive at 7 p.m. on the dot.

'You look amazing!' I say, as I open the door and give her a hug.

'D'you think?' she says, handing me a bottle of Prosecco.

'You're glowing.'

'Really? I've been on the Perricone, lots of oily fish. I feel like a penguin.'

'And your hair totally suits you longer.'

She reaches up and touches her neck. 'I'm growing it for the wedding. You don't think I'm too old for long hair, do you?'

'Don't be ridiculous, you're thirty-six. You didn't drive by the way, did you?' Polly, Dave and Maisie now live in a small village near Marlow in Buckinghamshire. It's only forty minutes by car, but if she's driving that means I'm drinking alone, which isn't good for anyone.

'My one night out and you think I'm drinking Evian? Dave gave me a lift in and I'll get a cab back. Is that smell what I think it is?'

I nod.

'How long has it been on for?' she says.

I check my watch. 'Just over eight hours.'

'I cannot wait, I've been looking forward to this all week! Will you email me the recipe? I want to make it for Dave.'

'I've got some copies of it, I gave one to Terry the other day,' I say, retrieving the recipe file I'd just returned to the hall cupboard.

'I'm so sick of eating mackerel,' she calls out from the kitchen. 'Shall we start this Prosecco or wait for Dalia?'

'*He who hesitates* . . . plus, it'll help the crisps go down more easily,' I say, opening a packet of Kettle Chips.

And it's just as well we don't wait for Dalia. Because twenty minutes later she sends me a text apologising profusely saying she can't make it, and she'll make it up to me another time, promise, kiss kiss.

'Look at this,' I say to Polly, showing her my phone. 'She doesn't even bother making excuses any more because she knows we won't believe them.'

'At least she's got the decency not to pretend she has a migraine, I suppose,' says Polly, handing the phone back to me and shaking her head.

'You would think she would at least pick up the phone rather than just text,' I say. 'It's rude.'

'Mark's probably there with her and she can't bear to drag herself away from his side for twenty seconds.'

'Do you reckon the sex is as good as she makes out it is?' I say. 'I've always thought Mark looked like the sort of man who would be entirely about his penis and not much else.'

'Me too!' she says. 'But apparently it's so amazing she says it's like a drug.'

'Huh,' I say. 'Well none of the drugs I've ever taken turned round and asked me if I wanted Botox for my birthday. Did she tell you about that?'

Polly nods. 'She's incapable of being on her own, though,' she says. 'She'd rather have someone than no one. I just wish that someone wasn't him.'

'I keep on telling her a man isn't the be all and end all.'

'That man's just the end all,' she says.

'Let's not talk about it, it'll just make me angry, and I've had a bad enough week as it is . . . Ooh, although I did meet a man.'

'A man?' says Polly. 'An actual real live man?'

'Hang on, I'll just put the pasta on and then I can tell you all about it.'

Two bowls of pasta, two bottles of wine and two helpings of cake later, I'm trying to remember all the reasons why I think Jeff is going to be my new boyfriend.

'And he noticed those earrings I bought in New York, the five-dollar ones from Old Navy that actually look quite expensive.'

'The moonstone ones?'

'Yes, and he actually knows what a moonstone is, but he's definitely not gay because he went out with another girl called Susie . . . with three Is . . . oh, and then he said that this chocolate sponge was my namecake, like namesake, because it's like a Suzy Q apparently. Isn't that funny? He's funny as well as handsome . . . and he used to live in New York and he's learning Spanish, and we like the same films, and he loves food!'

'Sounds perfect,' she says. 'Apart from one big thing.'

'What?' I say, suddenly worried that she has found a clue in something I've said that reveals he is not single. 'Polly?'

'It's obvious what the problem is, isn't it?' she says, waving her wine glass in the air.

'No,' I say. 'What's obvious?'

'The name, Suze, the name.'

I breathe a sigh of relief.

'It's up there with Tarquin on the list of worst men's names ever.'

'It's nowhere near Tarquin,' I say. 'It's a totally fine name.'

'Jeffrey?' she says. 'How many sexy Jeffs or Jeffreys are there? There's plenty of unsexy Jeffreys. Geoffrey from Rainbow. Geoff Capes, Jeffrey Dahmer. Yep, serial killer name,' she says, shuddering. 'Or a man in a golfing jumper. A golf-playing serial killer.'

'Jeff Bridges. He's a sexy Jeff. My God, have you ever seen a photo of him when he was young?'

She raises an eyebrow suspiciously.

'And Jeff Goldblum, kind of,' I say. 'Anyway, I'm in no position to be fussy about names at this stage of the game. If Nimrod Mcfartwhistle asked me out, I'd be hard-pressed to say no.'

'Does he have a beard?' she says.

'Jeff? Why do you ask?'

'It's a beardy name.'

'No,' I say. 'No beard. A little bit of stubble, but good stubble. And very very blue eyes. Just like Daniel Craig but with a less craggy nose. And he's bald.'

'So nothing like Daniel Craig.'

'Same eyes,' I say.

'Thank goodness he's not called Craig,' she says.

'What's wrong with Craig?'

'Who calls a baby Craig?' she says.

'Who calls a baby Spencer?!'

She laughs. 'Fair point.'

'So more importantly, tell me what's the latest on the wedding!' I say. 'I'm so excited, I can't wait!'

Her face lights up. 'The dress is sorted – Nanette's done the most amazing job ever – and I've found the perfect shoes, and they were a total bargain, forty quid in a shop in a village down the road from us.'

'Colour?'

'Silver,' she says.

'Comfortable?'

'Hell no! And the head-dress! Unbelievable. I found a woman on eBay who'd inherited her aunt's – Edwardian lace, totally beautiful, a hundred and ten years old this thing, worn once, and she only wanted sixty-five quid for it! And Dave and I have finally made our minds up about the food . . .'

'Are you going to tell me anything or are you keeping it a surprise?'

'Definitely a surprise. Although I think you'll like the cake.'

'Tell me about the cake at least?'

'No way!' she says, 'the cake's the best bit. Just be warned, the whole thing's not going to be as posh as first time round – the venue's just a little restaurant in Farringdon near the registry office. But all the money's going into food and booze this time!'

'Poll, I don't care if you guys get married in Nando's, I'm just so excited for you. You deserve this more than anyone.'

She squeezes my hand. 'I swear, Suze, it'll happen to you when you least expect it.'

'Oh Polly. I've been least expecting it for a very long time now,' I say, smiling.

She takes another sip of her wine and pours the rest of the bottle into her glass. 'Oh. And you'll never guess who's RSVPd and is coming without a certain evil other half . . .' she says, looking at me with a mischievous grin.

I put down my glass.

'Daniel McKendall's coming?' I say.

'Daniel McKendall's coming, and he asked if you were coming too.'

Daniel McKendall: best mate of Polly's brother.

I've known Daniel McKendall since I was twelve. We were born on the same day, in the same year. And from the age of thirteen through to fifteen, he was my best male friend and my sort-of boyfriend.

'I'm going to open another bottle,' I say, getting off the sofa and heading to the kitchen. I fetch myself a glass of water and drink it slowly, trying to figure out why even now, after all this time, just the sound of his name still has an effect on me.

'Bring me some booze immediately!' she shouts from the sofa. 'I don't suppose you've got any cider in the fridge, have you?'

Polly and I spent far too many of our teenage years drinking cider, wearing DMs and listening to The Cure. She was a proper bona fide Goth, hair dyed Naples Black, scary eyeliner, the works. I was just copying her because I was in awe of her, and because the DMs offended my mother in a way that I found hugely gratifying. Although there was no way I'd have got away with dyed hair living under my parents' roof. They'd have put me up for fostering.

'Polly, I haven't touched cider since I disgraced myself at your eighteenth. If you really want a blast from the past I can offer you Malibu, or I still have some Galliano left over from New Year's Eve 2004. It looks like fluorescent urine but it tastes far worse . . .'

'Malibu,' she says. 'And have you got any bad shit in the cupboard? I've chucked all the sweets out at home and I need something full of fat and sugar.'

'Chocolate raisins, jumbo Chocolate Buttons, peanut M&Ms, take your pick,' I say.

'Bloody hell, you're better than the Texaco. Buttons!'

I take the booze and the chocolates back through to her.

'Did I tell you Brooke's been living in New York for the last four months?' she says, taking a glass from me. 'Without Daniel . . .'

I take a sip of neat Malibu, wince at the sweetness, and pretend I haven't heard her.

'She said she can't bear to live in England any more because of the weather,' she says, with a raised eyebrow. 'Says the rain gives her headaches. More like it makes her hair go curly. God, she's such a spoiled princess,' she says, ripping open the packet of Buttons.

'It never rains in New York, does it,' I say, finding two Buttons that are stuck together. Almost as good as the mythical Kit Kat finger that's all-chocolate, no biscuit.

'Anyway, her family are so bloody rich they can probably blow the clouds away like the Chinese did at the Olympics . . .' says Polly.

'What do they do again? Finance?'

'Property, they're minted.'

'So she's moved back there and Daniel's still out in Kent?'

'It's only fifteen minutes on the train from Waterloo, Suze. That's less than an hour from here, door to door.'

'Have they actually separated though?' I say, trying not to sound a tiny bit hopeful.

I last saw Daniel five years ago, in the pub on Christmas Eve. Even then there'd been problems in his marriage. He'd flirted with me just enough to make me feel human, but not to the point where I felt like he'd meant anything by it. More just for old times' sake. Still, I remember when the clock had struck midnight, and we were all drunkenly hugging and kissing and singing carols, he'd given me a look filled with so much sadness and affection, I'd had to look away. Because I'd felt something.

'They're not separated yet,' she says. 'But it can't be long now. They're basically living separate lives. Apparently even before she moved back to the States she'd had him sleeping in the spare room for over a year.'

'A year?'

'That's what my brother said.'

'Hang on,' I say. 'They've got a little boy, haven't they?'

'He's nearly ten now. He's in New York with Brooke, the two of them rattling around in some Upper East Side penthouse . . .' she says, looking slightly less triumphant.

'But how does that work?' I say.

'How indeed,' she says, with raised eyebrows. 'Daniel's been flying over there every other weekend, but that can't make sense longer term.'

'He must be knackered. Why doesn't he just move to New York? I'd love to live in New York,' I say. 'Isn't that pretty selfish of him?'

'No! It's selfish of her! He's trying to get his business off the ground, he's been plugging away at it for years and he's finally doing OK. And you know his dad's not well, he's been in a home since last summer. Plus his brother's struggling through a hideous divorce. Daniel's got all that on his plate and then Brooke drags their son out of school a year before he's due to finish primary, so that she can swan around Barneys and get her nails done every day.'

'Bad timing. That must be hard for him,' I say, filing him back in the folder labelled 'unavailable'.

'Yeah, it's shit, by the sounds of it,' she says, shaking out the last of the chocolate. 'I think he's pretty messed up about the whole thing but you know what men are like, he says everything's fine. Maybe you can offer him a shoulder to cry on at the wedding. I'm putting you next to him at dinner.'

'Don't do that, Poll,' I say. 'He's married. And I mean, what's the point?'

'The point is, that marriage is as good as over. And it would be helpful for him to have an old friend talk some sense into him,' she says.

'*I'm* supposed to give him marriage guidance? I'm hardly a role model for successful living. No, stick me next to someone single.'

'I'll check with Dave to see if any of his mates are, but I don't think there are any single men coming,' she says. 'Apart from my brother, and he only seems to date women in their twenties nowadays. He's such a City Boy.'

'I remember he always used to steal the five-hundred-pound notes in Monopoly,' I say, laughing. 'Don't you have any single men on the list at all? Anyone – waiters, ushers, someone in the band?'

She shakes her head. 'Not that I can think of. Right, I've definitely had too much to drink, best call me a cab.'

I haven't thought about Daniel McKendall for years. Well, a few years at least. We're friends on Facebook, but the fact that I haven't even casually stalked him shows how low on my radar he is.

I remember Daniel's parents back in the day, must be over twenty years ago now . . . They were so much more exotic than mine. Daniel's mum, Krista, was a crazy Danish hippy; his dad, Robert, was a Scottish guitar teacher. When we first met, his parents were still listening to Joan Baez and smoking a lot of weed. (My parents listened to Vivaldi and to this day have never smoked a joint. When my mum found out I'd been smoking Consulate round at the McKendalls' house, she went ballistic. 'It starts with cigarettes, then you get hooked on the harder stuff. You'll be round the back of King's Cross, turning tricks for heroin if you don't cut that out right now!' If there'd been a 'rat on a rat' anti-nicotine hotline in the eighties, my mum would have shopped Daniel and me, taken her ten-pound reward, and still had a smile on her face when she put dinner on the table.)

Going round to Daniel's big, ramshackle house and twos-ing menthol cigarettes that we'd stolen from Krista

McKendall's crochet handbag was the most exciting, bohemian thing I had ever experienced. Daniel and I used to take a picnic blanket, sneak up onto the roof and spend hours lying on our backs, blowing smoke rings and staring up at the clouds. All that time, imagining what we would do with our lives.

Up on the roof we'd pretend things could stay the way they were forever. In our future it would still always be five in the afternoon on a perfect summer's day, with the sky so blue it felt like a child's drawing. Our parents would always stay young and strong and good looking and healthy and we would never have to think of them as actually being human. There would always be cold lingonberry lemonade so sharp it made your tongue curl waiting for us in Krista McKendall's fridge, if only we could be bothered to go down to the kitchen. Homework could wait. Tidying our rooms could wait. For now and always we would stay lying, side by side on this green and blue tartan blanket, looking up to the sky. Best friends who just happened to also like kissing each other.

Daniel and I were always happiest when we were together, just the two of us. The best days of my teens were spent with him. We had so much in common, and because we were born on the same day he used to joke that we were twins, separated at birth. 'The exact same day, that can't be coincidence! Look at the facts: your grandfather was Scottish and so was mine. It is technically possible.'

'He wasn't my actual grandfather,' I pointed out.

'Yeah, but he was the only one you ever knew,' he said. 'And look at the other things that are identical: both crap at art. You eat Breakaways the exact same way that I do, that must be genetic!'

'Clearly we're not twins. Your mum's Dutch. I wish I had her bone structure, she looks like Julie Christie.'

'For ten points, what's the capital of Denmark . . .?'

'Oh. Copenhagen. Sorry, your mum's Danish. I do know the difference, but you've got to admit they're confusing, they are quite close to each other. Anyway, why would you even *want* me to be your sister? That's messed up.' If we were siblings that would mean that all the medium petting we were doing up on that roof was technically incest. I'd read *Flowers in the Attic* though – maybe it wasn't so bad.

'What?' he said, looking confused.

'Think about what you're actually saying! Brothers and sisters don't do this. Oh God, just think about my brother . . . Gross! What's wrong with you? You're a pervert!' I said, pushing him away from me.

'Jeez, you're the one who's sick! I wasn't thinking about it like that! I just meant . . . If you were my twin you wouldn't have to go home at night. You could stay here with us. You could live in our house! We'd go on holiday together. We'd have fun all the time. That's what I meant.'

'Ah, so you're a romantic pervert at least. Well that's OK then,' I said, moving back towards him and kissing him on his beautiful mouth.

That's the thing about Daniel – he had an innocence about him. He always seemed a little bit lost but underneath that he also had a quiet confidence. Daniel was the first boy I fell in love with. Not just because he was good looking and tall and could blow double smoke rings. But because of that combination of sweetness and strength. And because, from the very first moment I met him on a hot July day in Polly's garden, I felt like I had always known him. He was the first boy I could truly be myself with, the first boy who made me laugh.

And then life got in the way, good and proper. Krista McKendall, that wild, crazy bohemian, ran off to Surrey with a balding accountant named Albert. And Daniel's heartbroken, cuckolded father took his boys back up to Edinburgh to be near their grandparents. And that was the end of that.

After Daniel moved to Scotland I wrote to him every week – heart-wrenching, embarrassing teenage letters telling him what I'd been up to, what films I'd seen: *Short Circuit II*! It's not as good as the first one. *Die Hard*! I bet you've probably already seen it but it is so brilliant! Go and see it, I know you will love it!!

And as is the natural evolution of life, he met a girl locally and his replies dribbled out, then stopped. And Polly told me to stop writing, what was the point? He was gone. But somehow I felt that if I could just remind him of how it felt to be up on that roof . . . through the power of my words on wonky lines on letters, then some day, he'd come back to London and we'd be together again and the sadness that had grown in my chest would shrink, then disappear, and everything would be OK.

Except off he went to Warwick University to study civil engineering. And in the summer holiday of his first year he met a beautiful girl from New York, and by the time he was twenty-five he'd married her. Done.

I'd get the occasional update via Polly who had taken an instant dislike to Brooke: 'She's beautiful, I suppose, in a no-carbs, groomed kind of way, but spoilt and cold. It'll never last.'

But it was lasting. These things often do. Still, it'll be good to catch up with him at the wedding. For old times' sake.

w/c 12 March

Status report:
- Get creative team – URGENT
- Visit Grumpy Marjorie

Monday

I do hate Mondays but this one's not too bad. When I give Sam his portion of brownie cheesecake from Saturday night he rewards me with some tasty gossip about Martin Meddlar's latest dalliance, and a packet of cool paperclips that look like penguins.

'Sam, you're not seriously going to eat that for breakfast, are you?' I say, as he unwraps the foil and sizes up the cake appreciatively.

'You're trying to tell me you've never done that?' he says.

I hate the fact that Sam knows me so well.

'Besides,' he says, 'it's easy for you – you know how to make this stuff. It's like in *Breaking Bad* – you're Walt, just sitting in your kitchen making crystal meth.'

'Sam, I can bring you in my recipe, then you can make it yourself.'

'If I wanted it I'd Google it.'

'You wouldn't actually, Mr Know It All, as this is my own recipe.'

'Bullshit.'

'It is! I stuck two other recipes together. It's awesome – take two good things and make them into something even better.' I can't quite bring myself to confess that I invented this pudding after putting two puddings in my mouth at the same time.

'I can't believe you can make up recipes like this and you're wasting your life in this place.'

'You're a fine one to talk about wasted potential. Anyway, this recipe's dead easy, shall I bring it in for you tomorrow?'

'No,' he says. 'I like the fact that you make things for me.'

'I don't make things for you, Sam, they're just leftovers. It's you or the bin.'

He smiles a little smile that suggests he doesn't quite believe me.

Before I know it the morning's gone and Rebecca's on the phone calling me for lunch.

'Give me ten minutes,' I say. 'I've got to catch up with Alexis about a creative team.'

'I wouldn't bother,' she says.

'Is she in a mood? Selfridges.com not got the McQueen in her size or some other tragedy?'

'Doubt it, I reckon she'll be in a great mood. She's in Paris with Fallon.'

'How do you know that?'

'She called in sick this morning, but there's a paparazzi shot of her and lover-boy on the *Mail* Online getting on the Eurostar yesterday afternoon, I'll send you the link.' Alexis has failed to grasp the fact that going out with an ex-*X Factor* contestant means she can no longer chuck sickies quite as liberally as in days of yore.

'This Fletchers brief is so late . . . fuck it, I'm emailing Robbie directly. See you in five.'

Rebecca's waiting in reception chatting to Sam. He always looks nervous when he talks to her and today is no exception. He's staring at his trainers while she's giving him full flirt mode, to no avail.

'Alright, Suze,' he says, looking up with relief in his face. He's taken off the sweatshirt he had on earlier and underneath is a blue t-shirt I haven't seen before that says 'Give Me All the Bacon and Eggs You Have'. Sam's eyes always look super green when he wears that shade of blue.

'Good t-shirt, Sam,' I say. 'Good slogan.'

He looks impressed. 'You've seen *Parks and Recs*?'

'Parks and what?'

He shakes his head in disappointment.

'Sam, come for a burrito with us?' I say. Great idea! If Sam's there, Rebecca won't dare try to hash over last Tuesday and he can protect me from a lecture.

'Yeah, come, Sam! We promise we don't bite,' says Rebecca.

'I can't handle the two of you together,' he says. 'Besides, I've got stuff to do.'

'What stuff?' I say. 'You've read the entire internet twice . . .'

'Nothing you need worry about,' he says and slopes off.

'He is so cute and such a loser,' says Rebecca, as we walk down the street. 'You do realise he totally fancies you?'

'Don't be utterly ridiculous! Why would you even say something like that?'

'You can't seriously tell me you've never noticed the way he behaves around you?'

'You are out of your mind, Rebecca. He fancies you more than he fancies me. He can't even look at you.'

'His face lights up when he talks to you. And he's always getting you stationery. And asking you to cook for him. He's desperate to impress you.'

'All he ever does is sneer at me because I haven't heard of the bands or TV shows that he's into. Besides, Sam doesn't do relationships any more. Some girl in Dublin broke his heart years ago, he's taken early retirement.'

102

'Oh I see. And you don't approve of that, do you?'

'Of what?'

'Letting the past hold you back.'

'Why would I approve of that? It's stupid. He's missing out on a lot of potential happiness.'

'Yes. Isn't he just?' She raises an eyebrow at me. 'Susie, trust me on this one. You just have to give him a bit of encouragement, that's all. Right, what are you having?'

'The usual with extra guacamole and a Diet Coke,' I say, fishing a tenner out of my wallet. 'Look, Rebecca: Sam asks me to cook for him because he likes food. He gives me stationery *because I give him food*. It's a straightforward, mutually beneficial friendship founded on basic physical needs being met. I believe it's called symbiosis. End of story.'

'Nonsense. I think it would be so sweet if you guys got together,' she says. 'You've been friends all this time . . . One chicken burrito, one chipotle chicken salad and two Diet Cokes please, extra guacamole on the burrito,' she says to the guy behind the counter who's gazing at her.

'And then we could sit at home together every night playing guitar? Hold on, could we have a bit more guacamole than that? Cheers . . . Rebecca, Sam's like a permanent student.'

'He just needs a push in the right direction, I don't think it would take much,' she says.

'I'm not interested in pushing or being pushed for that matter,' I say, as we take our food over to a corner table. I can feel the warmth of my burrito through the foil, and that mixture of excitement and anticipation that I feel rising in my chest is not a million miles away from the feeling I had when Jeff asked me for my number last week. Except that this burrito is entirely within my control and will definitely make me happy, whereas Jeff isn't and probably won't. I wonder when he's going to email . . .

I'm just about to tell her about him when I notice she's looking at me with her concerned-friend look – head tilted to the side at twenty degrees, lips slightly open, waiting for the perfect moment to say something I don't want to hear. Oh . . . here it comes.

'Listen, I've been thinking about you,' she says, 'and I know you're going to say no way, but I think you should give the online dating thing a try.'

'Let's not ruin my lunch before I've even had a bite,' I say, tearing the foil from the top of my burrito.

'Don't be like that, Suze.'

'No way. I'm not interested, Rebecca . . . oh my God, this is exactly what I wanted,' I say, taking a bite.

'I can't believe you won't even give it a try. Everyone does it. That's how you meet people nowadays,' she says, burying her fork into her salad.

Why can't *I* ever choose the salad in this place? I'm sure it's lovely. You still get coriander rice and a bit of guacamole. Still, ordering a salad, at Burrito Shack? That would be like going to Betsy's Cakes and choosing the oat and quinoa bar instead of the super-squidgy chocolate brownie: a point-less exercise in self-denial that would end badly.

Because then (hypothetically) you'd eat that oat bar and fail to be truly satisfied. So maybe you'd buy the brownie as well. Then eat the brownie on the number 88 en route to the last internet date you went on, wearing a white, Zara, dry-clean-only dress. Obviously you have no napkin; you're not the practical type who carries Kleenex in her bag. So you'd arrive at your date flustered, with dodgy brown smears on your dress. But then rapidly realise: the stains don't matter. You could be wearing a *Human Centipede* costume for all the difference it'd make. Because your date has lied about his height. By a mere eight inches. And while you can date a short man, you cannot knowingly date a liar. A liar who sends you a text, five minutes after your date has ended, to say, 'Your v nice but their was no physical spark 4 me'.

And then perhaps you'd kick yourself for not having bought a second brownie to eat on the bus home as conso-lation. But it all worked out fine because there was still half a tub of Ben & Jerry's Phish Food left in the freezer when you got home. And as everybody knows, Ben & Jerry's absorbs tears much better than Kleenex anyway . . .

I mean that's, like, one possible, hypothetical way that the situation might play out.

I put down my burrito and take a sip of Diet Coke. 'Rebecca. I don't want to have this conversation again. And you know full well I did try online dating, many times, before Jake. And it did not work out if you recall.'

'You didn't even go on a single date.'

'I went on two! The guy who licked my forehead, and the extremely short guy.'

'Oh. I thought the guy who licked you was the short guy.'

'Tongue wouldn't have reached.'

'Oh . . . That was so long ago. You were unlucky. And there are loads of new sites, some of them are actually quite cool. Emily White in art buying just got engaged to some guy she met on My Single Friend.'

'Well done, Emily.'

'And I've met loads of good men online.'

'Like who?'

'Paul . . .' she says.

'You liar, you said you met him in a bar!'

'He made me say that because he was embarrassed.'

'There you go, and with good reason too! Met him in a bar . . . I can't believe you lied to me all this time!'

'No, he was embarrassed to admit we met online because he's a macho old-fashioned idiot. Look, all I'm saying is that there are interesting, cute guys out there. I just think it'd be a good thing if you went on a few dates, got your confidence back. You know, take the focus a bit off . . .'

'Take the focus a bit off what?'

'I'm just saying . . .'

'What are you just saying?'

'The other night at Hawksmoor . . . I just think it's time you moved on, put a toe back in the water.'

'Rebecca. That guy in Hawksmoor was a dickhead. The stuff he was saying about women over thirty would have been justification alone for me to slap him.'

'This isn't about that guy. It's the . . .' she looks at me, then shakes her head, and then says, 'it's the Jake thing.'

'Jake? Jake who? I'm over Jake, if that's what you're talking about. Just because I might mention him occasionally doesn't mean anything. Naturally there are a few things that remind me of him . . . sometimes. And that's totally normal after a long-term relationship breaks up, and I'm a lot better than I was six months ago. Don't you agree?'

'Well yes, you're definitely better than you were, but still, I just think it would help you to see that there's hope out there.'

'Rebecca. First of all, hope is what kills you . . .'

'Stop trying to be funny.'

'I'm not trying to be funny. There's nothing funny about the death of hope. I hoped things would work out with Jake. I hoped I wouldn't waste four of the last good fertile years of my life with someone who ultimately mucked me about and wasn't who I thought he was. I hoped by my age I'd have found a job I enjoyed. Quite frankly I hoped I'd be married and settled and happy by now, like pretty much everyone else seems to be. And where has all that hope got me?'

'Susie . . .'

'I know your heart's in the right place and you think you're helping me. But there's just something about the whole online dating thing that I cannot bear. Everyone's a tick box. It's exhausting. It feels like shopping. And not fun shopping. Not "What's new in mid-length dresses this week on ASOS?" shopping. More like: "Do you like the right bands? Are you under thirty-five? Do you enjoy watching DVDs? Are you athletic or do you actually mean big-boned?" Are you going to finish that guacamole?'

'What?'

'Come on, hand it over if you're not eating it. If I ever open a burrito restaurant I won't charge extra for guacamole, it's just not right,' I say. 'Anyway, Rebecca, this whole online dating thing – I simply don't have time to spend hours wading through a bunch of profile photos of blokes with two thumbs up, standing in the snow. You're on a mountain. Wow, an actual mountain! No other male has ever been snowboarding ON A MOUNTAIN in the history of the universe . . .'

'But you're more than happy to spend hours looking at Jake's girlfriend's Facebook page . . .'

'I have *stopped* doing that.'

'No. You've just stopped telling me you're doing that.'

'I have not looked at her page for at least two months. And I know for a fact that you looked at Paul's new girlfriend only three weeks ago. So I win!'

'Yes, Susie, you win. Well done, doesn't victory feel great?' She shakes her head, exhausted. Hurrah, I've worn her down!

'I know lots of happy couples who've met online,' she continues.

No, I haven't . . .

'Look, Rebecca: I am ready to meet someone. I just want to meet him in the real world.'

'Since I've been online, I've met more men in the real world too. It helps give off an "I'm not desperate" vibe.'

'I am not desperate, Rebecca. If I was truly desperate, then I might consider it.'

'Being online just opens up your options. That's all I'm saying.'

'Fine. You've said it. I appreciate your concern, truly I do. Now pass the Tabasco please?'

'I've got a date on Saturday with someone from DoingSomething . . .'

'Name?'

'MrSalsa75 . . . you won't make that face once you've seen what he looks like,' she says, handing me her iPhone.

'He's like a better-looking version of that guy in *True Blood*! Is that his real photo?'

'There he is surfing on Bondi . . . that's him on the day he qualified . . .'

'As a surf instructor?'

'As a lawyer, darling. That's him with his niece at the zoo . . .'

'OK, OK. I get it. He's hot and smart and good with kids. Well I hope you have a lovely time . . . Ooh, and you've got what's-his-face, Hawksmoor barman too, haven't you?'

'We're going for drinks next week! He still thinks I'm called Susie . . .'

'You do realise you can't ever tell him your real name?' I say, smiling. 'But that's exactly my point, see? You walk into a bar or an office and you meet someone. It should be simple.'

'At least tell me you'll think about it.'

'No, because I have thought about it.'

'How about I buy you a three-month subscription to Lovematch.com?'

'How about you never mention it again and I'll buy you a cappuccino?'

'Just say you'll think about it.'

Wednesday

Such a phenomenal start to a Wednesday! An email sitting in my inbox with Jeff Nichols as sender. Sent at 8 p.m. last night, which is hugely encouraging. He could have just gone home at that time of night, sent this first thing today. But no, he stayed at his desk after hours to send it, which tells me two things. Firstly, I am not a task on his 'to do' list that he cares to procrastinate, so I am not entirely without significance. And secondly, if he had Miss Venezuela waiting for him at home I bet he wouldn't be working late.

Still no word from Robbie in New York though, which is a pain; this brief is getting later and later. In the meantime let's just see what Jeff has to say for himself. I click on the email with a tiny flutter of hope.

Hey Suzy Q,

Truly great to meet you last week. Hope you survived Tom's PowerPoint charts, sorry I had to dash, I wanted to stay. Let's meet up and I can show you my wares. How does next Monday sound, end of the day? Don't worry about that half piece of cake I know you're saving for me, I'll cook something nice for us on the day.

Have a great week and look forward to seeing you soon.

Jeff

Yes! So many excellent signs in this email, I don't know where to start. And an end of the day meeting – well, am I reading too much into it or does that clearly leave the door open for a drink after work? I spend a good half hour crafting a response and then panic that it's far too flirtatious, at which point I call Rebecca over, tell her all about Jeff and ask her to help me edit it.

'So exciting,' she says. 'A Fletchers client who isn't hideous!'

'I've earned it. Six years of Devron, I deserve a work crush, finally.'

'Sam will be heartbroken when he goes through your inbox.'

'Sam doesn't read my emails,' I say. 'I know he used to, but he's promised he'll never do it again. And stop with this whole Sam crush thing, it's nonsense, he's my friend.'

'OK . . . so I think maybe change that bit where you talk about the cake. He's not actually interested in the cake, he's interested in you.'

'Yeah, but I'm trying to flirt with him.'

'Be more obvious.'

'More obvious? Don't you think "Can't wait to see what's on the table" is pretty obvious? Actually I'm taking that out, it's too full on.'

'Ask him what he's up to at the weekend. That'll flush out whether he's got a girlfriend. Do it. Then you know whether to waste time fancying him or not.'

'Rebecca, it's a work email, I'm not going to ask him that. And besides, I don't think he has got a girlfriend. Honestly, there was just that chemistry there, you know, that instant rapport. I don't think you ever feel that unless the other person is giving off a major vibe too. It was way beyond politeness.'

'Oooh, this is so cool!' she says, clapping her hands with delight. 'What are you going to wear?'

'I haven't got that far.'

'Wear that black dress with the low V at the front that you wore for your birthday, you look gorgeous in that.'

'Meeting's in a kitchen, not a brothel.'

'With a white cami top underneath it's perfect. Great cleavage, big smile. He'll be totally defenceless.'

'What about the burgundy one with the little bow at the neck . . . feminine, quite quirky?'

'Men don't want quirky, they want sexy. Come on, Suze, I haven't seen you even vaguely bothered by anyone since . . . since last year; you've got to come out of hibernation with all guns blazing.'

'I'll figure it out at the weekend . . . Maybe that charcoal Topshop dress with the belt?'

'Perfect, feminine and sexy, although I'd argue more cleavage. And shoes, what shoes? How tall is he again?'

I think back to standing beside him when we were waiting for our coffees. He'd stood so close to me. 'Taller than Jake, just under six foot? But bigger, broader than him, solid.'

'Sounds hot. Wear your highest heels that you can still walk to the pub in after. OK, so put at the end of the email, "Can't wait for round two" or something.'

'That's far too much! You don't think we're getting carried away here? He might just be being friendly,' I say, suddenly filled with paranoia that I've misread the whole situation.

'Not at all, you know what the give-away is?'

'The end of day meeting thing?'

'No, that could conceivably just be his diary. It's where he says *us* – I'll cook *us* something nice. That, my friend, is assumed intimacy. It's like he's putting his arm around you already! Come on, just press send.'

'Alright. But I'm just leaving the sign-off as "Look forward to next Monday". That's what he said, so if I say it back I'm not exposed.'

'And I bet you something else, now that he's on the scene there'll be others crawling out of the woodwork too, that's what I was saying yesterday, just you wait and see!'

'Yep. I'll be waiting, Rebecca.'

Friday

My phone rings at midday. It must be Devron, in for lunch with Martin Meddlar but wanting to update me on the new pizza range name in person beforehand.

'Susie? Your visitor's here,' says Anita, our receptionist, whose sole job is to sit on a chair and look sexy. New clients sometimes get confused when they walk in to NMN, thinking they've stepped into a modelling agency: three beautiful women to welcome them, all nearly six foot tall, in white Lycra dresses. Everything in reception is white: thick white carpet, white sofas, and six giant white floor-standing vases filled with lilies that cost £50k a year.

And now we also have the white lights of the digital tickertape that runs along the back wall. Robbie installed the tickertape last year when he introduced 'Tweet of the Week'. He's made it my department's responsibility to run

116

a Twitter account for every campaign we do. 'Creative teams are still the Big Thought Leaders but you guys are the soldiers on the ground,' he'd said. 'Remember you need killer end lines, always: attack, attack!'

A little piece of my soul has died every week since. The tickertape runs a live feed, so one minute you'll have Berenice Tweeting: 'NMN ranks highest in industry survey! Client servicing is core to our values'. And then a minute later, the pessaries team: 'New campaign launches in Slovakia, well done Team Euro Bum!!!'

Devron's sitting in reception waiting, flicking through the *Sun*. 'S-R!' he says as he stands to shake hands and slips the reception copy of the paper into his briefcase. 'Just waiting for Marty, but I wanted to share the name, legal have finally signed it off.'

'Go ahead.'

'Gotta give you some background first,' he says, adjusting his stance so that his legs are a little further apart, as if he's about to leap onto a very small pony. 'So, a while back, me and Mands are watching *CSI*, she's eating a choc ice. Mands never eats fattening stuff, so I'm like what's the deal? She says, "It's a Skinny Cow." I'd never even heard of it but they make choc ices, ice cream, all sorts of frozen.'

'Yes, Devron, I know the brand.' And I can't believe you don't. Given that it's worth like a billion quid and it's owned by Nestlé and you're the head of food at a supermarket.

Next you'll be telling me about these amazingly tasty little beans in tomato sauce that you've discovered . . .

'Me and Mands thought it was a brilliant name. Obviously we couldn't call the pizzas the same thing but we brainstormed and came up with something even better.'

'Which is?' I say.

'Fat Cow!'

I do not respond. I'm trying to work out if this is a wind up, as it can only be a wind up. Ad yet from the self-congratulatory look on Devron's face it doesn't feel like a wind up.

'Don't look so stunned, S-R, I didn't mean you! I meant the name. Fat Cow!'

'Fat Cow.' I say. 'They're Skinny Cow and you're going to call yours Fat Cow?'

'Don't be daft, S-R! Of course we're not calling it Fat Cow.'

'Ha!' I say, relaxing. 'You almost had me there, Devron, you looked so serious.'

'It *was* Fat Cow but those jobsworths in legal wouldn't let us call it that. They thought it was too close to Skinny Cow.'

'Really?' I say, sympathetically. 'They thought Fat Cow and Skinny Cow were a little bit similar, did they? I don't think they're similar at all, are they . . . In fact they're the opposite of each other, aren't they, Devron? Fat Cow/ Skinny Cow. Miles apart. There's just that one little word that's the same. And it's only three letters . . .'

'That's what I said,' says Devron. 'Still, they started banging on about trademark infringement, I just said it's not worth the hassle. So me and Mands had another brainstorm, she's so good with ideas, Mands, she should come and work here.'

Yes, entirely what this building needs: another scantily clad young woman looking to spend quality time with a nice married man with a view to home-wrecking . . .

'And where did you get to, Devron?'

'We had a massive list,' he says. 'Pizza Skinnita, Slice-a-Nice, Chick-Pizzas, Thin Bottoms . . .'

'Are the bases thinner? Jeff's showing me products next Monday.' Yes, Jeff's showing me, just me, me, me.

'Nah. What other names . . .? Oh yeah, we thought we'd be single-minded, like you guys always say, so we had Shee-tzahs, like pizzas for shes. We had literally hundreds but it was spankingly obvious which name to go for.'

'So what is it?'

'Fat Bird.' He grins. 'I've shared it round the wider team and everybody loves it.'

'Fat Bird,' I say. 'Fat? Bird?'

'Fat Bird. And Nestlé can't touch us. So, in your face, Nestlé.'

I start to say something, then stop myself. 'Hang on a minute, Devron. Wasn't there a project last year on desserts that was called Fat Bird? And didn't it have to be pulled?' I'm sure I remember seeing something on our department status about a major cock-up.

'It was the wrong time to launch and the developer quit in the middle of the process.'

'Nothing to do with the name?' I say.

'The name's the best bit, trust me. Our PR guys say the tabloids will love it. And Tom's already briefed the printers on branded clothing. Play your cards right and come June there'll be a photo of you on page ten of the *Sun* in a Fat Bird onesie.'

You'll have to un-bury me first.

'Devron, who are these pizzas targeted at again?'

'Women who are a bit overweight. Tom's cluster researched the target audience and he's identified two core groups: Cellulite Sallys and Bingo-Wing Brendas.'

I take a deep breath and look at the floor. 'And you haven't researched the name?'

'Head, heart, guts!' he says.

'Isn't it possible that if you were a woman on a diet you might not love being called Fat?'

Devron crosses his arms. 'It's a well known fact that fat women have a better developed sense of humour than normal women. Look at Roseanne. And Dawn French.' This, right here is the biggest problem with my job: when a man like Devron says something like this it is considered unprofessional to slap him.

'If I listened to a panel of housewives before I made every decision, where would that leave me?' Good question, Devron. Better informed, perhaps? 'The public is fine with Skinny Cow,' he says, pouting like a petulant child

'There is a difference between being called skinny and fat,' I say.

'I'm not going to stand around arguing, S-R, it's not up for debate. Aaah, here comes the big man himself! Marty mate!'

I turn around and sure enough here comes the big man, Martin Meddlar. 'Big' being slightly misleading, as Martin's two inches shorter than me and that's including two inches of bouffant dyed-brown hair. Still – he does earn £1.2 million. And he drives a lovely shiny red Ferrari. So I guess maybe my ruler's broken and he is in fact taller than me . . . Martin's around fifty but he has that youthful glow that wealthy alpha males have: the glow that comes from the twin blessings of never having to worry about bills, and having access to plenty of rigorous sex with women far better looking than themselves.

'Devron, great to see you,' says Martin, giving him the full politician handshake – firm clasp with the right hand, left hand offering extra patting on Devron's arm. 'Susie darling, I haven't seen you for weeks.' He kisses me on the cheek and lets his arm drift down my back. 'Where have you been hiding?'

In the mail room, mostly, and sometimes in the basement toilets where no one can hear me scream.

'Perfect timing, Martin,' I say. 'Devron was just telling me the name of the new range.'

'Berenice tells me it's a game changer,' says Martin.

Come on, Devron, tell Martin and he can nip this whole Fat Bird thing in the bud . . .

'Fat Bird pizzas,' says Devron, giving me a smile that might as well be a middle finger.

'Terrific, I can see the spreads now!' says Martin.

'You don't think the feminists will get their knickers in a twist?' says Devron.

'No way!' says Martin. 'Susie darling, you don't think anyone would take offence?'

'I think there are probably less controversial names.'

'Darling, so many other brands out there competing,' he says, staring me in the eye. 'Sometimes you need to be a little bit provocative to get the attention you deserve . . .'

I return my gaze to the floor. 'It's a super-quick turna-round, Martin,' I say. 'Robbie still hasn't allocated a creative team . . .' And if there's any sort of fuck-up on this project Berenice will blame me and I won't get promoted and if I don't get promoted I can't quit and then I will kill myself.

'Darling, you're such a worrier, isn't she a worrier, Devron?' he says, rubbing my arm. Devron nods his head vigorously. 'Now, Devron, you and I have a little date with a Mr Ramsay I believe? Shall we?'

★

122

Back upstairs I pop to the fridge to grab my lunch, some leftover Moroccan chicken tagine that's been in my freezer for six months. I think it's chicken; it was entirely covered in ice crystals so I couldn't figure it out last night. I stick it in the microwave, then hurry back to my desk, hoping to see an email from Jeff.

No, nothing. It's been almost two days since I sent my email and suddenly anxiety creeps in. Have I over-flirted? Does 'Good to meet you too' actually come across as 'I'm not wearing any knickers'?

Maybe instead of typing 'Looking forward to Monday and your cake' I accidentally typed 'your cock'? I'd better check in my sent mail. It's been so long since I flirted with a man, I'm sure it's not supposed to be this traumatic.

No, all is fine. Back to the microwave, and I wolf down my lunch. It was actually lamb and pearl barley casserole. (I must remember to put stickers on my Tupperware before they go in the freezer.) The lamb was delicious; one of those slow-cook one-pot dishes that make you feel all warm and happy inside. I return to my desk in a much better mood than I left it in, only to be greeted by an email that is the exact opposite of what I want to read. It's so bad it actually makes me let out a small yelp of horror.

No, not Jeff telling me he's calling HR and Berenice because I'm sexually harassing him. And not Jake telling me he's impregnated his twenty-three-year-old girlfriend, and that he never loved me anyway. Worse than either of those. It's an email from Robbie, finally telling me which creative team will be working on Fat Bird.

'Sam, seriously, I should just quit now,' I say, as I storm into the mail room, only to find him dozing, head on the counter, with his hand covering his packet of fags protectively in his sleep like a nicotine security blanket. God, he looks so adorable and unsarcastic when he's unconscious.

He wakes with a start. 'Huh? What are you doing in my flat?' he says, before realising he's still at work. 'Christ, what time is it?'

'Don't worry, it's nearly the weekend. What have you been doing? You look like shit.'

He runs a hand through his hair. I have to resist the temptation to straighten it out for him. He has such thick, shiny hair; it really is a drag that he's chosen to opt out of relationships. Rebecca's right – he's a missed opportunity. If only he stopped smoking, stopped wasting his time in the mail room, changed those old jeans and did something with his life, he would be a decent prospect. 'I'm knackered,' he says. 'Been helping a mate with his website, didn't get to bed till 3 a.m. Anyway, what's wrong with you?'

'You know how I'm totally late on this brief, and now it has the worst name in the history of brands, and all I need is a team that can be grown up and sensible and turn around some scripts quickly? So guess who Robbie's given me?

'Dumber and Dumberer?' Benjy and Al, the pretty-boy coke-head Mancunians.

'If only!'

'Doug Lazy and Sir Dicks A Lot?' The twins, Doug and Dean – nicknames require no explanation.

'Much worse.'

'It can't be . . .'

'It is,' I say, as he rolls a seat towards me and I slump down onto it.

'Karly and Nick?!'

I rest my head on the counter. 'Those sadists are going to blow it for me.'

'Maybe it's not that bad, Susie. Maybe success has mellowed them . . .'

'It's only made them feel more invincible! They gave Sandra Weston a nervous breakdown last Christmas. Karly even had the nerve to Tweet about it!'

Sam shakes his head in disgust.

'The only thing that sets Karly apart from those feral girl gangs who terrorise people on the number 38 is the fact that Karly wouldn't get on a bus in the first place because her Louboutins would never recover . . .' I say.

'Her Louboutins? Is that the big bag she carries round like it's the cure for cancer?'

'That's her Birkin, the one Robbie bought her when they started shagging. Louboutins, Sam. Shoes with red soles, cost about five hundred pounds a pair.'

'Do they come with a built-in DVD player?'

'Oh Sam, where have you been for the last five years?'

'Working hard to keep you in Post-its.'

'Sam. Do you live in a cave? Do you not watch TV? Have you never read *Grazia*?'

Actually I do know the answer to all of these questions: Sam lives in a two-bedroom flat in Walthamstow – it's spacious and surprisingly tasteful.

He only watches American TV shows that he streams live online with some dodgy pirate software. He's always three seasons ahead of anyone else, and his greatest pleasure in life is being able to plot-spoil by saying things like 'You *still* haven't got to the ep where Big Louie gets whacked?'

As for print media? He has a subscription to *Uncut* magazine and enjoys reading about popular recording artists such as Steven Van Zandt (guitarist in the E Street Band, Silvio in *The Sopranos*, how can you not *know* that?). He never reads *Grazia*.

'Suze, how can a pair of shoes cost five hundred pounds?'

'Oh Sam, you're so innocent. Don't you understand luxury goods? Have you never been to Terminal 5 in Heathrow? The more something costs, the more important it makes you feel and the more other people will envy you. Anyway, you think five hundred pounds for shoes is expensive? It's a bargain compared to that bag. Guess how much?'

'One thousand pounds,' he says, like The Count in *Sesame Street*.

'Higher.'

'Go on then, two?' he says.

'Try eight.'

'For that Dalston market tut? How is that possible?' he says, with genuine distress in his voice.

'It's simple,' I say. 'The Birkin is not about what it looks like, it's about what it says.'

'Which is?'

'Which is: "I am rich. I mean proper-rich, Hermès-rich, not Marc-by-Marc-Jacobs rich. And what is more, I don't care if you think I'm a spoilt brat for jizzing the cost of a car just to wear on my arm. Because guess what? I am proper rich (well, my dad is). Now do excuse me while I finish my gold sandwich . . ."'

'Whoa. You can tell all that from a bag?' he says.

'It's brands, Sam. It's what we do in this building. Build something out of nothing. Find an object and give it significance, meaning, aspiration. This brick will make you happier, sexier, more popular. Then you can charge what you like for it.'

'Forget Karly,' he says, looking thoughtful. 'I'd be more concerned about Nick.' He suddenly looks worried. I never see Sam look worried. Even if Berenice calls down personally to shout at him that the world is going to end if her Boden delivery doesn't get brought up in two minutes flat, even then he never looks fazed. But right now he looks anxious. It's almost like he feels protective

127

of me. Maybe he's confusing me with his packet of fags . . .

'It's going to be bad,' I say.

'It is going to be bad,' he says. 'But . . . They're team of the year in *Campaign*. They won gold at Cannes. It could actually work in your favour.'

'What do you mean?'

'Suze – if you're going to be on the board you're going to have to get used to playing with the big boys. It'll toughen you up once and for all.'

Maybe I don't want to be toughened up that much, I think, as I head back out of the mail room and towards the weekend.

Sunday

I've lounged around all of yesterday and most of today and achieved pretty much nothing other than catching up on last week's TV, and making a rather good dark chocolate mousse. It's now 4 p.m., the guilt is about to overflow and I can no longer put off the inevitable: a visit to my neighbour, Grumpy Marjorie, who lives on the other side of Peartree Court.

My grandma and Marjorie knew each other well. They were not great friends.

On a good day Marjorie can be decent company: fun, vivacious even. She and my grandma would occasionally sit having tea, chatting about the horrors of growing old. Or gossiping about the Langdons, or the new couple in number 14 who definitely weren't married, and looked more like father and daughter, except they were always touching each other in public: 'Disgraceful, always pawing her like a wild bear.'

But Marjorie also has terrible black moods – she can turn from upbeat to aggressive in a moment. My grandma could go six months without exchanging a word with her. I wouldn't be surprised if Marjorie was bi-polar. Ironic, given that she used to be a psychotherapist. Mind you, psychotherapists must be properly crackers, sitting all day listening to other people's misery.

Marjorie has a son in his fifties but he lives in Brighton and they rarely speak. He comes round once a year on Boxing Day, stays for two hours, then flees back to the coast claiming he doesn't want to get stuck in traffic. 'Traffic, on Boxing Day?' she says, practically spitting. The only thing she's ever said about him is that he is the greatest disappointment of her life. All credit to him for visiting at all.

Still, since my grandma died and I moved into the block I've felt a weird sense of duty towards Marjorie. She doesn't get many visitors, although you can see why. I try to visit her, and Terry the caretaker pops in most days, though she once threw a can at his head a few years back. She'd had a bad fall and broken her hip, and he'd merely suggested it might be time to consider her options, perhaps move to a residential home. 'Why would I want to be around depressing old people?' No point arguing that misery loves company.

Today I head down to Waitrose to buy her a couple of punnets of raspberries and some seeds for her budgie,

Fitzgerald. I'll take her some bolognese I've defrosted too, and the chocolate mousse. She's a sucker for sweet things and mousse is her favourite – the only dessert I make that doesn't get stuck in her dentures.

'Who is it?' she says at the front door, though I know she'll be squinting through the spy hole at me.

'I have raspberries for you, Marjorie,' I say.

'Where from?' she growls back.

'Don't worry, they're not from Sainsbury's.' I wouldn't dare.

'Then you can come in.' She opens the door and greets me with a neutral expression; not huge on warmth, our Marjorie. She's wearing her usual floor-length grey robe and mid-brown suede sheepskin slippers. She has terrible gout and her ankles are purple with swelling. She shuffles slowly down the dark corridor and into her living room. The air is heavy; the smell reminds me of my junior school – a mix of canned soup and disinfectant.

'Marjorie, how can you see where you're going? It's practically pitch black in here, why don't you open the curtains? Let some light in.'

'What's to see?'

She slowly winds her way through the chaos in her living room: stacks of *Radio Times* are piled on the floor, and a collection of side tables house Sudoku books and mail-order catalogues; magnifying glasses bookmark pages of dressing gowns and neck pillows.

'Marjorie, do you want me to help you tidy up in here? It's getting a bit messy.'

She ignores me. She'd only tell me that she knows exactly where everything is and to mind my own bloody business.

Finally she reaches her destination and her face lights up. 'Look who's come to see us, Fitzgerald,' she says, bending down slowly to talk to the little green and yellow bird, twittering loudly on a perch in his cage. 'You're right, Fitzgerald, it has been a long time,' she nods at him. 'Yes, she does live very nearby, we could almost throw a stone, couldn't we?' I wouldn't put it past her. 'And that's correct, Fitzgerald, it wouldn't be so hard to visit us more often, would it, my darling? What a clever bird to remember where Susie lives when it's been so long. Isn't he clever, such a good memory?'

'I bought Fitzgerald a little treat,' I say, following her through the obstacle course and handing her the seeds.

'Oooh, look at what we get when someone has a guilty conscience!' she says. 'Your favourite, Fitzgerald! Sunflower seeds!'

'And I brought you some bolognese sauce and your favourite chocolate mousse too.'

She tries not to show that she's pleased.

'Just think,' I say. 'If I'd left it another month you might have got a whole suckling pig.'

She looks at me out of the corner of her eye. A tiny smile creeps up the side of her mouth.

'Put that lot in the fridge, make me a cup of tea and come and play a round of cards with me.'

Marjorie's fridge is the size of a shoebox. All that's inside is a pint of full-fat milk and three half-eaten, uncovered cans – one of Campbell's condensed chicken and mushroom soup, one of pilchards and one of steak and kidney pudding.

'Marjorie, shall I pop home and bring you back some clingfilm?'

'That stuff gives you cancer,' she says. There's no point in arguing with her, or pointing out that she's more likely to get ill from leaving food in cans, half-opened.

'Do you want me to cook you some pasta?' I say. 'I could do some nice shapes with bolognese?' I can't bear to watch Marjorie eat long length pasta. The sucking noise she makes and the mess that ends up all over her face when she eats spaghetti is gross. I mean, I'm sure I do exactly the same but I don't have to look at myself while I'm eating.

'I'll get the girl to cook it tomorrow, if she can boil water without burning it: a half-wit of the highest order this new one, even worse than the last. She can't understand basic English. She just looks at me with these big eyes like she hasn't a single thought in her head.'

I bet she does have plenty of thoughts, Marjorie: all of them about throttling you. I head back into the kitchen and make her tea, which she drinks whiter than milk. I don't know why she wastes money on teabags – I'm only allowed to introduce the bag into the cup for a millisecond.

It's like that quote about how to make the perfect Martini – hold the gin bottle next to the vermouth and let a beam of sunlight pass through. That's all well and good but there's no sunlight in Marjorie's flat to pass through this teabag anyway.

Those poor carers the agency sends round here: I have nothing but gargantuan respect for them. None of them have a hope in hell of ever hearing those immortal words 'thank you'. Quite frankly it's a good job most of them don't have English as their first language or they'd walk out a lot sooner, the amount of verbal she gives them. I know you're not supposed to say things like this about vulnerable old ladies with osteoporosis and gout, but more often than not Marjorie is a complete cow.

Now where's she hidden the kitchen bin today, I wonder . . . Marjorie's living room is like a junk shop but for some reason she can't abide the sight of a bin anywhere in her flat. Well probably those two things are connected, I suppose. She doesn't like throwing things away so she pretends bins don't exist. (Good grief, what's it doing in there? I know I'm a bit of a hoarder but at least I don't hide my kitchen bin in a shoe cupboard.)

Right. I'm done in this kitchen, it's too depressing. I take her tea through and set it down on the Duchess of Cambridge coaster on Marjorie's side table. She nods.

'Cake's still going strong?' I say, walking over to a Perspex case in the corner to examine my handiwork. For Marjorie's eightieth birthday last year, I'd baked a large cake in the shape of Fitzgerald's head. It had taken me ages to match the perfect shades of green and yellow for the buttercream icing, and two hours to pipe them precisely in short little strokes, like feathers. I suspect it would have tasted more of food colouring than of vanilla but no one ever managed to find out. Marjorie was so smitten with this replica of her beloved that she refused to let anyone cut into it, let alone eat his face. She's gone full Havisham and had it under Perspex ever since. God knows what they put in that food colouring – formaldehyde by the looks of it – but it's held up pretty well.

'OK,' she says, taking a deck of cards from her side table. 'Gin rummy, I'll deal.'

We play three rounds of increasingly frustrating rummy. I would probably let Marjorie win just to cheer her up but there's no need for that. She thrashes me every time. In each hand we play I'm just holding out for a couple of cards before I lay mine down, but she nips in and declares 'Gin', leaving me with a handful of deadwood. I swear she'd clean up in Vegas, she's a total card-sharp. Defeated, I head to the kitchen to make us more tea. She's still chuckling away to herself when I return.

'So what's going on with you?' she says. 'Still in that terrible office?'

I nod. 'I'm working on this one last project, and if that goes well I'll be promoted to the board. And then I'm going to leave.'

'What I don't understand,' she says, pulling herself forward in her chair with her elbows, 'is why you don't leave now, if you're so damn miserable. Makes no sense wasting time when you should be getting on, you're not young any more.' Marjorie loves to attack. It's her favourite pasttime and the main thing keeping her alive, along with bile and re-runs of *Columbo*.

'Well Marjorie,' I say, trying to be patient; we've discussed this before. 'There are three reasons, aren't there? I can't leave because I need my bonus.'

'Money's never a good enough reason!' she snaps. 'How much is this bonus?'

'Several thousand pounds,' I say.

'That's neither here nor there. You'll have to support yourself once you've left.'

'Well yes . . .'

'Your grandmother was never good with money either. I told her you can never go wrong with shares in ICI.'

Lay off the dead grandmother please, Marjorie. 'Of course I'll need an income,' I say. 'But that bonus money will give me a cushion, pay off my debt, that's all.'

'Nonsense, it's clearly fear, a classic evasion technique; you're not fooling me for a second.' I can only imagine what a delightful time Marjorie's patients must have had in their therapy sessions, being torn to shreds like this. 'I could write you a cheque for five thousand pounds right now and you wouldn't leave.'

'I would too!' I say.

'Bring me my cheque book,' she says.

'Marjorie . . .'

'Bring it to me, it's in my brown bag, in the hall. Bring it!'

I have no idea how much Marjorie has in the bank but I couldn't take her money even if she was rich. Still, to humour her, I fetch her bag and she writes me a cheque, signing her name in a frenzy and handing it to me with venom.

'That's your first excuse gone. Put it in your pocket. Do it, right away! OK, good. What's next?' she says, warming up now. I can see how much she's enjoying this, though there's a manic glint in her eyes that's a warning sign she's about to get nastier.

'Well, secondly, if I ever need to go back into working at an agency, I want to go in at board level. I couldn't bear to have to jump through all the hoops again.'

'Gobbledygook. What do you think, Fitzgerald? Flawed reasoning, failed before she's even started, self-defeatist, weak, cowardly. Yes Fitzgerald, I agree with your diagnosis.'

I feel my face flush. I know this is her idea of fun but I can think of many other things I'd rather be doing than sitting here: 'not sitting here' would be foremost.

'And what's your third reason? It had better be less flimsy!'

'Just because, Marjorie. It's the principle of the thing. I deserve it, I have earned it, and I'm not going to walk out of there till I have been recognised.'

137

'Ha, pride! And such stupidity! You must get that from your mother's side of the family because your grandma was no beauty but neither was she a fool,' she says.

'Marjorie, do you mind not bringing my mother into this?' I say. 'I know you're only joking but it's really not necessary.'

'I'm not joking at all,' she says. 'Though I can see I've offended you. You probably do get the over-sensitivity from your mother too . . .'

'Marjorie. I'm quite tired so I think I'm going to head off now,' I say, moving to stand up. I don't care if you're old and lonely. You are a rude old cow, plus you're not even a blood relative. And you can stick some Paxo up Fitzgerald's arse for all I care. I'm off.

'You've only been here an hour! You can't go yet, I'll have no one to talk to.'

You can talk to the bird, can't you?

'Marjorie, I've got a big week at work. I've left the food in the fridge and I can make you another cup of tea before I go if you'd like? Why don't I do that?'

'Don't bother,' she says. 'Fair-weather friend. And you can give me that cheque back right now, trying to steal my money.'

'Marjorie,' I say, putting the cheque on her side table. 'There's no need to be like that. I'm just tired. I've got an early start – Mondays are always the worst.'

She turns her head to the side and pretends I'm not even in the room.

'I'm going to go home now, but I'll come and see you soon,' I say. We both know this isn't true, and as I walk back to my flat I struggle to find some compassion towards her. No wonder she's lonely if she behaves like that to the people who are trying to be nice to her. She's not my responsibility and I refuse to feel bad about her. I've got plenty of other things to feel bad about as it is.

Oh, and something to feel good about too, I think, as I ponder tomorrow's wardrobe choice again. A date! Sorry, a 'meeting' with Jeff!

w/c 19 March

Status report
- Fat Bird – Pizza session with Jeff
- Brief creative team – TUESDAY A.M.

Monday

I have spent the whole of this morning looking at my watch and my inbox, willing it to be Jeff o'clock and worrying that he'll email me to cancel between now and then. It's now mid-afternoon and our department meeting has just drawn to a long, slow close. Berenice publicly savaged me for having failed to brief the creatives yet; when I explained that Robbie's only just allocated the team and that I'll be briefing them first thing tomorrow, she'd pursed her lips and said, 'It's super high-profile. It's not just you who's responsible.' (She means it's not just me who'll take the credit. Naturally I will be the only one who'll get the bollocking.) 'If you slip any further, make sure you keep me in the loop.' Given half a chance I suspect she'll be turning that loop into a noose.

I rush back to my desk to grab my things and when I look at my phone there's a text from a number I don't recognise: 'Pizzas ready and waiting, plus I've got a little surprise! J'.

I walk over to the Fletchers Head Office – sorry, 'The Building' – in my flats, checking my hair and make-up in as many reflective surfaces as possible along the way, then change into my heels on the corner of Wardour Street and head in.

Jeff Nichols doesn't make me wait twenty-three minutes down in reception! No, Jeff Nichols comes to fetch me within two minutes, which earns him brownie points in my book. And then even more brownie points when he takes me to the basement kitchens and presents me with some actual brownies.

'I baked these off earlier,' he says. 'We're doing trials on low-cal brownies and they tasted like an old sponge, so I thought I'd do a batch that weren't soul-destroying just to keep myself sane. What do you think?'

'Mmm, great,' I say. 'You've got salted caramel in there, haven't you? I'm getting the sweetness and then something cutting through at the end.'

'Good palate!' he says. 'I love that combo of salt and sweet. You know, for years, people thought that your tongue had different zones on it that tasted the different basic flavours.'

I nod encouragingly. We're a minute into this so-called

'meeting' and he's already talking to me about tongues. Could this be any more blatant?

'So when you first put something in your mouth, you'd taste sweetness, right at the tip of your tongue . . . and then you'd pick up saltiness on the sides, and then at the back you'd pick up if something had any bitterness to it.' He picks off a chunk of brownie and puts it in his mouth and I do the same.

'A Harvard scientist called, believe it or not, Boring, put that theory forward . . . but it's not true,' he says. 'Some bits of the tongue might be a tiny bit more sensitive than others, but you can taste everything, everywhere.'

'I did not know that!' I say. 'I wonder if he had a wife . . .'

'Who?'

'Dr Boring. Can you imagine being Mrs Boring?' I say.

'I can't imagine you ever being Mrs Boring,' he says, laughing. 'Right then, I suppose I'd better take you through where we are with this food.' He goes to the fridge and takes out three uncooked pizzas.

'Have a seat,' he says, pulling out a stool for me. 'Actually I'll sit next to you, it'll be easier to talk you through it.' He sits down next to me and our knees touch, and he doesn't move his away, though after a moment I feel so acutely aware of having turned tomato-red that I find myself moving my legs slightly.

'OK,' he says. 'So you know how we make our standard pizzas.' His eyes are so piercing and he has this way of

142

looking at me that's so intense it is all I can do to keep looking directly back at him. I nod and try to keep his gaze. 'The bulk of calories in a normal pizza is dough and cheese. If you're talking classic southern Italian pizza from Naples, it's not particularly fattening – just a thin base with a drizzle of olive oil and a little mozzarella, sometimes not even cheese if you order a marinara. Have you been to Naples?'

'No. My granny was Italian, but from the north.'

'Your grandmother was Italian?' he says. 'Your colouring's quite Celtic, that reddish brown hair with pale eyes . . .'

I feel myself blush under his attention. 'I look like my dad's side of the family more,' I say. 'But no, I've never been to Naples. I've always wanted to go, I hear it's amazing.'

'The drivers are insane but it's just one of those cities, like New York – it has an amazing energy. You should come out next time we do a research trip. There's this one pizza restaurant, Da Michele, they only have two pizzas on the menu, but they're the best two pizzas in the world . . . anyway, where was I?'

'Italian pizzas aren't fattening . . .'

'Right. But Fletchers pizzas aren't in any way authentic. We have our standard two-inch greased base, and then we load it up with fatty proteins – bacon, meatballs, cheese-burger bites, sweet chilli chicken bites, all the stuff our customers love.'

'So how are you cutting the calories?'

'You take out the saturated fat in the base and replace it with a liquid fat substitute.'

'Liquid fat substitute? Like the stuff you buy from the chemist if you're obese, that makes you . . .' I want to say anally incontinent, but of course I don't want to bring our light and flirtatious conversation on to that particular subject.

'Yes, liquid fat substitute – the stuff that means you can't get on the tube,' he says. 'And then instead of cheese you have low-fat cheese substitutes.' He picks off a handful of pale grey flaky matter from the pizza that looks more like a skin disease than cheese. 'But unfortunately, because there are no fat proteins in the cheese substitute it won't melt, even at two hundred degrees, so that's one of the problems we're looking at.'

'What's it made of?'

'Don't ask me that,' he says, shaking his head.

Can we go back to talking about tongues again please?

'Then there's the tomato sauce,' he says. 'Our standard tomato sauce has twenty grammes of sugar per hundred, to make up for the fact that the tomatoes are Chinese and have no discernible flavour.'

'Honestly, every time I think about Chinese tomatoes it makes me feel deeply unhappy.'

He laughs. 'What have you got against Chinese tomatoes?' he says. But he says this in a way that is *so* flirtatious he might as well be saying, 'I really need you to take your knickers off right now. Off.'

I laugh and recross my legs and almost fall off the stool, and have to steady myself by touching his thigh momentarily.

'Where were we . . . oh yes,' he says grinning. 'We've had to cut the sugar, so the tomato sauce now has sweetener in.'

'Rat cancer sweetener, like in the eighties?'

'No, just mouse cancer,' he says.

'OK, so you've got liquid fake fat in the base, plastic cheese flakes, and sweetener in the Chinese tomato sauce,' I say, trying not to laugh.

'Control yourself, my dear! I can see I'm making you ravenous, aren't I?'

'Tell me about the toppings, I want to hear about the toppings.'

'Are you sure you can handle my toppings?' he says.

That innuendo doesn't even make sense and yet I laugh like I've had three gin and tonics.

'OK,' he says. 'So Devron wants to launch with three flavours, and guess what?'

'What?' I say, grinning like a fool.

'None of them work yet! He's desperate to make the Meat Hoe Down half-cal.'

'It's the market leader, makes sense,' I say, sitting up straight and trying to resume some sort of professional demeanour, though frankly if we were in a bar we'd be snogging by now.

'But you can't have meatballs, cheeseburgers and chorizo on a diet pizza – it's impossible,' he says. 'The chicken pizza's easier, we use baked breast meat and add spinach. Devron wants to call it Sexy Chick and we're arguing about what constitutes a sexy ingredient. Devron thinks sweetcorn as it's Mandy's favourite. I'm not convinced.'

'What would you put on there?'

'Oooh, if I had my way, and we're talking quality ingredients? Asparagus maybe, though it's a bit of a cliché . The sexiest food for me isn't truffle or lobster. It's a rib-eye steak, medium rare, Béarnaise sauce and beautiful, salty, crunchy chips.'

'You'd stick a steak and chips on a pizza? Very Fletchers!' I say.

'No. Forget Fletchers, forget pizza. Just the steak on a plate. God, I could totally murder a steak for supper tonight . . .'

'Yes, me too,' I say. *Ask me! Ask me out for a steak tonight!*

'There's a thought. Anyway, finally there's the vegetarian pizza.'

'That should be easier on calories,' I say, thinking maybe I should repeat how much I too would like a steak tonight. Didn't he hear me properly?

'You'd think. But Devron's desperate for one of the three pizzas to come in at under four hundred calories, which means mushrooms, spinach and lettuce.'

'Hot lettuce on a pizza?'

146

'He says that in America they categorise pizza sauce as a vegetable; he wants our veggie pizza to be at least one of your five a day.' He puts two fingers to the side of his head and mimes pulling a trigger.

'Poor you,' I say.

He fixes me again with those eyes. He must be fully aware of how piercing those eyes are, how could he not be?

'Can I ask you a personal question, Jeff?'

'Fire away.'

'You seem . . . unconvinced by these pizzas.'

'What's the question?'

'No one else at Fletchers is quite as honest as you are about the food quality . . .'

'And what's the question?' he says, smiling.

'I don't mean to be rude, but if you love food isn't it hard to work on a project like this?'

He pauses for a minute and nods. 'That's an interesting question.'

'I mean, you were a chef, you ran your own place, and now you're working for a big company doing pizzas that have dubious side effects. Shouldn't it be the other way round? You work for a big company, then you go off and do your own thing?'

'Yeah, I guess,' he says. 'But you know, life just never turns out the way you planned, does it? On which note you'll have to excuse me. I'd love to stay and carry on talking but I have to see a man about some synthetic non-melting cheese. Let's catch up soon.'

I stand outside the Fletchers buildings as a rush of commuters flow past me heading for home. I hesitate, then pick up the phone. 'Are you free for a drink now?'

'What happened?' says Rebecca. 'I thought you were having a meeting with Jeff?'

'I was,' I say. 'And now I'm not. It just ended. I can't have a late one, I've got to be in early to brief the creatives, but meet me at The Flask in half an hour?'

'Let's go somewhere different?' she says. 'Clerkenwell? There's a new cocktail bar, same people as Colebrooke Row.'

'*No!* You know I can't go anywhere near that part of town.'

'Oh Suze, he's not going to be there. You've got to get over this.'

'I am over it. I just don't need to go anywhere near his postcode.'

'Clerkenwell is not Islington. You can't veto every postcode because of Jake.'

'I've told you I'll go as far as the Holborn–Farringdon borders. Just not tonight.'

'Fine. The Flask.'

'The Flask.'

'Fine.'

'I don't understand, it was all going so well,' I say, pouring a second glass of wine. 'He'd made me these amazing brownies, and he started the whole conversation talking about tongues. Then he was offering to show me his toppings; he even said I should go to Naples with them next time they go. I mean honestly, Rebecca, the way he was looking at me, I don't think I'm imagining this. But then suddenly mid-conversation he says he has to go, takes me back up to reception and that was that. Maybe it was something I said . . .'

'Like what?'

'Well I asked him why he worked at Fletchers, that it must kill him to work on that food . . .'

'And you think you might have offended him?'

'I don't think so . . . he doesn't seem the type to offend easily . . .'

'He probably just had to be somewhere,' she says.

'He said he had a meeting about cheese . . .'

'There you go! Nothing to do with you.'

'But I gave him this massive opportunity to ask me out for steak, and he didn't take the bait at all.'

'He's not going to ask you out for dinner during a meeting, is he? He probably doesn't know whether you've got a boyfriend. It is work, remember?'

'Oh now it's work? You're the one telling me to email him asking his inside leg measurements and now it's work?'

'Come outside for a ciggy,' she says, grabbing the bottle of wine.

'It's raining.'

'Come on. I just saw a hot guy go outside and his friend was alright too . . .'

Rebecca started smoking again when she split up with Paul last year. I hate her smoking. Not for my own sake – I'm quite fond of the smell of fags, reminds me of my youth – but because it reeks of self-harm, albeit in socially acceptable form. It suggests that she's not over her ex. I mean, I know I have my moments, but I'm relying on her to be wiser and stronger than me. The only upside to her smoking is that we do end up talking to even more men. Sure enough her fag's barely out of the pack before the guy we've followed outside leans over to light her cigarette – though his mythical good-looking friend is nowhere in sight.

Rebecca is so damn impressive when she's on the prowl. Within minutes they're practically snogging. She's turning round to show him something on the back pocket of her trousers, and he's touching her back pocket, pretending to be interested in the tailoring but clearly delighted to be copping a feel. I'm standing awkwardly next to them staring into the middle distance with a smile fixed on my face when the pub door opens, and his friend re-emerges with a couple more pints. He hands one to his mate, stops, looks me up and down in my dress, then nods a greeting.

Rebecca is right though – this man is attractive. Excellent teeth, dark hair, tall, wearing a lovely grey suit, cream shirt and a navy tie. He actually looks like a proper person with a proper job. Maybe Rebecca's theory stands up – maybe the mere fact of fancying Jeff means I'm now attracting more men into my universe.

'Is this us then?' he says.

'Is what us then?' I say.

'Your mate's going to get off with my mate, so we talk to each other?'

'Does this happen to you often?'

'A bit too often. I'd tell your mate not to bother with Gary,' he whispers. 'Seb, by the way,' he says, extending his hand.

'Susie. Why should I tell my friend not to bother? They look like they're enjoying talking to each other.' I notice Rebecca give Gary a joke slap, then press her hand to his chest in mock disapproval.

'I'm sure your friend's lovely,' he says. 'I just mean she's probably wasting her time.'

'Why? Is your friend a player?' Garys are always players now I come to think of it.

'You could say that,' he says. 'His wife would probably say that if she was here now . . .'

'Ouch,' I say, clocking his ring finger and noting it is bare. I pause for a second to try to work out why I feel so bothered on Rebecca's behalf.

'Are you married?' he says.

'Never,' I say. 'You?'

'No. Got kids?' I shake my head. 'But you want kids?' he says.

'Why are you asking me?'

'Don't all women your age want kids?'

'Er, no, Seb. And what age do you think I am?'

'Don't know, thirty?' he says.

OK, I shall stay in this conversation – for now. 'I don't know if I want kids. Not everyone's the same.'

'You're quite prickly, aren't you?' he says. 'I like that in a girl. Feisty.'

'It's quite a personal question. How about you start with something a little less significant?'

'OK.' He smiles. 'What's your favourite sandwich filling? Or is that too significant too?'

'Don't knock sandwiches – sandwiches are important,' I say, looking over to see what Rebecca's up to. I'm not sure if I should go over there and warn her Gary's married; I'll tell her in a bit, when I'm done talking to this . . . quite attractive person.

'I agree,' says Seb. 'I like roast beef, mustard and lettuce, with a packet of salted crisps on the side.'

'Good call on the crisps. Rocket or iceberg?' I say.

'Oooh, now you're asking . . . rocket, I think.'

Oh hang on a minute. Body language over there has changed slightly. I see Rebecca's hand come up to rest on her hip and she starts to shake her head. 'Seb, I think my friend has just found out that your friend is spoken for.'

'Oh that's a shame. You've only just forgiven me for that question about babies and now you're going to go off to another pub and we'll never see each other again.'

'That is a shame, isn't it,' I say, smiling in a way that I hope is encouraging.

'Ah well,' he says.

'Suze, shall we go?' says Rebecca, coming to stand next to me and raising her eyebrows with great emphasis.

'I guess I'm going now . . .' I say.

'Bye then . . .' And then after a pause, 'Are you going to give me your number or what?'

'07831 442 310,' I say, and I turn to walk away.

'Hang on a minute, let me put it in my phone,' he says.

'Come on,' I say, grabbing Rebecca's arm. 'Let's go.' I start walking.

'Don't you want to give that guy your number? He's standing there with his phone in his hand.'

'If he really wants it he'll catch up with us,' I say, as we walk away. With these good-looking ones you have to make them work a bit harder; they're usually quite arrogant.

'He's standing there waiting for you. He's not going to run down the street after you in front of his mate.'

'Oh. Is he not coming?'

'No. He's just standing there.'

'Well I can't go back now, I'll look silly,' I say. 'You go back and give him my number.'

'Seriously?'

'Just hurry up and do it, I'm too embarrassed now,' I say.

'You're a twelve-year-old sometimes, you know that?' she says, as she heads back to the pub, shaking her head.

Am not! I think, as I stick my tongue out at her.

'Fine. Done,' she says, coming back. 'Don't make me do that again. Can you believe that guy I was talking to was married? He wasn't wearing a ring.'

'I'm telling you, all Garys are love-rats. So meanwhile how was Mr Salsa, did you see him in the end?' I say.

'Ah, yeah, not for me,' she says, shaking her head. 'Lied about his height . . .'

I try not to smirk. 'You've got the hot barman this week though, haven't you?'

'Hot barman on Thursday. And yes, he still thinks I'm called Susie . . .'

'You can tell him your real name if you like.'

'He's taking me to some new pop-up speakeasy that serves alcoholic milkshakes.'

'Be sure to Tweet an Instagram the moment you get there . . .'

'Hopefully I'll have better things to do with my time,' she says with a smile.

Tuesday

One thing you do *not* want, when briefing Karly and Nick in their office first thing on a Tuesday is a cheap white wine hangover.

Another thing is Nick, lying on his stomach, playing *Grand Theft Auto* on his PlayStation and shouting 'Die, you slaaag!' at the prostitute on screen that he's shooting.

'Remind me why Robbie's given us this brief?' says Karly, tapping on her iPhone. Karly reminds me of Louise Brooks's evil twin. She has a fantastically expensive razor-sharp bob and a killer body – long legs, slim hips and collar bones like a Tiffany mount that snugly position a diamond skull at the pit of her neck. Along with a killer body she has the mind of a psychopath.

'It's a huge budget, it's very high profile, they want a star team.' I say, trying to locate some 'pep' in my tone of voice collection.

'Yeah,' she says, putting her phone down briefly. 'It's just not our thing. Pre-manufactured food? I haven't been to a supermarket for a decade. Are you sure Robbie meant this for us? He probably meant it for, like, Andy Ashford.'

'I guess he didn't want Andy on it because the budget's so massive . . .'

'How massive?' she says, picking up a copy of *W* magazine from a neat stack and flicking through it with an insouciance so practised it seems almost genuine.

'Four million quid all in. And Fletchers always use celebs . . .'

'Yeah, poxy no-name celebs.'

'Well I'm sure they'd be open to any celebrity, depending on budget.' And the fact that no one remotely credible would attach themselves to Fletchers in the first place. 'And Devron will want a big-name director . . .'

'We could use TK?' shouts Nick, still firing at the screen.

'Doing a feature with Kidman in Tokyo,' she says, chewing her bottom lip.

'Chad Breffen?' says Nick again. 'Take that, Guido, you little Mexican shithead!'

'Breffen . . .' says Karly. 'I suppose we could shoot in New York.' She picks up her iPhone again and starts tapping.

'"Hey Karlsie, you got such awesome vision, you gotta director's eye. Get behind my tripod . . ."' says Nick, in an attempt at a Brooklyn accent that sounds more like Cardiff.

156

'Piss off, Nick. It's not my fault he thinks I'm transcendental.' She turns to me. 'Yeah, alright. Leave it with us.'

'Great. And just on the brief, the range is called Fat Bird so in the scripts themselves steer clear of anything that's in bad taste – we don't want a double whammy of offensiveness. If in doubt err on the side of caution.'

'We don't do caution round here, love,' says Nick. Ah, little Nick, lying there in his ironic trucker cap, with his ironic facial hair.

'I'll leave you copies of the paper brief to read through,' I say. I've highlighted that pizzas are a bit like curries – most people assume they're fattening, and so the *great* thing about Fat Bird pizzas is that they're not as bad for you as you think. In the Essentials box I've put: *Avoid offence. Must have Fletchers logo and pack shot.*

'Did Robbie mention we'd like scripts by Friday week?' I say.

'Fine,' says Nick.

'Definitely?' I say.

'Yeah . . . Fuck you, die, whore!' (To the screen, not me, I think . . .)

All things considered, that went absolutely brilliantly.

Friday

Since Jonty returned from his course there's barely been a moment's peace in our corner of the office. He's just come back from an extended pub lunch with his friend who works at an agency round the corner. And now he's on the phone to his housemate laughing about their Thursday night, during which it appears they copped off with the same girl. Jonty's Facebook photos consist of glassy-eyed shots of mid-twenties blokes holding pints up to the camera at nightclubs with names such as Bhargeegees and Boubous. They sound like Eurotrash Tellytubbies. Mind you, so do his Facebook friends – he has one in Geneva called Mufmuf Van Lella. I wish he'd stop guffawing. I am trying hard to concentrate on urgent work – Jeff emailed me last night at 9.40 p.m. and I am trying to decipher the meaning in this latest correspondence:

Suzy Q,

*Apologies again for running off mid-chat on Monday.
I'd have liked nothing more than to stay – far more stimulating talking to you than to the plastic cheese man.*

*If I can be of any more help for now please call me.
Maybe we should have another session? Had a catch up
with Devron last night and I think the veggie pizza is
moving in an epic new direction.*

*Next time you're in 'The Building'(!!!) give us a shout,
we'll go down and have coffee in the kitchen. I have been
thinking long and hard about salted caramel brownies and
wanted to show you a tweaked recipe.*

Take care,

Jeff

Hugely thought-provoking, this email. And slightly trou-
bling. Polly's brother works in the City with a nob-end
called St John. In spite of having a worse first name (or
first two names?) than Tarquin, St John is what's known in
EC1, admiringly, as a 'swordsman'. He credits his prowess
with women (or Rat, as he calls them) on some guide to
seduction that recommends scattering your chat-up repartee
with sexual phrases such as 'long and hard' and 'go down'.
These are guaranteed, subliminally, to make ANY WOMAN
WANT YOU. My favourite recommendation of all is to
drop in the phrase 'new direction': if you say these two
words quickly enough, 'new direction' sounds like 'nude

erection'; women, rats, even hot twin gerbils will fall at your feet.

And so here in Jeff's email we have 'long and hard' *and* 'go down'! And look! Right there! Jeff has slipped in his very own 'new direction', and an epic one at that! Barely ten lines of text and we have three rat pellets in a row. That's a jackpot. This *cannot possibly* be deliberate.

And yet how can it be mere coincidence? Definitely going to have run this one past Rebecca in forensics. What else is there to analyse . . . 'Take care' at the end. That's annoying and patronising, that's what you say to an old person. But 'stimulating' is good, that's a compliment and I'll take it. And he's been thinking about me and wants to show me more baked goods. Encouraging, though of course that could be merely professional interest . . . Am I supposed to follow up on his offer of another session?

'Susie,' says Jonty, coming to stand behind my desk. 'Can you come do this conference call with me on Fletchers?'

I quickly switch back to the status report on screen. 'Right now?'

'Yeah, Tom's calling in to Boardroom Six, I'm not sure how to set up the system.'

'Couldn't you have sorted this earlier?' I say. I am beginning to sound like Berenice. 'I'll help you this time but try and be a bit more prepared in future.'

He nods. Nodding equals thank you for Jonty.

We sit by the triangular phone pad in the boardroom waiting for Tom to call in.

'What's the brief then?' I say.

'Piece of piss, new store opening at Marble Arch, small posters for the tube.'

'Busy station. Besides, even if you're just talking to one person, you do the best work you can.'

'Because of awards?' Jonty asks.

'Because your name is on the paper.'

'But there are always *so* many other things going on. I'm learning to prioritise. That course I went on said to focus on the big things, don't waste time on the little.'

'I think they meant don't spend a whole week pondering what type of moustache to grow for Movember . . . Show me this ad then.'

'I haven't got it in front of me.'

'Wouldn't it be a good idea to have it?' I say gently.

'I left it on my desk.'

'Do you want to run down quickly and fetch it?'

'But if Tom calls when I'm gone I'll look incompetent . . .'

'Would you like me to get it for you, just this once?'

'Good idea.'

I find the ad on Jonty's desk with a coffee stain on it that fails to cover up the name of the creative who did it: Andy Ashford. My favourite! One of the few old-timers left at NMN. He's early fifties, a relic in this industry

161

where you're either running the show or in The Priory by forty.

The poster has an image of Marble Arch. Andy's filled in a bar across the middle and made the right-hand pillar pale so that what stands out is an 'F'. At the bottom it says: 'Fletchers – now open at Marble Arch'. It's clear and smart. Fletchers will hate it.

'Ah, finally!' says Jonty, as I walk back in. 'We've been waiting for you.' He winks at me. 'So yah, the ad, you seen it, Tommo?'

'Yes,' says Tom nervously down the line.

'Good or what?' says Jonty, giving me the thumbs up.

'I did actually like the ad,' says Tom.

'Great,' says Jonty, punching the air. He doesn't realise, because he's not really listening, that Tom is about to blow out the poster.

'I thought it was very clever,' says Tom, working up the courage to reject it. There's a long pause. 'I just want to understand the *insight* behind it.'

Jonty rolls his eyes. 'Absolutely, Tommo. Your brief was simple: announce "We are open". Londoners are a savvy bunch, we thought we'd make it smart.'

'I think that's the problem,' says Tom. 'I'm not sure that *smart* is right for our brand.' Another long pause. 'Also, I'm not sure about Marble Arch. It's not the Eiffel Tower. It's not that famous. Could you use the London Eye instead?'

'The new store is *at* Marble Arch, Tom,' I say. 'That's why it's on the poster. If the new store was near the London Eye we'd use the Eye.' And if Parisians are ever foolish enough to let you into their marketplace we'll use the Eiffel Tower.

'The poster needs to say who we are, be more *strategic*,' says Tom.

'Everyone *knows* who Fletchers are, Tommo,' says Jonty, making a wanker sign with his fist. 'Don't go changing the brief on us, mate.'

'Tom,' I say, 'commuters rush past these posters. They need to be concise.'

There is a long pause, during which Jonty mimes head-bashing the desk while I try to think of a solution to this painfully common scenario.

Tom breaks the silence. 'It needs to say "Fletchers. The best supermarket, is now open at Marble Arch in London, selling groceries, magazines, alcohol and toiletries. And flowers. See in store for details" and then it needs to have our website. And our 0845 number. And loyalty card info and logo. And Facebook and Twitter. And then look at a different, better known landmark. I'll leave it to you though, you're the experts.'

Jonty's voice verges on panic: 'Oh mate, that would be a totes dull poster.'

'But I don't want dull, I want you to strategically fun it up. That's what our brand is about. Listen, team, I'm seeing new shelf wobblers in five. Can you go again?'

'No problem, mate.' Jonty flicks the off switch on the phone. I press it again to double-check the line has cut off.

'Shit for brains,' says Jonty. 'Why don't we just use the Statue of fucking Liberty.'

I say nothing.

'This isn't my fault, Susie!' he says, turning on me in a sudden panic.

'Calm down, Jonty, I wasn't saying it was. I'm just thinking how to fix it . . .'

'Couldn't *you* have done something more?' he says. Aaah, bless him, *he's* becoming more like Berenice every day. He'll probably make it to the board before me at this rate.

'None of that, Jonty, we're a team.'

'What are we going to do?' he says. 'I'm going to have to rebrief another team. Andy Ashford's too old for this game.'

'You will *not* brief another team. We're lucky to have Andy on this. Our job is to try to convince Tom to buy this ad. You can give Tom what he wants and still keep the visual. Add some copy, meet him half way. The idea itself is strong.'

'Tom said it's a rebrief.'

'Listen to what Tom actually said: get the ad mocked up with more words on it – first part solved. Then see what people think, go over to Marble Arch and show some Londoners.'

I can see a flicker of inspiration pass through Jonty's brain.

'And don't lie to me – or Tom – about the results. If the public like it, then Tom has no argument. And if they don't then maybe Tom's right and it is too clever. Only then can we brief in a new ad. With Andy.'

He sticks his bottom lip out. I'm not sure that there's anything less attractive in this universe than a boy who sulks.

'Come on, Jonty, stop pouting. It's nearly the weekend.' Two hours and twenty-one minutes to go. Not that I'm counting.

Saturday

Dalia feels bad about blowing me and Polly out the other week, so she's coming round later to help tidy my flat.

It was actually Marjorie who triggered the idea. I still feel guilty about walking out on her, but frankly I get enough abuse at work without her giving me extra. Yet the thought of her sitting, bitter and lonely in that dark flat has lingered in my mind all week. Am I going to turn into Marjorie one day? That would be horrific. Surrounded by nothing but junk . . .

All those magazine articles claim that the less physical clutter you have, the happier and calmer your state of mind. Maybe there's some truth in that – though I'm perfectly happy with the organised chaos that surrounds me. Still, Dalia's been itching to help me purge my flat for years, she says I live like a student. She's one of those super-organised neat-freaks whose kitchen counters are entirely bare – not even a bottle of olive oil is allowed to loiter. Her flat weirds me out – there's no stuff, anywhere. Aren't most serial killers minimalists?

I've agreed we'll tackle the kitchen only – small steps. There's no way I'll let her loose on my books, papers or clothes, but I have no emotional attachments to kitchen stuff.

I've promised her dinner at the end of it, but she texted last night to say she's on the Dukan diet and wants only protein and greens. I suspect the tidying session will be relentless and painful with no time for me to cook, so I'm making her Muriel's Chicken. No idea who Muriel is but I found the recipe on this great French blog and it's the easiest thing in the world. Stick a lemon up a chicken, stick the chicken in a pot with the lid on, stick it in an oven – then turn to a hundred and fifty degrees and leave for three hours. You don't have to pay it the slightest attention and it will still reward you with the most delicious, tender, fall-off-the-bone chicken that ever crossed the road.

I'm considering getting a cardboard box, putting half the contents of my kitchen in it, and hiding it under my bed, so that Dalia won't try to make me throw it away, when my doorbell rings. She's never normally on time, why today?

She breezes into my flat looking like she's walked straight off the pages of *Vogue*, wearing a beautiful teal belted wool coat, black skinny jeans and an expensive cream silk shirt. Her dark hair is looking even glossier than usual and she has perfectly applied eyeliner on. I'm in a pair of Jake's old paint-stained jeans and a purple Gap t-shirt that's lost its Lycra after eight years of wear.

'Why are you so dolled up?' I say.

'What? This? It's nothing,' she says, dumping her bag on my sofa and heading straight for my kitchen.

'Have you been at Mark's?' I say, following her through.

'What do you think of the hair?' she says, twirling a long strand between her perfectly manicured fingers.

'Looks so shiny! Have you just had it blow-dried?'

'I've had that Japanese treatment, no more frizz, so I don't have to worry about it when we're in Miami.'

'Miami?'

'I told you, didn't I?' She opens the tall cupboard and shakes her head in despair.

'Told me what?'

'Mark's taking me to South Beach for a long weekend, he's got to use up his air miles before July . . .'

'When are you going?'

'Flying out on the 19th of April . . .' she says, kneeling down to inspect the bottom shelf in an attempt to duck my response.

'Not for that whole weekend?'

'Uh-huh,' she says, reaching in and removing three jars of honey and placing them on the counter.

'You can't!' I say. 'That's Polly's wedding!'

'Do you think I don't know that?' she says, grabbing packets and bottles from the shelves and lining them up next to the honey.

'Have you told her?'

'Of course I've told her. So don't you give me a hard time as well.'

'But can't you go another weekend?'

'If we could have gone on different dates we would have,' she says. 'Besides, I went to her first wedding, I can't be expected to go to every wedding . . .'

'She's one of your best friends.'

'Yeah, and so she doesn't judge me. Right. What the hell was this when you bought it?'

'That's lavender honey.' Lavender honey that has now separated into solid orange fudge, topped with a thick, dark, treacly liquid.

'Bin it,' she says.

'Honey doesn't go off. It's one of nature's anti-septics.'

'Bin.'

'It cost six quid.'

'Shillings, more like . . . And these water biscuits went out of date last June,' she says, holding up the packet and inspecting the bottom.

'They're fine!'

'Fine?' she says, taking one out and squashing it between

her fingers. 'A water biscuit should snap. This one's as soft as a flannel, you could wash your face with it.'

'Maybe I will!'

She walks past me and throws the packet in the bin. When her back is turned I take it out.

'Preserved lemons: 2006.' She shakes her head again.

'They're *preserved*. They don't go off.'

'What the hell do you even use them for? Clearly nothing, as you haven't even opened them.'

'Right, so they'll be perfectly fine when I do.'

'Good grief, when did you last go through your herbs and spices?'

'Stay away from those.'

'These caraway seeds say use by 2002.'

'I don't use them much.'

'Good – then you won't miss them much.'

'I need them. Stop it!' I say, grabbing her hand as she reaches again for the bin.

'You have to get rid of some of this stuff, it's total clutter. It's not good for your feng shui.'

'Feng shui my arse . . .'

'You're the bloody cook around here. These spices are like Hoover bag dust. They literally have no smell, Susie. In fact they have the opposite of a smell. They are sucking the smells out of my nose and trapping them in their little glass bottles like some sort of reverse culinary genie. Look: you go through those and throw out anything that's more than a year out. I'm going into your fridge.'

'My fridge? There's nothing for you in my fridge,' I say, but it's too late.

'This ketchup is a year out.'

'Ketchup lasts forever,' I say.

'Your red pesto's gone green, and your green pesto's gone blue . . .' she says, pulling an appalled face at the contents of two jars that, to be fair, have seen better days.

'I didn't see those two, they were stuck behind the mustards . . .' I say, under my breath.

'Right. So stuff that's lingering at the back is going to get forgotten. Front line or bin,' she says.

'You're brutal.'

'What on earth have you got these old pieces of cheese rind wrapped in plastic for?'

'Parmesan rinds? They're brilliant for putting in soup, they add real depth of flavour. Don't you read Nigel Slater?'

'I'd have thrown them away months ago.'

'You never know when they'll come in handy. You can make something good out of these things.'

'You hold onto absolutely everything, don't you? Every last thing. Just get rid of this stuff. Christ, no wonder you can't get over that man . . .'

'What?'

'Oh, nothing. Listen, do you want my help clearing up or not?'

'Not,' I say. 'When you say "that man", I presume you're referring to Jake?'

She nods.

'Dalia, it's not like I cry myself to sleep every night.' (Just occasionally drink myself to sleep.)

'I don't think you really miss *him* anyway,' she says. 'You just miss having *someone*.'

'That's not true.'

'What do you actually miss about him?'

'Everything.'

She shakes her head. 'It's been well over a year,' she says, exasperated. She sounds just like Mrs Suddes, our GCSE maths teacher. *Susannah Rosen, why can you still not grasp the concept of quadratic equations? Because I can't – that's why!*

I know I shouldn't miss him any more but I do.

'If you do miss him that much then why don't you just call him?'

Every day I fight the urge to do just that. And that's probably why I've run out of self-control by the time it gets to alcohol.

'Is he still going out with her?' she says.

I shrug.

'Show me her Facebook pics again.'

'Why?'

'It might make you feel better about the whole thing. She's such a poseur, Jake must be bored out of his brains.'

'She literally has over a thousand photos of herself on Facebook,' I say.

'Such a pathetic need for constant validation,' says Dalia.

'And she posts on Twitter every five minutes: *In Selfridges, trying on new season Rag & Bone skinny jeans – AMAZING!!*' (I mean, I only know this because I'm following her Tweets, but that is NOT THE POINT AT ALL.)

'Anyone who spends that much time online isn't actually having fun,' says Dalia. 'She just wants the whole world to think she is. It's so insecure and attention-seeking . . . Go on, let's have a look.'

'OK then, you make tea, I'll get my laptop.'

'You do know your teabags are past their use by date?'

'Just put the kettle on.'

I sit on the sofa and log into my account. God, I hate Facebook so much; right, Little Miss Lip Balm, here we go . . .

'Here she is,' I shout into the kitchen. 'She's changed her profile pic *again*.'

'Let me see, let me see . . . oh God, she is so full of herself,' she says, looking at the photo of Leyla in a tiny silver bikini, standing making a star shape on a grassy lawn.

'She's got no body fat at all,' I say, thinking how actually this isn't making me feel better in the slightest.

'That tattoo is so trashy,' says Dalia. 'Go to albums . . . seventy-five albums? Jesus, that's more than the

Rolling Stones. They're all of her in no clothes with stupid accessories . . . that Russian hat is so try-hard.'

'You don't think she looks good?' I say.

'No. She looks like a fashion victim. Look at that one!' She points to the screen. 'Who puts photos of themselves in a see-through nightdress on the internet?'

I might, if I looked like that in one.

'And this one with the pole and the sunglasses, pouting like she's a supermodel, it's so embarrassing . . .'

'That's enough for one day,' I say, wearying of our bitchiness.

'Just one more, hold on . . . click on that – "Holiday Italia!"' says Dalia, clicking on an album with fifty-five photos in, added last week.

In this first photo, her bare, tanned feet rest against Jake's torso as he lies back on a lounger beside a swimming pool.

'I don't want to look any more,' I say.

'She's got horrible little feet,' says Dalia. 'And her toenails are weird.'

I stare at the next photo on screen, of Leyla on a beach, and my heart instantly aches.

'That bikini doesn't leave much to the imagination,' says Dalia. 'I don't know why she bothers wearing anything at all.'

It can't be *that* beach . . . it is, it is that beach damn it. How could he take her to *that* beach?

'You've gone quiet,' says Dalia. 'What's wrong?'

174

'You know what, let's not do this right now. I'm not in the mood.'

'OK . . .'

'Let me go and sort out some veg for you,' I say.

'For me?'

'For dinner,' I say.

'Did you not get my text?'

'Yeah, you said protein and greens . . .'

'I sent you one later saying I can't stay for food, Mark's bought cinema tickets.'

'You've got to be joking?'

'What?'

'You did not send me that text. And I've put the chicken in the oven already.' And it's Saturday night and you don't ditch your mates on a Saturday night twice in one month.

'I did send it, I'm sure I did . . .' she says, looking almost convincing.

'Whatever,' I say, sighing. 'I'm knackered, I'm going to go and have a lie down.'

'Don't be angry with me,' she says. 'Look, I'm sorry. I thought I'd sent it. My phone . . . it's so old I think it needs an upgrade . . .'

Yep – a bit like this friendship.

'Don't be pissed off with me,' she says, as I show her to the door. 'It was a mistake.'

I nod and kiss her goodbye.

A mistake.

175

I make a lot of those myself. Like looking up Leyla on Facebook.

That beach.

Three summers ago Jake and I went to Sicily. I had wanted to collapse by the pool every day but Jake, being Jake, was always looking for adventures. One morning he'd set an alarm for 5.30 a.m. so that we could drive along the shore to Marsala to catch a ferry to Favignana, one of three tiny islands off the west coast. 'It's too early, this is meant to be a holiday!' I'd wailed, as he pulled me out of bed, bleary eyed from the previous night's wine.

We'd nearly missed the boat. Five minutes before we were due to set sail Jake had insisted on darting back to the bakery we'd bought sandwiches in, to buy an espresso. He was so disorganised sometimes it drove me mad. He'd raced back across the quay as I'd stood with one foot on the drawbridge, pleading with the captain to wait just another sixty seconds for us. When we finally boarded I'd been about to bollock Jake for being so last-minute, always. But then from his rucksack he'd produced a small white paper bag in which nestled half a dozen mini chocolate and pistachio pastries, so warm Jake must have persuaded the baker to whip them out of the oven specially for us. 'Worth getting up early for, right?' he said, as we'd wolfed them down.

'Tell me about this place then,' I said, resting my head on his shoulder as the boat chugged steadily through the water. 'Why are we going here again?'

'Well . . .' he said. 'Favignana used to be a prison. And then it was a massive tuna cannery . . .'

'You've dragged me out of bed in the middle of the night to visit an old jail that smells of fish?' I said, raising my head and looking at his smile to see if he was winding me up.

'It's not a jail any more.'

'Seriously, tell me, why are we going here? What's so special about it?'

'Trust me, it'll be worth it. When have I ever let you down?'

We'd arrived at the dock, two of only a handful of tourists, and made our way over to a hole in the wall bike shop. For four euros we'd rented bikes from an old man with a face like a walnut. Jake had given him one of our pastries, and the man had called him *un uomo di mondo*: a man of the world. Jake had liked that nickname.

Even at 8 a.m. the sun was hot as we'd set off in search of Jake's mystery destination. We'd cycled and cycled along roads, then a sea path, a bumpy dirt track, and then back up into hills covered in wild fennel and purple flowers; all the while the sun was growing more fierce and beating down on our already tender shoulders. My thighs were burning from the heat and those hills – Jake was barely breaking a sweat but I could hardly breathe. And then, just when I was about to suggest we stop in the shade, or abandon this mission altogether – we'd probably already missed the turning – we'd rounded a bend and seen a small handpainted sign that said 'Cala Rossa'. Jake had turned down an even narrower track, cacti on both sides, and I'd followed him till we reached the edge of a cliff.

'Does that look like a prison to you?' said Jake, pointing down below us to a vast still bay of crystal clear turquoise water, seeping into aquamarine, peacock-blue and then navy out towards the horizon. Water so clear that even from up here you could make out each stone under the surface, each patch of seaweed. Surrounding it, high sharp white volcanic cliffs; the whole vista like something lunar, like nothing real I'd ever seen.

He'd held my hand as we'd stumbled up and down over the rocks for another ten minutes, weeds scratching at our calves, till we'd reached the far right curve of the bay. Along the way a smattering of men in tight white Speedos and mahogany women were laid out at strange angles on the rocks as if dropped in by alien tanning police. Setting our towels down in an isolated corner, Jake had flung off his clothes and launched himself off the nearest rock straight into the sea. I'd stepped gingerly over to where he'd jumped from, the soles of my feet burning on the hot stone.

'You have to come in right now, Suze,' he shouted, standing a short distance out into the water. 'You can see every last grain of sand at the bottom, it's so clean.'

The rock I was on was too high, but with one hand steadying myself I'd picked my way down through a series of ever smaller, slimier rocks till I'd found one about half a metre above the water. I'd sat, resting my feet on a stone, hypnotised by the red and green algae, miniature ferns swaying gently under the sparkling surface.

'Hurry up!' he shouted, and I'd had to force myself to slide down into the sea.

'OH MY GOD, SO COLD!' Ice cold. Freezer cold. But cold like the answer to a prayer. Almost like being punched awake. 'I think I'm in shock!' I shouted over to him.

'Just keep moving and you'll be fine . . . here, swim to me, my love.'

I'd moved quickly through the water. Further out, a sprinkling of little white boats dotted the horizon, but when I reached Jake it was just me and him, him and me. He put his arms around me tightly, pulling me to his chest, and his wet, cold mouth met mine and we kissed. Who knew salt could taste so sweet? He pressed himself against me and I could feel him, hard, against my thigh.

'How can you have an erection in this ice bucket, Jake? It's like minus twenty degrees in here.'

'It's you, it's you, it's always you . . .' he said, sliding his hand up and under my bikini top. 'You're beautiful,' he said, as I tried, half heartedly, to push his fingers away. His other hand moved slowly down into my bikini bottoms. 'Oh God I want you,' he said, slipping two fingers inside me as I turned to check no one was watching from the shore.

'I'm not doing it in the water, it's too teenage!' I said, laughing and pushing his hair back from his forehead. The sun rising above us shone right into his eyes, making them almost amber. I kissed him softly on the side of his mouth. 'Besides, we'll drown and none of those tan-a-holics will jump in to save us.'

'It'll be worth drowning for,' he said, trying to tug down my bikini bottoms and pulling my legs around his waist. 'I promise, we'll die happy.'

'I can't,' I said, moving his hand away. 'It reminds me of *Showgirls*.' I stroked the back of his neck. 'Kyle McLachlan from *Twin Peaks*, shagging that stripper in a swimming pool, all that over-the-top splashing about.'

'Oh I like that film! Isn't that the one with the scene in the dressing room where all the girls . . .'

'Trust you to remember that bit.'

'Hey, you've got goose bumps,' he said, tracing his finger along my arm.

'It's freezing in here, that's why!'

'I just offered you a shag, that'd warm you up a bit.'

'Piggy back instead?' I said, feeling his biceps. 'I'm sure there's a bit in *Showgirls* where Kyle gives his exhausted, overworked girlfriend a piggy back because he loves her so much, and it shows how big and strong and manly he is.'

'That sounds more like a Jennifer Aniston movie. But if it makes you happy . . .'

I'd clung onto him, my arms draped loosely over his chest, and we'd waded around in the water, the sun warming my shoulder blades.

'Does m'lady want for anything back there?' he said.

'I could do with a glass of cold Chardonnay, butler. But if not, then I'm just fine thanks. Are you OK – I'm not too heavy?'

'No, no, not at all. It's nice actually, you're protecting me from the sun.'

'Oh shit, I haven't got any sun cream on . . . Five more minutes and we'll go back, I just want to be in the water a little bit longer. Look at the way everything is magnified under the surface.' I pointed my toes to a small rock to our left. 'It's like a giant fish tank.'

'It's the nicest sea I've ever been in,' he said.

'It's amazing,' I said, kissing the back of his neck.

'It's amazing,' he said, tickling the bottom of my foot.

And it was. It was amazing, that beach.

Afterwards we swam back to the rocks and he scrambled up with ease, then held out his arm to help me out of the water. We spread our towels on a large flat grey rock and I lay on my back while he rested sideways, his head in my lap.

'Sandwich?' he said, stroking my tummy.

'Sure,' I said, reaching into his rucksack to grab the paper bag from the bakery. Inside were two tomato and mozzarella sandwiches on sesame-seed-sprinkled rolls. I took one for us, then wrapped the other for later. 'Here,' I said, tearing the soft bread roughly in the middle, trying to keep the bright red tomato flesh from spilling out.

Propped up on our elbows we ate in silence. Sweet, fresh tomatoes, springy, creamy mozzarella, and chewy fresh bread. A dribble of olive oil so fruity you could drink it, and a sprinkling of salt to make everything taste even more like what it was. Perfection.

'That's about the best sandwich I've ever eaten, ever,' said Jake, finally resting back in my lap.

'Not much in the world that's better than that,' I said, nodding. 'All you need, isn't it? Simple things . . .' I reached down to tousle his hair.

He turned his head to the side and kissed my navel, smiling softly.

'Do you think we'll always be this happy?' I said, staring up at a sky so bright and deep it was almost overwhelming.

'Of course we will,' he said, gazing up and fixing me with a serious look. 'We'll be at least this happy, perhaps even happier.'

'Now with more happiness . . .' I said, 'Sounds like a jingle.'

'Even more happiness, guaranteed, or your money back,' he said, reaching out to take my hand, holding it in front

182

of his face and kissing my ring finger, then placing my palm on his chest. His skin was dry already. I felt his heart's steady beat, warm, under my palm.

I'd never been happier than at that moment. I have not been as happy since. I did not want it to end.

So yes, I miss him, I still miss him, I do. I miss him.

Sunday

I dream the most vivid dream of being back together with Jake. In the dream we are sorting out laundry in his parents' house – the least exotic dream I've ever had – and yet I am filled with so much contentment within this dream that when I wake I feel momentarily happy. And then instantly deeply deflated and alone.

This is no use.

I get out of bed and make myself a cup of coffee and work out what I can do to cheer myself up. I'll make banana bread for breakfast for a start – with those three manky bananas in the fruit bowl. Then the flat will smell happy. And then I'll go and buy myself a new outfit for Polly's wedding!

Banana bread – the perfect silver lining to a hideous cloud: overly ripe bananas. I can barely eat a banana unless it's green. Yet if I miss that green window and they start

184

to go brown, then right at this point of grossness – when they're so soft the skin has almost melted into the flesh – they can be transformed, nay transmogrified, into something spectacular.

I've adapted a Nigella recipe to suit my needs: half the quantities – I'm a family of one. And I'm too impatient to soak sultanas so I leave them out and just add a good swig of bourbon and these cool mini fudge cubes I found in the Lakeland catalogue. It takes less than five minutes to assemble and just short of an hour to bake. I grab my recipe file and make a note that I've added an extra handful of toasted pecans that Dalia tried to throw away yesterday, just because they were four months out of date.

The loaf tin has been in the oven for all of five minutes when I hear Caspar clomping about upstairs. That's OK, I think. He's allowed to walk around. Why he has to wear hob-nail boots to do so I do not know, but still, let it be. Just as long as he doesn't whack on the Michael Bublé . . . oh for goodness' sake! It's 9 a.m. on a Sunday morning! He can't be having sex on a Sunday morning, and if he is, why can't he at least have a cooler soundtrack?

I have no choice but to turn my own stereo on to drown out the noises. I whack on Adele's 'Someone Like You' so loudly that the bass totally distorts, and then have to sit in the bedroom so that it doesn't deafen me. Ah, Adele – I do love you though. This song! It's so painful and sad and so *true*! How is it possible that you could read my mind?

185

How did you manage to write a song that speaks so entirely of my feelings about Jake? Well, more or less. I mean, I'm not happy that he's moved on, of course. But I do think about turning up on his doorstep rather a lot. I wonder what would happen if I did . . .

I'm in the middle of a fantasy about turning up at Jake's flat and him turning round and telling me he's never stopped loving me, he thinks about me every day too, and he totally doesn't like or even fancy his new girlfriend when my doorbell rings. No. It couldn't be . . . Jake? Oh my God, oh my God. I pull my dressing gown on over my pyjamas and run to the door.

The opposite of Jake: Caspar from upstairs, wearing a too-tight Abercrombie t-shirt and looking pink in the face. What the hell is he doing here? I pop into the living room to turn the stereo down, then go back and open the door an inch.

'Caspar,' I say. 'Been a while.'

'Yes, listen, your music? Could you not have it on so loud?'

'My music? It's not on particularly loud,' I say, congratulating myself for turning it down before I opened the door.

'Well, it was a minute ago.'

'Your ears must be too sensitive,' I say. 'Isn't that what you always say to me?'

'It was audible in every room of my flat.'

'That's because you chose to put in wooden floors which reverb,' I say.

'Could you turn it down a bit? My girlfriend's feeling a bit queasy.'

Not surprised, I would too if I was your girlfriend. Hang on a minute: girlfriend? Since when do you have an actual girlfriend? And queasy? How does he think I feel when I have to listen to him cough up phlegm and do . . . sex things – the cheek of it.

'Caspar: if you lay down some carpet, you won't have to listen to my music and more to the point I won't have to listen to you.'

'You're being unreasonable,' he says.

'Carpets, Caspar – they are your friend,' I say, and slam the door, feeling irritation rise up in me. How on earth has this man – the least attractive in North London – managed to find himself a proper relationship while I remain single, consoling myself with mouldy bananas? I know life isn't fair, but this *really* is not fair. I mean, I am now literally the last single person left in the world. Apart from Rebecca. But she's got another date with the Hawksmoor barman this week and no doubt she'll actually make it work this time and then it'll just be me.

I'm tempted to go straight back to bed, pull the duvet over my head and hibernate till Monday morning, but then remember that I have a dress to buy. And banana bread to eat . . . Forty minutes still to go. OK, I shall be productive

187

and find something to do with three-quarters of a roast chicken, some old caraway seeds and honey. I'm sure there'll be some inspiration online . . .

I type the ingredients into Google but can't find anything appealing. There are loads of tagines if it's only chicken and honey you need a home for, and various central European dishes with just chicken and caraway. But nothing that uses all three. Hmm, I'll sacrifice the honey and go for a chicken goulash – any excuse for sour cream. And then later in the week I could use the remaining sour cream as an excuse for fajitas! Done. Mind you, I don't like this chicken goulash recipe much. It's quite basic and it uses margarine. Maybe if I used olive oil instead . . . And I could add sweet paprika as well as smoked – not least because I love that gorgeous red and yellow tin it comes in. I'll chuck in some mushrooms too. Stroganoff and goulash must be related, I bet they're cousins . . . And I bet creamy, slightly smoky chicken and mushrooms would work amazingly in a pie too, with a puff pastry top . . . I grab a piece of paper and start writing down ideas, but then find myself side-tracked searching for fajita recipes, then flights to Mexico and then swimsuits for pear-shapes.

The oven timer goes off. I whisk out the banana bread and spoon a large portion into a bowl and pour some cream over the top. Thank goodness for the soothing properties of sugar and fat and bourbon. Calmer now, I get dressed. No point putting on make-up, it's a waste on a day like today. Instead I hide behind sunglasses and head out to find that killer dress.

I haven't treated myself to a dress for such a long time. Why bother? I never go anywhere remotely fancy, other than the work Christmas party. And with budget cutting the NMN party's been downgraded from champagne cocktails at a trendy East London members' club with bowling alley, to beer and house wine at our local Wetherspoon's.

But this is Polly's wedding! An epic celebration deserves a new outfit. I head over to Primrose Hill to one of those chi-chi boutiques you always see mentioned in the glossies. I'm willing to spend up to a hundred and fifty quid. Well preferably no more than a hundred, but a hundred and fifty if it's an absolutely amazing dress.

I walk into the shop and immediately feel like a tramp. What is it about the smell of these expensive candles that automatically makes me feel ungroomed? My nails aren't manicured, my hair could definitely do with a trim, my eyebrows need shaping. All this inadequacy just from an overpriced candle? Still, why should I be intimidated by melting wax? Or for that matter by those two assistants who just looked straight through me as if I'm wearing an invisibility cloak. Can't they tell that this invisibility cloak is new season Gucci?

I flick through the rack of clothes, each dress on a hanger separated by a good thirty centimetres. I can barely see what's in my wardrobe at home, all my clothes are crammed together like it's rush hour. Even the act of touching some of these clothes makes me feel like my fingers are dirty.

That's a lovely dress . . . who's that by . . . Phillip Lim . . . I've heard of him. Such pretty detailing at the neck, that'd be perfect. Oh. Ouch. Maybe not. *Seven hundred quid?* It's only cotton. When did everything get quite so expensive? (I'm sounding more like my mother every day.)

Ah, now the sales assistant is paying me some attention! But not good attention. No, a very blatant type of scrutiny. As if she suspects I'm about to do a Winona. So insulting! Don't fret, love, I'm not going to forget to pay. But now she's given me this look I feel I have to try something on, to prove that I'm not casing the joint. I'm not trying on anything that costs seven hundred pounds though. There must be something more reasonable . . . Five hundred and fifty . . . Eight hundred and ninety! . . . Ah, here we are – Day Birger et Mikkelsen. Two hundred and thirty quid, that's more like it. I have no intention of buying it of course, but I nod to myself as if I do, and head to try it on.

There is a girl in her twenties with long brown shiny hair, standing in the entrance to the changing room, the curtain held open by her friend. She stands there in black lace underwear and I find myself transfixed by the top of her thigh, where her leg meets her bottom. I try not to stare, but I find it impossible. Her body is amazing. Her thigh is so smooth and golden, and her bottom entirely pert and small but round. Her friend gazes on enviously too.

One of the assistants comes over, laden with clothes on hangers, and starts fawning over this girl as if she were Madonna.

'Katia darling, try this piece with the sequins,' says the assistant. 'It's totally you.'

The girl slips on the black sequinned dress and twirls at her own reflection. She tips her head to the side, then scoops up her long silky hair on top of her head, pauses, then shakes it down again in a shimmy. She pulls at the back of the dress and sighs. 'The eight's too big,' she says. *The eight's too big.* A phrase I have never said. A phrase I will never say.

'It's swimming on you. We'll see if there's a six, Petra! A six!' she barks, at her colleague. 'And try the Carven and the Rodarte pieces,' she says, holding up two equally beautiful dresses.

She slips on one of them, a tiny tomato-red silk slip with a lace trim at the bottom, and poses in the mirror, hand on one hip, one leg turned out to the side.

'You look amazing in everything,' says her friend.

'Yeah,' says the girl, her voice a stranger to doubt. She stands gazing at herself with her hands pressing down on her non-existent belly, then moves her palms onto her hip bones. She turns sideways and looks at herself over her own shoulder in the mirror.

191

'Stunning . . .' says the assistant. 'There isn't a six down-stairs in the sequins, but we'll get one in for you mid-week. Is Wednesday OK?'

'Sure,' says the girl.

'Great.' She pauses for the perfect moment. 'Shall we start ringing you up then?'

I take the dress I'm holding and hang it back up on the rack, but I'm too nosy to walk out just yet, so instead I hover near the till pretending to look at the overpriced necklaces that all have pistols or birds on them. I catch sight of my reflection in an ornate Venetian mirror on the wall. I really shouldn't leave home without make-up on any more – I'm too old. These dark, almost purple circles under my eyes never seem to shift. And I have these deepening frown lines above my brows that now seem permanent, not just when I'm frowning at work . . .

'I can't decide whether to head to New York in May for six months, maybe write a screenplay,' says the girl to her friend. 'Ray-Ray's got a place in the Hamptons so we could go there at weekends. Or I could go to Brazil, maybe Ecuador . . .'

'Ladies, sorry to interrupt,' says the assistant, 'but that's coming in at one-seven with your discount. Shall I bill as usual?'

'Yeah,' says the girl, sounding suddenly bored. 'What time's Roka?' she says to her friend. 'Do I have time for a massage?'

The girls leave the shop, laden with bags. For some reason the whole incident has left me miserable. That girl has triggered a horribly jealous reaction in me. Maybe it's the fact that she doesn't have to work? Just like Leyla, she's probably got rich parents who bankroll her every whim. Wouldn't that be nice, not having to work? But actually I'd be bored. Well, after a few years of doing nothing I'm sure I'd be bored.

Maybe it was her figure? She had the sort of body that you're either born with or you're not. And I'm not. Still, I thought I'd more or less made peace with my body over the years. It's not perfect, but it does the things it's supposed to. Though these last few years it's started sagging and wrinkling and even developing age spots. I had only just stopped hating it and now I have to start hating it all over again, but in different ways.

Actually I think it's simple. She's young and rich and beautiful and has her whole life ahead of her. She can still afford to make a thousand mistakes. Time is on her side, and it isn't on mine.

I come away feeling so disheartened that my legs subconsciously walk me over to Melrose and Morgan where I buy myself a consolatory pear and frangipane tart. Ridiculous, I think, as I bite into the crumbly sweet pastry. You're thirty-six, not ninety-six. Besides I don't even need a new dress anyway. I have that lovely jade one from Anthropologie that I wore for the last wedding I went to.

It'll do just fine, more than fine – it's a perfectly good dress . . . Oh, sorry – 'piece'. And I don't wear it nearly enough. It's not like there are going to be any single men at the wedding anyway.

When I get home the flat still has a faint smell of golden warm banana bread, but it is being drowned out by something toxic coming down from Caspar's flat. No doubt he's laying on a mackerel fest to avenge our earlier argument . . .

I go into the kitchen and wrap a thick slice of the banana bread in foil for Sam for the morning. I consider taking some over to Marjorie but I can't handle a further downer this weekend. Instead I wrap up two more chunks, one for her and one for Terry, and pop them down to him. He can give it to her tomorrow when he's doing his rounds. Cowardly I know, but it's better than nothing.

I go to bed early. I didn't think I'd ever find myself looking forward to a Monday at NMN merely because it meant that the weekend was finally over. Just as I turn the lights out my phone goes off – a text. I wonder if it's Dalia apologising for yesterday . . . Maybe it's Jeff? Please let it be Jeff from Fletchers . . . Urgh. Bloody hell – it's from Fletchers alright, but it's their marketing round-robin, announcing twenty per cent off sandwiches tomorrow. I don't even subscribe to these texts, but they send them to me anyway. I delete it in a rage, and am about to turn my phone off when it beeps again. What now, twenty per cent off plastic bags too? Leave me alone!

But no! It's from that guy I met in the pub last week. I'd almost forgotten about him. 'Fancy dinner this week? Seb.'

About time too . . .

w/c 26 March

Status report:
- Get scripts & sell scripts – URGENT
- Get Jeff to ask me out

Wednesday

Things are beginning to look up. I have a date on Sunday night with Seb at a gastropub in Camden. He's texted me several times already. His texts are quite amusing, if a little long, though he does seem to text quite late at night. And so far this week I have had eight emails from Jeff Nichols – and it's only Wednesday. Some of his emails are just sweet and chatty and about food:

'Do you know what is smaller than a petit-four?' he wrote.

'A petit-two?' I replied, wondering if he was trying to make a joke.

'No, a mignardise. Just been to a seminar on bite-sized snacks. Good word, isn't it?'

And then some of his messages are ragingly flirtatious – in my opinion at least.

'Wish you worked with me, that'd be fun. Can't you apply for a job as my sous-chef??'

However, none of them has brought me any closer to a date. For example, this latest one:

'Having a day from hell! Sexy Chick pizza now has no actual chicken, just re-shaped chicken-flavoured pieces. Do you ever think about running away from it all? Have you ever been to Costa Rica? I think you would love it. I can imagine you, sitting in the shade wearing a large hat, sipping a tropical cocktail.'

Suggestive, surely? Does he imagine sitting in the shade next to me? Surely that's the sub-text. I'm currently at my desk pondering how to reply and move things on when Robbie's PA, Alexis, calls.

'He wants to see you,' she says. 'But hurry up, he's due in Creative Autopsy in five.'

I rush up to his office where I find him sitting behind his cherrywood desk lining up three small amber glass bottles of Bach Rescue Remedy in a line to the right of his notepad.

'Blossom,' he says, looking up suddenly. 'Isn't that an amazing word?'

Not as amazing as 'script' or 'here are your mega-strategic urgent scripts' . . .

'Hear the resonance,' he says. 'Blossom, blossom, blossom. Melodic. Extraordinary. I can lose myself in words for hours, like Rothko in paint.' He smiles at me. He has one of those rare faces that is less attractive when he smiles – all gums.

'Have the team shown you scripts yet?' I say.

Robbie turns his head to study his bookshelf on which are stacked rows of awards – Perspex squares, bronze statuettes, yellow D&AD pencils. He nods his head at all fourteen of them individually, then turns back to me.

'Susie: do you know how long the Sistine Chapel took to paint?'

I do actually! Because it's a Trivial Pursuit question, and I have a brother who memorised every answer on every card when we were kids so that no one else could ever win. Robbie is about to tell me but foolishly I can't keep my mouth shut.

'Just over four years,' I say.

His smile falters. 'OK. Ergo . . .'

Please don't tell me you're heading in *that* direction . . .

'. . . Da Vinci didn't paint the Sistine Chapel in seven days, so please don't expect Karly and Nick to give you the scripts by Friday,' he says.

On one level of course Robbie is entirely correct. Da Vinci did not paint the Sistine Chapel in seven days. In fact he did not paint it in four years. He did not paint it all; Michelangelo did. I sit, still as a statue, as the urge to point this out sweeps over me, then eventually passes. To be fair, if it wasn't for my brother becoming obsessed as a kid with the Ninja Turtles, and giving me those lurid slippers with Michelangelo Ninja Turtle on them that I still wear, I would not have retained this fact.

I contemplate what it must be like to make statements like Doggett just has with a straight face. I mean, why stop at the Sistine Chapel? Why not compare the agency's latest leaflet for haemorrhoid cream to *Hamlet* while you're down there?

'The thing is . . .' I say, getting out my timing plan on the basis that he will be entirely disinterested in facts or my problems but at least it will move us away from the whole Karly-and-Nick-are-genii conversation . . . 'Scripts are urgent. We're going to be late otherwise. The airdate's in six weeks and there's really no fat in this timing plan.'

'Don't make your problems into my problems. Work around it.'

'The airdate is fixed,' I say. 'When I briefed this in, the team were clear they could deliver on time . . .'

'Things change,' he says. 'Karly now has a medical condition that needs to be addressed.'

I'd hardly call getting a B cup bumped to a D cup a medical condition. Then again, Robbie probably doesn't know that I know about this. Of course I do! Sam told me about it jubilantly last week: 'It's Dr Redfern, same surgeon who did Robbie's eyelids! When he's doing a boob job he goes in under the muscle, minimal scarring. You can be back at your desk the next day,' he'd said, putting me right off my chicken schnitzel sandwich.

'Karly's in today though,' I say. 'They must have done the bulk of the work already?'

'Do you think she needs harassing at a time like this?' he says.

'Can't Nick take me through the work? Devron will go mental if we don't show him something this week.'

'You'll have to buy some time. Now, chop-chop,' he waves his hands at me. 'Go hustle.'

Buy some time indeed . . . The minute I tell Devron he won't see the scripts till next week, he'll pull rank, pick up the phone and have a tantrum down the phone to Martin Meddlar. Martin will then shout at Berenice who will shout at me. And then Martin will take Devron to lunch and all will be forgiven, temporarily . . .

I have got so many better things to do than sit in the middle of this crossfire: like plan what to make for dinner on Saturday. I have six friends coming round and I'm debating whether to serve Italian lamb stew with risotto. Then I could try making arancini the following day with the leftover rice. I love arancini – deep-fried crispy golden rice balls with melted cheese in the middle. Once a year I manage to persuade my mum to make them. She sets up her deep-fat fryer on the patio and stands in her garden like some lesser-spotted mythical frying fairy. She then turns magician, making them all disappear – for five minutes anyway, to cool down so that my dad doesn't demolish them instantly.

And maybe for dessert I could make a chocolate bread and butter pudding. If there's any left I could make it into a trifle on Sunday night. Would that work, I wonder? Maybe the texture of the pudding wouldn't be dry enough to soak up the sherry . . .

Actually, what am I talking about? I can't stand around deep-frying balls of rice on Sunday, or making trifle. I won't be doing any cooking on Sunday because I have a date. With Seb. An actual, real, live date.

Saturday

I've ended up making lasagne. It's a total labour of love, but when I woke up this morning it was so cold and damp outside it felt like winter again – and I thought it would be ideal. I know it's not posh but it's one of those dishes that everyone loves.

I've got about eight lasagne recipes in the file – one with spring veg and ricotta, one for later in autumn when the first Jerusalem artichokes are unearthed, and an excellent winter vegetarian one with butternut squash and sage. But tonight I've made the classic – actually a twist on my grandma's version. She'd have turned her nose up at dried sheet lasagne, but you have to draw the line somewhere.

Along with Polly and Dave I've invited Debbie, who used to live in my block, and her husband Sean. I'd rather have just invited Debbie, but you can't choose your friends' partners. The last time I saw her she'd drunkenly confessed that they hadn't had sex for nearly two years and 'because of this' he'd had an affair with a girl at work. She thinks Sean's infidelity was her own fault. She's thought about leaving him but would never do that *for the sake of the kids*. I sort of understand this, and I sort of don't. Do children really want parents who don't like each other, don't talk except in resentful accusations, and are way past affection?

And then there's Andrew and Franny, who are a little too affectionate at this point, certainly in public anyway. Andrew has been my friend since I was seventeen and I love him dearly and, thankfully, only platonically. Thirty-six, handsome, solvent, tall, fun, he listens and has no hideous sexual tics. Every woman wants an Andrew: he is a Willy Wonka Golden Ticket in the London dating game, hence he also gets to be a kid in a sweet shop. He has so many lovely girls to choose from that he simply doesn't bother choosing. He can live in this perpetually adolescent state of honeymoon dating for years to come: six to nine months of bliss, then find a few flaws and go on a quest for someone perfect. Though Franny might be the one – she's sweet and funny and they clearly adore each other: joined at more than the hip. We've christened them Frandrew.

Three couples and me. I probably should have roped in a mate. Rebecca's out with the barman though, and I'm still pissed off with Dalia. All my single male friends are a bit useless nowadays: since his divorce Josh spends his weekends training for marathons. I think he's trying to run away from himself. Toby's just signed up to AA. He's not even an alcoholic – not by my standards anyway – but apparently the meetings are very social and there are loads of hot women there. Maybe I should have invited Sam. It would be nice to have him round again one of these days. We used to hang out more when I first joined NMN, but then he and Jake didn't really get on.

This morning started well: I spied Caspar at around 10 a.m., loading up the Range Rover with a large overnight bag and the girlfriend. The prospect of a mini-break – spending the entire weekend having fun somewhere lovely with someone I fancy – is such a remote one at this point. Nonetheless, maybe tomorrow might be the start of something with Seb. Or maybe next week I'll get a date with Jeff. Regardless of any of that, I've had a very happy, solitary, peaceful day of cooking and pottering. I have been content.

I've made two lasagnes. If you're going to put the work into one you might as well do two – you can always freeze it. I've gone all out and used three cheeses. I'm trying to save money for The Great Escape, and the price of cheese these days is ridiculous. But cheese matters, and I can't bring myself to scrimp on food like this. I found a chunk of gruyere at the back of the fridge that was totally fine (yes, Dalia, totally fine). And I already had parmesan. So it just meant buying mozzarella. How could I possibly deprive my friends of the joys of stringy melted cheese?

These are five-layer lasagnes. Apparently there's an incredible thousand-layer lasagne, though how anyone could have the patience to make that I don't know. And who'd have a big enough mouth to eat it? No, five layers is plenty. Pasta, meat sauce, béchamel, cheese, and again, and again, and again, and again. Five layers is the point where the preparation stops being meditative and satisfying and starts being hard work. I don't want to resent my supper.

But looking at my guests now, sitting round the table relaxing back into their seats, I think it was worth all the effort. We have polished off the first lasagne, and are trimming inches at a time from the back-up lasagne. Everyone has drunk a lot and everyone is merry.

'We loved the fourth series of *The Wire*,' says Andrew.

'We loved that, but did you see *Romanza Criminale*?' says Polly.

'Amazing, we thought,' says Dave.

'We just don't understand why everyone raves about *Borgen*,' says Sean.

'Really? We thought it was amazing. Well, season one is brilliant, two wasn't quite as good,' says Polly, and Dave nods in agreement. 'Oooh, and have you seen *Wallander*?'

'We love it! We've just started one of the books,' says Franny.

How do two people read one book at the same time? I can picture Frandrew on a park bench, sharing headphones on one iPod – that's sweet, romantic. But reading a book together?

'Who writes those again?' says Andrew.

'Jo Nesbo does *Wallander*,' says Sean.

'It's Henning Mankell,' says Debbie, wearily.

'We love that Scandi crime stuff,' says Sean, ignoring her. 'We just watched *The Girl with the Dragon Tattoo* on Netflix, the remake. Pretty violent stuff . . .'

'We couldn't get past the first fifty pages of the book,' says Polly. 'All those street names . . . and every five minutes he's having coffee, having a sandwich . . .'

'I know what you mean,' I say. I am the only I. It's my own fault for inviting three couples for a meal. But if I don't invite my friends-in-couples round as couples, I don't get to see half of them. And they rarely invite you back for couples get-togethers; it makes for odd gooseberry-flavoured dinners. Still, why can't one of them, just once, express an opinion on a box-set or a book that is entirely their own? *We* do this and *we* think that and *we* go here and *we* like there . . . I'm sure they're not doing it on purpose but I swear, if one of them wees in front of me again . . .

Polly must sense something as she changes the subject to something she thinks will cheer me up.

'Hey Suze, we're going to The Alford Arms in a couple of weeks!' she says.

'We went there a couple of months ago, didn't we?' says Andrew.

'We had the lamb,' says Franny.

'We had it too, gosh, that was years ago . . .' I say,

remembering that Jake and I had been there when we first started dating. That lamb was delicious – seven-hour slow-roast shoulder, with buttery mash. Franny looks at me strangely. Ah, but of course. She wasn't around when I was with Jake; she only knows me as the perpetually love-thwarted Aniston of the group. She doesn't know that once upon a time *I* was a *we*.

'Didn't we go there for your birthday a few years ago?' says Sean to Debbie.

Debbie nods and takes a large gulp of wine. I remember her telling me that Sean had picked a fight with the waiter over the cheeseboard and then sulked for three days.

'We thought the food was good but the service was fucking shocking,' he says. Debbie says nothing. It seems we are not amused.

'We thought we'd leave Maisie with Mum overnight, go for a nice long country walk, get really pissed,' says Polly. 'I'm so jealous of you, Suze, you can just do what you want, when you want. You never have to think about babysitters.'

'Speaking of which,' says Dave, 'we'd better go, sweetheart – we said we'd be back by midnight.'

'We had a great time,' says Polly. 'Amazing food, as always.'

'We must have you over soon,' says Debbie.

'We had such a great night,' says Andrew.

'We did too,' I say.

★

207

Memory's a bitch; those little details that hijack you out of nowhere.

That day Jake and I went to The Alford Arms: on the train home I'd fallen asleep and when I woke Jake had been staring at me, smiling, like he was keeping a secret. Back in the days before he started keeping secrets.

A week later he went to buy furniture for his new flat. I remember him calling me from a bathroom shop in Islington, summoning me to meet him in the rolltop bath at the back of the store, the one with the cast iron feet. We'd kept our clothes on, but we'd had a good session in that bath before the poor manager, coughing loudly as he approached, asked if we needed any help.

Two weeks after, Jake had phoned me, drunkenly, at 2 a.m. on a Saturday night out with the lads to tell me that he thought about me all the time, and that I had to promise not to take the piss, but that he thought I was made of magic. And the following day turning up sheepishly with a hangover and a bunch of orange tulips from Columbia Road to say that he didn't know where on earth 'made of magic' had come from, but he stood by it nonetheless.

And eight months later, a surprise mini-break to Ludlow for our anniversary, to the cosiest little hotel in the world. They had the best breakfasts ever – they made their own jams, breads, even their own butter. The best breakfasts and the best bed. I really hope he hasn't taken her there.

My whole life spent, living in the past.

Sunday

It has been years since I've been on a real date, as opposed to an in-my-head-only Jeff date. I have to call Rebecca up and disturb her while she's on some idyllic walk along the Thames with Luke Barman.

'Subecka speaking,' she says, a giggle in her voice as she picks up the phone.

'I need help! I'm meeting that guy from The Flask tonight. At Koko's of all places. What do I wear?' The last time I went to Koko's was in 1988, when it was still called The Camden Palace, and I was dressed like all four of The Bangles.

'I thought he was taking you for dinner?' she says.

'He was, but then he said he had tickets for a gig so we're doing that and then food.' A nightclub, on a Sunday night . . . I'm too old for this.

'Heels, jeans, low-cut top,' she says. 'Just make sure there's cleavage. My over-arching impression of him was that he was staring at your chest.'

'Really? I don't remember that at all,' I say, thinking *What do I remember?* He was good looking. He liked roast beef sandwiches, crisps on the side. He was confident. He was a bit annoying, that comment about women wanting babies, a little bit boorish maybe . . . but I probably over-reacted, I'd had a few. Anyway, I don't feel too nervous about this date. The fact is I have been focusing most of my mental energy on Jeff, with some lingering thoughts of Jake, so I have not invested *that* much hope in tonight. Probably for the best.

As I walk towards the venue I have a small smile on my face, rather than the expression which I should adopt – one of neutrality. This means that when I do catch sight of Seb it is Munch-screamingly obvious that I am disappointed, whereas had I worn a straight line instead of a smile I could have passed off my frown as confusion over which entrance we were meeting at. It's that Justin Timberlake knitted beanie hat. Absolutely fine if you are Justin Timberlake or skiing fast. But Seb is neither. It's not me being fussy about clothes. It's that a handsome man like this, standing in a hat like this, screams male vanity. It is so precisely arranged to come down *just so* over his right cheekbone that it can only be the result of five minutes of positioning work in front of a mirror. A man who spends that long on his hat does not spend enough time thinking about other things – he will be arrogant, shallow and probably immature. I know Rebecca would tell me not to read so much into a hat – it is only a hat – but she'd be wrong.

We've been in the club for twenty minutes; it's dark and it smells sickly – of Red Bull, stale fags and staler sweat. But so far Seb and I have been getting on fine. I'm not convinced I fancy him, though he is definitely good looking and quite funny. He's been telling me about his crazy week at work, and how he narrowly escaped being fired after he accidentally emailed his client a copy of a rude email *about* the client. He's been a little too touchy-feely, but that might just be me being over-sensitive. I mean, I guess this *is* a date: he's flirting, that's what you do on dates.

He's gone to the bar for a second round and I'm standing waiting on the balcony overlooking the stage, my feet sticking slightly to the manky floor. I am so the oldest one here. No one has lines on their forehead, no crow's feet, no bags. Everyone is young and everyone looks great and everyone looks sort of the same. I feel like the odd one out in a Nokia ad.

A skinny kid over to my left is staring at me – he can't be much older than twenty. He's wearing a green t-shirt with a picture of a horse on, which says 'Ketamine – just say neigh!' He grins at me – I smile awkwardly back – and this encourages him to sway over.

'Dyoowah-sah dirtykittee?' he says, beaming at me with slightly glazed eyes.

'I'm sorry?'

'Sah dirty kitty?'

Erm. No? Maybe? 'Did you say dirty kitty?'

In his hand he holds a small plastic tube that looks like a party popper. He unscrews the lid and removes a spatula with some grainy yellow-white powder piled on it.

'Dirty kitty!' he says, his face stretching shiny and tight like a balloon.

'Ah! Do you mean Meow Meow?' I say, suddenly very excited and pleased with myself. I've just deciphered a cryptic crossword clue – something I have never done in real life. Kitty = code for Meow. I read *Metro*, I am informed about kids today and their drugs of choice.

The boy nods and gurns, offering me the mini spatula. If I'm going to end up looking anything like him I'm going to have to decline his kind offer. I look over and see Seb still waiting at the bar, tapping his head along to Dizzee Rascal.

'Gwon . . .' the boy mumbles, shoving his spatula towards my nostril.

'No, honestly, thanks, I don't . . . my nose is a bit bunged up anyway,' I say.

'Dyo wansuh MD? Gotta 3.5 bomb?' He pats himself down, trying to find his pockets.

Hmm. MD . . . 3.5 bomb . . . Ministry of Defence? How many letters? Give us a clue.

212

'MD . . .?'

'MD. MDMA,' he says. Oooh, it feels like charades at Christmas, but with class As instead of *The Sound of Music*.

'That's very kind of you,' I say, 'but I'm with someone.' I point at Seb. 'And I'm just, I'm not in the market. Thank you very much though, that's very generous.'

The boy shrugs and stumbles off. I don't mind being exposed to all this youth culture, but there's only so much I can take. Why couldn't we have just gone to a gastropub like Seb originally suggested? Besides, I'm properly hungry now. I could do with a seat, a shepherd's pie and a nice glass of red.

Seb returns with the drinks and I suggest we move to the seated area upstairs.

'Like your thinking, cosy up there,' he says.

We sit in a red plastic booth and he puts his feet on the drinks table in front of us, so that his right knee rests against mine. It would seem churlish to move my leg – he's just being flirty; I should relax and see where this goes.

'Do you date much?' he says, resting his hand on my thigh, but again so casually that to flick it off would seem an over-reaction.

If I say no it will sound like nobody wants to go out with me, so I shrug. 'How about you?'

'I've had like three serious relationships in the last ten years, and then bits and pieces.'

'When were you last seeing someone?' I say.

'I was living with someone last year but we broke up and I've just been having fun since. But I always seem to be the one who ends up having to finish the relationship.'

'You've never been dumped?' I say.

'Never.'

'That's not normal, is it? Surely when you were fourteen someone dumped you?'

He shakes his head. 'Nah,' he says. 'And nowadays it's hard. Girls all seem to want to settle down with me for some reason, and I'm not looking for that at this point in my life,' he says looking pained. The hat! I knew it! Full of himself, arrogant idiot.

'Then what are you looking for?' I say, draining my drink and wondering if he's going to buy me dinner, and thinking I'm not sure I actually want him to buy me dinner . . .

'I suppose someone who's on my wavelength,' he says. 'A girl who's independent . . .'

I'm pretty certain that in modern dating parlance, *independent* actually means *won't expect me to call her after sex*.

'A girl who takes care of herself . . .'

That means *zero body hair* . . .

'Who's generous . . .'

Loves giving blow jobs . . .

'And open minded . . .'

Into butt sex.

'Do you do any online dating?' I say.

'Sometimes . . .' he says, stroking his fingers along my thigh. 'I'll do it for a month or two, then I just get sick of it.'

'I don't like it myself.'

'I went on this terrible date a few months ago, this girl I met on PlentyofFish – she looked nothing like her pictures. She must have eaten the girl in those pictures! I should have known – all her photos were headshots. I put my coat on half way through the first drink and she still didn't get the hint!'

I down my gin and tonic. Would now be an OK time to leave? How has it taken me this long to realise he's a prat?

'Let me get you another,' he says, 'same again – double, wasn't it?'

'You know what, I might go and get some food.'

'I'm not hungry,' he says.

'That's fine. We'll just finish these and then I'll eat at home.'

'No! The band'll be on in a sec, I'll get you something,' he says, rushing off before I can protest, and returning with a gin and tonic, two Sambuca shots and a pack of pistachios.

'So you,' he says, squashing up next to me and putting his arm around me. 'You're very aloof, aren't you? I find that very sexy.'

I'm not aloof, I'm annoyed; you have, within the last

thirty minutes, reminded me why I should never bother leaving the house again, because there are men like you out there, and I truly would have been better off making a trifle and saving myself the bus fare.

'Down in one.' He hands me a Sambuca – a drink even more odious than a Jäger Bomb.

'I can't drink shots on a Sunday night,' I say – but then figure maybe that's the only way to get through this, so I drink the Kool-Aid and instantly regret it. Urgh, so disgusting . . .

'Tell me more about you,' he says. 'I really think we could be on the same wavelength.'

'What do you want to know?'

'I don't know . . . When was the last time you had sex in a nightclub?'

'Never,' I say.

'You've never had sex in a nightclub!'

He makes it sound like I've just announced that I've never tried toast.

'OK . . . how long's the longest you've gone without sex?' he says.

'Do you want to talk about anything apart from sex?' I say. 'Because otherwise this is going to be a very short conversation.'

'Oooh, OK then! What do you want to talk about?'

'I don't know . . . Where are you from, what do you like to do in your spare time?'

'Born in Leicester, moved to London when I was thirteen . . . let me see, went to university in Manchester, studied estate management, I work in property . . . What do I do in my spare time? Dunno, watch sport, have a laugh. See my mates, go to bars, meet sexy girls like you, go clubbing.'

'What sort of music do you like?' I say.

'All sorts, house, a bit of rock. I just turn on Spotify and see what's new . . . By the way, when was the last time you were sexually screened?'

'Why on earth are you asking me that on a first date?'

'I was recently tested and I know that I'm safe.'

'And?'

'If we're going to be intimate I just want you to know that it will be at my risk.'

I am without the vocabulary to reply to this.

'Do you want to touch my penis?'

And again.

He grabs my hand and moves it over to his crotch. I rapidly whisk it away.

'Don't worry. It's dark, no one will see,' he says.

Yep – because being seen was the thing stopping me . . .

'I'm going,' I say, standing up.

'Sit down, sit down, I was only joking. Joke.'

'Look. I don't know you. I have to go now, I've got work in the morning.'

w/c 2 April

Status report:
- Fat Bird: Get script from Karly and Nick – URGENT
- Fend off Devron in the meantime
- Then sell script. MEGA-URGENT
- Get date with Jeff – PRIORITY RED

Monday

'Count yourself lucky. At least you got some pistachios out of it,' says Rebecca, as we sit in our department meeting on Monday afternoon, listening to Berenice talk about cost-cutting. 'Pistachios are expensive.'

'Rebecca, there are some clouds that have no silver linings. Don't you dare try and make me feel better about last night,' I say, as she tries not to laugh. 'And the lunatic even had the nerve to text me at midnight asking when he's going to see me again.'

'And what did you reply?' she says.

'Are you joking? I've deleted his number.'

'Well at least you gave it a try,' she says.

'That is *not* the moral of this story. The moral is *don't ever* give things a try.' I fold my arms and try to sit up straight and focus on Berenice's lecture. No more free stationery for anyone below board level? Why don't they just sell our chairs and make us stand at our desks?

The minute our department meeting is over, Berenice drags me to one side to scream about the delayed scripts. 'I've had Martin on the phone this morning, Devron is furious!'

Not any more he isn't. I spoke to him before this meeting. He'd just returned from a mega lunch at Nobu with Martin and sounded in fine fettle. I told him he'll have scripts by the end of Friday; Martin filled him with so much expensive sake that Devron said end of the week was fine, then accidentally said, 'Love you, darling' instead of goodbye.

'I told you, Susannah,' says Berenice, 'you will be defined by this brief. And yet you're falling at the first hurdle.' Her face is so close to mine I can almost taste her Smint.

It is not *that* big a deal, I want to say. The scripts will be a few days late. No one's dead. No one's even sprained a toe. Instead I take the bollocking, feeling the tendons in my neck tighten like dental floss round a finger. The whole time she's telling me how incompetent I am, all I am focusing on is how Sam is going to work his way round this new stationery ban. If I can't even have nice pens and Post-it notes then, really, what is the point?

Friday

I've had Devron on the phone all week. Once his sake hangover wore off, he realised he wasn't at all happy with the delay and has been increasingly irate about these scripts. I have promised him on pain of death that he'll have something today. He's now on some media jolly at Pennyhill Park, but he's got a golf club in one hand, a whiskey and an iPhone in the other, waiting. Waiting.

I'm waiting too – for Alexis to summon me to the script meeting, but in the meantime I've come to see Sam for a pep talk. He has assured me that there are a myriad of ways round the stationery ban, and he can't quite believe I doubted his skills. And as for how to handle a script presentation with Karly and Nick, the key, apparently, is to go to the Happy Place.

'Sam, could you possibly take your headphones off your neck for one minute and explain yourself? I can hear Bruce

222

Springsteen coming out of your collar and it's rather disconcerting.'

He slips them briefly onto my ears: 'Thunder Road'.
'You've got to admit that is a class song,' he says.

'Yes I am a big fan of that song, Sam. Now help me,
please.'

'Right. So, the thing you have to do with Karly and
Nick is just not struggle, don't argue back in the room.
Let it all sweep over you. It doesn't matter what you
think. What matters is what the client thinks and what
the public thinks. Your opinion counts for nothing, you're
the world's best-paid ketchup fetcher, stick with that
thought, right?'

I nod.

'Keep your comments to yourself. Don't point out the
flaws in their work. Those two take great delight in
provoking. Do not play up to them. If the script hasn't got
a woman in a burka or a threesome in it, count your blessings. Just nod, play nice, deal with it outside the room.
You're a diplomat. You're Tony Blair. You're the Dalai Lama.
Go to the Happy Place in your mind, lock the door and
stay there.'

I take a deep breath. OK, I can do this. I don't want to
do this, but I can.

My phone rings. Alexis. 'Yup. Be there in a second.'

'Thank God – it's only going to be Nick, Karly's not
around,' I say.

'That's half your battle done. Good luck,' he says, nodding sternly. 'Remember: go to the Happy Place.'

Don't worry, I think, in the lift on my way up to their office. They *are* the agency's star team. And they *have* had sufficient time to make this work good. It *will* be good. It had better be good. It had better be the Sistine bloody Chapel of pizza ads. And the Mona Lisa . . .

I find Nick perched on the side of Alexis's desk, trying to impress her with his new Terry Richardson-style over-sized plastic glasses. 'They're Moscot Originals,' he says. 'I picked them up when we were shooting in New York.'

'You look like a pervy geography teacher,' she says, laughing.

He seems slightly disheartened that his five-hundred-dollar glasses have not turned out to be the roaring, knicker-loosening success he'd hoped for.

'Sorry to interrupt,' I say, 'but you've got scripts for me?'

'Wait here – I'll be back,' he says to Alexis.

'Right,' says Nick, closing his office door and handing me a piece of paper that turns out to be blank. 'I want your first impressions of each script as I read them out. You're the target audience for this product, aren't you, Susie?'

'Not really.'

'You are demographically: ageing, weight-conscious, that's the deal, isn't it?' he says. 'Whatever. The first route is called "Naughty Naughty". And it's based on the insight you gave us: pizzas are like curries – you don't expect them to be low-calorie.'

'Right. Good.'

'These pizzas look like they're bad for you but in fact they're not. Yeah?'

I nod.

'So it takes that metaphor – something that looks bad, but is in fact full of goodness – and Usain Bolts with it.'

'OK . . .' I say. Sounds reasonable enough.

'We open on Penelope Cruz in a red basque and suspenders . . .'

'A Penelope Cruz look-alike?' I say.

'Penelope Cruz. Or Monica Bellucci if we can't get Cruz. Megan Fox at a push. She's in a dark room. Candlelight. You can't tell exactly where. But she looks sultry and smoking hot. Think film noir. Steven Meisel. Dolce & Gabbana. There's music in the background. Christina Aguilera's "Dirrty". Sung by the Welsh Male Voice Choir.'

Don't worry, I think, trying to calm myself. They'll never be able to afford the music, let alone Penelope Cruz.

'The whole ad is an extended reverse striptease. Penelope bends over, puts on her sussies, g-string, push-up bra, then finally, right at the end, her habit . . .'

'Her what?'

'She's a nun, isn't she? And then an Italian voiceover comes on and says, "Some things in life look a LOT

225

naughtier than they are. Like new Fletchers Fat Bird pizzas. Lose the guilt. Find a tasty new habit. Thank heavens for Fletchers.'"

He looks up over the top of his paper. 'Why aren't you writing anything down?' he says. 'Write something down and then I'll go on to route two.'

'I don't need to write anything down, Nick.' Because there are two chances of that script getting made: fat chance and no chance.

'Write something, I want your immediate reaction.'

Trust me, Nick, you don't. Instead I write down 'Catholic issue?'

'What have you written?' he says, leaning forward to peer over the top of the paper.

'Just the PR angle . . .'

'That's the whole point? Massive PR, all those free tabloid inches. It'll be the most talked-about ad of the year.'

'What's the second route?'

'Karly wrote the second route, it's the girly one.' Karly – as girly as Tyson. 'It's called "What It Means to Be a Woman" – and it's based on insights of what real women feel about being real women. It features four women talking about emotional stuff, but they're going to be CGI women, not actual women.'

'Real women played by pretend women?'

'It gives it an edge. The girls are CGI but we film the backgrounds. It'll be totally fresh.'

226

'I can't quite . . .'

'Look: like this,' he says, bringing up a YouTube video on his Mac that has had eighty-seven million hits. 'Some kid in Wisconsin did this. Ours would look like this. Get it?' I nod.

'So we've got a blonde, a redhead, an Asian and a black girl. We open on a close-up of the redhead in a bikini on a Caribbean beach, and she says: "You know that awful feeling when you're on holiday and you suddenly realise that you've forgotten your tweezers?" That'll be shot in Mustique or St Barts, somewhere where the light is that granular, golden light you only find in certain parts of the Caribbean.'

Certain parts of the Caribbean where you want to go on holiday, Nick. Mind you, I wouldn't say no to a week on the beach . . .

'Carry on,' I say.

'Then the blonde says: "Ever had a bikini wax that went really wrong? Like, seriously wrong?"'

'Is that on a beach too?' I say.

'That'll be in a rainforest, Fiji. Then we have a close-up on the Asian bird: "The day before I'm due on all I want to do is cry or shout. My boyfriend stays in the pub all night." That one's shot in Barcelona. And then the black girl's in Buenos Aires and she says: "My boyfriend cheated on me with my sister. All I want to do is put on pyjamas and eat, eat, eat." Then we cut to a black screen that says: "bad-day-just-got-better.com".'

227

He pauses for a whole minute.

'OK . . .' I say. 'And then?'

'Write something down,' he says. 'Why aren't you writing anything down?'

'Because I'm waiting for you to finish the script,' I say.

'What do you mean?'

'The pizzas? I'm waiting for the bit about Fletchers pizzas.'

'That's the whole point!' he says. 'We don't mention the pizzas.'

'Sorry, Nick, you probably think I'm being a bit thick but could you explain that?'

'The point is, when something bad happens to a woman, she inevitably turns to food. It's a truism – we don't need to spell that out. That would be *so* patronising and *so* hackneyed. Instead we show these vignettes and let the viewer do the maths.'

'OK . . . I can understand a link between being dumped and eating chocolate, or even a pizza, but I'm not convinced that forgetting your tweezers is one of those occasions where you'd automatically think *must eat pizza.*'

'It'll be much more interactive for the viewer. That's why this script is so powerful. Doggett *loves* it,' he says.

'Go ahead with the third one,' I say, remembering Sam's advice and trying to enter the Happy Place in my brain but realising I've forgotten my keys.

'This one's called "The Truth". We've lined up the perfect celeb. Warm yet cool. Earthy yet sexy. Trendy yet relatable. Aspirational yet just like the viewer. We shoot her in her kitchen. And it's addressing this massive taboo, which is that women claim they're happy when they're fat – but actually that's bullshit, all women want to be thin.'

'What?'

'All this Dove stuff, love your flab, accept yourself as you truly are. It's a crock of shit: women hate themselves if they're not thin and we're going to be brave and come out and say it. Like an anti-Dove stance but more feminist.'

'Is this Karly's idea?'

'Do you remember when Kate Moss said "Nothing tastes as good as thin feels"?'

'Yeah, well, I think she regretted saying that in the end . . .'

'But the point is, it hit a nerve, because it's true. So: the celeb speaks to camera throughout. We see her in her kitchen. Smeg fridge. Large marble-topped island. "Let me tell you the truth about my body. I used to be a whopping size fourteen."'

'Size fourteen's not whopping,' I say.

'Just let me read,' says Nick. 'She walks across to the fridge, opens it. It's full of healthy food. Her hand hovers over a chocolate milkshake, then chooses skimmed milk. "The truth is, when I was big I was only pretending to be happy. Secretly I wanted to be thinner. As much as I hated models in magazines, the truth is *I hated myself*. I couldn't admit I was jealous; we're not allowed to admit that, are we, girls? But that's the truth. No one likes being fat. The truth is I love eating and I can't control myself around delicious food." We then cut away to her sitting at a banquet table alone in her pyjamas, eating handfuls of doughnuts and burgers.

'Then she says: "But the truth is I can have it all – with no compromise on taste! With new Fat Bird pizzas I can still enjoy that great pizza taste without worrying about being a Fat Bird ever again. And that's the truth." She takes a large bite of Sexy Chick Pizza and finishes with: "Right down to the last slice."'

'Well?' says Nick. 'What do you think?'

The truth is, it is loathsome, so awful it makes me feel sick. Perhaps the least awful of the three but it is truly awful.

'I'm not sure what to say.'

'How about provocative? Brave. Searingly honest. Insightful. Game-changing,' says Nick. 'That's what Doggett said.'

Of course he'd say that. The more worrying thing is, I suspect Devron might actually like these scripts.

I'm going to have to find a way to kill all three of them. (The scripts, that is.)

'Who's the celeb?' I say.

'Celina Summer,' he says. 'She's a mate of Karly's, apparently she'd be up for it.'

Celina Summer . . . Celina Summer . . . that name sounds familiar . . . URGH. 'Celina Summer who's married to what's-his-face in that band?' Who wrote that recipe for a chicken sandwich in the newspaper that was chicken, bread and lettuce? Who knows nothing about food whatsoever?

'Her new book *Eat Music, Dance to Food* is top of the charts,' says Nick. 'She's going to be the next Nigella, we need to get her now before she hits the big time.'

Top of the charts? How does one even dance to food? I bet my recipe folder's ten times better than her book and yet here I am, biting my tongue to shreds for fear of saying what I mean in front of this dickwad.

'I'm not finding your silence hugely motivating,' says Nick.

'I'm thinking . . .'

I'm thinking that this campaign will bomb and I will never get promoted and I won't escape. If I don't escape I'll still be here in my forties. I'll become so bitter and angry that I'll turn into a fully-fledged alcoholic rather than a trainee alcoholic. What remaining physical attractions I have left will rapidly diminish. No one will go out with me again, I will never ever have sex again, and then one drunken Saturday night in five years' time I will crawl upstairs on my hands and knees to Caspar's flat after drinking two bottles of white wine to proposition him and he will probably say no and then that truly will be the end of me.

231

So you see, Nick, these scripts are a much bigger problem than you could possibly realise.

'If you don't like them speak to Doggett,' he says, closing his folder and standing up.

Bollocks: I thought he might say that. I absolutely have to send something to Devron this afternoon, there's no time left to waste, so I have no choice but to speak to Doggett. I look past Alexis's shoulder and see that he's in his office talking to Berenice. It never rains . . . Mind you, I should grab them while they're together – Berenice at least should be sympathetic. She won't want awful headlines about sexism and misogyny for NMN. Plus she has zero sense of humour and won't know where to insert her pretend laughs when she sees the scripts.

But how to get past the Rottweiler . . . Alexis will make me wait till Monday for an appointment on point of principle. There's only one thing to shift her from guard but I can only pull this trick once a year or she gets suspicious . . .

'Alexis,' I say. 'I think Sam said there's a massive parcel for you from Space NK downstairs.'

And she's off! Faster than you can say Touche Éclat . . .

I knock on Robbie's door. 'Sorry to interrupt but . . .'

'Be quick,' says Berenice. 'I've got to be somewhere in two.'

'OK. I've just seen the Fletchers scripts and . . .'

'Amazing, right?' says Robbie.

'Have you seen them, Berenice?'

'Robbie and I were just talking about how taboo-breaking they are.'

'They are both singular and multiple,' says Robbie – a point I can't argue with because I don't understand what it means.

'I agree about the taboo thing,' I say. 'I am concerned that they push it just a bit too far . . .'

Robbie nods his head, making slow forward circles with his neck. 'Such as?'

'OK. Well the Cruz one is potentially going to cause offence to Catholics.'

'Go on . . .' says Robbie.

'And the CGI one . . . it's just a bit unsavoury talking about bodily fluids on a food ad. Plus, it doesn't even say the words Fletchers or pizzas, it just has a URL at the end . . .'

Robbie smiles benignly at me. Berenice looks at me as if I've just used her favourite orchid vase as a toilet.

'And the Celina Summer Truth one . . . personally I'm a size twelve to fourteen and I don't find her message very . . . endearing. And I just wondered if we could tone anything down a bit or whether there are any other scripts I could show?'

'Fascinating,' says Robbie. 'You appreciate that the Cruz script is incredibly witty? And you are aware that comedy is binary?'

I open my mouth but all that comes out is a small puff of confusion.

'As for sticking the client's name or logo on a script, that's *so twentieth century*.'

Berenice is nodding so fast and hard I'm surprised she doesn't slide off her chair.

'We live in an attention economy,' says Robbie. 'We are battling with thousands of brands to win the consumer's heart and mind, and what do consumers want?'

'Killer end lines,' says Berenice.

'Killer end lines,' says Robbie. 'And lucky you! Because we've given you three scripts with three killer end lines.'

'I'm worried Devron will buy them but that customers will complain,' I say.

'Ah! So you think you know better than me, your creative team and your client? I suggest you endeavour to sell your scripts. Brave and fearless, Susie, brave and fearless.'

I feel almost sick with loathing as I close Robbie's door on my way out. My face is still scarlet when I bump into Martin Meddlar in the lift on my way back down.

'What's wrong, darling, you look troubled?'

It is entirely inappropriate to discuss one's day-to-day work problems with a man of Martin Meddlar's ranking, in a lift. Then again, it is entirely inappropriate for a man of Martin Meddlar's ranking to have grabbed my hand and to be swinging it now, gently, like we're on some weird adult play date.

'It's nothing, Martin . . .'

He gives my hand a gentle squeeze. 'Talk to me, Susie, I'm here to help.'

Alright then: if you're going to squeeze me then I'm going to share some of this pain with you.

'It's these Fletchers scripts. I know you said be provocative, and I know it's great to get PR, but I'm concerned they might alienate our female shoppers.'

'I'm sure they're fine, darling.'

'There are three routes and they all feel too extreme, but Robbie and Berenice disagree.'

'If you're that worried, stick them into research. No point losing sleep over it.'

'Devron's not the biggest fan of listening to his customers. Plus Robbie and Berenice will be pretty unimpressed with me for even suggesting it.'

'Tell them all I said to do it. How big's this campaign?'

'Four million pounds.'

'Fine, do one group, that's a couple of grand, say the agency will pick up the tab. I'll get Finance to tuck it on another client's job number.' That's the reason Martin runs this place – he's as wily as they come.

'Thank you,' I say, sincerely. 'This is a big project for me. I appreciate your advice.'

'You know you can call me any time,' he says, as we reach the ground floor. 'Have you got my mobile, darling?'

'I don't think I do.' I take my phone from my pocket. And it is my sheer bad luck that at the exact moment he is giving me his number the lift next to ours opens and out walks Berenice.

Still, there's no time to worry about her reaction. I have to get these scripts off to Devron before 5 p.m. I email them over, writing a soul-destroying spiel about how strong the ads are; 'how powerful, how original, how hard it must be to have to choose only one . . .'

And then I sit back and cross my fingers that he will hate them all, and insist on moving the airdate back three months and then I can get another team on the job who will do an award-winning script. And then Ryan Gosling will turn up at the awards ceremony with the world's largest tub of chocolate mini-bites and when I say 'But Ryan, won't these make me fat?' he will reply, 'No Susie, they will make you even thinner and younger and prettier than you already are.'

And who says I'm not an optimist?

Saturday

Dalia has suggested an early evening drink at Boccarinos in Mayfair before she heads off to meet Mark for dinner.

Boccarinos is one of those places where silver-fox titans of industry go for breakfast, to eat two poached eggs for fourteen quid. In the evening there's a real scene: you could be in Italy in 1985, the amount of gel that's slathered on the men's hair. Over there in the corner is that miniscule billionaire who's always in *Hello!* with what looks like his nurse but is in fact wife four. And across the counter from me at the bar are two high-class escorts, all tits and teeth, Choos dangling off heels.

Dalia loves it here – she loves Eurotrash-watching. She doesn't love it quite enough to be punctual, and when she does arrive, twenty minutes late, she immediately announces she can only stay for fifteen minutes, as she totally got confused about her timings and thought dinner with Mark was at 9 p.m., when it's actually at 7.30 p.m. Third time in a row she's mucked me about because of him. Three strikes and she's still not out . . .

'I've bought us a bottle!' I say, secretly cursing the fact that this wine cost thirty quid and I'll either have to drink the whole thing alone here at the bar, or ask for a cork so I can take it home on the bus. Which is totally unacceptable behaviour at Boccarinos, even if it is sort of acceptable on the top deck of the number 13.

'I'll neck a glass with you now,' she says, sitting and taking her coat off to reveal a scarlet silk dress with a plunging neckline.

'Wow, beautiful, is that new?' I say, as I notice the man next to her do a double-take.

'Thanks – it's Issa,' she says.

'Not cheap!'

'Well it's an important dinner for Mark. He asked me to make an effort.'

'Did he buy it for you?' I ask, staring at my glass to avoid her having to lie directly to my face.

'. . . I had a voucher for Selfridges from work for my birthday . . . it wasn't that expensive . . .'

'And what's this dinner you're off to?'

'Some charity gala, Mark's mother's on the committee.'

'You're finally going to meet the mother?' After two years of not being allowed anywhere near family members.

'No,' she says, taking a large sip of wine and immediately fishing in her clutch bag for a mirror to check her lipstick. 'She's in Venice, some arts thing . . .'

'Do you think he'll introduce you to her one of these days?' I say.

'I don't want to meet her,' she says unconvincingly. 'She sounds like a complete dragon. Besides Mark and I are . . . you know . . . we're trying not to put too much pressure on our relationship at the moment . . . keeping it open, you know . . . We're just hanging out.'

'You're just hanging out . . .' I say, smiling, and re-adjusting her black lacy bra strap that's slipping slowly down her shoulder.

'What's that supposed to mean?' she says.

'What? Nothing! . . . I mean you're hanging out of your dress!'

'I know you and Polly don't like Mark . . .'

'Dalia . . .'

'You think he's using me, and that I'm some sort of an idiot or something. But he *is* a good guy. And I'm telling you it is *the best sex* of my entire life. I am talking full on, heated, rampant, can't-concentrate-at-work-because-I'm-thinking-about-it, bloody-great, pin-me-up-against-the-wall sex.'

'Alright!'

'And I *personally* refuse to live without that,' she says. Dalia thinks I should at least find myself a fuck-buddy. But

I don't want to segregate my heart from the rest of my body. So I am learning to live without that sort of sex. And I am almost used to not having it; almost at a point where I don't miss it.

Not almost enough.

'And what's more,' she says, 'I refuse to apologise for the fact that I am a passionate person who knows what she wants.'

'For goodness' sake, Dalia, all I was doing was tucking your bra strap back in – nothing more! You don't need to go on and on about it like that.'

She takes a deep breath. 'Fine. It just feels like you judge me all the time.'

'How's work?' I say, with forced jollity. 'Boss still off?'

'Yeah,' she says, glancing at her watch. 'I can't believe it – a month off with stress, after she threw her iPhone at the work placement's head! Still, at least she's not micro-managing my every move. How's yours?'

'I'm off at Christmas, as soon as they promote me.'

'You'll leave?'

'I hate it,' I say, realising that hate is a strong word – yet, thinking about Nick and his scripts, perhaps not strong enough. 'I'm not learning. It's not fun. The only good things are my friends, and I'll still see them if I quit.' Funny, that's what Jake used to say and I'd always shoot him down.

'It's a bad time to be out of work, they're talking triple dip recession.'

'You sound just like my mum,' I say.

She looks at her watch again. 'Shit, I've got to go or he'll be pissed off. Let me give you some cash,' she says, checking her make-up again. She holds the mirror an inch from her eyes, and prods gently at her cheekbones before shaking her head. 'Mark's right – I do look old and tired. I think I'm going to have to start getting filler.'

'Nonsense. You look beautiful. You are beautiful. Wine's on me. Go. You don't want to be late.' For a man who tells you how knackered you look . . .

She gives my arm a quick squeeze as she goes. I can tell she feels slightly bad about ditching me again on a Saturday night, but not as bad as I feel now, slightly tipsy Norman No-Mates with my bottle of wine. I turn the bottle round and pretend to inspect the label. I sense the man who'd given Dalia the once-over glance briefly at me. When he's stopped looking I glance back.

Old. Expensive suit. Portly. A thick shot of white hair. He too has a bottle of wine all to himself, and not even the cover of a now-vanished friend to share it with. His booze is considerably finer than mine, however, and sits in its own shiny silver bucket. He has a couple of small plates of food – one with meatballs, another with what look like tiny mozzarella balls in a pale sauce. Without my glasses I can't tell. They look too shiny to be cheese . . . They look tasty . . .

'Excuse me,' I say, my wine getting the better of me. 'Is that mozzarella?'

241

'Quail's eggs. With tuna. Try some?'

'That's OK,' I say. 'I was just trying to work out what they were.'

'They're terribly good.' He pushes his plate towards me.

'Only if you're sure.' I hastily pull the plate nearer. 'And do you mind, the bread basket?' In for a penny . . .

'Verdict?' he says, as I swipe a soft square of focaccia through the sauce.

'Totally delicious. Thank goodness someone's got the patience to peel a quail's egg.'

'I come here often,' he says, looking around the room as if it's his. 'I'll have a few bits here, then go next door for my main course.'

'What's next door?'

'Lydia's.'

'I've always wanted to go to Lydia's!'

'I've been a member since 1958. Lydia and I were great chums, used to ski a lot together,' he says. 'If you fancy dinner, we can go there now?'

I look at him carefully. He is unfit, overweight, double my age. His complexion has the glowing redness of sunburn but I suspect it's a lifetime of long lunches. If he tried to attack me I reckon I could hold my own. Besides, people don't get abducted from swanky members' clubs in Mayfair. Unless of course he slips me a Rohypnol . . .

'So if you used to hang out at Lydia's in the sixties did you know Lord Lucan, then?' I say.

242

'Bastard won a Jag off me playing backgammon.'

'What's your name?' I wonder if he's a politician.

He suddenly looks wary. 'You ask a lot of questions.'

'I can't go to dinner with a man whose name I don't know.'

He pauses for a moment to consider this. 'Peter.'

'And your surname?'

'You don't need to know that.'

Maybe I do, maybe I don't. Either way I'm going to Google him when I go to the loo in a minute to check he's not a murderer. The man used to gamble with Lucan – I mean, who knows?

'Help me finish this Chablis,' he says, clicking towards the barman for a clean glass, then filling it almost to the rim. If he is going to slip me a Mickey Finn right now is when. I watch the pour carefully. No sign of white powder falling from his Savile Row sleeve.

'Back in a sec,' I say, heading to the loo, smartphone at the ready. I type in 'Peter', 'Lydia's nightclub' and 'Lord Lucan' and come up with five possible old aristos called Peter, then add in 'backgammon' and 'Jaguar' and find him – thank you, internet, for once you're on my side!

Peter Emerson-Black, born in 1940 . . . yes, double my age. Made his money in the City in the eighties . . . Owns cars, a small plane, a football team – yep, he can pay for dinner. One ex-wife, no children . . . and no history of murder.

I check my face in the mirror. Why is he asking me to dinner, I wonder. I look OK tonight, quite well turned out I suppose in a knee-length navy dress with a high neck. And I guess I look quite classy compared to some of the women in here who are in head-to-toe leopard print. Why am I going for dinner with him is probably the question I should be asking. I don't remotely fancy him.

But it's Saturday night, I've been ditched by my friend. I'm drunk. I'm hungry. And I've always wanted to go to Lydia's to see what all the fuss was about. All those famous paparazzi shots over the years of people falling out of its doors at 3 a.m., with people they shouldn't be falling out of doors with. This might be my only opportunity to get in. So it's that or go home for a fish-finger sandwich and *The Killing*. Though I do love Lund. But I guess I could catch up on iPlayer . . .

I can't possibly go home at 8 p.m. on a Saturday night when everyone else in London is out having fun. Besides, I'm here now. And Lydia's is right next door. And Peter looks lonely. He does, poor old man, sitting with a bottle of wine and no one to drink it with . . .

'What sort of food do they do at Lydia's?' I say, as Peter helps me on with my coat.

'They can make you whatever you want,' he says, as we head out of the door and turn right. I wonder if they would make me a fish-finger sandwich – it's actually what I really fancy.

244

A doorman in a bowler hat greets Peter warmly and ushers us through a heavy black door. Inside we climb a staircase and walk through gold curtains and into a low-ceilinged dining area. The walls are lined with purple velvet and guests sprawl on banquettes drinking champagne under chandeliers that I'm sure I've seen in Homebase. There isn't a woman over forty in this room with the face she was born with. One diner moves a fork unsteadily across her plate like it's a fawn on ice. If eating is cheating, why go to a restaurant?

The maître d' seats us at a corner booth and before I've even eyeballed the menu Peter has ordered for us both. 'You do eat meat, don't you, Sarah?' he says as an afterthought.

I nod. I think about correcting him on my name but don't really see the point.

'You like food, don't you?' he says.

'Who doesn't?'

'You're not a nutritionist by any chance?'

'No. Why?'

'I put my back out in Barbados at Christmas, haven't been able to play golf since. I need to lose three stone.'

'Not three,' I say, assessing his paunch. 'Maybe one at a push.'

'You're an angel,' he says. 'But my friends say I look terrible.'

'Get new friends,' I say. 'It's simple. Eat less, move more.

245

There are six hundred calories in a bottle of wine, all of which are nutritionally empty.'

'Six hundred, you say? Is that a lot? You know, I think you'd be perfect for the job.' He reaches out and grabs my hand. His small hand is unexpectedly dry. I smile anxiously, willing him not to move any closer. 'Sarah, say you'll be my nutrition advisor, please?'

I have no idea what I'm dealing with here. Is this code? Is he actually propositioning me for sex? Does he genuinely just want advice? Or is he a lonely old man, looking for an excuse for a conversation? His hand gives mine a gentle squeeze. Is there any way, in any conceivable universe, that I could imagine dating this man? Fundamentally he is far too old for me. He is also shorter than me – though I could probably get past that. Also I suspect he's an alcoholic – I don't really want to have to get past that . . .

His face is inoffensive though. And his eyes do have a certain sparkle and warmth. He's generous. And smart. And he hasn't tried to move my hand to his crotch yet . . . Oh it's no use. There's just no way. He's far too old. Does that make me terribly shallow?

'I'd make sure you were remunerated appropriately,' he says.

A meal ticket out of NMN . . . No more of Berenice's crap . . . I could be like that girl in Primrose Hill, shopping all day. I'd never need to worry about the price of cheese.

246

'I can give you some simple advice but I can't take your money,' I say.

He looks confused. 'Are you some sort of operator?' he says, slurring slightly.

Terrific. He thinks I'm a prostitute. Ironic, really, given that the woman on the table next to us surely is. She's the blondest, largest-busted woman I've ever seen. Dressed in an Hervé Léger white minidress, she's sitting on the lap of a wizened old Monty Burns look-alike. I'm sure I've seen him in *ES Magazine*. I think he owns all the steel in the world. Or maybe it's all the copper mines.

I'm contemplating how to reply to Peter's question without sounding offended, when the waiter comes over and presents a bottle of wine. Peter swirls the golden liquid ostentatiously round his glass, then swigs it back with an appreciative gasp.

'My ex-wife insisted on serving Montrachet at our wedding,' he says, staring at the ceiling. It is covered in black velvet with little diamante sparkles throughout, which cast a weird shimmer over all the flesh in the room. 'Yet when we met she'd never even heard of Montrachet.' Well then she and I have something in common.

He takes a large sip of wine, pauses to look at the remaining liquid, then downs it. 'Though I dare say she'd heard of a patsy . . .' He gestures to the waiter to pour him another.

'When did you get divorced?'

'Last summer,' he says, gripping the stem of his glass tightly. 'We were only married for eleven months and yet she tried to unburden me of four million pounds.' He shakes his head. 'Does that seem just to you?'

Depends on how bad a husband you were, I guess.

'I take it you're no longer on speaking terms,' I say. He snorts a response.

'Are you tempted to try again?' Perhaps he's given up on love at his age. Burnt financially, emotionally . . .

'Why ever not? I've got twenty good years left!'

That's the spirit. I wonder if I should try to fix him up on a date with Rebecca's mum? Make it clear that I'm not interested and at the same time do a bit of matchmaking. Of course, Marjorie would be more his age but these rich old guys don't want to date women their own age. Plus, Marjorie gave up on intimate relations and politeness around the mid-1970s. Rebecca's mum on the other hand is another matter. Divorced ten years ago, she's gorgeous, probably fifty-five but passes for forty. She's sparky, lots of fun, well travelled . . .

'My friends are trying to set me up with some women. Met a charming lady the other day,' he says. 'Flew her to St Tropez, had a marvellous dinner down there, an excellent Pauillac from '78.'

'That's quite full on for a first date.'

'She'd never been to France,' he shrugs.

'Never been to France? Is she English?' Maybe she was one of those mail-order brides . . .

'Sure, she's English.'

Hang on a minute. 'How old is she?' I say.

'Mid-twenties, I suppose. Ah, food!'

The waiter descends on us with a tray bearing two plates covered by giant silver domes. He places them in front of us and I catch sight of my reflection. Even though the curve of the dome is distorting my face you can still register my shock.

'Tournedos Rossini,' says Peter, poking his fork into a nugget of meat placed perfectly in the centre of a large white plate. 'Nothing better than a bit of foie gras.'

'I was actually going to ask if you'd be interested in taking my friend's mother out? She's lovely.'

'Her mother?' he says, doubtfully. 'How old is she?

'Early fifties?'

'No use I'm afraid, I need someone who's fertile. Early thirties, thirty-four maximum.'

I find myself involuntarily pushing my plate away. Marvellous. I am having dinner with a seventy-three-year-old who considers me too old for him! I had grudgingly accepted that every man my own age wants to date younger. But where does this leave me? What is left out there? A hot centenarian who might be persuaded, just this once, to lower his standards?

'Not hungry?' he says, reaching out for my hand, which I quickly move to my lap.

'Actually I feel a bit peaky,' I say, holding my napkin to

my mouth while I think. If I race over to Bond Street tube now, I can still be home for *The Killing*. I bet the murderer's that good-looking guy . . . I'll open that nice Malbec that Frandrew brought round, drink away this whole tawdry experience.

'Come! Have a dance,' he says, grabbing my hand from my lap. 'That'll wake you up.'

I don't want to be woken up! I want to go home to bed, scream and then cry a bit.

But instead I let him drag me to the mirrored dance floor, just as the electro-whine of *Gangnam Style* kicks in. Peter starts lassoing his arm through the air and boinging to the left and right. Occasionally he breaks his horse-inspired routine to spin me violently. After ten minutes of increasing dizziness I plead a time out, but sitting proves to be a mistake. Peter orders another bottle, then a third. I keep thinking 'just leave', but he is now telling me about his dead brother and how can you possibly walk out on someone while they're telling you about their dead brother? All I can do is keep knocking back this expensive, delicious white wine, though I'll be the one paying the price in the morning. It is only when he moves my hair to one side and tells me what a delightful jaw line I have that I sense a window, and an urgency to jump through it.

'Thank you so much for your generosity but I must go now.'

'It's still early, Sarah! You're such terribly good fun, do

stay.' He clutches my hand, awkwardly grabbing my fourth and fifth finger in his fist.

'I have to go.'

He is still holding onto my fingers for dear life while he reaches over to kiss me goodbye. I turn my head quickly but he still manages to plant his mouth next to mine. His top lip is moist from the dance floor and his wet lips linger. It is all I can do not to wipe his sweat from my skin until I'm back out on the street, walking away as fast as I drunkenly can.

Sunday

I wake at 11 a.m. and the first thing I feel is a throbbing headache, followed by a low, deep ache of sadness. Alcohol's a depressant, I reason. This is just a particularly emotional hangover. It's normal to feel miserable – that's why people become alcoholics: when they feel like this they carry on drinking. And hangovers are harder to recover from in your thirties than in your twenties; a bit like relationships.

Why did I let myself get into that situation with Peter last night? And the week before with Seb? I was drunk both times, yes. But drunk on loneliness more than anything.

Speaking of Seb, when I check my phone there's yet another text. Eighth one this week. How has he not got the hint? I'd taken the view that any response from me would encourage him but I should have put my foot down at the start.

Hey sexy lady. U have not responded to my texts. Y not? Last Sunday u were v friendly, touching my leg 1 minute, then totally cold the next! U have given V mixed signals. Perhaps u r frigid – no wonder u r single ☺. I do think u r rude though – ESPECIALLY when someone buys u drinks and snacks. Anyway: rightly or wrongly I think u do NOT want to c me again. If I am reading these signals wrong and u call me tmrw and say hey Seb crossed wires Seb v sorry OR I lost my phone – then no harm done. If u do I think we could have a REALLY good time. If u r around and r genuinely sorry I look forward to date 2. And if not – your loss, S, your loss ☺

I phone Polly to share the lunacy of this text but it goes through to her voicemail. Only two weeks to go now till the wedding, she'll be totally hectic. I can't wait for that wedding.

Rebecca and I had vague plans to go to the cinema, but while I'm in the shower she calls and leaves a hugely apologetic message saying she's still with Luke, do I mind if we take a rain check? I could really do without her turning into Dalia marque two. On one level of course I'm incredibly happy for Rebecca that things are going so well with Luke Barman. And on another horrible level I'm a bit bothered that it's working out. My partner in crime has abandoned me, and while I want her to be happy, I don't want to be left alone.

So . . .

Sunday . . .

What to do with a day?

Since when did days become so long? When Jake and I were a couple the weekends never felt this drawn out. We usually had something fun to do but when the diary was empty that was fine too: we might do nothing other than eat a late breakfast, bumble around and watch a box-set and yet the time would fly. But nowadays some weekends feel like a long journey home in the rain.

I think about calling Sam. He'd be fun to hang out with, we could watch a DVD or something. Is that what it all boils down to? Trying to find people to share or avoid the loneliness with? Should I be brave and text Jeff? I can't bear the thought of spending a day waiting for him to not reply. Besides, next week at the research group I'll pin him down properly.

I'm definitely not in the mood to see Marjorie. But I don't want to sit here thinking about things and people I shouldn't. I should go to Westfield and find a dress for Polly's wedding, but the thought of shopping with a hang-over is too heinous. Besides it's cloudy out. I'll make lunch and then I'll be able to think of something.

There is only one dish to make on a day like today – *the* go-to, cheer-me-up-post-hangover pasta: conchiglie with cream, bacon and parmesan. How could there be a better designed pasta shape for this dish than these shells? That delicious creamy sauce, held safe and warm in those private little sanctums. I myself would like to climb into a giant pasta shell on a day like today.

I've got carried away and made twice as much as I can eat. Still, it'll keep till dinner. It looks like the sky is beginning to clear. I flick through last week's Sunday supplements. There's an article about Being Single: it says that the key to happiness is to treat yourself like you are your own soul mate, spoil yourself with flowers, take yourself out on dates.

You know what? I would really like to go to London Zoo – I haven't been since I was about five and it's only twenty minutes away. But I can't picture myself going to the zoo alone. Though actually I could go for a long walk in Regent's Park . . . Clear my head, get some exercise. Perfect. I love a walk in the park. It's one of my favourite things. I feel most myself when I'm in Regent's Park in particular – even though it's always busy it still always feels calm. And it's so beautiful – so much better than Westfield at the weekend.

I walk round the Outer Circle and then head to Queen Mary's Gardens. The roses here are breathtaking. It's like something out of a fairy tale – I can't believe they don't charge people to see such a spectacular sight, not to mention the scent! And the names of these roses are so random – this one's called Ice Cream, and this phenomenal deep yellow one's called Keep Smiling. I wonder who makes up these names. That would be a lovely job, making up names for roses.

I pop over to The Cow and Coffee Bean and treat myself to a cappuccino and a slice of awesome carrot cake, and then walk all the way round to the lake to look at the birds. Unbelievable – these little black ones with white collars, so chic! And these, with the glimmering purply-blue feathers – stunning.

That was a delightful date with me, if I do say so myself. I would totally ask me out again!

I'm in such a buoyant mood that I decide to go and see Marjorie on my way home. I just about have time to pop to the supermarket. I don't think she deserves it after how rude she was to me, but still it'll be up to me to be the bigger person. I trek to Waitrose, buy some raspberries, some seeds for Fitzgerald, a *Mail on Sunday,* a bunch of purple tulips and a tin of old fashioned mixed-fruit travel sweets. White flags and olive branches aren't on deal this week.

I pop back to mine quickly and put the leftover pasta I was saving for dinner into Tupperware for her, and head over. When I get to her door she doesn't answer. For a moment I panic that she might have had another fall, but when I prop open her mailbox I can hear the TV blaring out. I knock loudly again and after three long minutes, during which I begin to regret making the effort, she comes to the door.

'What do you want?' she says, through the inch she's willing to give.

'Hello Marjorie! I've brought you a few things.'

'I'm in the middle of *Columbo*.'

Columbo's on every hour of every day.

'OK,' I say. 'If you just let me in I'll give you the stuff, make you a cup of tea and then I'll leave you to it. Would you prefer that?'

She nods grudgingly, opens the door, then shuffles back to the living room.

I flick the kettle on, put the flowers in a vase and the fruit in the fridge, and head back in to see her. This room is even more of a tip than before – it's depressing. But there's no point in me offering to help tidy it, she'll only have a go at me. I notice the cheque she wrote for me last time is still sitting on her side table. I'm amazed she hasn't ripped it up.

She is entirely serious about not wanting to be disturbed. I try having a chat, but she shakes her head and points to Peter Falk, who's just said 'One more thing . . .'

I wait until the episode is over, but it's straight into another episode, and when I try to offer her another cup of tea she tells me to shut up or go home. And so I thank my lucky stars that for once she doesn't want me to stay and I leave her to it.

I've given her my dinner, so I take some fish fingers out of the freezer and make that fish-finger sandwich. I get in to bed with my laptop and catch up on *The Killing*. Maybe I'll move to Copenhagen. All the men there are so handsome, even the serial killers.

I turn the lights out at 9.10 p.m. Big week coming up, research group with Jeff, and of course that whopping major work problem on the scripts . . .

I'm asleep before I even have time to worry.

w/c 9 April

Status report:
- Get script signed off – URGENT (subliminally persuade Devron to research)
- Jeff date – FORCE THE ISSUE THIS WEEK

Monday

Oh dear. First thing Monday, Devron's on the phone: he loves all the scripts. Mandy too loves the scripts. Their next-door-neighbour Keith who was round at the weekend watching the match thinks they're blinding. And Keith's wife Lorraine does too, though personally she's not a fan of that Penelope Cruz, and thinks Lana Del Ga Ga or whatever her name is would be a better choice.

Why don't I just let this play out? Let them make a terrible ad, waste four million quid – it's not like it's my

259

money. Because: the minute a single viewer at home complains about the ad, it will be entirely my fault, no one else's. Don't ask me why, it makes no sense. Same as quadratic equations – I cannot explain it.

'I can't decide which one will work best for the brand,' says Devron. 'The Cruz script – that'll get great PR but there's not much pizza in it . . .' True, there is no pizza in it, I think, as I doodle an un-smiley face on my to-do list.

'Then those CGI girls . . . love that, and those locations will look *so* aspirational . . .' He means Mandy's already bought a new bikini.

'But then that Truth one with Celina Summer – it just has so much honesty, so much raw truth to it. I think it'll really speak to our customers in their own language.'

'Tricky,' I say. 'If only there was a way of finding out what your customers actually think . . .'

'Yeah . . .' he says. And then falls silent. He can't bear to suggest research because he doesn't want to look indecisive or weak.

'I'm not sure if it's at all possible,' I say, 'and I'd have to ask a massive favour from Martin Meddlar . . .'

'Yes?' says Devron.

'But just this once would you allow us to commission some research? We'd pay for it, of course. I mean, we're the ones putting you in this awkward position . . .'

'How soon can you do it?'

'If we're lucky we can get it sorted this week . . . Thursday at 6 p.m.?' I say, clicking send on the email I've already drafted to our research agency giving them the go-ahead.

'Done,' he said. 'Just this once.'

'Oh, just one thing, Devron. I think it would be incredibly helpful if that chef of yours was there . . .'

'Jeff?'

'That's his name, Jeff. There might be some NPD feedback for him . . .' And 6 p.m. on a Thursday night will be a good time for me to get some feedback from him.

'Alright, I'll bring him,' he says.

Now that, Rebecca, is a cloud with a silver lining.

Thursday

It's 5.50 p.m. and I'm applying a second layer of mascara and a bit of extra cover-up under my eyes in the ladies' toilets at the research centre. Jeff and Devron are two minutes away. Karly is sitting scowling in the viewing room, tapping away on her iPhone and bitching about her time being wasted.

I'm wondering if this tight red dress Rebecca made me wear was really such a good idea. It has a very low neck-line and you can see the top of the middle bit of my bra, but she assured me that this is a good thing. Too late to change now, and if I pull up the top part I'll only end up revealing too much leg.

Still, it's dark in the viewing room, I think, as I go back in. It's dark so that we can look through the one-way glass at the five loyal Fletchers shoppers on the other side. These are the 'Bingo-Wing Brendas' that Tom identified as the main audience for Fat Bird pizzas: loyal Fletchers customers in their thirties and forties who are trying to lose weight. In return for their opinions on the three scripts they'll get a twenty-pound Fletchers' voucher and ten per cent off their next shop. They sit there, shyly helping themselves to crisps and sandwiches from the table, a couple knocking back the free wine.

The door opens to our viewing room and in come Jeff and Devron. Jeff is looking seriously good. He's wearing a denim shirt over a white t-shirt, which makes his eyes look amazing, and he's clean shaven today, which somehow makes him look even naughtier than when he has stubble.

Karly perks up significantly when she sees him and suggests he sits next to her, but fortunately that's the spare seat between her and me that she's left to make it obvious that she doesn't want to sit next to me. (Her and Nick are *deeply concerned* about this research group. It is *not how they like to work* and *really insulting to their seniority* and *if anything needs changing on these scripts, someone else will bloody well have to do it.*)

'Would you like some wine, Jeff?' I say, and pour him a particularly large glass to kick-start proceedings.

'Ssssh, they're about to start,' says Karly, though she's busy tap-tap-tapping away on her iPhone as always.

Eileen, the researcher, begins by asking the group what sort of pizzas they like. When one woman says she likes Sainsbury's Taste The Difference pizzas, Devron has his first tantrum. And when five minutes later one of the other women says she once had food poisoning from a Fletchers pizza, Devron says to Jeff, 'She probably ate three pizzas at once, look at the size of her.' Coming from Devron of all people!

Things go seriously downhill when Eileen takes them through the three scripts. They think the Penelope Cruz route is 'tacky', 'disgusting' and 'cheesy'.

'Perfect – so are the pizzas,' Jeff whispers to me and I snort down a giggle.

The CGI script is 'vile', 'sexist' and 'stupid' and 'what on earth has it got to do with food?' When one of the group says that it was clearly written by a man, as no woman could ever have written such misogynistic tosh, I see Karly grip the sides of her chair like she's giving birth. And the Celina Summer script is 'the best of the bunch', except that 'all the words in it need changing' and 'she's utterly obnoxious' and 'horribly smug about being thin'.

'Looks like I'm going to have to find a new career!' I say, as Karly bitches loudly in the background about how stupid these women are; how they haven't got a clue about humour or creativity; how customer feedback is meaningless; and why are we even researching these scripts two weeks before the shoot anyway – whose dumb idea was *that*?

'What would you do instead?' says Jeff. 'Something with food, right?'

'Totally! I had this crazy idea for a blog but it's stayed in my mind for so long – I think maybe there's something in it.'

'Tell me,' he says.

'It'll sound really silly,' I say.

'No, tell me. I want to know.'

'Well my grandma, the Italian one, used to say that there's always the perfect pasta to suit any occasion.'

'So what, like if you're starving then spaghetti with meatballs, or something lighter if you're not that hungry?' says Jeff.

'No, no, no. Way more sophisticated than that,' I say. 'For example, if you've been out and got drunk with an old man you met randomly and felt sorry for, but turns out he's a randy old goat, and then you wake up the next day feeling sorry for yourself – then that would be conchiglie with bacon, cream and parmesan.'

'That is quite specific,' he says.

'Yes! That's the point. Or I'll give you another example. Say you've just found out that your ex has taken his new girlfriend to "your" beach in Sicily, and you're annoyed because now he'll always associate that beach with her and not you. And also I mean like why does she have to post every single photo on Facebook anyway? . . . That's how specific I mean,' I say, aware that I now sound entirely crackers.

'That is most definitely specific,' says Jeff. 'So then what would that pasta be?'

'OK. That would be . . . cream based, because it's ultimately about comfort. And bacon, because salty fat is the heart stone of all medicine. And peas, because they're little balls of green delight. And maybe tomato, so you don't feel like you're going to get fat off the back of bad news. And then a shape that's distracting and that can take your mind off it. So that might be bucatini – like spaghetti but with holes down the middle that you can try to whistle through. Or strozapretti. Which means "priest stranglers". Because it's sort of unusual and interesting and would take your mind off your ex too, but in a different way because you'd be thinking about strangling a clergyman. Do you get it?'

For some reason Jeff thinks this is all quite funny. 'You're insane but I really love that idea,' he says.

'What idea?' says Karly, suddenly interested, though still tapping away on her iPhone.

'No, nothing,' I say, embarrassed.

'Tell her!' he says. 'It's a great idea!'

'Honestly, Karly, it's just this dumb thing . . .'

'When Susie was little,' says Jeff, 'her Italian granny . . .'

'Shh!' I say, knowing Karly will try to humiliate me in front of him.

'Her granny told her that there's always the perfect pasta for any occasion and so she's got this idea that there's always a perfect shape and sauce for whatever happens to you.'

266

Karly looks directly at me for a long moment, seems to actually think about it, but then goes back to tapping at her phone.

Jeff shrugs.

'No, go on,' says Karly, a smirk creeping across her face. 'Like what, Susie?'

'Oh gosh. Like erm . . . you've got an important decision to make, say, and you're confused . . . so then you might make a straight shaped pasta, like penne – but smooth penne, not ridged – and combine it with a smooth sauce – no lumps. It just helps you think clearly if you don't have wiggly pasta or a chunky sauce.'

She keeps typing and I turn to Jeff and shrug. 'I told you so,' I whisper. 'Now she's going to think I'm even more stupid than she did before.'

'I don't think you're stupid, I think you're great,' says Jeff.

'What's pesto for then?' she says, suddenly.

'Do you mean fresh pesto made in a pestle and mortar?' My grandma used to make the most delicious *pesto di noce* with walnuts. I've never attempted it – you need a good heavy marble pestle and mortar.

'Pesto in a jar,' says Karly.

My grandma would never have dreamt of eating pesto in a jar. Still, it works for me, or rather it would do if Dalia hadn't thrown my jars away . . .

'I guess that's the fastest, easiest way to mainline salt, cheese and oil and still feel mildly healthy . . . So that would be a mid-week supper after a not-too stressful day, early in the week when you're still feeling virtuous and have good intentions, say on a Tuesday.'

'That makes absolute sense,' says Jeff.

'Which pasta shape?' she says.

'The quickest shape to cook that can also grip the sauce – so ridged penne for that one would be perfect.'

But Karly's tap-tapping away at her iPhone and ignores my reply.

The door opens and Eileen, the researcher comes in, shaking her head.

'What's the verdict?' says Devron.

'Well . . .' says Eileen, trying to be diplomatic but struggling to know where to start. 'I'd say the Penelope Cruz route and the CGI with tweezers route are a no-no . . .'

'What??' says Karly. 'You're seriously going to listen to five drunken old housewives? They don't know what they're talking about.'

'I always thought the Truth script was the strongest,' says Devron, nodding sagely.

'But . . .' says Eileen, 'I think the feedback on the Truth script is worth taking on board. I do understand that the insight behind the script was some sort of confrontational honesty . . . but I don't know that this audience particularly warms to the way in which it's currently expressed.'

Karly is shaking her head so violently she's making me dizzy.

'Perhaps . . .' says Eileen, 'a slight change of direction. You could still use Celina Summer but soften it, have her be a little more sympathetic about how hard it is to stay slim, rather than bragging about her own body . . .'

'I'm sure we can find a way of doing it if we just have a little look at the words,' I say, looking at Devron. 'And frankly if we don't, we'll have empty airtime in the central break of *Coronation Street* in a few weeks' time, so it's up to us all to be a little pragmatic at this point.'

'As far as I'm concerned,' says Devron, 'if Celina and the pizzas look great and she says the word truth a lot, I think that's the main thing.'

Karly pulls my arm and takes me to one side. 'If you change a word on our script, you'll lose the whole idea. And you'll lose us. We're not doing any revisions, I'm telling you that right now. Nick and Robbie are going to go ballistic when they hear about this.' She grabs her Birkin bag and heads for the door.

'Right, better get back to Mandy,' says Devron, putting on his coat. 'Jeff, are you coming?'

He looks at me and I make the universal gesture for glass of wine and hope it doesn't look like the universal gesture for hand job.

'I think I'll just have a catch up with Susie,' he says, and Devron nods and leaves.

★

269

Finally! I'm sitting in a cosy corner of a bar in Soho with Jeff. Quite drunk. It's nearly 10 p.m. and we've been drinking and having a total giggle since we left the research group. It's only taken me five weeks to manoeuvre this, but I got there in the end.

Jeff is amazed and appalled at all the things I'm telling him about Karly and Berenice and the agency. He can't believe the sort of bad behaviour that goes on. I try to explain that it's this weird chemical reaction that happens when people of average talent get paid far too much to do a job that isn't that significant.

'But they're surrounded by all these arse-lickers pandering to their egos, they become convinced they're mini-gods,' I say. 'The power goes to their heads.'

'And other bits of them too by the sounds of it,' he says.

'Ha! Yeah. Oh and then Robbie, the one who's always quoting Nelson Mandela, except Robbie's about as compassionate as Genghis Khan. He's now making us do this ridiculous "Tweet of the Week" on all our projects. I've had to set up a Twitter account for Fat Bird pizzas so that I can be the voice of Fat Bird. Have you ever heard of anything so ridiculous? Like the world is holding its breath to hear what a person pretending to be a chicken pizza has to say about Kate Middleton's hair . . .'

'What's the account name?' he says.

'Fat Bird pizzas, would you believe,' I say. 'But I haven't started Tweeting yet . . .'

'I'll be your first follower,' he says, getting his iPhone out.

'First and last. What's your Twitter name?' I say, holding out my hand for his phone.

He pauses for a moment, then hands it over.

Jeffanjill. 'Jeff Anjill?' I say. He nods. 'What's that about?'

'Just a log in,' he shrugs.

'Go on then, show us your Tweets.'

'It's boring,' he says, taking his phone back. 'Boring stuff. It's more just when I'm bored, I've got a handful of mates who follow me. I'm too old for Twitter.'

'Show me,' I say, peering over his shoulder.

'Alright.' He looks awkward, and hands me his phone.

I scroll down through his Tweets, giggling.

'What's this one?' I say, clicking on a link that says 'Old Boys Reunion'.

'That's just me and some mates from college at the boat race,' he says.

I click on it anyway. 'Ha, you look really pissed in that photo. Actually you look a little bit like Jason Statham in that photo . . . hmmm . . . but you've got nicer eyes.'

'You've got to be joking,' he says, shaking his head in embarrassment.

'Let's see some more . . . oooh, what's this one?' I say, clicking on a link that says 'Saturday Morning Footy', which has a photo of him playing five-a-side.

'Phwoar. You look hot in shorts!' I say, as I enlarge the

section of the photo with him in it. 'Nice legs.' I give his thigh a little squeeze.

'Cheers,' he says, uncomfortably.

I scroll down a bit more and come to a Tweet from about a month ago that says 'Birthday Fun!!!'

'Hey! I bet you're absolutely hammered in this one!' I say, laughing, but he's suddenly gone quiet. The air between us has changed. It's almost imperceptible but there's a sense that he has sobered up while I am still drunk. I pause for a moment before clicking and then my finger hits the screen.

Ah. That'll be why. She's terribly pretty. They look terribly together. They look terribly happy. I feel terrible; overwhelmed by embarrassment to the point of mortifica-tion. And it must be obvious from my face that I am shocked. And yet I have no right whatsoever to be shocked. I never asked him properly if he was single. He never lied and said he was. I just assumed that he was because he was flirting with me. He *was* flirting with me. Boy, was he ever flirting with me.

I swallow hard and try my damnedest to make my face seem exactly the same as it was sixty seconds ago. *Of course* I knew he had a girlfriend, why on *earth* would I feel any sense of disappointment? I haven't been thinking about him much or waiting for something to happen *at all*. I always flirt outrageously with colleagues and squeeze their legs and letch over them, I see it as the height of professionalism . . .

272

He has a guilty look on his face. He knows I didn't realise. He knows I am a tad crestfallen.

'That looks like a super fun night out! Shall I get us another round?' I say, my voice slightly higher than before.

'You want another drink?' he says. He's now the one looking shocked.

'Yeah, yeah, oh absolutely, yeah,' I say, nodding, as if nothing whatsoever has changed, and no significant revelation has happened, or even if it has, so what? I am Mrs Super-Flirt, not Mrs Boring, after all!

I spend the next gin and tonic furiously over-compensating for the fact that I feel so humiliated. I am so relentlessly upbeat I could get a job presenting on CBeebies.

Jeff looks mildly uncomfortable throughout, and when we say goodbye his sense of relief is so palpable I could wrap my arms around it.

Sunday

Is it called lying low because you only do it when you're feeling low?

I can now confirm that it is not the worst thing in the world to lie in bed watching Ryan Gosling movies all day Saturday and most of Sunday. Unfortunately Ryan's body of work is not quite extensive enough to last me through until Sunday night but it's done pretty well nonetheless. *Blue Valentine* is so brilliant and so real and so sad – Michelle Williams is such an amazing actress. And *The Ides of March*, that's a classy film, and those glasses make Ryan look so intelligent. *Crazy Stupid Love*? I laughed out loud at that scene where they go to the mall. I didn't realise Ryan could do funny. Ryan, Ryan, Ryan: how did you get to be so handsome and so versatile? And *Drive*? That scene in the lift where he kisses Carey Mulligan. Honestly? I thought I might pass out from Ryan's sheer hotness.

You know what? I don't have to feel bad about any of this.

First of all, it's the weekend before Polly's wedding and so I've managed to catch up on beauty sleep, paint my toenails, floss twice each day and exfoliate. If I'd gone to a spa I'd have paid a fortune to do those exact same things.

Second of all, that whole misunderstanding with Jeff. Yes I am still utterly humiliated to the point of feeling nauseous, though maybe that's this quite acidic Sauvignon Blanc that's been keeping me company.

But it was just a work crush. A big old work crush. Everyone needs a work crush to get them out of bed in the morning. Jeff doesn't know quite how much I actually fancied him. He has no idea that I feel like a pinball, sprung onto the dating table post-Jake, being flung painfully between creepy young men, creepy old men and no men at all. He doesn't realise that I need someone to help me shift this heartache; it's too heavy to move on my own. How could he know that this, this latest disappointment, this Could Be Something but Actually It's Nothing, feels like just that little bit too much to bear.

And more to the point he is *the* most outrageously flirtatious man I have ever met. He is utterly incorrigible. And I am encourageable. Or am I? Is that even a word? Well, according to Jacob's Creek it's a word. There really should be laws that say you are only allowed to flirt at that level once you've fully disclosed your relationship status. I mean really, 'A girl like you deserves cake' and 'I think you're great'. I could practically sue him for something or other, no doubt. Not that I'll ever be in the same room with him ever again, I'll make sure of that.

Thirdly, I haven't only been lying in bed indulging in a Gosl-a-thon. No, I have been industrious in the extreme.

I've written down two awesome pasta recipes that are appropriate for a post-Jeff concussion. Pasta with crab, chilli and garlic, and pasta for when all hope is gone and all butter . . . I even took photos of the dishes while I cooked them, and have been teaching myself how to do a blog. It's so straightforward I can't believe I haven't started one earlier. Literally all you have to do is type whatever you're thinking and then upload photos from your phone or laptop – it is *so* easy and so much fun! I've called my blog 'Some of my best friends are pasta' and indeed that is how it seems to me this Sunday night . . . And another thing, did you know that De Cecco's rigatoni number 24 is the perfect pasta shape of all time? Pretty, pretty curlicued edges, perfect length, I really love you, rigatoni . . .

So, life, I just want you to know these important things:
- I am productive.
- I am not a loser.
- I am not drunk.
- I am going back to bed now.

w/c 16 April –
three weeks to airdate

Status report:
- Get revised Celina Summer script from new team
  – URGENT URGENT
- Avoid Jeff at all costs
- Give up alcohol (after the wedding, and before the wedding, just not at the wedding)
- Book taxi for wedding
- Tinker with some-of-my-best-friends-are-pasta.co.uk

Monday

Worst. Monday. Evah . . .

Even if I didn't have a violent hangover, this mauling I'm sitting through in Berenice's office would be intolerable.

'. . . You've destroyed Karly and Nick's motivation . . .

We'll have to find another team with no time left . . .
Personally I am deeply disappointed by what I've observed
of your working style . . . For someone who was hoping
to be promoted at Christmas . . .'

There is no point explaining to her that I've done them
all a favour – saved Fletchers from a potential PR disaster
– and that she should actually be presenting me with a
magnum of champagne. And as for Karly and Nick walking
off the project? That right there's a reason to pop the cork . . .

'Really, Susannah, I don't know what you think you're
playing at, suggesting that we research scripts so late in the
day. A colossal error of judgement.'

'I didn't actually suggest it,' I say, realising the minute
that it's out of my mouth that I should not be drawing her
attention to this point.

'Whose idea was it then?' she says, scornfully.

'Well . . . Martin Meddlar's . . .'

'Why on earth would Martin be advising you on that
level of detail?' she says. 'Oh. But of course you've been
spending time with him . . .'

'No! Not at all.'

'I saw you together the other week.'

'Berenice, I bumped into him in the lift and he asked
me how it was all going.'

'If you need advice at senior level I am here for you.
My door is always open. I am your first port of call.' Yes,
and what a warm welcome you give . . .

She tips her head to one side and looks at me. I sense her change tack. 'You do realise, Susannah, that Martin has certain . . . proclivities, don't you?'

Yeah of course. Sam tells me everything about what goes in or up anyone in this building.

'And he is extremely charismatic,' she says, nodding sympathetically.

I feel my face flush with shame though I have done nothing wrong. I mean, the man could be a double for Gollum, though she's right, Martin is charismatic. Mind you, I suppose so is Gollum, in his way.

'Berenice. I don't have any interest in Martin Meddlar like that.'

I actually want to say that I have no interest in him because I find him to be oleaginous and a bit scary; but regardless, she should mind her own bloody beeswax. But I can't say that for obvious reasons. I don't know how to pronounce oleaginous (is that g hard or soft?) I can barely spell it. And I'm not entirely clear what it means, apart from sort of slimy. And I mean, obviously I can't tell Berenice to mind her own beeswax.

'It's not you, it's him,' she says. 'He doesn't just go for pretty little things . . . He probably looks at a thirty-six-year-old unmarried woman and sees an easy target.'

Wow. Ouch. Wowch.

'I'm just looking out for you,' she says. Interesting – feels quite the reverse.

'Berenice, I'm meant to call Devron with an update now, so do you mind if I head off?'

She shakes her head and raises both hands in the air in exasperation. 'This is a disaster.'

Tell me something I don't know.

I need some fresh air to clear my head and work out what to do about this Celina Summer script. As I head out of the revolving doors I see my new best friend Martin standing in the street, waiting.

'We must stop meeting like this,' he says, giving me a kiss. We must if Berenice is spying on me from her window . . . 'How did your research go, darling?'

'You haven't heard? Ah. Well it brought some clarity, in that all the respondents hated the scripts.'

'Ah. Well, some you win, some you lose. At least we discovered that before we went ahead and made the ad.'

'Exactly! But now I need a new creative team urgently, to tidy up Karly and Nick's script, and I'm just trying to figure out how to broach the subject with Robbie . . .'

'Would Andy Ashford do?' he says. 'We're off to Rules now for a catch up, I'll see how busy he is.'

'Really? Andy Ashford would be the perfect person. But don't I need to go through Robbie?'

'No no, Robbie does what I tell him to. Leave it with me.'

Friday

Given that we're shooting the biggest ad of my career next week and we have no script; given that Berenice has accused me of trying to seduce Martin Meddlar and insinuated my demotion is imminent; and given that I've spent the last five days having to email Jeff about work and pretend that whole thigh-squeeze thing didn't happen last Thursday night, I'm surprisingly un-suicidal.

The only reason why is because I'm in Andy Ashford's office. Andy is my favourite creative in the building. He's a dream: talented, polite, genuine, accommodating, helpful – if I could work with him on every brief then I don't think I'd drink quite so much. Even though he's the oldest creative here by a good fifteen years, he has a vitality and a twinkle in his brown eyes that other teams lack.

He's actually made *me* a cup of tea – unheard of! And

when I sit down and deliver him the brief from hell he's totally unfazed.

'Have one of these, it's elevensies,' he says, reaching over with a pack of dark chocolate digestives as I apologise for the sixth time since entering his office for dumping this on him.

That's another thing I love about Andy! His office! It doesn't have Pirelli calendar girls on the wall. It doesn't have rude words illustrated in Gothic fonts, or framed Chelsea shirts. It has posters of his favourite ads of the last fifty years, including one with my favourite line of all time. It's from an old campaign for Rich Tea biscuits: "A drink's too wet without one".

Brilliant; it gives you an excuse to eat a biscuit every time you have a cup of tea.

'So Susie, all you need me to do is tidy this up, make Celina a bit more likeable and say the pizzas are half the calories?' I nod. 'Does 2 p.m. sound alright?' he says, smiling.

I go round and give him a little hug. 'You're a life-saver, Andy. It's better than alright.' Because now I can send Devron a script this afternoon that I know he'll approve. And then I won't have to think about work, and instead I can think about enjoying myself at the wedding.

I bump into Sam as I'm leaving the office at 6 p.m. 'You look remarkably happy,' he says.

'Happy client, for once; he's just signed off the new script,' I say, smiling and feeling a little bit of excitement about tomorrow start to creep in.

'You should do happy more often, Susie. It suits you.'

Saturday

Today's the big day: Polly's wedding!

Most of my friends got married in their late twenties. Back then, every other month saw us trekking to Hampshire or across to Bath or up to Derby, to beautiful old churches, and country house hotels and marquees. Mostly my friends had classic wedding cakes, iced and white, flowers and bows. And then there was the occasional cake that was a cheese cake – not a cheesecake, but an artful piling up of cheeses, tiered to look like a cake, with jars of 'Ben and Lucy's Wedding Chutney' for every guest to take home. Back then there were no wedding cakes that were stacks of cupcakes.

The last wedding I went to was four years ago, out in Cape Town. Jake's boss, Steve-O, a confirmed bachelor, was tying the knot with a South African girl he'd met seven months beforehand. It had been a lavish affair, a different wine and wine glass with every course, champagne all night and a sparkling view out over Camps Bay. I'd worn this dress for it: a lovely jade silk number from Anthropologie. Yet standing looking at myself now in my bedroom mirror I suddenly have a horrible flashback to the way I had actually felt at that wedding: desperately unglamorous compared to all the women wearing statement jewellery, micro-clutch bags and Gina platform heels.

Weddings are all about accessories, I figure, and that's one thing I'm rubbish at. I should have made more effort to keep on top of trends. That's another thing that's making me feel . . . not *old*, just not *young*. I need a spruce. This outfit just looks boring. Nice. But boring. Anthropologie dress and a blazer from Zara. Classic round-toed black heels. Nice. Boring. Nice. Boring. I could be going to an AGM dressed like this. It doesn't feel fitting for the occasion.

I've booked an appointment at a chi-chi hairdresser in Hampstead that has fifty per cent off with Groupon. I'm due there in half an hour – my timings are already screwed as it is. But this will not do. I never thought I'd find myself in urgent need of a fascinator, but I definitely need something – something sparkly or frivolous, to put some oomph into this outfit.

Oh no! Maybe it's actually the dress that's wrong . . . Why did I not treat myself to a new dress for this wedding? I knew I should have. Why did I let those silly girls in the boutique deter me so easily from my mission? I should have gone to Westfield instead of Regent's Park; or Selfridges one night after work last week.

And now I look at myself it is most definitely the dress that's the problem, not just the lack of accessories. I hate this outfit, *I hate it*. I take off the blazer and fling it on the bed. This is a party, damn it! A celebration of hope and of love and of happiness, not of increased profitability and like-for-like growth.

I wade through my wardrobe . . .

No, too short.

Too tight, that never fitted properly first time round . . .

Too pink, need a tan for that one.

Ah, now this dress could work, but where's the belt? Can't find the belt, doesn't work without the belt . . .

How about this one? Black: lace, slightly-off-the-shoulder from Autograph. It's sexy and ladylike. This is fail-safe usually, though today it's making me look drained. I thought little black dresses were always meant to save the day. Brilliant. I've got nothing to wear at all.

Oh, but hold on. Hold on one minute . . . Now this one I love. I've forgotten all about this dress because it's too nice to wear, and if you spill something on it then it's a hassle because it's dry-clean only . . . But the colour of it is so fabulous! Purple, like an iris, and for some reason that colour makes my hair look more auburn than mouse. And with those two ribbon straps at the shoulder that form a low V at the back, classy yet really understatedly sexy.

The last time I wore this dress . . . I think it was my second anniversary with Jake, and oh yes, that's right . . . We'd gone to Claridge's for a drink, and while he was in the loo and I was standing at the bar waiting, a beautiful Argentinian man had tried to chat me up. He'd said that I was the most elegant woman in the bar, which was the first and last time anyone's ever said that to me. He'd kissed me on the shoulder when he'd said goodbye. All credit to the dress – it's that kind of a dress. Yes, this is the one. And damn the discomfort, I'm wearing the five-inch silver strappy heels. If my feet hurt I'll just drink my way through the pain.

Midday already! I pull on my jeans and a t-shirt and race out to the street. No time to walk or get the bus so I hail a cab to the hairdressers – so much for trying to save money.

'I've got a 12.15 p.m. with Shelley,' I say. 'A wash and blow-dry with a Groupon voucher.'

Her interest slightly wanes. 'Have a seat, she's just finishing someone's colour, she won't be a moment.'

But she's more than a moment. It's now 12.40 p.m. and I'm shampooed but still waiting in the chair, anxiously looking at my watch. The wedding starts at 2 p.m. I should never have cut it so fine, I shouldn't have chanced this to Groupon. I'm an idiot. I can't be late. I'm going to be late. I can't be late.

'Excuse me, could someone else do the blow-dry? It's just I'm late . . .'

'She won't be a sec, can I get you a coffee?' says one of the other girls.

'No, but you can get me a hairdryer?' I say. 'I'll start drying it myself, if that's OK?'

'Better wait for Shelley,' she says.

'Please just get me a hairdryer,' I say.

12.55 p.m. and I've dried the underneath parts OK, though not as straight or as shiny as I'd like. Now Shelley's here and she's obviously not happy that I've taken the law into my own hands, because she's pulling my hair really very hard from my roots, and a few hairs have actually pinged out in the process. Still, she does a good enough job and I pay her thirty pounds for eight minutes of labour, then race out of the door.

OK, it's fine. If I get a cab from my house at 1.30 p.m. I'll be there at 1.55 p.m., it'll be OK. I call my local minicab firm as I speedwalk down the hill but they've got no cars till 2 p.m. I hang up, panic rising in me. I call the other local cab company and it's the same story. What the hell is wrong with me? Why didn't I book this cab earlier? I meant to. Every wedding, every holiday Jake and I went on, I used to have to organise every detail and I've never missed a flight or been late before. Why today? By the time I get back to the flat, red-faced and sweating, it's 1.12 p.m. I'm going to miss the ceremony.

'Terry!' I say, spotting him talking to the Langdons in the forecourt. 'Terry, I'm so sorry but is there any chance you can find me a cab in the street, I'll be down in ten?'

The Langdons give me a filthy look. First of all I've interrupted them complaining about the proposed new paint colour for the radiators in the communal hallway. And secondly, this is not an appropriate request to make of the caretaker.

'I wouldn't ask normally, but it's my friend's wedding and I've mis-timed everything.' I point at my jeans and un-made-up face.

'Not a problem, love. I'll see what I can do,' he says, delighted to have an excuse to rid himself of the Langdons, at least temporarily.

I race up to the fifth floor, and have the world's quickest shower – sixty seconds – keeping my new hair well away from the water. Thank goodness I shaved my legs this morning, but make-up needs doing. Shit, 1.19 p.m. already . . .

I put on foundation and blusher and calculate if I have time to curl my eyelashes – yes, just about, ten seconds' squeezing time each side in the little metal mangle. OK, don't rush the eyeliner now or you'll have to start over. Please let there be a cab out there, please Terry, don't let me down. I can do the mascara in the cab. OK, dress on. Christ, nearly forgot deodorant. Calm down. Dress on, deodorant, perfume. Oh, and another tooth clean, bollocks! I have forgotten how to be a lady. It has been too long.

By the time I've sorted out cash, keys, bag, make-up touch ups, and locked my front door, it's 1.35 p.m. I could almost cry when I see Terry downstairs, chatting to a cabbie, looking in my direction.

'Thank you, I owe you big time,' I say.

'You look stunning,' he says. 'Terrific dress. Mind you don't break your neck in them shoes.'

Finally. In the cab, on the way. Shit! I've forgotten my phone. Doesn't matter, you don't need a phone at a wedding . . .

At every red traffic light I put on a little more mascara, then lip liner and a little gloss. OK, it's actually OK. You look nice. You've done OK.

We pull up at the registry office with two minutes to spare, and as I bolt up the stairs as fast as these heels will allow I vow I will never be such an idiot again. I'm nearly thirty-seven years old. I've been dressing myself and moving myself round this city on time for a long time now.

Everyone is already seated, looking expectantly at the door. I must be the last one in as the door shuts behind me. I take a seat at the back, smiling awkwardly and waving at Polly's parents and at Maisie as I shuffle along the row, banging into knees and the backs of chairs. Dave is standing at the front, hands clasped nervously behind his back, looking excitedly at the door. He looks so handsome in his three-piece navy suit, a cream rose in his buttonhole. I give him a warm smile and he gives a little wave back.

Made it to my seat! And with sixty whole seconds to look around and take in the atmosphere. It's a small ceremony – maybe sixty of us gathered. Apart from Polly's family, everyone else is in a couple holding hands, apart from me and one other woman, about my age, in the back row. Impossible to avoid your own single-ness at a wedding. That's fine, I think. You're not here to pull, you're here to celebrate with everyone. I don't recognise many of these faces though, apart from her family. Polly and I have always been close, but she and Dave have a group of friends that I don't know at all.

This set up is quite different from her first wedding. That was in St John's Church in Holland Park – beautiful, traditional – and she walked down the aisle to Handel's *Queen of Sheba*. Lovely, of course, and I cried immediately. But it was all very formal. Spencer's parents were raging West London snobs. I could almost see the disappointment on their faces that Polly, this rag-tag regular North London girl, who'd been to a *comp*, not even a public school, had scrubbed up quite so spectacularly, and they couldn't find anything to be snotty about.

This time round, though, Polly has decided to be true to herself. There's a moment's hush as the door opens again, and then Polly takes one step into the room and all our eyes light up, at fireworks. She looks extraordinary. Standing there in a silk crepe, Edwardian bias-cut dress the colour of the sky after rain just before the sun breaks through. It has a low neck and tiny flowers with seed pearls and crystal beads adorning the bodice. The sleeves are made of lighter silk with a tiny puff at the shoulder, and behind her flows a train of the same silk with the initials 'P & D' made into a flower, like a Rennie Mackintosh rose.

Her red hair hangs softly around her shoulders and at the crown of her head is pinned a cream lace head-dress with tiny silk rosettes sewn into the border, which falls in waves down her back. In her hands she holds a simple posy of palest pink and ivory roses and sweet peas. She looks so amazing that even though I have vowed not to blub at this wedding I immediately start to cry.

She stands there and pauses for a minute trying to compose herself but already she's teary-eyed and can't contain the huge smile on her face. And then the music starts. And it's so very Polly, still a Goth at heart. No Handel this time. Instead she's chosen The Cure's 'Just Like Heaven'. And as the opening bars start and she saunters down the aisle I know this is going to be a special day.

The service is wonderful. Second time round, simple vows, we'll try our best. I've no doubt these two are going to make it work. They belong together. Look at them, holding each other's fingers, both trying not to cry and laugh as they repeat their vows. There is just one reading, at the end. Polly's dad recites a poem by Raymond Carver, called 'Late Fragment'. Just six lines, six lines about love, but oh what lines. Even Polly's brother has to borrow a tissue from his girlfriend. She really does look young, that one. Even if Jake wasn't also going out with someone in her early twenties, I'm sure I'd still think it was slightly tragic. She makes him look older than he is, not younger.

It's all over so quickly though, and it's only as we're standing on the steps of the registry office, confetti in hand waiting for the bride and groom to emerge, that I realise something was missing from the service. Or rather, someone: Daniel McKendall. I feel a little punch of disappointment, like a promise has been broken. I had so been looking forward to seeing him. Even at Christmas that time, I remember coming away from the pub thinking, above all else, I like who this man has become. I like talking to him. I like being around him. Still, probably just as well. He's no doubt gone to New York to visit his wife and son, where he should be.

On the coach on the way to the restaurant, I sit next to the other single girl who was on the back row a few seats along from me during the ceremony. I smile at her but she gives me only the faintest smile back. Maybe the ceremony made her feel more single too. Still, we're all in this together, aren't we?

'It was a lovely service, wasn't it?' I say.

'Beautiful,' she says.

'And didn't Polly look amazing? That dress, I can't believe it wasn't some mega designer.'

'It wasn't?' she says.

'Her friend Nanette made it, she's brilliant,' I say.

She nods.

'You must be a friend of Dave then?' I say.

'I'm Amy. I used to work with him when he was at the *Guardian*.'

'Ah right. Are you still there then?'

'God no, I left six years ago. I can't imagine working in an office ever again. I hated it.'

'So what do you do now?'

'I still do graphic design, but I'm freelance now and my fiancé is an illustrator, so we can work from anywhere. We're just back from a year in Amsterdam and thinking about where to go next.'

Fiancé? Ah, yes. She has a ring. God, I'm even disappointed when the women I think are single are actually taken, let alone the men.

'Is your fiancé not coming to the wedding then?'

'He's coming to the party, he couldn't make the service, that's all,' she says.

Oh. I thought I'd have someone else who was single to hang out with.

'That's nice,' I say. 'And when are you getting married?'

'August Bank Holiday weekend, down in Rye.'

'At The George?'

'You know it?'

I do. I was lying in a bed at The George on my thirty-fifth birthday weekend, Jake in the shower, when I realised he wasn't in love with me any more. I remember staring at the lamp on the bedside table for about twenty minutes while it dawned on me that our relationship was not what he wanted. Was not what I wanted. And that I really didn't know what, if anything, I was going to do about it.

Nothing, as it turned out. I left the doing to him.

I hate that hotel.

The coach pulls up at the restaurant and as we climb out all I can think about is how quickly I can get to the alcohol. We leave our coats with the door check, walk through a short corridor, and then we're in a room so gorgeous that it instantly banishes the ghost of memory that was hovering over me.

In the dining area, six long weathered wooden tables are laid out with simple white linen cloths, china plates, and silver cutlery. Instead of flowers there are glass vases from which stem dark wooden branches that have handmade paper cherry blossoms along them, and a scattering of tiny little blue feather birds nestling. Between the vases, antique silver tea light holders cast a warm, reflective glow over the room, creating pools of shimmering light.

Over to the right is a dance floor decked out with a canopy strung with warm white star-shaped fairy lights. And on a table at the back is the cake, which is hands down the best wedding cake I've ever seen. I can't believe Polly managed to keep this a secret from me – it's phenomenal. Five square tiers of white chocolate buttercream cake are stacked on top of each other. Each layer of cake is bordered by tall panels of white chocolate, at alternating heights, like a delicate, edible fence. Between each tier is a two-inch ledge that has been filled with tiny wild strawberries that mark out a scarlet border between each layer of the tower. It looks like the world's tastiest skyscraper, the fruits gathered on each layer jostling for the best view.

A waiter comes over with a tray of Proseccos with fresh raspberries floating on the surface like jewels. I carefully take one and wander through the room, smiling randomly at people I don't know and hoping to strike up small talk. I'm sure these people are normally friendly. But a single woman in her mid-thirties with a drink in her hand at a wedding is not so much a potential liability as a grenade. Having had a lovely chat about golf with Polly's great uncle Cecil and caught up with her parents, I walk back over to the dining tables to have a closer inspection, putting on a smile that's meant to convey *I'm never happier than when I'm alone at a wedding* . . .

I haven't seen a seating plan anywhere, but on the back of each wooden chair, tied to the top with string, is a little cardboard luggage tag place card. On one side is a silver heart motif, and on the other is written each guest's name. I wonder whom Polly's seated me next to in the end. Hopefully it's not that girl on the coach or her boyfriend. And I could do without sitting next to great uncle Cecil . . .

Let's have a look, where's my tag then . . . no, no, not me . . . where am I? . . .

'You're next to me,' says a familiar voice behind me that makes me jump so suddenly I nearly spill my drink down the top of my dress.

I turn.

It's him.

It's been five years and four months since the last time. Twenty-three years and nine months since the first time.

And still, still he's as gorgeous as that very first day in Polly's garden, lying back on the grass smoking a cigarette and looking like the coolest thing I'd ever seen. If anything he's getting better with age, bastard. His dark brown hair is untouched by grey, and his pale blue eyes are still full of sparkle and mischief. He has the most beautiful mouth of any man I've ever known. Or maybe it's not the mouth. No. It's the space between his mouth and his chin: a perfect indent between his bottom lip and that straight, square jaw. Good old menthol-smoking Krista McKendall and her perfect Danish bone structure; well almost. Daniel's beautiful, straight nose, that I used to love tracing my finger down, broken by a rugby ball when he was in the sixth form up in Edinburgh. And now that bump in his nose just makes him even more handsome.

He gives me a hug that lasts about half a minute, then puts his hands on my almost bare shoulders and looks at me. He breaks into a huge smile, and I automatically do the same, though for some reason I try to hide it, which must look peculiar.

'I was looking forward to seeing you,' he says, 'you look so well!'

I stop myself saying 'It's the blusher and the blow-dry.' Instead I say, 'You look well too, old friend.'

'Wow, Susie, I mean it, you haven't changed at all really . . .' he says, looking at me thoughtfully. He shakes his head. 'I can't believe how great you look.'

'I found my first grey hair the other day! You're not supposed to pull them out, are you?' I say, as we take our seats at the table.

'Seriously, you look exactly the same as I remember you, up on the roof all those years ago.'

'Ha, the good old days on your roof! How's your family?' I say.

'Dad's OK, I was just with him earlier. Getting old, it's no fun at all. And Joe's on the mend . . .'

'How's Krista? She still with Albert?'

'No, she kicked him out, wants to do her own thing. She's gone to some massively expensive ashram to focus on her inner goddess or something,' he says, laughing.

'She was always that way inclined . . .'

'So Polly tells me you're doing really well in your job,' he says. 'Sounds very glamorous.'

'Let's not talk about work at a wedding! But more importantly, how are you? I hear you've got a lot going on?'

He shakes his head slightly. 'Been a difficult year . . . let's not talk about that either.'

298

Well if we don't talk about work or family or relationships, what's left to talk about? Plenty, as it turns out. We
natter our way through mozzarella, figs and Parma ham,
then roast lamb and dauphinoise potatoes and finally the
amazing cake, without stopping for breath. Two hours pass
and it feels like five minutes. He is on such good form, I'd
forgotten how much we think alike, even though our lives
have gone in such different directions. We should have
made more of an effort to stay friends over the years. It's
such a shame that you often lose your male friends to their
relationships. Mind you, I suppose we were always more
than just friends.

I can't quite get over how good he looks. I glance around
the room – it's full of couples. Daniel and I must look like
a couple. A new couple though – still in that excited,
discovery stage, though we also share the past. I catch a
glimpse of Dave. He has this look on his face, like he can't
believe his luck, to have found this woman, to have found
such joy. Sod being self-sufficient: I want a man to look at
me that way again.

This is how I would have wanted my wedding to be.
There is singing. There is laughing. There is toasting. There
is an awful lot of drinking. And above all there is dancing.
Polly and Dave have chosen Roxy Music's 'Let's Stick
Together' as their first dance, and after that each song is
better than the last, no duff choices at all. There's The
Cure, of course, but then The Eurythmics, Erasure, good

early Madonna, The B52s (but 'Rock Lobster' not 'Love Shack'), Happy Mondays, Stone Roses, Guns N' Roses. Daniel and I used to go down to Our Price on Saturday afternoons to buy this music; I bet I've still got half of these on cassingles in a shoebox somewhere at home.

Daniel grabs my hand and drags me to the dance floor the minute 'Sweet Dreams' comes on, and for four hours we dance like maniacs, only stopping to rehydrate with wine, then gin and tonics and then brandies. We are the last ones on the dance floor.

At 1.30 a.m. the lights go up and the last record goes on – Roxy Music again, this time 'Avalon'. My eye make-up has smudged, my hair looks a mess and my foundation has slid off. My feet are in tatters from these ridiculous shoes and I couldn't care less. I feel high.

'Shall we share a cab back north then?' says Daniel, finally helping me on with my coat.

'North?'

'I was never going to make the last train from Waterloo . . .'

Is he inviting himself to stay at mine? Should I offer him my sofa?

'Where are you going to stay?' I say.

'At Joe's in Kilburn,' he says. His brother. I'm relieved and disappointed in equal measure. 'You're still in your granny's place in Swiss Cottage, right?'

'You remember!'

'Course! I loved your granny. She used to make that amazing custard pudding.' I love the fact that he remembers this.

In the cab back to mine he puts his arm around me instinctively and I rest my head on his shoulder. I do this without thinking and it is only once my head has been resting there for a moment that I realise this might not be a good idea. I can't bring myself to move though. It feels so natural, so comfortable being this close to him again, and I love listening to him talk. That voice that sounds like he's just got out of bed: warm and deep with a smile in it always.

As we pass the petrol station about half a mile from my flat he asks the cabbie to pull over.

'Fancy sharing a pack of Consulate for old times' sake?' he says.

'I don't smoke any more but you go ahead,' I say.

'I don't either,' he says. 'Rarely, anyway. But I have a sudden craving.'

'Sure,' I say. 'Shall I wait in the cab?'

'How about we walk back to yours from here and I'll pick up another cab when I've seen you safely home?'

My heart starts to beat a little faster. We are both drunk. I have never been in this situation and I don't know how this works or what I should do.

'Are you sure?' I say. 'What if you can't find another cab? It's late . . .'

'We'll be fine.' We. We. We not I.

We sit on the wall outside my block and we talk. We talk about all the things we wanted to do in life and all the things we can't believe we actually did, and all the things we still plan to do but at this rate never will.

It is only when the sky has lightened to grey and we are looking at our morning-after faces in the light that he finally looks at his watch.

'Shit. It's nearly six! I'd better bust a move,' he says. 'I promised Joe I'd go to Ikea with him. It's bad enough normally, let alone with no sleep and a hangover . . .'

'Do you want me to call you a minicab?' I say, a tiny twinge in my heart as I think how much I'd like him to stay by my side, just a little bit longer.

'It's fine, I'll head over to Finchley Road and get a bus or a tube or something . . . Man, it was so good to see you, Susie. I can't believe how good it was . . . you're just . . . yeah . . . you look great . . . it was great . . . You're such great company . . .'

He wraps me in a big hug, then holds me away briefly while he smiles and looks at me, and then kisses me on the mouth, for a moment, for quite a long moment. Before I have time to react he's walking away and I watch his back, wishing for all the world that I could see the expression on his face right now.

I stumble into my flat, kick off my shoes, unzip my dress and let it fall to the floor, then climb into bed in my underwear. There is no one in the whole world who had more fun than me tonight, I think, as I finally rest my head on my pillow as the birds start to sing.

I feel like I have woken from a deep sleep.

I remember how it feels to be happy.

w/c 23 April – SHOOT WEEK

Status report:
- Sign off budget, location, wardrobe
- Shoot – Thursday/Friday/Saturday
- Buy chocolates for Mum and Dad before Sunday

Thursday

Andy Ashford and I have been scrabbling around with a production company doing location and casting and budgets for the last three days. I have been working till midnight flat out and thank goodness for that. It's meant I haven't had too much of a chance to think about last weekend. Why did Daniel kiss me? Why did I let him? Why did I let him leave without giving him my number? Because he's a married man, that's why. Now get back to work.

Today Andy and I are finally on set, on day one of our three-day shoot for Fat Bird. We're on location in a five-storey house in Notting Hill, in a vast room that's designed to look like Celina Summer's kitchen. The set looks gorgeous: white painted brick walls, a marble-topped kitchen island and six stunning over-sized hanging pendant lights with bright pink interiors that cost eleven hundred quid each. For a light!

I can't believe we've actually made it after all the pain of the last two months. We would never have made it to this point if Karly and Nick were still on the job because Karly would have said those lights were too cheap, and this house was too small, and actually now they've had a chance to really think about it, the only person who could possibly direct the script is Martin Scorsese and he's not available until 2018.

Karly would have insisted on executive directing Celina's wardrobe personally – escorting a stylist down to Selfridges and then picking out everything she wanted from next season's look books – then walking off set with them at the end of the day. Luckily Andy Ashford's not the type to combine a floral Erdem bomber jacket with a monochrome Louis Vuitton skirt and Prada geisha-style wooden heels, so I haven't had to worry about the budget being blown on clothes.

Devron's sitting over there in the director's chair next to Mandy, reading the paper and eating his way through a bowl of Celebrations. I've been despatched twice already to the organic shop on Westbourne Grove to fetch Celina some vegan cheese, and then some supergreen juice. I have no idea why Celina agreed to advertise pizzas made with wheat and dairy if she's truly allergic to them, though I suspect she's faking it – I'm sure I saw a Twix in her handbag earlier. Actually I know exactly why she's agreed to advertise these pizzas: all two hundred and fifty thousand reasons.

All Celina has to do today is talk directly to camera and say this: 'The truth is, it's tricky to stay in shape when there are so many temptations. The truth is, staying slim can be such hard work. But with these new Fat Bird pizzas from Fletchers, you get all the flavour, with only half the calories. Delicious – ain't that the truth!'

(Devron forced the end line onto the script, but it's not too bad, all things considered.)

The rest of the ad will be made up of 'money shots' of the various pizzas that we'll shoot tomorrow and Saturday.

So: a script with fifty words. You'd think, if you were being paid five thousand pounds for each word you had to say, that you might perhaps have found the time to practise at home beforehand? Or even in the Mercedes that picked you up from Hampstead and drove you here this morning? But no, it seems Celina finds the whole talking and looking to camera thing super-challenging. And that is why we are still here at 10 p.m., on Take 86 of the final line . . .

My phone's been on silent all day – you can't have a phone ringing in the background when you're filming, as Devron is finally beginning to comprehend . . .

And so it is not until we wrap for the day at midnight, and I am finally sitting in the back of a taxi on my way back to my flat, that I actually check my phone.

Four missed calls:

Dalia. (No doubt back from Miami and feeling guilty.)

My mum. (No doubt checking I haven't forgotten I'm due for lunch on Sunday.)

Sam. (Probably checking I'm still sane and haven't walked off set.)

And one from a number that I don't recognise, but they've left a message.

I call voicemail and my heart leaps when I hear his voice. It's Daniel. I feel a flutter of happiness which lasts for as long as I remember that he is not actually single. Perhaps two whole seconds.

He hopes I don't mind but he got my number from Polly's brother and he just wanted to check in and say hi and to call him back and that's all really.

Friday

The whole of Friday morning has been spent filming The Cheese Pull.

The Cheese Pull is the money shot, the wonder lick, the ultimate in melted cheese in motion. The most important five seconds of this ad, without a doubt. If Devron could have continuous Cheese Pull for thirty seconds he would; in fact he'd have twenty-four-hour Cheese Pull TV. The Cheese Pull is the action from the moment a slice of pizza is lifted and separated from its neighbouring slice, to the moment where it disappears out of shot. According to Fletchers' extensive research there's a direct correlation between the length of Cheese Pull in an ad and their share price – it's Pavlov's dog in Dolby stereo.

As well as being incredibly important, it is also incredibly hard to film. The cheese snaps too soon, or is too stringy or is not stringy enough. The home economist has been working flat out with Jeff since 7.30 a.m. to try and get the viscosity of this cheese right; it's not easy with regular cheese, let alone this scary low-calorie substitute. I watch them work together over in the corner and I witness Jeff in action with another woman and it is enlightening.

This is the first time I've seen him since the pub, though we've spoken quite a bit on email, mostly about work. I have calmed down considerably and, while I'm still embarrassed about the leg-squeeze thing, I have come to realise that I over-reacted slightly. For Jeff is one of those men who loves the attention of women just for the sake of it; he loves to flirt and he's terribly good at it. He is like a male version of Rebecca – a massive flirt, for whom flirtation is like breathing – they don't even think about it, and they don't mean any harm by it.

The only other man who flirts with me as heavily as Jeff does is Martin Meddlar, whom I consider to be a letch because I don't fancy him. But Jeff is more attractive, and therefore Jeff is not a letch. Also I suspect Meddlar would follow through with me, whereas I think Jeff would not – for him, flirtation is a hobby, not a goal-based mission.

I was embarrassed because I didn't know Jeff had a girl-friend. But if that first time I'd met him when I asked 'Do you go to the cinema much?' and he'd said 'My girlfriend and I go a lot' then I would have been embarrassed in a different way. In a way that says, 'You don't need to shout that you've got a girlfriend, I was only trying to make polite

309

conversation.' Though at least it would have saved me rather a lot of time spent daydreaming. The Jeff incident has reinforced what my mum always says: if a man wants to call you then he'll call you.

Which reminds me. Daniel called me. I must call him back.

I have not called Daniel back earlier because once I call him then I will have called him and that will be that. I'll have nothing left to look forward to. And what if he says, 'I kissed you because I was totally drunk' or 'I kissed you because I felt sorry for you' or something awfully mean about that almost-kiss on Sunday morning? Though Daniel's not the mean type; he's never mean at all.

When we finally break for lunch I take a deep breath, take my phone out of my bag and step outside to call him. As it rings at his end I feel my heart start to beat a little faster; I feel nervous, a little excited.

'Hey you!' he says. 'I had such a great time the other night. I haven't had that much fun in years.'

'It was fun, wasn't it,' I say, thinking that this is the first time we've ever spoken to each other on a mobile phone. Back in the day it was landline to landline, usually with my brother or his brother trying to eavesdrop at one end.

'I've missed talking to you,' he says. 'Even though we haven't seen each other for such a long time, it felt like we could just pick up mid-conversation.'

'I know what you mean,' I say, feeling a little wave of

happiness surge up inside me. 'I had a really good time too.'

'Hey, can we hang out again? You know I'm up in London quite a lot, and you're only a few stops from my brother. It'd be so nice to see you, to have a mate to hang out with.'

'You must have plenty of other mates,' I say.

'Sure,' he says, 'but it's just nice hanging out with a girl who's a mate. I don't have many girl mates left. Brooke's quite jealous.'

'What does she have to be jealous about?'

'Nothing, obviously!' he says. 'Listen: I'm off to New York this weekend, but maybe we could do something next weekend? I'm with Dad next Saturday morning and then I'm meeting Joe on the South Bank at 6 p.m., but we could meet somewhere central-ish around 3 p.m.?'

I can't think of any reason not to meet him. Other than that it's a bad idea.

'Shall we say Marylebone High Street at 3 p.m. then?' I say. 'Up at the top, near the church – we could grab a coffee and go for a walk in Regent's Park?'

'Perfect, see you then.'

Sunday

A trip to see my parents will take my mind off Daniel McKendall.

They live out in Chesham and I get stuck in traffic from Brent Cross all the way along the M1. I wonder what Daniel's up to in New York? I wonder if he's thinking about me at all? Do they stay in the city at the weekends or go upstate? I turn on the radio to distract myself . . . thanks Radio 4, a documentary on the history of Ellis Island, helpful . . . And now on Money Box a discussion about the hidden costs of divorce . . . What's on Heart FM . . . 'Jolene' . . . Consider myself thoroughly distracted.

I finally pull up outside my parents' house at 12.30. 'You're late,' says my mum, opening the front door and giving me a brief kiss. 'I hope you're not hungry. There's only a few bits and pieces.' She heads back to the living room to finish her knitting.

Every time I come round here, my mother cooks enough food for a medium-sized wedding reception. No doubt it's her subliminal hint that my nuptials are long overdue; 'How come Polly's managed to find two husbands and you haven't even found one?' I'm not sure she's forgiven me for that brief fling I had six years ago when she thought I was going to end up with the next James Dyson. 'He's not that sort of genius, Mum. He works in the Apple Store.'

My parents have gone past the point of fearing I might be a lesbian. They've gone past the point of hoping I am a lesbian and that I might meet a nice girl. Mum thinks the problem is that I'm too fussy. How do I explain that fussy doesn't come into it? I just can't settle down with a man who tries to get his nob out in a nightclub on a first date.

I take off my coat and follow my mother through into the living room.

'Hello darling,' says my dad, his eyes glued to the test match. 'Good week?'

'It is now,' I say, walking into the kitchen and seeing lunch: a roast chicken, a huge tray of crunchy potatoes roasted in butter and olive oil, a beautiful green salad. And most importantly, a large avocado on the side! The dinner table of my childhood was a scene of combat played out over avocados. My brother's job was to lay the table, mine was to clear. But if a meal involved an avocado then my dad – a man who normally never set foot in the kitchen – would leap to help like a Girl Scout on her first day.

If a salad crowned with those pale green jewels ever made it to the table un-pillaged, there'd ensue a series of moves and counter-moves as my family did battle for equal share. Sleights of hand, sleights of mouth, an occasional slap. As the youngest and weakest I invariably ended up with the least. Perhaps my mother was trying to teach me to assert myself via the salad bowl. Dog eat dog/dog luckily not eat avocado.

I consider cutting open the avocado and eating half, just to see my mother's reaction, but figure that I'm going to annoy her enough once I start telling her about my latest master plan – no point antagonising her prematurely.

'How was the wedding?' she asks, as I set the table and she finally manages to drag my father from the cricket. 'Don't let me forget I've got a little present for Polly.'

'It was so beautiful,' I say. 'I'll send you a photo when she's back from honeymoon.'

'Did you meet any single men?' she says, picking out the crunchiest potato in the tray for herself, then thinking twice and putting it on my dad's plate. She is softening in her old age. My dad is normally the sentimental one – he cries if England win the cricket. My mum would take a crossbow to a kitten if she thought the kitten was eyeing up her space in the Waitrose car park.

'No, Mum, there are no single men left. Though guess who I sat next to?'

'I can't remember who's who . . .' she says.

'Daniel McKendall.' Just saying his name gives me a little thrill.

'I hope you weren't smoking again?' she says. Aah, she can't remember who's who, but she can remember I smoked a few fags with him twenty-three years ago . . .

'He's hasn't changed at all,' I say. I find myself wanting to talk about him to someone, anyone, just so that I can have him in the room with me. 'We're having coffee next weekend.'

'Didn't he get married years ago?'

'Yes, but his wife lives in New York.'

'So he is married.' That's one way of looking at it . . . But here's another way: he was mine before he was hers.

'Oh, forget I mentioned him. He's just a friend. Anyway, I need to talk to you . . .'

'Don't tell me,' she says. 'You're thinking of leaving your job.'

'Don't say it like that, Mum! I am. And I just need you to prepare yourself for the fact.'

'You've been saying this for years,' she says. 'Forgive me if I don't take you too seriously.'

'I fully support you,' says my dad. 'Miserable sounding place. I don't mean support you *financially* of course, but if you've got a good idea, you should go for it.'

315

'You're out of your mind, the pair of you,' says my mum. 'Don't you read the papers? This recession's worse than the Great Depression. You'll be foraging for food in bins like those poor people I read about in the *Observer Food Magazine*.'

'Mum, they're called Urban Foragers and it's very trendy nowadays. Anyway, why can't I have a normal conversation with you about this? I am going to pursue an alternative, more creative career.' I daren't mention the word blog to her – she'll think I'm trying to be the new Belle du Jour . . .

'If you are actually serious about leaving the agency, Uncle Alfred's looking for someone to help run his business,' she says.

'Mum, I have *zero interest* in the finer points of screeding. I don't care about comparative pour rates of glue viscosities, Uncle Alfred's office doesn't even have the internet, in fact I'm pretty sure it doesn't have an inside toilet, so will you please never mention Uncle Alfred's business to me ever again!' This is why I don't come round here more often – I instantly revert to being a teenage brat.

'You can't go off to your room in a huff, dear,' says my dad, trying not to laugh. 'Your mother's using it as one giant wool cupboard.'

'Your brother's talking about buying a second place in France,' says Mum, pointedly.

'Bully for him.' I say.

'If you are serious about leaving, darling,' says Dad, 'then you should sit down carefully and work out how much you need to live on and still pay your bills.'

'Yes, of course I'll do that. I will do that today.'

I clear the table just to cut short the conversation.

'Make sure you take some of that chicken home with you, dear,' my mum calls out. 'There's too much just for the two of us.'

'Yeah, yeah, yeah,' I say, already wrapping it in foil.

'Now make us some coffee and then you can help your father sort out all your piles of old junk in the spare room,' she says.

My dad looks at me with his eyebrows raised. I shake my head.

'Cricket doesn't finish till around 6 p.m.,' he says to my mum. 'We can do it next time.'

'Besides,' I say to her. 'I'm actually going to go home in a bit and do this spreadsheet.'

'Believe it when I see it,' she says, picking up her knitting and settling herself into her chair for the rest of the day.

Laptop out, and I'm an hour into this spreadsheet of how little I can afford to live on.

Seven hundred and fifty quid just for the roof over my head every month. And then all the normal utilities of course. And council tax will be going up again . . .

There's no way I can live without a mobile phone, that would be ridiculous.

And I guess I need contents insurance . . . And the internet – I mean, obviously I can't run a blog without the internet . . . oh, and the TV licence . . .

And then my car, insurance, MOT, tax, monthly costs of running . . .

Sweet lord, I'm surprised I can even live on my current salary. There's no way I can give up my job. How can anyone afford to live in this city?

It's not even like I go anywhere fancy or buy expensive clothes.

OK, let's strip this right back. What can I compromise on and what can't I live without?

No new clothes for a year, apart from maybe tights if I run out of pairs without holes in. I can work through all my old clothes, I've got plenty stashed in the wardrobe.

No eating out. Well, no eating out apart from one burrito per month plus guacamole. No cinema – I can make do with TV and I'll get Sam to show me how to watch things online.

Stockpile cotton wool and deodorant at Costco next time Mum and Dad are going.

Drink booze only two nights a week. I won't need to drink every night because I won't be stressed from my day job. And no posh coffees.

Bugger. Haircuts. I could learn to cut my own hair? How hard can it be?

If I eat less, and eat only lentils, pulses and rice on weekdays, then I could afford avocados and cheese at the weekends . . .

Bollocks. I still need fourteen grand before I even set foot out of the house. Oh what's the point? I'll never be able to leave that place . . .

w/c 30 April – one week to airdate

Status report:
- Post-production edit with Andy
- Friday – Happy Hour with Robbie
- Plan what to wear for Saturday's coffee
- Try to remember Saturday's coffee is not a date
- Google how to cut own hair

Thursday

Andy and I have been sitting in an edit suite in Soho all week trying to make this ad half-decent.

We spent all of Monday looking through the rushes of the pizzas and of Celina. Since then Andy and an editor have been painstakingly working through it all, trying to cut the footage into a polished thirty-second ad. The pizzas all looks terrific. The pizzas are not the problem. But there are precious few takes of Celina where she's looking at the camera and saying her line clearly. In most of them she either looks glazed or fluffs the script.

'Fast forward . . . a bit more . . . yep, pause,' says Andy to the editor. 'So if you cut at 2.06 and take three seconds of that shot, you can intercut with the mushroom shot from reel seven, then cut back in again on the other take, where she stumbles on the word "truth" but then finishes the line well.'

Andy is amazing. He has such great attention to detail that he's able to shape and mould this mess into something that ends up looking totally brilliant by the time we finish late on Thursday night.

'How on earth did you manage to do that, Andy?' I say.

'Oh, I love the editing,' he says. 'Finding those perfect little moments and picking them out. It's like a jigsaw. And there's always something brilliant just to the side of where you're expecting it. You can have a shot that seems like a total disaster but then if you look closely, see, where this take finishes, Celina gives this beautiful, natural smile – because she thinks the take is over. She's actually looking relaxed for the first time right there. And we can stick that smile on the end of the first shot and make it look seamless.'

While Andy's been glued to the screen all week, I've been obsessing about what I'm going to wear to meet

Daniel for coffee on Saturday. What *am* I going to wear? Do I look slimmer in jeans or a skirt? Will that small, subcutaneous spot have surfaced and disappeared again by then, or will it just be breaking through? Should I get my hair done? Maybe I should get my hair done? Last time Daniel saw me my hair was 'done' and it does always look better when the hairdresser blow-dries it . . .

I have to keep reminding myself that this is just a coffee, nothing more.

But I feel so excited about seeing Daniel that I find it impossible to keep this thought in my brain for long enough to over-rule my happiness.

And I know this is probably a bad thing.

Damn emotion, failing to be controlled by logic.

Friday

I'm finally back in the office after being out for more than a week. All I have to do is make it through today and then it'll be the weekend and I get to see Daniel. But before I'm released from this luxuriously carpeted prison that is my second home, I have to sit through Happy Hour.

Happy Hour. Officially called 'Inspiration Hour' – though that doesn't sound too inspiring. In actual fact it should be called 'Boredom Hour' or, on Sam's suggestion, 'Just Kill Me Now-er'. Happy Hour was introduced two years ago and was designed to ruin our Friday afternoons in spring and summer. During these sessions, one of our senior team deigns to share their 'Original Blue Sky Thinking' with the rest of the agency. A modest bunch, my colleagues; from the way they pitch it, you'd think NMN was a cross between Apple, Harvard and NASA. You'd never guess our most profitable client was a thrush cream.

To break this tedium we occasionally have external speakers from diverse backgrounds, selected to stimulate our minds, bodies and souls. We've welcomed Shirley Hanigan from our software providers. Shirley spoke at great length on 'Perfect Presentations: Empowerpoint Yourself!' (Berenice's choice, clearly.)

We've also had Robbie's personal yogi, Marco Nirvana. Marco presented us with his 'Venn of Zen'. (A Venn diagram illustrating how to better balance our souls and our day jobs: Marco's blue circle = 'Ways to Find Meaning in a Materialistic World'; his red circle = 'Ways to Succeed In the 21st Century Media Jungle'. The purple overlap = 'Marco's spirituality course in Crete, only £1499 this summer, including all soft drinks and one session of Reiki or a head massage'.)

But my absolute favourite of all time was Lieutenant Colonel Gordon Hattenstone: ex Black Watch, and undoubtedly The Hardest Man Ever to Set Foot in an Agency that has bottles of £24 organic Sicilian lemon handwash in its toilets. Gordon had killed loads of Taliban, rescued even more Afghan women and children, and raised £100k doing an Ironman for charity. Gordon showed us a testosterone-charged video of soldiers doing battle; all the boys in the audience nearly wet themselves with excitement. Gordon roused us with talk of 'Ultimate Team Work' and 'Fighting the Good Fight'. And then we all went back to our desks and updated our status reports. (Although the following Tuesday I did lay out the napkins for my breakfast meeting with Devron with military precision.)

Before they promote me I'll have to stand up and do one of these sessions myself. I hate public speaking but it's an NMN rite of passage, like a frat-boy hazing but hopefully with less urine drinking. I've been avoiding thinking about my own speech for months now. What could I possibly speak about with any expertise? The joys of being dumped? The best use for old parmesan rinds? I've still got a month to work on it though, so for today I can relax and enjoy/endure the talk. First I have to swing by the mail room to pick up Sam.

I find him leaning over three chocolate muffins, picking the chocolate chips off the top and holding them up to the light like diamonds before filing them in a line on the counter.

'What now, Sam?' I say.

He holds up one finger.

'Sam. I know for a fact that you have a 2:1 in maths from Leeds and that it has been entirely your choice to waste your education on a decade of idleness in this room. I don't know the exact reasons why you've chosen to underachieve – I suspect it's something to do with your mother, or perhaps a fear of failure – these things usually are. However, this is a new low in time-wasting, even for you.'

'Can't you see I'm concentrating?'

325

'What exactly are you looking for in those chocolate chips? If it's the face of Jesus, it's actually in a piece of toast in Las Vegas.'

'I'll know it when I see it.'

'Explain yourself now, Sam, or we'll miss the best seats.'

'Alright, alright.' He stops and turns to me. 'Who is the laziest person in this agency?'

'Other than you, Sam?'

'I'm not lazy, just under-utilised. OK, lazy and light-fingered, nicks loo roll, could give the guys from Enron a run for their money, Freebie Gonzalez . . .'

'Steve Pearson, obviously. And?'

'Well, Suze, as you say, I've spent a fulfilling yet constantly challenging decade in this mail room. And in that time Pearson has never once brought down his own parcels. Until today, when he came in early for a quickie with Julie in Boardroom Three. CCTV's got a lot to answer for,' he says, shaking his head in horror.

'Sam, remind me never, ever to piss you off.'

'Anyway, Pearson then saunters down here with this jiffy bag, three muffins inside, home address on the label. He's couriering them home to himself!'

'Ridiculous; why wouldn't he just carry the muffins home, Sherlock? Why spend twenty-two quid of company money on a bike?'

'Same reason anyone in this place ever does anything that's out of order,' he says, putting a chunk of muffin into his mouth. 'Because they think they can get away with it.'

'The chips, Sam?'

'I'm hunting for one perfect chip to put back in the bag to send to his house. Aha! This is the one.' He nods to himself and carefully places one chocolate drop back into the envelope.

'He'll know you've opened his mail,' I say.

'He's hardly going to bollock me for stealing his stolen muffins though, is he?'

'Why on earth would you waste your time doing that?'

He looks out the window and up to the sky. 'Because it amuses me.' He pauses. 'Because it feels like justice.' And finally, 'Because I can.'

'Well let's get a move on because if we don't get the best seats I'm going to blame you,' I say, as we head out of the mail room and race up to the boardroom.

'You've got to admit that was the perfect chip, worth the quest, no?' says Sam, as I pull open the heavy boardroom door, and see with relief that the best seats are still free. The best seats = the back row: the only conceivable place to sit if one is to survive. Sam, Rebecca and I hide here, whisper and try not to laugh or weep too loudly.

The rest of the agency are already seated – Robbie's the speaker today, so everyone's on time, and wants to be seen at the front. There is the usual low-level chattering, punctuated by the occasional guffaw, but the moment Robbie enters there is silence. He's wearing a pair of black Prada trousers, limited edition snakeskin Nikes and a black t-shirt with a photo of Steve Jobs on that says 'Stay Hungry, Stay Foolish'.

'He's half way there at least,' says Sam, rolling his eyes.

After surveying the crowd Robbie takes out his iPad Mini and presses a button controlling the sound system, which blares out 'Imagine' by John Lennon. This mixes into 'Video Killed the Radio Star', then into Katy Perry's 'Last Friday Night'. Milking every second, Robbie glides to the podium across a carpet as thick and cream-coloured as he is.

'A bonus point for anyone who can connect the dots on that little soundtrack,' says Robbie, looking pointedly round the room.

'Unholy musical trio,' whispers Sam.

'I thought you liked John Lennon?' I say.

'Lennon was a genius, unquestionably, but come the mid-sixties he was basically taking acid every day. McCartney held the band together, he's the true avant-gardist.'

'Yeah – "Frog Chorus",' I whisper back. 'Doesn't get much more cutting edge than that.' Rebecca lets out a small giggle.

'Anyone at the back?' says Robbie. 'I'll give you a clue, something in the Katy Perry lyrics.'

There is some conferring in the audience. Jonty sticks his hand up. 'Is it something to do with Fridays? It's

Friday today. And the Katy Perry song is all about Friday nights?'

'Epic fail I'm afraid,' says Robbie, allowing himself a little laugh. 'Any more takers? No? One last clue.' He presses the remote back on: 'Islands in the Stream' plays out, at which point Steve Pearson's hand shoots up.

'Mr Pearson?' says Robbie.

'Is it the Beatles?' says Pearson. 'John Lennon was a Beatle. "Video Killed the Radio Star" – the Beatles were the first radio stars. And Katy Perry, doesn't she go out with George Harrison's son or something?'

'And "Islands in the Stream"?' says Robbie.

'Oh. I don't know,' says Pearson. 'Written by a Beatle?'

'Written by the Bee Gees, you muffin-stealing bozo,' says Sam, under his breath. 'And the title was taken from an Ernest Hemingway book.'

'Are you sure about that, Sam?' I say.

'It's true,' he whispers, 'I'll bet you a fiver.'

'The answer is *not* the Beatles,' says Robbie. 'I'll have to enlighten you: it's the w, w, w, the digital highway, the internet.'

'How on earth is the answer the internet?' says Sam, shaking his head.

'These songs are all connected,' says Robbie. 'Just as *we* are all connected. The internet connects us in ways we could never have imagined. Katy Perry's song talks of posting pictures on the internet. "Video Killed the Radio Star" is

329

about the death of the radio medium, and many people think the internet is the death of paid-for TV advertising.'

'"Video Killed the Radio Star" is actually about Kenny Everett,' says Sam to me. 'And actually Kenny Everett was mates with John Lennon . . . And now I come to think about it, Kenny G has a cameo in that Katy Perry video . . .'

'Too much time on your hands, Sam,' I say.

'And Kenny Rogers sings "Islands in the Stream"! The answer should be Kenny!' says Sam indignantly.

'Imagine,' says Robbie. 'Well, who could have *imagined* even ten years ago how indispensable the internet would be to us? Who could have imagined Foursquare?'

'Yep, civilisation would definitely end if we didn't know that Jonty has just entered Starbucks on Oxford Street,' mutters Sam. 'Besides, you can't have "Imagine" as a clue just because it has the word imagine . . .'

Sam puts his hand up. 'What about "Islands in the Stream" then?'

'Streaming? Islands, floating, like clouds.'

'What's he talking about?' I say.

'Cloud computing, it's like a big virtual memory bank. It's pretty amazing actually. Though remember, if you write it, you can never delete it.'

'If you delete it from your trash can it's gone though, isn't it?' I say.

'It's *never* gone,' says Sam.

'What does the G in Kenny G stand for?' says Rebecca.

'Let me play you a little something,' says Robbie, and turns on the projector. Up on screen comes the clip from the Olympics opening ceremony illustrating the internet, where a girl loses her phone and a guy finds and returns it to her. Robbie watches the screen, lips pursed together smugly. Once the clip is over he turns, pauses, then starts:

'Technology is changing faster than the blink of an eye. In the year 2000 there were less than a million homes with the internet in the UK. This year that number will top eighteen million. Today we laugh online, we cry online, we can even meet the love of our lives online.' Rebecca gives me a sharp jab in the ribs.

'Most importantly for us warriors in the media battle-ground,' says Robbie, 'more consumers than ever use the internet to shop . . .'

'For porn,' whispers Sam.

'So now more than ever we must fight for the best ideas. Be original, be creative. There's so much digital white noise – think how your campaigns can stand out! Grab that consumer by the throat. Have the killer end line,' says Robbie. 'Remember your Maslow! The consumer has basic physiological needs: water, breathing, sleeping . . .'

'Sleeping is my basic need at this point,' says Sam.

'And then there are more sophisticated needs,' says Robbie. 'Fulfilling employment, sexual intimacy, self-esteem.' I'm still working on all three of those.

'And it is advertising's role to meet these emotional needs,' says Robbie. 'Successful brands fill gaps in consumers' lives that they can't articulate for themselves. It's our job to get under their skin, pre-empt their desires. To do this well you need to understand the hearts of your brands. You are the midwives of your brand's soul.'

Sam wriggles in his chair. The phrase 'brand soul' always makes him shudder.

'Which brings me finally back to our working-class hero John Lennon,' says Robbie. '"Life goes by while you're making other plans." *Carpe diem*, guys: make the campaigns you're working on today the greatest you can.' He raises his hands in the air like a preacher. 'Every Tweet, every banner ad. Accept nothing less than excellence. Be brave. Be fearless. Thanks for listening.'

'Martin Luther Doggett,' says Sam, pretending to wipe a tear from his eye.

'I hate that John Lennon quote,' I say, as the rest of the room filters out. 'Reminds me of all the years I've wasted here.'

'Robbie misquoted him, as ever. That's not even what Lennon said,' says Sam. 'And besides Lennon borrowed it off a journalist, it wasn't even Lennon's own.'

'Then it's the perfect quote, seeing as half the campaigns on this agency's reel are *borrowed*,' I say. 'Meanwhile what the hell am I going to talk about when it's my turn?'

'Gorelick,' says Sam.

'What?' I say.

'G is for Gorelick. Kenny G. His surname is Gorelick.'

'Sam — I honestly don't know what I'd do without you,' I say.

Is that a little blush I see blossoming on his cheeks?

'Are you coming for a drink after work?' he says. 'It's Jinesh's leaving do, we're going down The Crown. Come. I haven't seen you properly for ages.'

'Can't, I've got something urgent I have to do,' I say, as I grab my bag and head for the door. Something urgent that I don't really want to do, but I feel I should: go home and call Daniel again.

I've drunk a glass and a half of red wine and I can't put it off any longer so I pick up the phone and dial his number.

'Daniel McKendall,' I say.

'Hey, Susie Rosen! I was just thinking about you.' You were?

I take a deep breath. 'Listen. I'm sorry for the short notice but I can't see you tomorrow.'

'Don't tell me, those pizzas are eating into your weekend?'

'Oh no, that's all done. We're in the central ad break in *Corrie* on Monday night if you fancy a laugh?'

'I wouldn't miss it for the world,' he says. 'So what *are* you up to tomorrow then, anything exciting?'

'I just can't make it, that's all.'

'Why?'

'I just don't think it's a very good idea if we hang out.'

'Why not?' he says.

'Because . . . I don't think it's a good idea.'

'What's wrong?'

'Because all I've been thinking about since I last spoke to you is what I'm going to wear when I meet you,' I say, feeling ridiculously exposed, even as the words come out of my mouth.

'Right . . .' he says. 'That's sweet.'

'And that's not normally how my brain works when I'm thinking about having a cup of coffee with a mate.' I mean, I didn't even sort out my dress to Polly's wedding till an hour before the ceremony, but you really don't need to know that.

'What are you saying?' he says.

'I'm saying I think I fancy you. I'm sorry. It's messed up. This is embarrassing. But I'm kidding myself if I say that you're just a mate, because you're not just any old mate. Not that you're not a mate, but . . . I'm just trying to be honest with myself and with you because this feels like a weird situation,' I say.

'Oh sweetheart, that's really flattering,' he says. 'It's fine, we're not going to do anything, we're just hanging out. We can be mates, can't we? I was really looking forward to seeing you.'

Now I feel really stupid. What am I even thinking of? I've made it sound like I'm in love with him. All it boils down to is this: I fancy him. He's married. We have a history, and because of the other night I feel nervous. And that's understandable. He's a good-looking man. There was an almost-kiss. But I am totally able to control myself. I'm seeing him for two hours in broad daylight. And in this phone conversation I've made it sound like I'll be trying to dry hump him in the street.

'You're totally right,' I say. 'Ignore me. Of course we can just hang out. I'm being an idiot.'

'Good,' he says, laughing.

'Ignore me,' I say again. 'Honestly, 3 p.m., in that little park opposite the Conran Shop, up by the church. I'll be wearing jeans. Or maybe I won't be,' I say. 'No, jeans, ignore me. OK, I'm going to hang up now. See you tomorrow.'

I hang up. I am nearly sick with embarrassment. Why on earth did I say those things? Just because they're true, does not mean they needed to be said.

335

Saturday

So what *am* I going to wear for this not-date? If I was being good, I should go wearing tracksuit bottoms and no make-up. I shouldn't care whether Daniel McKendall fancies me. I should not be trying to attract him in the first place. But clearly I want to look pretty and feel pretty. Alluring and yet effortless – that is the look I need. That is a look I find impossible to pull off. I've never been one of those girls who can work layering and gilets and multi-length necklaces. I try on various skirt and top combos but they all feel too try-hard and end up on the bedroom floor. In the end I settle for my jeans, and a super soft t-shirt I bought a few years back that's on the verge of wearing through. A bit too comfortable and dressed down. I go heavy on the mascara.

I feel so excited about seeing him. Foolish: I am setting myself up for another massive disappointment, and yet I can't control the fact that this mixture of excitement and familiarity is the thing about falling in love that's so wonderful.

In love! What am I even talking about? This is pure loneliness, morphing itself in my brain into something totally different to what it is.

He's waiting in the little park next to the church, sitting on a wooden bench holding two coffees. The sight of this beautiful man in jeans and a dark wool coat – looking at me in the same way that I'm looking at him – makes me so nervous that I want to turn round and go home. Except I don't. Instead I pick up my pace and walk around the cobbled path to join him, trying not to smile too broadly. God, but he's handsome: those ultra blue eyes, that nose, that perfect mouth above all things.

He stands to give me a hug. His body feels so strong and solid, I try not to hold onto him too tightly.

'I have a plan,' I say, slightly too quickly. I talk too quickly when I'm around Daniel McKendall. I have so many things I want to say to him, and I'm scared he's going to disappear on me again and so I have to say them all, right now, at the same time.

'A plan!' he says. 'That sounds extremely organised.'

'I think we should go to the zoo! It's only ten minutes away and I haven't been since I was a kid.' And more to the point: the zoo is an innocent and non-sexual

337

environment. Other than the possibility you might see two mammals humping (and surely the zoo keepers make sure that doesn't happen in front of the kiddies). The zoo is not erotic. There are bad odours throughout.

'Sure, let's go to the zoo!' he says, his face lighting up. 'But I want to see the lions, and can I please have an ice cream when we get there?'

He takes my arm and we walk, giddy like lovers, up to Regent's Park. I want to keep walking with him, to have his arm interlinked with mine like this. I could walk round and round the park all day and be entirely content just to be holding onto his arm like this.

'Isn't this nice?' I say.

'It's perfect,' he says. 'One of my favourite things in the world, a walk in the park.'

'Me too,' I say.

'It's beautiful, but it's also calm,' he says.

'Totally,' I say, smiling.

'A walk in the park is when I feel most like myself.' He pauses to look at me. He seems almost embarrassed by what he's just said. He gives my arm a little squeeze, then says, 'We'd better pick up the pace, looks like it might rain.'

'I don't care if it rains.' I don't. I could walk through a storm with Daniel McKendall and it wouldn't bother me in the slightest. 'If it rains you get wet,' I say, laughing at how silly I sound.

'One of the great philosophers of our time,' he says,

grinning. 'I forgot you were so gifted.' He reaches over and musses up my hair gently.

'Yes, well, Harvard did call earlier for my opinion on this year's *X Factor* line up, but I don't care to brag,' I say.

'Of course you don't . . . modest and brilliant. And looking rather radiant today, if you don't mind me saying so?'

I don't mind in the slightest. Say it again.

The sky is clouding over now, and when we get to the zoo it is relatively empty. We are the only people here in our thirties who aren't accompanied by kids, and it occurs to me only now that a Fun Family Venue was a bad choice on my part. It will remind Daniel of his own family, the almighty elephants in the room. I make a note to bypass the actual elephants, though when we look at the map it turns out there are no elephants in the zoo. And no pandas. The zebras are being re-housed and the tigers have gone to tea.

He stands studying the map and it is all I can do not to reach up on tiptoes to kiss the side of his neck. That stretch of exposed skin, just below his ear . . .

What's wrong with me? I must pull myself together.

'Let's go to the aquarium,' I say. Maybe being surrounded by cold water will help dampen my ardour. Besides it will be a safer environment generally – dank, otherworldly, full of alien distractions.

In the Coral Reef Hall we spy tiny, thin metallic silver shrimpfish, vertical knives of light, sliding up and down in the water. And beautiful neon tang fish in yellow and blue and turquoise – swimming jewels.

'Look at that.' I point out a small fish, maybe two inches long, that's a ravishing hot pink. 'Unbelievable. Why would a fish evolve in such a bright colour? Surely it doesn't make sense, from a predator point of view?'

'Bright colours are nature's way of warning that something's dangerous. They're meant to ward off attackers,' Daniel says, looking slightly confused as he says it. 'I think I read that in the *Encyclopaedia Britannica*, back when Google didn't exist.'

'Can you even imagine living without Google?'

He shakes his head. 'Don't say such things!'

'Surely these fish are just asking for trouble looking so damn pretty, drawing attention to themselves like that?' I say. 'Why don't they wear camouflage? Something watery coloured, some nice khaki fins . . .'

'Same reason you didn't wear some nice khaki fins to Polly's wedding . . .' he says with a little smile.

Thank goodness it's so dark in here and he can't see me blush.

'Ooh, stingrays!' I say, wandering over to a giant tank in the corner. I spot a flat black and white polka-dot fish pulsating like a strange pancake at the bottom of the tank. 'They're so weird.'

'Come over here if you want something properly weird,' he says, from over the other side. As I move towards him I see him in profile, transfixed in front of the glass, one hand pressed against it. His face is illuminated from the bulbs in the tank; his expression is full of wonder. It reminds me of how he used to look when we would lie on his roof, gazing up at the clouds. Boyish and awestruck and innocent. Such a sweetness about him.

The tank is full of piranhas.

Mesmerising. Unlike all the other fish who dart or glide or flicker through the water, these dozen black fish hover, static, in place. All in profile facing to the right, they hang like an army biding their time, waiting to attack.

'They get a bad rep, poor things,' he says. 'It's not true that they go after humans. Generally they mind their own business.'

I look at their sharp little mouths, sharp little teeth. 'The way they hang there playing dead. It's creepy . . .' I say, shivering.

'Don't worry, sweetheart,' he says, putting his arm around me. I feel a jolt of nerves grip my stomach. 'There's four inches of glass between us and them. If it breaks, I'll protect you from the little fishies.'

I'm sure you will. But who's going to protect me from myself?

'Let's get out of here,' I say. The aquarium, while dank, is also dark, and under cover of this darkness we have ended up in an almost embrace. I need to move us somewhere less dangerous. 'Time for a llama?'

A perfect choice, if I do say so myself. Llamas are boring. They're not daredevils. They don't do anything cool. When they chew (and they chew a lot), they look like old people contemplating decrepitude. Their coats look like they were bought in a flea-infested secondhand shop near a village train station. Best of all, the llama enclosure smells bad. Really, truly bad.

Daniel's attention is drawn to a sign by the enclosure with a cute hand-drawn illustration that reads *Llama – proud, curious, spitty.*

'Hey Suze, does this sound familiar to you?' he says, laughing. 'I could have that written on my tombstone.'

'Proud, curious, spitty? I'd say more flatulent, judging by the smell around here.'

'I don't want flatulent on my tombstone,' he says.

'I meant the llamas, not you. No: I wouldn't use those exact words to describe you, Daniel.' I stare at him. His eyes in daylight are incredible: the bluest, but with those tiny flecks of pale green near the pupil.

'What words would you use then?' He stares back at me without breaking my gaze. Does he know how gorgeous he is? He never used to when we were young.

'Well, my long lost twin?' he says. 'What words?' He smiles, that smile. That smile is inches from my smile.

Gorgeous. And Gorgeous. And Unavailable.

'Complicated,' I say, with a sigh.

He raises an eyebrow but says nothing.

I take a deep breath. 'And decent,' I say. It is the opposite, I suspect, of what is on his mind. But I want us both to be better than this. And I do believe he is good, because if he is good then that means I can be good too.

'And flatulent,' I say, as I watch the tension in his face disappear into a smile. 'That's enough about you – how about me, Daniel McKendall? How would you describe me, in a nutshell . . .'

'You, Susie Rosen? You're a walk in the park on a beautiful day,' he says, without missing a beat.

I really wish he hadn't chosen those words.

We part at 6 p.m. – he's already late to meet his brother – and we stand at the entrance to Baker Street station hovering between friendship and the desire to do bad things.

'I'm off to the States next weekend but are you around the weekend after?' he says. I think he feels the same way that I do: I'm not done yet. I want more.

'Let's see how we go,' I say.

Right at this moment all I want is to hop on the tube with him to see Joe, hang out with the McKendall boys, then go back to Daniel's house in Kent, climb into bed and spend tomorrow and the rest of my life with him. Or even just a week with him. Or even just a whole day.

I didn't think I'd feel these things again after Jake. Relaxed, happy, optimistic, less out of sorts, more like my old, better self.

'Thank you, Susie,' says Daniel as he takes my hands and kisses me goodbye. 'I was so excited about seeing you today but I suppose a part of me was worried that maybe we wouldn't get on as well as we did the other night at the wedding. I know that sounds daft.'

No it doesn't. I know what he means.

'But I can honestly say,' he says, with the sweetest of smiles, 'that this has been the best three hours of my whole week.'

That is exactly what I would want a man to say to me. That is exactly what I feel too. For the first time in such a long time there is a mutual feeling. I had forgotten how your heart can actually feel like it's expanding from just a few simple words that somebody says. I'd forgotten this feeling of hope.

Daniel has made me realise that perhaps there is some hope.

But actually what use is this hope if it's going in the direction of Daniel McKendall? I think it's worse than no hope at all.

w/c 7th May – AIRDATE!

Status report:
- ON AIR! Keep senior team updated on results
- Happy Hour – plan speech – MEGA URGENT
- Try to remember Daniel McKendall is still married
- New Fletchers brief – check on timings – due any day?

Thursday

Our thirty-second TV ad for Fat Bird pizzas, featuring the lovely Celina Summer, went on air for the first time during *Coronation Street* on Monday.

By the close of business on Tuesday, Fletchers had sold out of all their stock, which was supposed to last through until Friday. They've had to double the number of lines and workers in the factory, and they're running night shifts too, in order to meet the unexpected demand.

It's been the biggest success since the launch of the Triangulicious pizza in the mid-nineties. Devron has been whoop-whooping down the phone to Martin. Ton of Fun Tom has been whoop-whooping down the phone to me. Jeff sent me a funny email yesterday describing the double high-fiving and low-fiving that's been going on around their office.

Berenice is fully abreast of the phenomenal sales figures.

And do you know who we have to thank for this 'amazing, stellar, dazzling performance' – according to Robbie's email that went out this morning?

Of course I knew it wouldn't be me, I'm not entirely naive.

But Andy Ashford, maybe? Nah . . . Andy who???

Why, it's Karly and Nick of course! The heroes of the piece.

I'll be getting a new brief on the next Fletchers project in a couple of weeks and perhaps I should chase for it now, but I'm not in the mood so I pop up to Andy's office with a gold tin of Fortnum and Mason Chocolossus Biscuits, to commiserate.

'These are for you, Andy. To congratulate you on doing such a great job and for being so gracious about it. I know you're partial to a biscuit, and having conducted extensive biscuit research on your behalf, I think you might like these.'

'Oh goodness, you shouldn't have!' he says, beaming. 'It was my pleasure.' He gestures for me to have a seat.

'You know, Andy, I think it's so unfair that those guys are getting the credit when you're the one who saved this ad from being a total disaster.'

He shrugs. 'I was just doing my job.'

'Doesn't it bother you though?'

'What?'

'The email that Robbie sent out? It didn't even mention that you're the one who did all the hard work.'

'I'm far too old to pay attention to any of that nonsense. I ignore all the politics, I just keep my head down, come in and do the work. I'm probably lucky to still have a job in this business at my age.'

I nod.

'And I really love the work,' he says. 'It's the greatest luxury in the world to do a job you actually enjoy.'

'I'll have to take your word for it,' I say.

'You sound a bit down on the whole thing.'

I nod and look round his office at the posters on display. 'Here's the thing: I look at all these great ads on your wall – Boddingtons, Volkswagen – and I remember why I wanted to work in advertising in the first place . . . When I was thirteen, watching that first Levi's ad on TV, Nick Kamen taking his jeans off in a launderette . . .' Maybe I just wanted Nick Kamen in his pants, not the job in advertising . . .

'Levi's was a brilliant campaign,' says Andy.

'But I feel like over the years I've lost my way in this business,' I say. 'Or maybe this was never the way for me.'

'There's no shame in admitting you made a mistake,' he says. 'And I can never quite understand how you guys on the third floor put up with so much grief from all directions. I've seen the people who get on in this industry and, forgive me for saying it, Susie – I mean it as a compliment – but you're not quite like them. You don't play the game.'

'It's just I know how to do this job, Andy. I don't love it but I know how to do it.'

'Just because you know how to do something, doesn't mean you have to do it,' he says. 'My father wanted me to follow him into law, but I would have been a very average lawyer. It took me five years to figure it out, and another five to work up the courage to leave.'

'Maybe you're right,' I say. 'Well anyway, I just wanted to thank you properly, even if Robbie didn't. I know it's only a packet of biscuits but they are very fine biscuits.'

He smiles warmly. 'You know, I can't remember anyone in your department ever saying thank you before!'

Saturday

Dalia calls. I haven't seen her since Boccarinos, and since then I have not been too hasty in returning her calls.

'Are you free today?' she says.

'I'm off to Maltby Street now to buy some ingredients, and then I'm going to do some recipe work on this blog thing tomorrow. So no, not really.' Not if you're going to give me the one hour of your time when Mark is busy doing something else.

'I can meet you at Maltby Street,' she says.

'I didn't think you ever went south of the river, Dalia.'

'I'd really like to see you.'

'As you like. I'll be at Monmouth Coffee at midday.'

I take the tube down to London Bridge and wander the back streets and under the railway bridge, through to the arches of Maltby Street. It's so much quieter here than at

Borough Market, and yet there are all these fantastic food places hidden away. An amazing cheese shop, a greengrocer where it all looks so beautiful you want to buy every last bit of produce – I have to get these broad beans, ooh and the peas look amazing too. And then there's the best place of all – St John's Bakery, where they do the greatest custard doughnut in the world. I think about picking one up for Dalia but what's the point, Mark won't let her eat it. Well, she won't let herself eat it rather . . .

I head back to the coffee shop for noon. Dalia's already there, sitting at a table outside.

'I got here early, managed to grab us a space,' she says.

'Thanks.' I take a seat and feel the sun warm my face.

'I got you a cappuccino, and a brownie for us to share.'

'You eating brownies nowadays?'

She smiles gently.

'How was Miami?' I say. 'You've still got a bit of a tan.'

'It was fine,' she says, nodding. 'And I hear I missed the wedding of the year. I saw Poll yesterday, she showed me the photos.'

'It was wonderful,' I say, thawing slightly.

'And I hear you had a good time with Daniel McKendall?'

I spoon the froth off my coffee. 'What did Polly say?'

'She said you were all over each other on the dance floor, that his marriage is on the rocks, and that you're going to run off into the sunset together . . .' she says, giving me a warm smile.

'That is beyond stupid,' I say.

'And you went on a date to the zoo?'

'Just as friends,' I say.

'You might as well shag him,' she says. 'Get some action, why the hell not.'

'He is mar-ried.'

'But you're not.'

'Oh Dalia, it is bad karma. And of *all* people I am not the type. And nor is Daniel, I'm sure.'

'He's still a man though, isn't he? Sooner or later they all do it.'

'That is totally not true, how can you say that?'

'Come on! My ex cheated. And Polly's ex cheated,' she says, counting out on her thumb and forefinger. 'Oh, and so did yours.' She holds onto the dark red nail of her middle finger. 'Three out of three. Isn't that a jackpot? Or even a Jakepot?'

Ouch.

'Sorry,' she says slowly rubbing the end of her finger softly. 'That was unnecessary. I . . . I'm having a bad week . . .' She shakes her head.

'Which of your exes cheated?' I say.

She takes a deep breath. 'You mean Polly didn't already tell you?'

'Tell me what? Oh. Oh I see. Oh! I'm sorry.'

'Look, there's no need to pretend you're upset about it, I know you guys don't like him.'

351

'I'm still sorry that he let you down.'

She nods slowly. 'I can't really imagine the thought of not seeing him again,' she says.

I nod. 'It's hard.'

'I just feel so good when I'm with him. Like really alive,' she says, her eyes starting to fill with tears.

'But not so good in the times in between . . .' I say.

'I guess so,' she says, taking a tissue from her bag.

'Is it definitely over?' I say. They've been on and off for so long now, I don't know whether this is finally it.

'Who knows . . . yes. I think it only happened once, maybe twice. Some girl he met in a bar.'

'Oh. No. I meant you and him.'

'I don't know . . . I don't want to think about any of that.'

'Fair enough,' I say.

'And I'm sorry I've been giving you a hard time about Jake. I suppose now I get why you're still so hung up about him.'

'What?'

'You know, you kind of block that stuff out.'

'What are you talking about?'

'Oh, it doesn't matter,' she says, quickly shaking her head. 'I didn't come here to have a row.'

'Well then explain what you're talking about,' I say, feeling myself start to get angry.

'When I was last round at yours . . . oh forget it,' she says.

'Say it.'

'Well I asked what you missed about him, and you said . . .'

'And I said everything.' I nod.

'Like what?' she says.

'His smile, his optimism, his energy,' I say, counting out on my fingers. 'The fact that he always gave people the benefit of the doubt. His sense of fun. The way he used to . . .'

'. . . stay out till 4 a.m. on a week night and you didn't know where he was or who he was with?' she says.

I ignore her. 'The way he used to get the papers for me on a Sunday morning, even if it was pouring with rain . . .'

I can see she's itching to say something. Something along the lines of, 'He was probably leaving the flat just so that he could text her . . .'

I really don't want to have this discussion. 'Dalia, you can slag off Jake all you like. The point was, regardless of how it ended, he was on my side. And I miss having someone on my side.'

She grabs my hands in hers. 'Susie: we are all on your side. I'm not trying to upset you. But you see that relationship through rose-tinted glasses. You never remember the bad bits. I'm not saying he was a total wanker but he was far from perfect.'

'I do know he wasn't perfect,' I say quietly. 'But no one is.'

And of course I'm selective with my memories. Why would I want to remember every last thing?

A year of feeling paranoid, except it wasn't paranoia.

Of Jake staying out drinking late with work mates. Or maybe just that one work mate.

Of him picking fights. And that awful birthday weekend, when it hit me like a rock – we weren't going to make it. And then it was OK, because we had a good week, and then it wasn't OK because we had a bad month.

That last Christmas, the way he'd looked at me when he'd unwrapped the watch I'd bought him: delight, rapidly followed by guilt.

And then that awful phone call.

'It is what it is,' he'd said.

No excuses.

No apologies.

Five little words – two of which he'd used twice, and that were so piddly they'd get a terrible score in Scrabble.

My grandmother had an expression Jake used to love.

'*Hai delle fette di prosciutto sugli occhi.*'

'You must have ham over your eyes.'

You must have ham over your eyes which is preventing you from seeing the truth.

I think perhaps I've had a whole ham sandwich.

Sunday

I am proud of myself. I've been working hard. I now have a total of twenty recipes up on the blog. I made myself eat pasta for lunch and dinner; tough job but someone's got to do it.

Today I wrote up posts for these seven recipes:

1) Pasta for a dreary, cold Monday night after a long and tedious day in the office.

2) Pasta for a hungover Wednesday night in front of some trash TV, incorporating two of your five a day!

3) Pasta for a lazy weekend day when it's raining outside and you have a dear friend coming for supper.

4) Pasta for when you Google Image your ex's new girlfriend and find a photo of her, arm in arm with

355

your ex, drinking champagne at a fashion party on Bond Street:

Stortini are small, smooth, semi-circular tubes – a younger cousin of macaroni. While their primary function is as a soup pasta (their size means they cook quickly) they also provide the perfect shape for this troublesome and unsettling occasion. What is needed is instant happiness, combined with something to bite on. Stortini take only eight minutes to cook and offer a hugely satisfying mouth feel for such an itty-bitty shape. More importantly, stortini closely resemble smiles: genuine smiles, not fake fashion-party smiles. And 100g dry weight of stortini provides you with 436 of these smiles. (This number is accurate. Believe me, I have counted.) If 436 little smiles smothered in lightly salted butter don't cheer you up, try opening a bottle of wine. Picpoul is a nice, dry white and hugely effective in removing any lingering bitterness that the aforementioned photo might have brought to the fore.

5) Pasta for when your oldest friend has just put a total downer on you by bringing up your ex's bad behaviour, which you'd been doing such a decent job of burying.

6) Pasta for when you realise that you *really* might die alone without even an Alsatian to eat you, and that Helen Fielding has a lot to answer for.

7) Pasta for a productive Sunday in spring, for when hope, and new season broad beans, have returned:

Broad beans are almost as big in Italy as the scale of Silvio Berlusconi's sexual ambition. Broad beans are also known as fava beans, and so will forever be associated with Hannibal Lecter. While Dr Lecter might not be your ideal dinner guest, you can't knock his taste in legumes.

Beans, legumes, are they the same thing? If not, what is a chickpea? You can ponder these, and other significant questions, such as 'Will my upstairs neighbour ever move out?' and 'How did Ryan Gosling go from being this slightly skinny, sweet-looking guy in The Notebook *to being the world's biggest sex symbol?' while you are podding your broad beans.*

Then, after a three-minute boil in salted water, comes round two – the double-podding, where you can further ponder the important questions raised in your earlier podding session: 'If my upstairs neighbour gets someone pregnant, maybe then he'd have to move out?' and 'In Gangster Squad *Ryan manages to look even hotter than he looked in* Drive. *How is that even possible?'*

Double-podding a bowl of fresh broad beans is an excellent way to spend an hour or two on a Sunday

afternoon. It is immensely therapeutic. It is also physi-
cally quite soothing – popping out those perfect little
beans from their velvety green bunkers.

More importantly it is symbolic: an act of hope, a sign
that you are investing in the future. Yes, it takes time
– one bean after another, after another – but it is worth
it. Put in all that work, go the extra mile, and eventually
you will be rewarded on the plate.

Add a touch of fresh mint, right at the end, before
serving.

When I climb into bed I feel a little tingle of excitement
start to spread through me.

This could actually be something. This could actually
be something good.

w/c 14th May

Status report:
- Chase new brief
- Write Happy Hour speech – URGENT
- Do more on the blog

Wednesday

I've chased Fletchers for this new brief but Ton of Fun Tom has been uncharacteristically quiet on the subject. Strange. I'd have thought there'd be at least some mumblings about the next hugely game-changing, mega-strategic project. But nothing, except an email from Tom saying, 'Devron will be in touch.'

I've chased Devron. He's made vague noises about 'gestation periods' and 'work in progress'. But for now I have nothing to do but sit and wait.

I hate not being busy at work.

It so rarely happens that I actually forget I'm much happier when I have too much to do, rather than too little. Not only am I happier when I'm busy, I'm more productive. But now that the only urgent thing I need to get on with is to draft my Happy Hour speech for two weeks' time, I find myself unable to write a word.

What am I going to say? The truth, the whole truth? Not even close to the truth, of course. No doubt I'll end up sounding just as tedious as every other speaker that gets up there, wanking on about brands and consumers, when what I'd really like to be talking about is my top fifteen pasta shapes of all time. Oh, and I need to source some music too, for the opening. I'll speak to Sam about that.

Still, not being busy means I can leave work on time, and in the evenings I've been researching other blogs, and working out a better layout for this pasta blog that disguises the fact that I'm not terribly good at taking photos. I'm really enjoying the whole thing.

And of course all this free time means I can't help but think about Daniel.

We've spoken quite a few times on the phone this week. He rang me from the airport the other day to ask if I still like Toffifee.

'They've got them on two for one in duty free.'

'I don't think I've eaten one for about twenty years, Daniel. Not since that time we OD'd on them up on your roof.'

'Me neither. We've got a lot of making up for lost time, you and me. I'll bring you a box next weekend. What am I talking about? I'll bring you two.'

I feel like we're becoming friends again, but with a flirty undercurrent. But not a Jeff mega-flirty undercurrent; something quieter yet more significant. The foundations of our relationship are already in the ground, immoveable. I know how Daniel thinks, I know what he cares about, I know that when he smiles a certain way it's actually because he's feeling sad.

And I know how he smiled at me when we said goodbye the other day at the tube station. I know what that smile means too.

Daniel and I: we knew each other pretty well back in the day. We may have grown up but neither of us has really changed. Though I guess along the way we've both learnt – the hard way – about love and disappointment.

Maybe the universe has a backlog of unanswered teenage prayers and it's only just getting round to dealing with mine now: please let him come back to me, I'll be good, I promise, I'll even tidy my room, I swear.

The other day Daniel texted me a photo of these beautiful lavender fields down the road from his house in Kent. Fields of lush, bright purple-blue flowers as far as the eye could see. I thought they only had lavender fields like that in places like France; I didn't realise it grew so happily just an hour from my door.

Daniel McKendall is starting to inch back into my world.

I'm getting used to hearing his voice every couple of days. Having someone ask me about my day, and tell me about theirs.

Having someone to share the tiniest things with.

It's nice. It's so nice. It really is.

Saturday

It's a gorgeous spring day and Daniel is sitting in my flat drinking a cup of tea. We were planning a walk up to Hampstead Heath but Daniel is transfixed by the view from my window.

'It's amazing,' he says, staring out across the City. 'That's the London Eye!'

'And then there's the Post-Office Tower.'

'Hold on, there on the left, is that Canary Wharf?' he says.

'See the skyscrapers? And then those ones a bit to the right are Liverpool Street . . . there's the Gherkin,' I say, pointing it out to him.

'Ooh, look at the Shard! Have you been up it yet?'

'No, have you?'

'Me and Joe are planning on buying tickets. It's supposed to be phenomenal.'

'It's so big, it's insane. You can't really see the scale properly from here, but if you see it from the roof it makes St Paul's look like an Iced Gem.'

'You've got a roof terrace?'

'Yes. Well no. Sort of. It's amazing up there, really, the best view ever – well, maybe not quite as good as the Shard, but you don't need a ticket, and there are no queues . . .'

'Let's go up!' he says, a glint in his eye.

I'd love to go up there and show him the view. It would make him happy. But I'm not meant to take anyone up there. Least of all a married man. Still, nothing untoward's going to happen on a concrete roof in broad daylight.

'Come on, let's do it,' I say. 'We have to stay low so the Langdons don't see us. But it's perfectly safe.' Well, it's perfectly safe when I'm not up there with you.

Me and Daniel McKendall, up on the roof again, talking about clouds.

Just like old times. Lying on our backs, looking up at the blue, blue sky. Pretending nothing's about to happen.

The only thing that's different from twenty-three years ago is that now Daniel has a wife. And a son. And a wedding ring. Just those three little things. Things that mean I shouldn't be up here with him, horizontal, our sides lightly pressed together from shoulder to foot.

'You were the first girl I ever fancied who was also a

mate,' he says. 'In fact I don't think I've met another girl since who I can talk to about anything and everything and just feel so comfortable like this.'

'Are you comfortable?' I say, propping myself up on one elbow so that our heads aren't so close together. 'This concrete's killing my back. We should have brought up some cushions.'

'Take this.' He sits, and as he reaches his arms over his head to pull off his cotton jumper his t-shirt rides up, showing three inches of reasonably flat, firm stomach. I resist an urge to lay my hand there. It has been more than a year since I've been this close to a body I desired – I don't know what a normal response is any more.

He balls up his jumper in a makeshift pillow for me and I lie back down, feeling a sense of expectation tightening inside me. I'm starting to worry that something might actually happen. *Something might happen* . . . Funny how my brain makes it sound like this *something* is nothing whatsoever to do with me and entirely out of my control . . .

'You know what I mean by comfortable, Suze. I mean comfortable mentally, not physically,' he says. 'Just being able to talk to you. It feels . . . like coming home.'

'What about your wife? I say quickly. 'Surely you talk to her all the time about everything?'

He turns on his side to look at me. Don't turn on your side, I think. That'll mean more of your body is in contact with more of my body.

'Yeah,' he says, his voice sounding suddenly defensive. 'Of course we talk. Well. We talk about stuff. Like bills. And who's going to pick who up from where . . .'

'But that's just having a kid, isn't it?' I say. 'Lots of logistics. You've got to be a team. Being a parent forces you to grow up. You can't just sit around chatting nonsense.'

'Sure, no, I know that,' he says. 'But I mean I don't ever remember doing that with Brooke. It wasn't ever really like that.' He turns again onto his back, and his palm reaches up to rub his forehead, as if he has a mild headache.

Like a photoflash I remember a story Polly once told me, about how Brooke had thrown a tantrum the night Daniel proposed. She'd berated him for asking her against the wrong backdrop – a local pub rather than a Michelin-starred restaurant or at Tiffany's. She'd refused to speak to him for forty-eight hours. When Polly told me this story, she'd said, 'He's so dumb and loyal to that woman. He should have left her there and then.' I guess the loyalty's starting to slip . . .

For a moment I feel so sad for him I want to reach out and put my hand to his face. Then a thought stops me: he has all the things that you want – a spouse, a family to belong to, security. What on earth gives you the right to feel sorry for him? He probably feels sorry for you, you deluded cow.

'Oh, you must have had a lot of fun at the beginning,' I say. 'Besides, talking nonsense is just the honeymoon phase of a relationship, isn't it, before you actually get to know the real person.' I don't believe a word of what's coming out of my mouth. Whoever I end up with, I want to be talking nonsense to them when they're ninety.

'You don't mean that though, do you, Suze?'

I shrug.

'Are you happy?' I say.

He looks at me and smiles. 'I love hanging out with you.'

'No, I mean in your marriage.'

'Oh. Pass.'

'Why don't you talk to your wife about the way you feel?'

'She's not that type.'

'You should try.'

'I've given up trying.'

'Well, how *do* you feel?' I say.

He pauses, as if it's never occurred to him to really think about it before, as if feelings are an indulgence and not the point.

'I suppose I'm upset . . . with the timing of it all. She moved back to New York when I've got so much on with work and Dad and Joe. If it had been in a couple of years then maybe I could be there full time, but it's not the easiest commute in the world. And more than anything I miss seeing my son every day,' he says. 'And being a dad is the best thing that's ever happened to me.' He breaks into a smile.

'Can't you ask her to come back to England?' I say.

'She thinks the schools in New York are better, or at least the parents she wants to socialise with are . . .'

'I guess I don't understand where you go from here,' I say.

'I'm trying to work it out,' he says.

'How do you feel day to day?'

He blows out a long breath. 'I feel like I'm on a psychiatrist's couch!'

'Sorry. You don't have to answer.'

'No, it's good to talk about it. I suppose . . . I suppose I feel lonely,' he says.

Bloody hell. You're not actually supposed to say those words out loud, ever. Doesn't he know that?

'I wonder,' he says, turning again onto his side so that I feel his chest, firm against my arm. 'What would have happened if you and me . . .' He smiles at me, and I feel myself staring at his mouth, and that beautiful space between his bottom lip and his jaw. I want to rest my lips there . . .

I swallow hard. My heart is beating so loudly I'm amazed the Langdons can't hear it from the third floor.

I take a deep breath that comes out like a small but audible sigh. 'If you and me?' I say, trying to sound only mildly interested in the rest of his sentence.

'I miss this,' he says, as he gently brushes a strand of hair away from my face and tucks it behind my ear. 'I miss this closeness.' His voice cracks slightly with the sadness of all the things he has put to one side.

I suddenly think that my roof is a very dangerous place after all.

I don't know what is going to happen between us in these next few seconds.

I don't know what I want to happen.

I know exactly what I want to happen.

I want him to kiss me so much that I can hardly breathe.

I feel my heart, a trouble-making, weak, bad-intentioned stone, weighing me down, keeping me lying on my back like this when what I should be doing is the right thing. Standing up. Going indoors. Telling Daniel how nice it was to have tea, but that it's really time for him to go home. That is the right thing.

Daniel looks at me. His soft sad half smile moves an inch closer to mine.

I try not to move a millimetre. I don't know whether to edge towards him or away. Maybe if I don't breathe, we can freeze this moment and stay just like this for a while. After all there's nothing wrong with looking at each other, is there? Maybe if I stay like a statue then whatever happens next won't be my fault.

And then he gently moves over. He kisses me and I kiss him, and we kiss.

And nothing that I can remember has ever felt as right as this kiss.

I don't know how long we kiss for. It could be twenty minutes or forty. In the vague distance I hear a car alarm and a siren, some mild commotion from downstairs. But all my attention is focused on the spaces between us. The weight of Daniel as he lies on top of me. The feel of his thick, soft hair under my fingers, warmed by the low strong sun that beats down on us. The gentle but firm touch of his fingers as he touches my face, and pulls me to him. The feel of his mouth on my mouth, his tongue as it moves to meet mine. He is the best kisser, and even though all we do is kiss, it is so intimate that it feels like sex.

It is only the sound of my mobile ringing that finally makes me break away from him, though he shakes his head, no, don't answer . . .

It's Terry.

Shit.

I press reject and Daniel moves back to me and we start to kiss again but Terry immediately calls back. I push Daniel gently away, stand up and move to the side of the roof to see if Terry's outside. Sure enough, he's standing down in the courtyard looking up and waving for me to come down.

Double shit. The Langdons have obviously spied me up on the roof – no doubt Mrs Langdon's got the binoculars out. She probably thinks we're having sex, even though we're fully clothed. Now I'm going to be known as The Harlot of Peartree Court, for copulating outdoors in full view of spying neighbours and passing helicopter pilots . . . And Terry will make me give him the key back, so I've lost my roof terrace access as well as my morals in the space of five minutes.

'Oy, Susie, come down!' he shouts up at me.

He's obviously seen me come up here with Daniel. Shame colours my face. I go back over to Daniel who's looking slightly rumpled and hot, perched up on one elbow. The late afternoon sun warms his face and makes his eyes look the colour of a swimming pool. He smiles at me like he's just spied me naked. 'What's wrong?' he says. 'I was enjoying that . . .'

'Come on, we've got to go inside, you've got to go . . .' I say, grabbing his hand and pulling him up.

'What's wrong?' he says. 'Who was on the phone?'

The phone rings for a third time. 'Bloody hell,' I mutter, 'why is he calling me again?'

'Sorry, Terry, sorry, sorry, sorry . . . I'm just going back to the flat now . . . I won't do it again . . .' I say, as Daniel creeps up behind me and pinches my arse. I try not to giggle down the phone and turn to shoo him away.

'You'd better come down,' says Terry, sounding solemn.

His tone of voice feels like a glass of cold water poured over my head. Suddenly I feel stupid and silly and bad. I've broken Terry's trust, but worse, I've given in to temptation with Daniel without putting up the slightest resistance at all.

'Terry, I'm sorry,' I say, remorse and guilt attacking from either side. 'I'll bring the keys back right away.'

371

'Don't worry about the keys,' he says. 'Just come quick. It's Marjorie.'

I run downstairs, leaving Daniel the keys to my flat and strict instructions to stay put and wait for my call.

'What happened, is she OK?' I say, trying to catch my breath, as I catch up with Terry in the courtyard.

'She's had another fall,' he says.

'Where is she, is she in the flat?' I look up at her window where the dark curtains, as ever, are drawn.

'No, she's been taken to UCH in an ambulance about a half hour ago.'

I suddenly feel sick with panic. 'An ambulance? Is she going to be OK, what shall we do, is anyone with her? I should be with her . . .'

'They wouldn't let me in the ambulance,' says Terry, 'and besides, I can't really leave this place for long. I've called her son, he's driving up, should be at the hospital in about an hour . . . but yeah, I think if you can get down there now . . .' he says. 'If you're OK to get away . . .' He looks at me with an expression I can't read properly.

'That's just a friend,' I say, 'it's fine. I'll get a cab right now . . . shit, my bag's upstairs, shall I go and get it, what should I do?'

Terry's already got his wallet out and stuffs thirty pounds into my hand. 'That should get you there and back. Call me and tell me what's going on as soon as you can.'

This is my fault, I think, as the taxi drives into town and I stare out the window, wishing I could go back in time to the point this afternoon where I decided it was a good idea to go up on the roof and get off with a married man.

If I hadn't gone up on the roof, Daniel and I would have gone for a walk on the Heath, and when I returned I would have seen the ambulance downstairs and I could have gone to the hospital with Marjorie. Held her hand so she knew I was there, so she didn't feel scared or alone. I hope she's OK. How dare her son not live nearer to town, how irresponsible to move an hour outside of London when you have a frail mother. What is he thinking, selfish man?

Oh God, please let her be OK. I have been a terrible neighbour. All those times when I didn't want to go round and listen to her moan, having to sit there and absorb her loneliness, putting my own needs above hers – when she can't even leave her four walls. All those self-justifications of why I couldn't go round there: *too busy, too tired, back too late from work, I'm not even a relative*. And the other day I should have insisted on tidying up her flat, clearing away some of those piles so that she wouldn't have tripped – rather than secretly being relieved when she told me to go away.

The reception in A&E stinks of alcohol. There's anxiety in the atmosphere, as contagious as a bug. The receptionist has a large handwritten sign in capital letters saying 'POSITION CLOSED' but he's dealing with the couple in front of me – a boy of about seventeen, leaning heavily on his girlfriend. He's done something bloody to his ankle. The receptionist tells them to sit and wait, then sits, refusing to make eye contact while I stand in front of him waiting for him to look up. After about a minute I say, 'My neighbour, Marjorie Horstead . . . she's just arrived in an ambulance . . . could you please tell me if she's here?'

Eventually he looks up, points to the sign that says 'POSITION CLOSED' and says 'Can you not read?' then heads into a back office, muttering.

I want to shout through the glass: *You were helping the other guy just now! This is a hospital. I'm scared about Marjorie. Be less of a dickhead.* But I'm silenced by anxiety. The smell of this place alone makes me short of breath. Instead, I stand on the verge of tears and wait. After about two minutes, another woman comes out from the back office, and after I explain the situation, sends me through the heavy door into the main admissions area and tells me to head for the recovery room.

The corridors are lined with people in various states of worry. I head down to the recovery room, past half-drawn green curtains behind which lie various bodies in states of shock or distress. One man sits alone, head drooped forward like he's just been pulled from an explosion. Two skinny, hairy legs stick out from beneath his blue gown and hang limply over the side of the bed. He sways forward a fraction, as if in slow motion.

I hover outside the open double doors of Recovery until a handsome male nurse comes and asks if he can help.

'Ah yes, Mrs Horstead, bed three. Follow me,' he says, leading me into a pale yellow fluorescent room with rows of beds and complicated floor-standing machines lined up. There are bins all over the place – brown bins with black bin liners, blue bins, white bins with orange bin liners, and all I can think is that Marjorie must be going mental – she hates the sight of a bin as much as anything.

Bed three is partially sealed off with a floor-standing screen, but I know Marjorie's here because I can see her sheepskin slippers poking out from the end of the bed, the mid-brown suede dotted with large drops of blood. The sight of these drops of blood makes me want to cry again, but I tell myself to stop being so pathetic. This isn't the morgue; she must at least be conscious if she's in this room.

She's talking quietly with a doctor, and I stick my head round the screen and give her a weak smile. She looks first confused, then a tiny bit moved by emotion, and then quite quickly, furious. Her lip is bloody and swollen, and there are flakes of dried blood under her chin. Her beige house-dress has dark, almost brown blood stains on the chest, then a few longer trickles down the skirt and then the splotches that have spread out on her slippers. Her left wrist is bound in plaster and a drip feeds into the thin, pale blue flesh on her right hand. In this harsh, sickly yellow-green lighting her skin gleams, a chalky grey. She looks so small and weak and defeated I have to force my smile to stay up.

The doctor nods at me. She's dressed in a pretty purple print dress, and looks at least five years younger than me, but has a calm gravitas I don't think I'll ever have, even when I'm fifty. 'Are you Marjorie's grand-daughter?' she says.

'Neighbour,' I say. 'Marjorie, your son's on his way, he'll be here very soon.'

She makes a low grunt of acknowledgement.

'What happened?' I ask the doctor.

'She can't remember, but from what the ambulance guys saw, it looks like she tripped on a rug, hit her head on a table on her way down and landed on her wrist.'

Marjorie lets out a moan of annoyance and pain.

'It's a compound fracture. It's unstable. We've tried to set it but it's slipping back. We might need to take her to theatre,' she says.

Behind me a new patient is being wheeled in. She's lying on a trolley with her head wedged between two large red stabilising blocks, and from this angle it looks like she has no head of her own other than a large red plastic square. She's wheeled into place in the bay next to Marjorie, and all I can see now are the soles of her feet, soft and pale pink and so naked in this room. The noises coming out of her sound like they're from a wounded beast – low, groaning sounds followed by deeper, more guttural wails.

'Her white cell count's normal and her chest is clear, but I'd like to x-ray her left hip,' says the doctor, looking down at her clipboard. 'Marjorie,' she says softly. 'This is the third fall you've had in three years, isn't it?'

Marjorie ignores the question. She knows exactly where this is leading: the further removal of her independence.

'It says in your notes that you broke your hip in a fall two years ago . . .'

Marjorie turns her head away from the doctor and stares sullenly at a trolley, pretending to study the red, green and blue boxes of latex gloves.

The noises from the patient next door are getting louder. She sounds like she's being smothered with a pillow, then repeatedly stabbed, then smothered again. A low buzzing noise from a computer sounds every five seconds, like the noise on *Family Fortunes* when you guess the wrong answer to 'Things You Might Find in a Rucksack'. The woman keeps making different noises, as if in the hope that the correct groan or scream will cause the buzzer to stop. A male doctor's voice says 'You're doing really well', in a soothing tone. Her response is a low but urgent, 'Somebody, somebody help me please.'

'Marjorie,' says the doctor. 'I've asked the bone specialist to come and see you. In the meantime, I'd like you to look at my finger. Up . . . Down . . . Up . . . Down . . .' She moves her finger gracefully through the air as if through water.

'I've hurt my wrist, not my brain, you silly girl,' says Marjorie, her voice sluggish from the sedatives but still with an edge of anger unquelled by the drugs.

'Up . . . Down . . . Up . . . Down,' says the doctor, and Marjorie eventually rolls her eyes upwards, then downwards, then closes them in protest.

'Are you left or right handed, Marjorie?' asks the doctor.

'Right,' she says in a low voice flat and heavy with misery. The doctor looks at me and shakes her head.

'Just go away,' murmurs Marjorie. 'I don't want you here.' I don't know if she's talking to me or the doctor – both, I suspect. 'Go away!' she says now, summoning as much force as she can.

'We'll give you a moment to rest, shall we?' says the doctor, pulling the screen across, taking my arm and leading me over to the x-ray monitor on the side.

'What's going to happen, are you going to keep her in?' I say. There's no way she can go home like this on her own. 'I can stay with her tonight? And for a couple of nights . . .'

The doctor shakes her head. 'We'll move her to a ward for at least a couple of days. I suspect she'll need more surgery. And she won't be able to manage a walking frame with her wrist in plaster like that on her own . . .'

'Her son might be able to look after her,' I say, doubtfully. She wouldn't want that any more than he would, I'm sure.

'No. We'll look for an interim bed. The main issue is her longer term care. With her osteoporosis and history of falls she's probably too high risk to live alone any more. Her notes say she was offered a place in a facility the last time she was admitted but refused on the basis that she'd agree to work with a physiotherapist to improve her mobility. It seems that hasn't been happening with any sort of regularity . . .'

A middle-aged, balding man in a dark grey sports jacket has walked into the room and is hovering to my left, his gaze switching nervously between the doctor and me. 'Excuse me,' he says, breaking into our conversation, 'but I'm looking for my mother, Marjorie Horstead? She was brought in this afternoon with a broken wrist.'

'Your mother's just having a little rest,' says the doctor, turning to him.

'Is she OK, what happened?' he says, his face clouded by panic.

'I should go . . .' I say, suddenly feeling like I'm in everyone's way and that I have no right be here.

The doctor and Marjorie's son have already moved to the x-ray monitor and are examining the photo of Marjorie's bones. They look so spindly and thin. Strange, how we forget that we're all just a collection of the same joined up bones. I move slowly away, then poke my head around the screen to see how Marjorie's doing. Her eyes are closed and she's snoring gently, a whistling noise coming from her nose as her chest moves heavily up and down.

I turn and head quickly out of the ward. As soon as I'm back out on the street I call Terry to update him, and ask him to check in on Fitzgerald. It is a beautiful evening, cooler now but with some heat lingering. I decide to walk home in the fresh air – air that doesn't smell of bleach and blood. And then I suddenly remember that Daniel is waiting for me in my flat and that I had forgotten entirely about what happened a few hours ago.

I can't see him. I can't lean on him. He belongs to someone else.

I send him a text saying I won't be home for a while and to let himself out. He immediately calls but I let it go to voicemail, then switch off my phone.

I don't know what I'm doing.

I don't know what happened today but I know that it feels like the start of something.

Sunday

I can't sleep. I can't sleep at all. I feel rotten about Daniel, and worse about Marjorie.

I must doze in the end because I wake with a jolt at 6.23 a.m.

The only people who are up at this time on a Sunday morning are people with young kids. I ring Polly.

'Polly, can you meet me at Maidenhead station in a couple of hours?'

She's sitting in the car waiting for me when I arrive, armed with a box of tissues.

'I don't need tissues, Poll, I just need advice.'

'He's the one who's married, not you,' she says. 'You're not doing anything wrong.'

'How can you say that after what Spencer did?'

'Because ultimately Spencer wasn't right for me. And Brooke isn't right for Daniel. And I've always thought you and Daniel would be much more compatible long term.'

'But I know it's wrong. I wouldn't want it done to me. It's bad karma . . . look what happened with Marjorie, it's a sign.'

'Oh Suze, that's not how the universe works. Marjorie fell over because her flat is a mess and she's old and she's stubborn and she won't accept help.'

Those things are true. I turn my head and gaze out of the window at a group of ramblers who are just setting off from the station car park, rucksacks on backs, chatting animatedly as they charge up the road.

'How was the kissing?' says Polly. 'I bet it was good.'

'Oh God it was so good,' I say, thinking back to how great it had been. Perfect kissing. The sort of kissing that cannot stay in one place. The sort of kissing that has to end up somewhere else. 'I know if I see him again it will happen again and we'll probably end up shagging.'

'And so what if you do? It could be the start of something.'

'I can't.' I shake my head, trying to convince myself as much as her. I agree with her that Daniel and I are very compatible when it comes to the things that really matter. I know who he used to be and I know who he is now. And I can't rid my brain of the idea that we've done a lot of the groundwork already: if we started again now we might actually stand a chance of making it. We could be happy; we could fall in love and maybe even stay in love.

'That marriage is *never* going to last,' she says.

'He needs to work that out for himself though. He might never leave her.'

'But you could give him a reason to leave,' she says, resting her hand on my arm.

What? And be like Leyla? 'I can't be the other woman.'

'You were there first,' she says.

'Yes I was. But that was a very long time ago. And I don't want to be his stepping stone.'

'But maybe he could be yours?'

'Maybe,' I say. 'But maybe he's already been that. He's the only one since Jake who made me feel some hope. Look, Polly, Daniel is married, and he's not getting unmarried any time soon.'

She nods. 'And Jake . . .'

I open my window half way and turn to look out over the empty train track. 'I still miss him, Poll. I can't pretend I don't. It still hurts. And I'm embarrassed to say it, because he so wasn't worth it . . .'

'It's that final year that did the damage. You wouldn't miss him if you'd left earlier.'

'Who ever leaves at the right time?' I say.

'You're allowed to miss him,' she says. 'But what you're not allowed to do is let that get in the way of giving the future your best shot.'

'It shouldn't still hurt,' I say.

'It will pass, I promise.' She gives me a small smile and tucks a strand of my hair behind my ear.

I nod and take a deep breath. 'I know you must be right. It must have been so much worse for you with Spencer . . .'

'Heartbreak is heartbreak, Susie. You don't need a marriage certificate to prove it. One thing Mum said to me when things fell apart was that you rarely get everything in your life functioning well at the same time – friendships, love, work . . . But two out of three's good enough.'

'I've only got one out of those three,' I say.

'Exactly. So let's work on the things that are in your control. Your job. You've been threatening to quit forever.'

'And I will, this Christmas.'

'Sometimes you have to cut your losses, quit while you're behind. Like you just said: no one ever leaves at the right time. Come on, Suze, you're totally capable of a million things. What else could you do?'

I pause. I still feel silly talking about it, but it's actually starting to look pretty cool.

'I had an idea for a blog, based on my grandma's pasta theory. There's a story behind each recipe. They're all good recipes. And who doesn't like pasta, right?'

'Everyone likes pasta,' she says. 'I made your bolognese for Dave the other night, he hasn't stopped talking about it since.'

'So I started working on it, about a month ago. I was a bit drunk, but I've done quite a lot on it since then. I mean, I know it wouldn't make money for ages, if at all . . . But if I could earn £14k with a local job or something . . . And I've been thinking I might ask Sam to help me with some more advanced technical stuff . . .'

'Sam – the cute one at work?'

'I work with him, yes.'

'Right: that's a plan Go home now and do some work. And go into the office tomorrow and ask Sam to help you. Just do it. Stop waiting for someone or something to save you. You've got to save yourself.'

And of course she's right.

On the train back home I think: 'No one ever does leave at the right time.'

Why is that?

You don't leave a relationship when your instinct first kicks in telling you that it's not going to work.

Because you want it to work. Maybe it will work. You're in love. Plus you've invested time, and energy, and hope.

If you leave then you'll have to start over. If you leave then you're admitting failure. If you leave then the worst thing in the world will happen – you will be single, a statistic in a magazine article about twenty-first-century loneliness. And so you stay. You live with dysfunction. You bury your feelings. And then a year or two later, when one of you can't ignore those niggling doubts any more, someone cheats, or thinks of cheating, or leaves.

And that's the main reason why this Jake thing haunts me.

Because I knew for so long that it wasn't right, but I was a coward. I just sat there doing nothing about it, because I was scared. Same way I'm sitting at NMN, knowing that even after they promote me I'll probably be too scared to actually leave.

I have been scared about a lot of things since Jake left.

Scared Rebecca would find a boyfriend and I'd be the last singleton left.

Scared I'd made a fool of myself in front of Jeff.

Very scared of how I felt about Daniel – too much longing for someone I shouldn't long for.

Most of all I was scared I'd never get over Jake, scared I'd never feel OK again. But Polly's right. I will.

And there's only one person who can help me: me.

I call Daniel back that night.

'Are you OK?' he says. 'I was worried about you.'

'You don't need to worry about me,' I say. 'Sorry I had to run off.'

'Is your neighbour OK?'

'Sort of. Terry spoke to her earlier. She's going to be in there for at least a couple of weeks I think. They're going to have to reset the bone in her wrist.'

'Sounds painful,' he says.

'Yep. Perils of old age. I'm going to head down to the hospital to see her tomorrow after work. Visiting hours are only till 8 p.m. but I should be able to escape the office more or less on time.'

'That's so sweet of you.'

'Not really, I feel like it's the least I can do. Terry's going to look after her budgie this week and then we'll work out a plan once we know when she'll be coming out.'

'You're not going to fight Terry for custody of the bird?'

'No way. Do you know how noisy budgies can actually be? I've just finished making Marjorie some of her favourite dark chocolate mousse. That's my one good deed for the day. It'll be nicer than the food in the hospital, though I don't know whether she'll be in the mood to eat it.'

'Well if she's not, then I always am!' he says.

'Don't worry, I'm sure I'll find a home for it.'

'No, I'm serious, I love chocolate mousse.'

'I know you do.'

'So why don't you save me a little bit and I can pop over tomorrow night when you're back from the hospital and say hi?'

I wish.

'No,' I say. 'I don't know what time I'll actually be back.'

'OK then, how about Thursday? I'm round at Joe's for dinner but we could go for a drink first. I could meet you after work in town?'

'I can't. I'm sorry. I wish I could,' I say.

'Why can't you?'

'Because I like you too much to see you – if that makes any sense?'

He pauses. 'Not really; that doesn't make much sense at all.'

'What happened yesterday,' I say. 'I feel bad about it. But not that bad. I know I wouldn't stop myself next time.'

'Look: we can just be friends,' he says. 'We are friends.'

'We were friends,' I say. 'And we will be friends, I hope. In fact I'm sure of it. But we just can't be friends at this precise moment in time.'

He is silent. I can't bear it when he's silent. I have to force myself to speak again. 'Daniel: I have to focus on other things for now that are more important in my life. And so do you.'

There is more silence. Silence which I want to fill with the words: 'Actually forget everything I just said and come round now, right now and I'll open a bottle of wine and make us a lovely dinner and let's see what happens . . .'

But I don't. Because I am finally doing what Jake told me to do years ago: growing up.

w/c 21st May

Status report:

- New brief – chase
- Happy Hour – plan. URGENT
- Write five more recipes for the blog and investigate cameras

Wednesday

Where is this new Fletchers brief?

And where is Jonty? He's been to-ing and fro-ing like mad these past few days, and when I ask where he's going he just looks blank. It's 9 a.m. already and if he's chucking a sickie he should at least have called in by now with that pathetic pretend-croaky voice he puts on.

Hopefully he's interviewing at another agency and then I can recruit someone less work-averse . . . Though I'm sure Berenice has a file marked 'Nepotism', full of replacements already lined up . . .

Speak of the devil, he's calling now . . .

'Susie, you've got to help me out.'

Do I?

'I'm at Fletchers and I've just realised I've left the new script on my desk. Any chance you could scan and email it to me?'

'What? What do you mean, new script?'

'Oh. Shite. Have you not spoken to Berenice yet?'

'About what?'

'Ah, well, I don't have time to explain but basically could you just scan it for me?'

'Just call the team and ask them to email you,' I say grumpily. What on earth is going on? Jonty's not meant to look after TV briefs, he's not experienced enough yet . . .

'I can't speak to the team,' he says.

'Why not?'

There's a pause on the line. 'Because I'm scared of them.'
Scared of them? It can't be.

I head over to his desk. 'Jonty . . . where is this script?'

'Somewhere . . . fuck . . . on the left maybe? Under the status report?'

'Hold on . . . this one here . . . with Karly and Nick's name at the top?'

'Yeah, that's the one. Please hurry up, I can't screw this up, it's a big meeting.'

I look at the script. I take a deep breath. No. It can't be. It cannot possibly be.

'Jonty, I'm afraid I'm going to have to call you back.'

'What *are* you talking about?' says Berenice, looking at me as if I'm speaking Dutch. Or Danish.

'That whole script is *my* idea based on *my grandmother's theory* and I cannot believe Karly is putting my words in Celina Summer's mouth – Celina Summer hasn't even got an Italian grandmother! And Jonty, running the project? And no one even mentioned it to me? I'm sorry, Berenice, but I don't understand how this has happened.'

I can feel my face burning with rage, my arms feel fuzzy with adrenaline.

She sighs. 'It's quite simple. Devron was obviously keen to turn around another script quickly with Celina in it, to capitalise on the success of Karly and Nick's last campaign. And Robbie and Karly talked about this idea a while back. And there's nothing sinister about the fact that we gave it to Jonty. Frankly, after all the bad blood between you and the creative team, how could we *not* give it to Jonty? I thought you'd be relieved. I have no idea why you're quite so angry.'

'I'm sorry, Berenice: "I'm Celina Summer and when I was little, my granny used to say there's always the perfect pasta for whatever life throws at you. Take pesto with penne . . ."? That is practically verbatim what I said to

Karly during the research group. Apart from the words "I'm Celina Summer" . . .'

'Oh really, Susannah. It's not your idea.'

'Jeff from Fletchers was sitting next to me when I was talking about it; he'll tell you it was my idea.' Except we were both a bit tipsy and while I'm pretty sure he'd vouch for me I'm not entirely sure how much detail he'd remember.

'Even if you did have a vague conversation on that general subject, Karly's the one who turned the raw nugget into a script. Ideas and scripts are not the same thing. You could have an idea about a man wearing jeans, that doesn't mean you wrote a Levi's ad.'

'Berenice,' I say, shaking my head. 'It was not a raw nugget. It literally is my idea. My words. My grandmother. And I don't want Fletchers to use it.'

'You can't copyright an idea, Susannah, it's not intellectual property. I've had many ideas in my time that I've shared. Besides, Devron's signed off on the concept already, we're just finessing the details.'

'But I might want to do something with that idea myself.'

She pauses to consider this. 'If what you're actually saying is that you're interested in doing a week's work placement in the creative department then that is something we could potentially discuss with Robbie.'

'No, that is not what I'm saying at all! Fletchers pay us a hundred grand a month for creative ideas, and that particular idea is mine – not Karly's, and not this agency's.' And it is my escape route out of this hell hole! I've put in all this hard work and now it'll look like I've copied Celina Bloody Summer!

Her voice takes on a sharper edge. 'Now is not the time to be throwing your toys out of the pram. I find it quite surprising that you would be so disruptive, after all the problems you created on the last brief, given that you're presumably still hoping for some sort of promotion at year end.'

'Hold on. Are you saying you'll definitely promote me but only if I let this slide?'

She twists her head slightly.

'Is that what you're saying, Berenice?'

'If you do what is expected of you, and what is right for the brand and for this agency, then that will be taken into consideration in due course . . .'

'And that means . . .'

She turns her head to look out of the window, then gives an exhausted sigh. '*Yes*. We can do that for you at Christmas.'

'Right. Jolly good. At Christmas,' I say. 'Fine. See you at Happy Hour next week.'

I am still quivering with rage when I walk into the mail room.

'Sam,' I say. 'I need you to do me a favour.'

'I'm not very good at cutting up bodies,' he says, looking at me nervously. 'I can chop up Karly, but I can't do Nick too.'

'You know that Cloud thing you mentioned in Robbie's Happy Hour?'

He nods.

'Can you tap into Karly's old text messages and notes file on her iPhone with it, or is that not something the Cloud keeps?'

'The Cloud keeps all of it.'

'Even if she's subsequently deleted a file?'

'All of it. What dates do you need?'

'Just the one: Thursday 12th April, at around 6pm for an hour.'

'OK,' he says. 'I might need to pull a little favour but is Monday morning OK?'

'That'll be fine.'

I am still angry when I get home.

Not Oscar the Grouch angry, that's just a grump. No, I am full on Tony Soprano furious.

OK. Pasta for an angry night, a very angry night, pasta to calm one's ire and help one think straight . . .

Right. Rigatoni: it's nice, it's short, it's precise, and it will help me formulate a nice, short, precise plan. And arrabbiata sauce would be the obvious choice – it literally does mean angry. But I fear chilli will only work me into a greater state of apoplexy.

No. Calm. Simple. Clarity of thought: butter, parmesan. Strip it right back to basics:

Fletchers are going to use my idea whether I like it or not.

I could rush out a load more recipes for my blog now – but it'll take months and months to build up an audience and by that time people will associate my idea with Celina.

Even if I can prove Karly stole it – and with Sam's help I'm sure I can – then it won't do much good.

The only thing NMN would worry about is a negative story in the trade press . . . Damage to their reputation . . . Whistle blow . . . So all I can do is encourage them to keep me away from that whistle . . .

All I want to do is quit anyway . . . Hmm. Tricky . . .

By the time I've finished my final bite of pasta I've figured it all out.

Sunday

I have called Sam and asked him for another favour.

I have explained the first part of the plan to him and he actually used the word 'genius', although I suspect he might have meant 'lunatic'. And now he is sitting on my sofa with his laptop waiting to brainstorm ideas for an alternative blog with me.

Since my conversation with Berenice last week, I have been so busy thinking about what's going to happen next week and, more importantly, the weeks after that, that I have not been anywhere near a shop and now I look in slight despair at the contents of my fridge.

'What time's lunch?' calls Sam from the living room.

'I might have to buy you a pizza,' I say, taking out a bowl of mashed potato from last night and wondering if I could make it into potato cakes or bubble and squeak . . . But I promised Sam lunch, and boys – well this particular boy – likes meat. There is that nice chicken stew in the freezer that I could defrost . . . I think that it might just about stretch . . .

Sam comes through into the kitchen and looks in horror at my fruit bowl. 'Jesus Christ, were those once bananas?' he says.

'Perfect!' I say. 'Do you fancy some banana bread?'

'Not if you're using that old shit in it,' he says. 'They're disgusting.'

'Sam, that's how you make banana bread,' I say, shaking my head. 'The bananas have to be totally over-ripe. You've had my banana bread before.'

'Yeah, but I didn't realise it was made with bananas that looked like that. And what's that stuff in the bowl?' he says, looking over my shoulder at the cold mash.

'Just go and sit back in the living room and find that thing you were talking about . . . the digital platform what's-its-face . . .'

'Alright but promise not to poison me if you want my help,' he says.

I defrost the chicken stew and then find a bit of cara-melised onion chutney in the back of the fridge that's like the crack cocaine of condiments. I stir a dollop through the chicken, stick the potatoes on top with a bit of extra butter and some grated cheese, and shove it in the oven. I'll give Sam a beer or two now and then he won't notice if it all tastes a bit weird . . .

'Actually, Sam, do you want to help me make the banana bread?' I say, calling through to him. 'That way you can make it when I'm not around every day.'

'I'm not touching those bananas,' he says. 'Division of labour, you do what you're best at and I'll do the same.'

Fair enough . . . I mash the bananas, weigh out the flour, sugar and eggs, and chuck in some dark and milk chocolate chips as I'm out of fudge pieces, and stick that in the top oven.

I go back through to Sam who is looking at a website about affiliate marketing and clicks per thousand and all the things I need to start getting my head around. He talks me through the basics, which is all well and good, but I'm avoiding the major problem, which is that I no longer have an idea, as it's been nicked.

'I know what I want the new site to look and feel like,' I say, showing him Ms Marmite Lover's blog, and Dash and Bella. 'These two blogs look totally beautiful but they're also brilliantly written, they have a point of view . . .'

'OK,' he says. 'Well, you're never short of things to say, are you?'

'Yes but my idea has gone!' I say, as I hear the oven timer go off.

'If you can have one good idea you can have lots,' he says.

I open the oven door. Oooh! This chicken thing's turned out alright! That melted cheese on top's done the trick. Actually it's better than alright, it looks delicious.

'Lunch is served,' I say, as I take it through to him.

'Smells amazing,' he says. 'What is it?'

'*Pollo rimasto*?' I say.

'What does that mean?'

'It's Italian for leftover chicken. Try it, it's an experiment.'

'Yep,' he says, taking a forkful. 'Good. Really good.'

I watch him as he eats. I love it when someone's enjoying a meal and they're oblivious to everything around them – lost in simple pleasure. When he's finished I offer him the final three bites from my plate and he eats them with gusto. There's the tiniest bit of mashed potato stuck just above his lip, and I smile to myself, waiting for him to notice. I resist a little urge to lean over and wipe it off with my finger.

By the time I've cleared the plates and come back through it's gone, and he's settled back on the sofa, laptop resting on his knees, typing and scanning the screen intently.

'Sam, are those new jeans?' They're darker denim than the ones he usually wears at work and they're smarter. In combo with that navy cotton sweatshirt he has on, he actually looks rather stylish, almost French.

'Huh?' he says, looking up briefly.

'Oh no, nothing, forget it. Anyway, so, ideas, ideas . . .' I say. 'I want the website to be about food, obviously, but I want to do more than just recipes. There are so many brilliant blogs out there, I have to do something different enough to actually stand out and make money.'

'Agreed, too much competition already.'

'Right, so I'm thinking maybe do something more visual, like Pinterest . . .'

He nods.

'Or maybe have an area of the site where users could swap recipe ideas?' I say.

He pauses to consider this. 'They could swap stuff, not just ideas?'

'Like what?'

'You know, cookbooks or kitchen bits.'

'Oh, like Freecycle but with more lemon squeezers?'

'Yeah exactly. And you could do a social thing too, I don't know, like a community . . .' he says.

'Or even a dating thing! But instead of people saying *I like walking* and *I like laughing* they could talk about what they like best in a sandwich. That's more useful information in a prospective partner, isn't it? Find people who have similar tastes in food to you, matched appetites . . . Or even unmatched, like Jack and Mrs Sprat . . .'

'Perhaps you could combine the community idea with the dating idea,' says Sam, scratching his cheek. 'Get together with people in your area who like similar food.'

'Like a group date, but not in a bunga-bunga way,' I say. He laughs. 'More like in a *take the pressure off the date* kind of way . . .'

'See?' says Sam, pointing at me. 'I told you ideas don't happen in isolation. You're full of them.'

'Yes, but I still don't have a theme. I don't want to do something overtly British, that feels dated already, all that stuff last year with the Olympics and the Jubilee . . . And puddings have been done to death, and so has baking. And I'm not going anywhere near cupcakes . . .'

'Doughnuts?' says Sam. 'I'm a massive fan of doughnuts. You'd be good at doughnuts, Suze. I think they could be your true calling.'

'I am a fan of doughnuts, Sam, but I'm not sure that I could build an entire online empire based around them. Besides, it needs to be broader than just one food type. Apparently Peruvian's the new big thing, but I don't know anything about Peru. I think perhaps something Italian. That feels like the obvious direction to go in, but not pasta . . . I don't know. Maybe it should be wine, not food . . .'

'Whatever it is, just make up your mind so we can get started.'

'OK,' I say, feeling a sudden burst of energy. 'I'm going to go and have a look through my recipe files now and start having a proper think.'

'Do you want me to stay and help?'

'No, no, you've been great, but I want to get cracking,' I say, standing up and walking him to the door. 'Oh shit, I nearly forgot, the banana bread . . .'

'That smells amazing,' he says, following me through into the kitchen and peering over my shoulder expectantly, as

I take it out of the oven. I hold the hot tin out for him to smell: how could anyone fail to be moved by this warm, vanilla-y, buttery sweetness, with the melted chocolate coming through?

'Susie, I've thought of another thing I could do to help you out,' he says, hovering as I place the loaf tin on a cooling rack.

'What's that, Sam?' I say, turning to him.

'I could take this cake off your hands?'

He has set his facial expression to earnest and helpful but as I look at him he breaks into a grin.

'You would seriously actually do that for me, Sam?'

He nods.

'But, Sam, I couldn't possibly impose on you any further. You've done so much for me today already . . .'

'As long as you promise I'm not going to die on the way home because of those Stone Age bananas . . .'

'Ah Sam, there are no guarantees in life. But OK, if you honestly wouldn't mind relieving me of this horrendous burden, you really would be doing me an *enormous* favour.'

The cake's too hot to remove from the tin so instead I double-wrap the whole thing in foil and put it in a bag. When I hand it to Sam, he looks properly chuffed – like four of his numbers have just come up on the lottery.

'Can I actually do this, Sam?' I say, as we stand by my front door and he puts on his jacket.

'Of course you can. It's about time. It's more than time. You're finally manning up.'

'And you're sure you're happy to help me with all of this? I mean, I can't pay you at this point, other than in cake, and it will be a lot of work over the coming months.'

He shakes his head. 'It's fine, I'll enjoy it. Just hurry up and think of your theme.' I think he's almost as excited about all of this as I am.

'And this thing tomorrow with Karly's Cloud,' I say. 'You're not going to get into trouble for that, are you?'

'No. Come and see me first thing and I'll have a printout for you.'

'Why are you doing all this for me, Sam?'

'Because I'm on your side,' he says, without a moment's hesitation. He pauses to consider it further. 'And because it feels like justice.'

He hovers in the doorway and allows himself a little smile. 'And because I can.'

By the time I get into bed I am so buzzy with nervous energy that I can't sleep.

I lie there and I think:

Sam seems a lot more grown up when he's not in that mail room. And those new jeans fit him so much better than the old ones he wears at work.

And I think:

I wish I hadn't given him all of that banana bread. It would have made a brilliant base for a trifle, I could have had a layer of butterscotch custard under the cream. That would have been delicious.

And I think:

I wonder how Daniel McKendall's getting on. I hope he's getting on well. I hope he's happy. I want only good things for him.

And I think:

Having kids forces people into being grown ups. And if you don't have kids then you can live in prolonged adolescence for a really long time. But then you'll wake up one day and you'll be fifty years old and behaving like a teenager. And that is not a good look.

But there is an alternative and you do have a choice. You can push yourself into being an adult.

And finally I think:

If you can take on Berenice then you can take on Karly too. And if you can do that you can literally do anything. She's a bully. They are all bullies. And if you don't stand up to bullies, they keep bullying. And it's time to fight back.

And if you don't do this now you will never do it at all.

w/c 28th May

Status report:
- Take a deep breath
- Catch up with Sam and then Karly
- Happy Hour – speech

Monday

I didn't think it was technically possible to feel any angrier than I did last week, but my rage is re-ignited when Sam shows me the exact wording of what he's retrieved from Karly's iPhone. I still cannot quite believe she has done this; though why is that? It's not like I'm the first.

My dad says never do anything when you're feeling very angry; sit tight. But this extra burst of fury is probably the force that finally propels me up to the creative floor and towards Karly's office.

'She's got no time in her diary until next week,' says Alexis.

'Don't worry,' I say, 'this won't take long.'

'You can't go in there without an appointment,' she says, but I'm already at the door.

Karly's sitting flicking through *Campaign* with her feet up on the desk, electric blue Louboutin boots flashing their red soles at me.

'Hey, Karly,' I say. 'I know you're busy but I just wanted to check something with you on your new pasta script for Fletchers.'

'What about it?' she says, looking over the top of her magazine suspiciously.

'It's really good,' I say. 'I like the idea.'

'Yeah. Cheers.'

'It just occurred to me that it's exactly the same idea I was talking about in that research group you were at . . . do you remember?'

'Not really,' she says.

'You remember Jeff, that good-looking guy from Fletchers, who was sitting next to me?'

She shrugs.

'Because he remembers that conversation too . . .' I say.

'All I remember is that you were quite pissed and you were coming out with all sorts of weird shit about pasta . . .'

'And then you asked me about pesto . . . ?'

'I have no memory of that,' she says, slowly turning the page of her magazine.

'You did, Karly, you asked me about pesto.'

'If you say so. Believe it or not, I don't keep a diary of conversations I have with account people in the middle of research sessions that shouldn't even be happening two weeks before a shoot.'

'Fair enough,' I say. 'But actually you were writing something on your phone, do you not remember?'

'No,' she says.

'You were. You were typing while I was talking to you. I remember because, believe it or not, most people don't continuously type while other people are talking to them.'

'Whatever you say,' she shrugs.

'You were writing some notes on your iPhone, weren't you?'

'Actually?' she says angrily, putting her magazine down on the desk. 'If you must know, I was texting Nick to tell him what a nightmare that session was.'

'Yes, that's quite right,' I say, fury running through my veins. 'So you were. But after you texted Nick telling him what a stupid bitch I was, you wrote some notes on your phone. And those notes were my exact words, and the exact words that are now on that script.'

I say nothing. I look her directly in the eye, hoping like mad that I'm not showing any fear.

'What are you getting your knickers in a twist for anyway?' she says finally, picking the magazine up from her desk again. 'It's not that big a deal. We take our inspiration from everywhere.'

I know that, Karly. But you do not take it from me.

Back at my desk and I only have to wait nineteen minutes before my phone rings. I've only just stopped shaking.

'Martin Meddlar!' I say. 'To what do I owe the pleasure?' Although we are both fully aware.

'Have you got five minutes?' he says, brightly.

'Now?' I say.

'No time like the present . . .' He hangs up.

I could not be readier.

'I hear you had an interesting chat with Karly, who subsequently had an interesting chat with Robbie. I'm not sure how you came to know the contents of her iPhone but let's put that to one side for now. Let's focus on how we can help you at this point?' he says.

'Last week Berenice offered me a week's placement in the creative department. But I've been thinking. And I'd like a slightly more generous offer than that, to reflect the fact that my idea is the basis of this new campaign.'

'What were you thinking?'

'Well, Fletchers pay you £100k a month as a retainer for creative resource. And we give them a half decent idea on average about once every three months, if they're lucky – so I'd say my idea is worth around £300k.'

'*Three hundred grand?* You can't possibly think . . .'

'Obviously I'm not expecting you to pay me anywhere near that amount. Because here you have lots of overheads, like those premium chocolate biscuits and so forth . . .'

'Tell me you'll settle for a month's worth of biscuits . . .?' he says, grinning at me.

'I *shall* take a month's worth of biscuits, seeing as you've offered – along with a fair payment for my idea. So how about a very modest five per cent of what Fletchers are paying for creative resource?'

He fixes me with a look that is part admiration, part lust, part surprise, and part fear.

'I'm not convinced your idea is worth fifteen grand . . .' he says finally, tapping his fingertips together slowly in front of his chin.

'Well, I'm not really sure that spending fifty grand a year on white lilies for reception is worth it either,' I say.

'Is that really what we spend on flowers?' he asks, looking appalled.

'Berenice's peonies cost another twenty . . .'

'Well, ten grand is the going rate for the board's bonus at Christmas,' he says.

'Actually it was fifteen grand last year. That's what Steve Pearson was paid.'

He pauses. 'I'm quite surprised you discuss these figures amongst yourselves.'

Yes, well Sam and I discussed it. After Sam looked up the finance files . . .

'Fifteen grand is what I'll be getting when you put me on the board this Christmas,' I say. 'But I would like my bonus and promotion now, I don't want to wait till December.'

'I think that's not unreasonable,' he says, looking relieved. 'And this is on the understanding that we move forward with a clean slate.'

'Absolutely,' I say. 'No point looking back. The future's bright and all that.'

'OK. We'll look into getting you your bonus and promotion at month end,' he says.

'No, I meant I'd like them now, as in *now* now,' I say. 'I'd like my promotion signed off and a CHAPS payment today. I'm doing my Inspiration Hour on Friday and I'd be so much more *motivated* if the money was already in my account.'

He pauses to consider this. 'I don't know if finance can do a CHAPS payment mid-month . . .'

'They managed to when Sandra Weston had to be paid off after her rather unfortunate difference of opinion with Karly. That was on the 12th of January. A Thursday, I believe . . . I'm sure these things are possible, with a little persuasion . . .' I say.

'You're bloody good on detail, I'll grant you that,' he says, standing up with a half smile that's verging on respect.

'There's one more small thing . . .' I say. He hovers, not knowing whether to sit or stand.

410

'And what would that be?' he says.

'I would like you to get Karly to apologise to me.'

His face falls. 'Susie: I can get you the money. And at a push I can probably get you the biscuits. But there's only so much I can do: you do realise I'm not Merlin?'

You know what? He's right. I am being unreasonable. Because even if he did manage to make her apologise, she wouldn't actually be sorry. She'd merely be sorry she'd been caught.

'I just thought it was worth asking,' I say, shrugging. 'Right then – so you'll authorise a CHAPS payment for me?'

'It'll be in your bank account by end of play,' he says.

'OK,' I say, holding out my hand to him and smiling. 'I think we have a deal.'

He smiles broadly back. 'Why *haven't* we promoted you earlier?' he says. 'I think you might have what it takes to go far.'

Oh I am going to go far, Martin. Very.

Watch me.

Friday

It is Friday. It is Happy Hour. And it is my turn to speak.

I thought long and hard about what music to play as I walked up to the podium. Sam suggested the theme tune from *Rocky*. I was thinking more like the Rolling Stones, 'You Can't Always Get What You Want'. But in the end I decided to have nothing. The only words I have to say today are my own. And this won't be a normal Happy Hour. I reckon it'll be more like a Happy Four Minutes.

I stand with my speech on a scrap of paper in front of me and look out at my audience. A few faces I love, a few faces I don't; most in between.

There are moments in life when I've thought: 'I could change my world in a heartbeat. I'm driving at seventy miles an hour along the M1 and if I jerked this steering

412

wheel five inches to the left, I'd crash. Five inches between me and a fiery death-ball.'

Or I could call up Jake and tell him 'There are times when I literally ache from still missing you, so could you please change the past, and large parts of your personality so that we can be happy and I will never have to feel lonely again?'

I would never do either of those things because I'm not crazy, I don't want to die. And even more than dying, I definitely don't want to be rejected. And besides, I do understand that you can't change the past and you can't change other people.

So I have not been foolish, but I have not been brave at all either. I have stayed in the safe area, in the comfort zone for a long time now, in emotional limbo.

But there are moments in life where staying comfortable has become so uncomfortable that it's not an option to keep your mouth shut any more. And I know, as I look at Berenice and Robbie and, for the first time in the front row, Sam too, that this is my moment. It is now or never.

I am on. The audience look at me, a few smiling, most already bored, fiddling with their apps. I can feel my heart beating in my chest, and a little voice in my head saying do it. Just do it. Not in a Nike way, like Robbie would think. Or in a JFDI way, like Devron would. But in a Polly way.

'Hello everybody,' I say, giving the microphone a gentle tap. 'I hope your Friday's been good. I hope your whole week has been good. Steve Pearson, how was your week?'

Steve looks up in surprise, mid sex-text – and says, 'Yeah. Fine, cheers.'

'I'm glad,' I say. 'It's good to talk. Good to talk to each other. You sit next to me, I say good morning, hello, goodbye. It's nice. Human. Rather than you emailing me from four desks along asking for a favour and then ignoring me when we pass in the corridor.' I say this with a smile on my face – you can say anything you like when you're smiling – people think you're being jolly.

'Today's Happy Hour is just a few simple thoughts from me. We've all sat here over the years and listened to the great and good tell us lots of fascinating facts, and I thought I can't really compete with that. Plus we do all know how to use Google by now. So I'll just tell you a few things I've been thinking about recently.

'When I was young, I fell in love with the Smash Martians. Do you remember them?' There are a few smiles and nods in the audience from those old enough to remember.

'These funny little talking aliens charmed the pants off people; they made us want to go out and buy powdered potatoes. I loved them so much they could probably have persuaded me to buy a powdered steak.' Sam nods his encouragement from the front row.

414

'And the reason those ads were so persuasive was because they had an idea in them. And they had charm, and they had wit.' Robbie nods and Berenice allows herself a pinch of a smile.

'But nowadays it seems we don't have those sorts of ideas very often. We're "inspired" by ideas that we "discover" on the internet. We "borrow" a new animation style from some kid in Idaho, or "pay homage" to a brilliant idea from a girl in Leeds, and just don't quite get round to giving them credit. I've been working recently on a big pizza campaign for Fletchers. Berenice, when you briefed me, you said that the project would define me. It was called "The Truth". It did really well.

'Now we talk a lot about truth in this building. Getting *to the heart of the brand*. Being *the midwife of its soul*. But the truth is this: brands don't have hearts, and they don't have souls. People do. Well, some of them.

'The truth is, I am not defined by a brief for a pizza. None of us here should be defined by our work, no matter how big the budget is. We are defined by how we treat other people. I've been at NMN for six years. When I joined I had hope, a bit of confidence, joy and some energy. I lost them in this place, maybe in the lush carpets, or in one of the giant lily vases in reception. But last weekend for the first time in about three years I found them again.'

I pause for a moment, feeling my heart pounding in my chest.

'"The truth will set you free" apparently. You might have heard that quote before? It's from the Bible, though I think you'll find that Karly came up with it first. Well, the truth has set me free, in its own way.

'Robbie, I have one thing I've been meaning to say to you for such a very long time: Leonardo Da Vinci did not paint the Sistine Chapel. It was Michel-bloody-Angelo. Michelangelo. He was a painter. Italian. And if you don't believe me, look it up on Wikipedia.' I take a deep breath and take my piece of paper from the podium and turn to go.

I hesitate for a moment and turn back.

'Oh, and one more thing,' I say. 'I almost forgot!' I take a deep breath and force myself to stay calm.

'Robbie: you always said that you're a huge fan of the killer end line. Well so am I. How's about this for one? I quit.'

I walk out of the agency.

I head north and I keep walking.

I turn left and walk through Regent's Park and then out past the long parade of perfect cream Nash Houses.

I take a right and then walk all the way up to the top of Primrose Hill and sit on a bench looking out over this beautiful grey city.

I almost cannot believe what I have done. But I have done it.

It is foolish and perhaps it is brave and perhaps it is insane. But whatever it turns out to be, at least I will have tried.

So come on then, life.

Let's see what you've got for me.

One year later

30th May

As the minicab pulls up outside the Hilton on Park Lane I take Sam's hand and give it a little squeeze. His fingers are strong, though mine are shaking.

I'm so nervous that I accidentally tip the driver the change from a twenty rather than a ten and only realise when I'm half way down the stairs to the Great Room reception area. Oh well – what goes around comes around. I suppose I've had a pretty good year on most fronts.

The lobby's already bustling – gorgeous girls in sequins or one-shouldered numbers or tuxedo-style jackets, lots of perfectly groomed brows and highlighted cheekbones.

After much consideration I have opted for the purple dress I wore to Polly's wedding. I admit, I dithered; it makes me think so much of that amazing night with Daniel. But it's OK to think of Daniel a little bit. We can be friends. We are friends, from a distance. His life goes on and my life goes on and maybe one day his situation will change. And maybe if it does and if I'm single, and if we both feel like it, then maybe we'll go for a drink. But that's a lot of ifs and maybes. And one thing I have learned is that you cannot live your life in ifs and maybes . . . You cannot live it in week commencings. You live it right here. You live it now.

Sam and I head over to where a couple of girls with clipboards are standing under a silver banner that reads '*Style and Food Magazine* Awards – Short-List Finalists' to pick up my name tag. I scan the names for Leyla's – her blog is on the list too, but her tag's already gone.

'Are you sure you don't want to do this bit for me, Sam?' I say. 'I wouldn't be here if it wasn't for you.'

'You can't blame any of this on me,' he says, putting his hands gently on my shoulders and smiling. 'It's all your work. It's all you. In fact it couldn't be more you.'

'Let me just pin this name on you for a little bit . . . just till after the speeches.' I make a grab for his lapel. My, but this boy does scrub up well. I can't quite believe how dashing he looks in his suit. He has even managed to get a good haircut, and he's promised he won't pop out for a fag till midnight.

'You know I can't be trusted speaking in public,' I say. 'Not after the last time!'

'Oh I don't know,' he says. 'That was one of the highlights of my time at NMN. That and the time Steve Pearson got locked in the toilet overnight.'

I don't expect to bump in to Jake immediately. I was hoping to neck a couple of glasses of champagne at the very least, to calm my nerves. But of course things never ever turn out the way you play them in the fantasy in your head. He's there, of course – with her, of course. And the first thing I feel when I see him is a tiny jolt of shock, followed by a balloon-burst of disappointment. I've waited so long for this moment and now that it's here how could it be anything other than an anti-climax?

He looks fine. Not amazing, not terrible. A little bit chunkier than when I last saw him. A little bit older. So do I, I'm sure. Does he look happy? He looks a bit tired and a bit bored. Not unhappy. But he doesn't look as happy as me.

I instinctively check his left hand to see if he's wearing a ring. He isn't, and she's not wearing an engagement ring. And I realise that I would actually feel OK even if she was wearing a massive rock: she has ceased to be shrapnel. And then I suddenly understand that over the last year something truly wonderful has happened. The feelings of love I once had for Jake have become something better. They have gone through pain and turned into indifference. And when you truly don't care any more, you are finally free.

Because Polly was so right. If he hadn't left me, then sure, maybe none of the bad things would have happened in these last two years, but none of the good things would have happened either. If we'd stayed together I would have

420

just bumbled along. I'd have always had someone to come home to, to watch a DVD with. And I would have hidden in that relationship and put him first, so that I never had to try or fail at anything that was all my own. He pushed me onto that path to freedom, though I didn't want to be pushed. Freedom. That's a much greater luxury than a Birkin bag.

So I really should go over now and thank him. But I'm not going to. Not because I'm going to ignore him. I'm not. I give him a little wave and a smile. Just for old times' sake. No, I don't go over to him because I have somewhere far more important that I'm meant to be: front row table in the Grand Room, taking my seat for the ceremony. And there's a few VIPs already sitting there who I need to say an urgent hello to.

Polly, six months pregnant with baby number two. Rebecca and Luke, holding hands under the table. The pair of them look like they should be in a Kooples ad, they're so perfectly beautiful together. Frandrew, still together and still snogging like teenagers at the back of a bus. Debbie, without that idiot husband of hers. Dalia, back with that idiot boyfriend of hers. Mum, Dad, Terry! Marjorie's sitting next to Terry, almost smiling. And there's lovely, sweet Andy Ashford with his wife.

This time last year, all I could think about were the things I didn't have: a boyfriend. Someone to go on mini-breaks with. Younger skin. Size ten jeans that fitted me. A really good marble pestle and mortar. A promotion. Something solid in the ground to say 'I've done OK, I'm not a total failure.'

I wanted so many things that I didn't have. But I look around me now at the people gathered at this table and I no longer think of all the things I don't have. But of all these things I do. Because it's not about scrabbling in the void for people to share your loneliness. It's about filling the void with the people you love, to share the good times.

The ceremony has started and everything is such a blur that I don't hear my name called out as the winner is announced but suddenly my mum is grabbing my arm and whispering loudly.

'Hurry up, get up there before they change their minds . . .'

I take a long slow sip of water, then a quick gulp of champagne, then a bit more water, and I move slowly to the stage. I feel a wave of nerves push me up the steps and carry me over to the microphone.

I take a deep breath. And another. And then I begin.

'Good evening, ladies and gentlemen. My name is Susie Rosen. I run a blog called The Leftovers.

'I started writing this blog twelve months ago and I had three people reading it, only one of whom wasn't a relative. Last week a lady called Jenny Knight in Norwich became my 100,000th subscriber. Waitrose signed up as my biggest advertiser. And you, *Style and Food Magazine* (my favourite magazine, by the way, I have always been a fan!) voted me as your best new website of the year.

'Leftovers started out as a collection of tasty, budget-conscious recipes with a clever search engine that my very talented friend and business partner Sam designed. And now it's grown into something a bit bigger. It has a scrap-book section where readers post photos of their own recipes. And there's a Swapsies section, where you can exchange or give away bits of kitchen equipment you don't use any more . . . And then there's the newest section of the site which is like a dating website but based on food. It's called Meet Up/Eat Up. You don't have to go out one-on-one either – if there's a few of you who are single you can go out for a meal as a group.

'Leftovers. It's a funny old word. To some people it might sound a little bit negative. Like the things that got left on the table, the things that no one really wants. A dollop of mashed potato. Two chicken thighs that didn't get eaten because you were saving room for that more exciting dessert. The last scraping of caramelised onion chutney in the bottom of the jar, the square of Cornish Cruncher cheddar at the back of the fridge that you failed to wrap properly.

'But take that slightly hard cheese and grate it. Warm the potato, stir the cheese through. Add a lump of butter. Add a lump of butter to everything. Take those pieces of chicken and spread that not-quite-enough scraping of onion chutney on top, then layer the potato on and put it in the oven. In twenty-five minutes you'll have a dish I call "Sam's chicken". Tender chicken, golden cheesy mash, with a sweet, sharp hint of caramelised onion.

'And there you were, thinking of throwing all that in a bin.

'That's the thing about leftovers. With a little thought, a little imagination, a little faith – you can see the potential in what's left on the table. You can put in some work. And you can make something.' I resist the urge to look at Sam, though even against the bright lights of the stage I can still make out his expression – a huge grin, full of pride.

'You can make something worthwhile,' I say, feeling hope rise up in me so strongly I have to take a breath.

'You can make something good.' I allow myself the tiniest of smiles in Sam's direction.

'Maybe something even better than you started with.

'My name is Susie Rosen.' And I am a Leftover.

Pasta for when you've just finished a book that you enjoyed and there's a little hole in your life to fill while you ponder what to read next

This pasta is my slightly indulgent take on an Amatriciana – the classic Roman sauce of tomato, bacon and cheese. It is nowhere near authentic, but it is easy, delicious, comforting and not that bad for you, in a relative universe. These quantities make enough sauce for two people, but I've written as a 'serves one', so that if there is one of you, you can eat the leftover sauce the following day once you're engrossed in your new book and can no longer be bothered to cook.

Serves 1

Ingredients:
100g linguine
70g cubed pancetta
A knob of butter
1 tbsp olive oil
1 medium onion – red or white – or 1 echalion/banana shallot, chopped
1 large clove of garlic, thinly sliced
A pinch of red chilli flakes
A pinch of sugar
A pinch of salt

A tin of Italian tomatoes – preferably peeled cherry tomatoes
40ml of single cream
Pecorino (or parmesan)

Method:
Heat the butter and olive oil in a saucepan over a medium heat until the butter has melted.

Add the onion/shallot and cook over a gentle heat for five minutes, stirring occasionally.

Add the pancetta and garlic, and cook for a further ten minutes, stirring, so that the onion starts to turn golden, but doesn't turn brown.

Add the tomatoes, chilli flakes, salt and sugar. Stir, and leave to cook on a low heat for 30 minutes.

Meanwhile cook the pasta in boiling salted water.

Two minutes before the pasta is ready, add a dollop of single cream to the tomato sauce, stir, taste for seasoning and bring back to a simmer.

Drain the pasta, pour the sauce over it and grate some fresh pecorino on top immediately.

* You can see a more visual guide to cooking this recipe on my blog - pastafriends.blogspot.co.uk – if you find that sort of thing helpful, which I do.

For what it's worth, my recommendations as to what to read next are as follows:

If you're looking for something very funny, try *Bossypants* by Tina Fey.

If you'd prefer a smart, sharp thriller, try *Gone Girl* by Gillian Flynn.

If you want a proper book, I'm a big fan of *Beyond Black* by Hilary Mantel, *The Stone Diaries* by Carol Shields, and *The Poisonwood Bible* by Barbara Kingsolver – all brilliant in very different ways.

And of course if you want a darkly comic book about love and cake, you could do worse than *Pear Shaped*.

Gino D'Acampo's spaghetti del poveraccio
(Pasta with anchovies, breadcrumbs and garlic)

The very talented and handsome Gino D'Acampo has written two excellent books on pasta, and has kindly shared with me his recipe for spaghetti del poveraccio, poveraccio being Italian for 'a very poor man'. This dish makes brilliant use of leftover breadcrumbs, and is the perfect store cupboard supper for a mid-week dinner when your fridge is bare . . .

Serves 4

Ingredients:
500g dried spaghetti
8 anchovy fillets in oil, drained and finely chopped
100g white breadcrumbs
4 cloves of garlic, peeled and cut into quarters
1 medium hot red chilli, deseeded and finely chopped
3 tablespoons of freshly chopped flat leaved parsley
6 tablespoons of olive oil
Salt to taste

Method:
On a low heat, gently fry the garlic in the oil until golden all over. Remove the garlic and place the chilli and the anchovies in the oil. Cook for approximately 3 minutes, or until the anchovies are melted into the oil. Set aside.

In another frying pan, toast the breadcrumbs until crispy and golden brown. Set aside.

In a large saucepan, cook the pasta in the salted boiling water until al dente. To get the al dente perfect bite, cook the pasta for one minute less than instructed on the packet.

Once the pasta is cooked, drain and tip back into the same pan you cooked it in.

On a low heat, pour over the anchovy oil, the parsley and the breadcrumbs. Stir everything together for 20 seconds, allowing the flavours to combine properly.

Serve immediately.

Ms Marmite Lover's Leftover Brioche and Marmalade Pudding

'Some things are just good to eat,' says Ms Marmite Lover. If you look at her blog, marmitelover.blogspot.co.uk – or better still, buy her beautiful cook book, *Supper Club: Recipes and Notes from the Underground Restaurant* – you will see that everything she makes looks very good to eat indeed.

Serves 4-6

Ingredients:
8 slices of leftover brioche
½ a jar of marmalade
300ml single cream
300ml whole milk
60g sugar
2 eggs, beaten
100g unsalted butter
Sultanas soaked in Cointreau (an orange liqueur), if you like a touch of booze

Method:
Butter a baking tin. Cut the brioche into slices and butter both sides. Spread marmalade on the side facing upwards.

Place brioche in the buttered baking tin.

Mix the cream, milk, sugar and beaten eggs together. Pour over the brioche..

Drain and sprinkle the plump sultanas on top.

Bake at 180°C/356°F/Gas Mark 4 for 15 minutes or until golden brown.

Serve with double cream.

* NB. This recipe can be made with any leftover bread, preferably sweet – try pannetone, or challah (a braided egg bread available from Jewish bakeries).

The Goslathon

I am embarrassed to admit that as recently as two years ago, I would get confused between Ryan Gosling and Ryan Reynolds. Both were good-looking, mousy haired and thirty-something, and I couldn't really tell them apart. I'd never seen them in the same room or film; it's possible they were the same person.

Now I look back and I am amazed and saddened that my younger self failed to invest sufficient attention towards Gosling. I had opportunities. I'd heard rumours, talk of 'the hotness' from friends and breathless media alike; but I was in the middle of a weird Alec Baldwin crush and paid no heed. While regret is a futile emotion and achieves nothing beyond self-flagellation I can honestly say that I regret this failure to notice and thus appreciate Ryan G. And while this is truly the worst pun I've ever typed, and I regret it too, let me say it in French anyway: je regrette Ryan. For in those pre-Ryan years, while I thought I was happily making my way through life, it turns out I was merely sleepwalking.

Then one day, I was so bored of people telling me how brilliant the soundtrack from *Drive* was, that I decided to watch the damn film, just so I could tell them they were wrong. And they were wrong! The soundtrack is monotonous and whiny, I'm sorry, it is.

But they were right about Ryan.

When I revealed to my now ex-boyfriend that I had a late-onset crush on Ryan Gosling, he said something rather insulting about Ryan. I can barely bring myself to say exactly what that something was it is so patently ridiculous, but still...he said that Ryan Gosling...give me strength now...he said that Ryan Gosling *looks like Rodney Trotter in a denim jacket.*

Seriously? I'm sure he was just trying to get me back for the countless times I've said that Rose Byrne is average-looking. It's hard not to be jealous sometimes, I admit it. (Of course Rose is a beauty). But still, Ryan as Rodney Trotter? I Really Don't Think So.

Nonetheless, it did strike me as strange that this random Canadian had gone from Disney Mickey Mouse Club child actor, via years of steady, stable acting in interesting, indie roles, to suddenly BOOM! The Sexiest Man on the Planet. So I decided to investigate the development of Ryan's hotness. Maybe in doing so, I could find myself a geeky ex-Mickey Mouser and mould him into my own private Ryan.

Having obsessively studied the oeuvre de Gosling (not the worst homework, by the way, better than quadratic equations), I am now in a position to report back on what are the key eight films in his repertoire. Here for you now are my findings. You're welcome.

United States of Leland *(2003)*

Plot: Ryan plays Leland P Fitzgerald, a very sad, gentle teen, who is in love with the girl from *Donnie Darko*. He commits a terrible crime, though possibly not as terrible a crime as the film's scriptwriter. The plot is unconvincing.

Hot: If you had to bet a fiver on which actor in this movie would go on to become a bona fide heartthrob, you'd almost definitely place your money on Chris Klein from *American Pie*'s broad shoulders, rather than the young Ryan who stars. You would barely recognise this reedy Ryan with his thatch of murky brown hair as the same Ryan from the shower scene in *Crazy Stupid Love*, and yet they are one and the same. At no point in this film is Ryan hot, though he is endearing.

The Notebook *(2004)*

Plot: Super-shmaltzy love story about a young couple falling in love, told in flashback. Ryan plays Noah, who is desperately, unwaveringly in love with Rachel McAdams, whose snobbish parents don't approve of young Ryan because he is a simple, working-class lad. You will be moved to tears by the end, whether you like it or not. Watch with ice cream.

Hot: An interesting film from a transitional hotness point of view. At the start you're still thinking *I don't get it, he's skinny, a bit weedy, boyish, lanky, his lips are a little thin* and then suddenly POW! He grows a BEARD. He drinks a little too much BEER. He gets ANGRY. He makes things out of WOOD. And he becomes H-O-T. He becomes A MAN.

Stay *(2005)*

Plot: Complicated psychological thriller, almost impossible to follow at times. Equally distracting (along with the holes in the plot) are Ewan McGregor's many pairs of badly cropped trousers. Ryan plays Henry Letham, a psychologically troubled art student, who seeks help from a shrink – *or does he?*

Hot: Ryan's hair is often dirty in this film, and in a few shots he has a disturbing touch of the Macaulay Culkins, before Macaulay turned to the dark side. Gosling still looks way better than McGregor and his dumb trousers; but not better enough to justify the 99 minutes of your life you just kissed goodbye. Avoid.

Fracture *(2007)*

Plot: Extremely entertaining thriller, pitting Ryan as hotshot southern lawyer, Willy Beachum, against a psychotic wife-murderer played by Anthony Hopkins. Lots of twists and turns, and great casting, including a sterling performance by Rosamund Pike, whose hair looks brilliant.

Hot: Ryan's character is charming, cocky and on the side of good. He looks supremely handsome throughout, wears some sharp suits, and even manages to carry off a diamond and gold lucky horseshoe ring. If you watch closely there is a shower scene, and a work-out scene, but you see nothing, damn it, NOTHING.

Blue Valentine *(2010)*

Plot: Heartfelt, painful story of a couple's relationship and its deterioration over time. This film is ferociously depressing, but not necessarily in a bad way – it feels entirely authentic. Besides, if my relationship with Ryan Gosling was breaking down, I too would be ferociously depressed.

Hot: Flashback Ryan is super-hot as Dean, particularly when he woos Michelle Williams, and serenades her with a ukulele while she dances in a shop doorway. As life and alcohol take their toll, Ryan's looks go to pot – his hair suffers terribly – and yet he remains hot because a) he loves his wife so much, b) he looks like he's a great shag, and c) he is Ryan Motherfucking Gosling.

The Ides of March *(2011)*

Plot: Ryan plays Stephen Meyers, a staff member working for would-be presidential candidate George Clooney. As one of the key team members in charge of spin, Ryan gets

437

embroiled in a potential scandal and has to take care of business.

Hot: One of the reasons Ryan is so fiendishly sexy is that he is very good at playing intelligent characters and therefore one assumes (rightly or wrongly), that he must be intelligent in real life. His cleverness in this film is underlined by accessories, namely, some rather fine dark-rimmed, non-ironic spectacles. He even wears them in bed, while typing on a laptop, *that* is how clever he is. Not just a very pretty face. Also, note how his eyes study Marisa Tomei's features in the early scene where he is flirting with her. Imagine for a moment that you are Marisa Tomei. Good, right? Now imagine that Ryan is actually Nicholas Lyndhurst. No longer good.

Crazy, Stupid, Love *(2011)*

Plot: Ryan plays Jacob Palmer, a serial womaniser, who decides to help Steve Carrell rediscover his manhood after Carrell's wife asks for a divorce. A charming, funny, silly movie, with excellent casting. Interesting to note that the girl who plays the babysitter came to fame in *America's Next Top Model*, cycle 11. Who knew?

Hot: Ryan looks very, very hot throughout, but in particular: the scene at the mall where he's wearing shades and eating a slice of pizza; the naked scene in the shower where Steve Carrell's head is sadly covering Ryan's crotch;

the scene where he takes his shirt off and reveals his insane body to Emma Stone.

Drive *(2011)*

Plot: Ryan plays Driver (correct, no name allocated to his character. Poor The Ryan). He is very good at…driving! And so makes a living in Los Angeles as a stunt driver, with some dodgy business on the side. Then he meets Carey Mulligan and things start to go wrong. Violent – avoid if you don't like eyeballs being pierced with forks.

Hot: Arguably the hottest example of hotness to date. This is not just because of the tight t-shirts Ryan sports throughout. Nor is it solely because the director does an excellent job of filming Ryan at angles that showcase his incredibly straight and pretty nose. More than anything, it is because his character is so damn silent. What could be more attractive than a strong, quiet man? He never whines, he barely even talks. He is the opposite of neurotic; he concentrates, and he takes care of business. And then there's that kiss, in the lift, obviously, that kiss…

While undertaking the extensive research behind this filmography, I happened to visit the cinema to watch *Silver Linings Playbook* and realised something rather disconcerting: I fancy Bradley Cooper 3% more than I fancy Ryan Gosling, which actually breaks the laws of science, as I didn't think

439

I could fancy anyone more than I fancy Ryan. It was too late to rewrite this book and change all the references from Ryan to Bradley. Nonetheless, some consolation was to be found in the fact that Bradley and Ryan star together in *The Place Beyond The Pines*, which is coming soon to a cinema or computer near you, and also stars the rather average-looking Rose Byrne.

Loved *The Happiness Recipe*? The don't miss this hilarious
novel from Stella Newman.

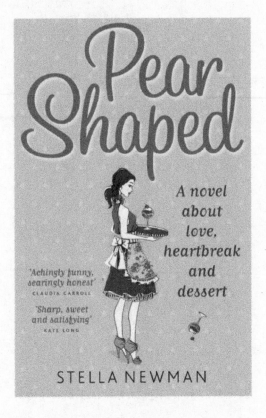

Girl meets boy. Girl loses boy.
Girl loses mind.

Two girls walk into a bar. There is no punchline.

I'm the girl on the left in the wildly inappropriate black and white spotty summer dress. It is the snowiest February in thirty-eight years but I flew back from a month in Buenos Aires three days ago and this tan ain't going to waste.

A month in Buenos Aires: sounds glamorous? Ok: a month in a £6 a night hostel in the Boedo barrio – think Kilburn with 98% humidity. No air con, no overhead lighting, shared showers. I'm thirty-three. I earn okay money. I don't like sharing showers, not least with 18-year-old Austrians proclaiming *Wiener Blut* the greatest Falco album ever released. Wieners aside, Laura and I have the time of our lives.

Laura is the girl on the right in the bar. Best friend, tough crowd, northerner. She's wearing a polo neck and a woolly hat. Together we look ridiculous; we don't care.

It is one of those evenings. Whether it's the outfits, the tans or the sociability that a snowy Friday night in London brings, we end up being the epicentre of it all. One guy, Rob, has been trying to impress me for the last twenty minutes. He's too pretty for my taste and he's spouting off about knowing Martin Scorsese's casting director.

'I can see you playing a gangster's moll in that dress,' he says. 'Those big green eyes. Real curves.'

I laugh. I'm a size 10, with tits and an arse, and the girl he's abandoned at the bar talking to his mate is one of those girls you can count the vertebrae of through her silk shirt.

'Are your eyes real?' he says.

'No, they're mint imperials, I paint the irises on every morning to match my shoes,' I say.

'I like your brushwork,' he says, smirking.

'Your girlfriend's getting pissed off,' says Laura.

'She's with my mate,' says Rob, fiddling with his watch. 'Actually, do you girls want a drink? Two more margaritas?' He heads to the bar. Before he's even back there, his mate, who is less pretty and far more my type, heads towards us.

'He doesn't waste his time . . .' says Laura.

I say nothing. I look at Rob's friend and a rare but familiar feeling grabs me: something big is about to happen.

'Why are you talking to Rob?' he says to me, grinning. 'You don't fancy him.'

'What business is it of yours?' I say. 'Do you fancy me?'

He looks at me for a heartbeat. 'Yeah.'

'Well, then you talk to me instead. What's your name?'

'James.'

'James what?'

'James Stephens.'

444

'Like the poet.'

'Ooh, a clever girl.'

'I'm not,' I say. 'My granny has a poem of his she likes to quote.'

'A love poem?'

'Yeah, it's about a man who throttles his over-attentive wife to death.' He laughs.

'I can tell you're smart,' he says. 'And warm. It's in your eyes. Don't waste your time with Rob, waste it with me.'

So I did. I talked to him, danced a tango round the bar with him, sank three margaritas with him and at the end of the night gave him my number.

He calls when he says he will – the next day. Why do I feel so grateful for this? Because the world of dating has deigned this sort of behaviour too keen.

'I want to see you again,' he says.

'Good.'

'But I'm going away for a fortnight tomorrow.'

'Oh.'

'It's work. I travel quite a bit.'

'Where are you going?'

'China.'

'What do you actually do?' I'd imagined he was a high-end builder or something to do with running a warehouse. He's very masculine, hefty, a bit rough round the edges, and his shirt last night didn't quite fit.

'You'll laugh,' he says.

'Are you an international clown?'

'No. I sell socks.'

'What, like in a shop?'

'Sort of.'

'Everybody needs socks,' I say.

'At least two pairs,' he says. 'I'm back in a fortnight, I'd like to take you for dinner.'

'Great. I like dinner.'

'But do you like to eat?'

'Are you joking? It's what I do.'

'You're not one of those girls who orders salad and just pushes it round the plate? You're pretty skinny.'

'You've got the wrong number.' I have slender arms and a small waist. You can fool most of the people most of the time with this combo.

'Good. I know the perfect place. I'll call you in two weeks.'

I work in a twelve-storey shiny building in Soho. Up until six months ago, I had one of the greatest jobs in the world and one of the greatest bosses. I am a Pudding Developer for Fletchers, one of the biggest supermarkets in the country. I worked for a genius called Maggie Bainbridge. She never compromised on quality and had bigger balls than any of the men here.

Six months ago she quit after management fired a bunch of our top talent and brought in a grunt of accountants, intent on putting the bottom line above everything else. Even our loo roll has been downgraded to that tracing paper crap from the 80s that you have to fish out of a cardboard slit.

Maggie's started up a one-woman brownie business, 'Happy Tuesday'. Even though we speak often, I miss her, and daydream about running off to work with her again.

So, I still have a great job, but I no longer have a great boss. No. I have Devron.

Devron used to work for a supermarket that was chewed up and spat out by a large American supermarket. He was regional manager for London South East, which is a Big

Deal in Retail. Apparently he was very good at driving up and down motorways in his BMW.

His sole qualification for being head of my department seems to be that he is fat, ergo he 'knows food'. Devron would be happy eating every meal from a service station on the M4. He thinks he's an alpha male, he's actually an aggressive little gamma.

The first thing Devron did when he joined was to make us all switch desks. Wanting to make his mark, and attempting to convey his profound creativity he decided to arrange us alphabetically. I used to sit with 'Hot Puddings', 'Family Treats' and 'Patisserie'. Makes sense – we share the same buyers, technical advisers and packaging team. We liaise constantly about pastries, sugar prices, trends in the Treat market – all elements that are pudding specific.

But now, because I do Cold Desserts, I sit between Lisa, who does 'Cocina' – our fake-a Mexicana range of variety nachos, and Eddie: Curry. Devron says 'we can learn a lot from talking to our colleagues'. True. I have learnt that Lisa, Eddie and I all agree: Devron is a nob.

The only thing more moronic than splitting us up from the people we need constant contact with, is Devron's introduction of 'cross-discipline platform solutions'. He has dumped a marketing wang on our bank of desks: Ton of Fun Tom.

Tom always wants to show me some great viral on YouTube featuring a gorilla or a dancing mouse. Tom's knowledge of marketing is like my knowledge of Chechen history: he knows three random facts and feels guilty about not knowing more. However, I do not try to bullshit my livelihood as a Chechen historian.

Laura has come for lunch at the Fletchers' canteen en route to do a voice-over for a car insurance website who want her husky Yorkshire accent to add 'honest northern values' to their shonky brand. Laura only has to do two voice-over sessions a month to pay her mortgage, and spends the rest of her time helping her boyfriend Dave run his eBay business selling vintage magazines.

This week's canteen theme is 'Pre-Valentine's Value' and we have the choice of heart-shaped pork bites or asparagus pasties. Sounds better than the falafel Eddie ordered last month, within which lurked a dog's tooth.

'James sounds keen,' says Laura.

'D'you think?' If he was that keen, he wouldn't wait two weeks to call me.

'He wouldn't let go of you the other night. You were dancing for ages.'

I love dancing. My ex, Nick, an introvert, danced with me once in five years: quarter-heartedly, for thirty-eight seconds, at his best friend's wedding, and only after I'd threatened to embarrass him by dancing on my own if he didn't.

'Bet his friend wasn't pleased,' says Laura.

'Rob's an arse,' I say. 'That girl with them was Rob's fiancée!'

'She's stood there while he chats you up?' I nod. 'You're going to have some fun double dating . . .' says Laura.

'Early days, love. He might meet some sock model in China and never call again.'

My mother phones from California. She lives in an apartment in Newport Beach, OC heartland, with her second husband Lenny, a retired orthodontist and professional doormat.

'Have you spoken to your brother?' she asks, saving the pleasantries for another time.

'Why?'

'It's Shellii.' Or 'the-scrawny-tramp-who-is-bleeding-your-brother-dry-with-her-spirituality-crystals-and-Lee-Strasberg-acting-classes'.

'What now?'

'She's bloody pregnant.'

'That's good news, isn't it?' It means you won't harangue me to have children for at least another two years.

A heavy silence on the other end.

'Mum, she's not that bad.' Shellii's so much worse than 'that bad', but I never agree with my mother on point of principle.

'Huh. What's news with you? How's the flat?'

'The flat's fine. I'm fine.'

'Job going well?'

'I'm heading up cold puddings.'

450

'Good, well eat some. Your grandmother said you're looking very thin.' My mother speaks to her ex–mother-in-law twice a year and it seems their sole remaining common ground is my weight.

I am currently slim and mostly toned but by no means 'thin'. I will never be 'thin' – the Kleins are big boned. But since I split up with Nick last summer, I have lost a stone and a half through exercise and taking proper care of myself. For the first time since I was twelve, I'm almost happy with my body, save for a few inches around my bottom.

My mother takes my weight loss as a personal slight. A rejection of body fat is a direct rejection of what unites our family and everything she stands for. Food equals love, too much food equals Jewish love. At weddings, my genetically freakish thin cousin is the subject of whispered snipes about anorexia and suspect parentage. My mother feeds Lenny three large meals and half a cake every day. She will feed that man to an early grave and then overfeed everyone at the shiva (think full on Irish wake, but with egg-mayo sandwiches instead of whiskies).

'Lenny's just walked in, I've got to start lunch.'

Two weeks later James calls from Beijing airport. 'Remember me?'

'Clown school's out for summer?'

'You should see what I can do with three chopsticks and a scorpion.'

'Sounds painful. Anyway, how can I help you?'

'Tell me when you're free for some spaghetti.'

My favourite. 'A week on Wednesday.'

'Too far away. I want to see you before then.'

Then you should have called me before now. 'Sorry.'

'Seriously, what are you doing between now and then?'

'All sorts. Wednesday week, then?'

'Okay. I'll call you nearer the time with a plan. Got to go, they're calling my flight.'

Acknowledgements

A massive thank you to my first draft readers – Belinda K, Priya B, Ann F, Dalia B, Keren B, Michelle G, Anna T, Ben K, Sophie S and Kerry W – for your ever-constructive feedback, given in double quick time (apart from you, Little Raynus).

To my editor Claire B, for immense patience and encouragement, and Becke P and the entire team at Avon for all your hard work; and Becky T at William Morris for doing such a good job.

And to all my other friends who have given me endless love and support in a pretty tough year. If I thanked you already in *Pear Shaped*, I'll just say ditto; trees don't grow on trees and all that:

Alex E-W – for investing so much time in cutting out little photos from the colour printer and finding new places to hide them, and for dancing the Annabel's dance better than any hooker ever could.

Ana S – for the Spanish lesson.

Andrew H – for being one of the good guys.

Anna P – for gin and jam, what more could a girl ask for?

Cassie S – master chef, dance partner extraordinaire, reorganiser of kitchen drawers with or without permission. The secrets of The Notebook are safe with me. I mean, it's not like I'd ever put them in a book or anything...

Chris and James – for Frandrew.

Dom – the best eyes in the business.

Harriet J – for amazing attention to detail, and for helping me through the hardest times.

James H – you said you wanted to be in my book, so now you are in my book. Happy? (P.S. that beard *totally* suits you).

Jinesh P – for the many, many coffees.

Henry F – for such a valiant effort.

Jenny K – for never failing to make me laugh.

Kathryn F – for being so lovely, generous and supportive, always.

Mark L – for the rooftop memories.

Massi – for the Italian lessons.

P-Hill – for putting up with my Ryan fixation, and never forcing me south of the river.

Polly C – for letting me use so many of your beautiful things.

Rachel G – for being there, always.

Ruth S – for helping me to feel un-lonely at the wedding.